## The Buzz on *Flabbe*

"Amazing. A novel with no illicit sex, bad words, racial slurs, or crime that is simultaneously serious, hilarious, and impossible to put down."

—*Dallas Morning News*

"Blackston's first novel is refreshingly honest in its portrayal of young, single Christians. Good writing and an ample dose of humor make this as charming as *Bridget Jones's Diary* from the male point of view. Highly recommended."

—*Library Journal*

"Blackston's imaginative first novel is sometimes brutally honest but always refreshingly funny."

—*Library Journal,* Best Genre Fiction 2003: Christian Fiction

"Blackston's tale is a zany take on twentysomething life in the shadow of the steeple—and proof that when it comes to courtin', less can definitely be more."

—*Fort Worth Star-Telegram*

"Seafood, marshmallow roasts, spray-painted mosquitoes, ghost stories, and a couple of near-death experiences force reexamination of the outlook on life in the here-and-now, and life in the hereafter. Ray Blackston captures the easy ebb and flow of Southern culture—complete with all-day-singin' and dinner-on-the-grounds—with grace and charm. He is equally adept at describing the loneliness of single life and finding humor in the absurdities of American dating rituals while weaving a healthy dose of religion and romance through both. Blackston's light and breezy style makes *Flabbergasted* an ideal reading choice for a lazy summer night."

—*Bookpage*

"If you only read one novel this summer, let this be it!"

—*Crossings Book Club* main selection

"Lad Lit with great buzz and a voice very much like Nick Hornby, *Flabbergasted* is well worth checking out."

—*Bookreporter*

"With a colorful cast of quirky characters and a plot full of surprises, this is one of the feel-good novels of the year. A fun, lighthearted, and thoroughly enjoyable relational 'gumbo' of a novel . . . quirky and very satisfying."

—*CCM* magazine

"A narrative in three acts, the humorous odyssey in Ray Blackston's superb first novel unfolds through the eyes of stockbroker Jay Jarvis. Underlying Blackston's story is the theme that God is in control, planning behind the scenes what we often perceive as detours, and leaving us flabbergasted at how he weaves unadorned surprises into life."

—*Christian Retailing*

"Ray Blackston takes an amusing look at the Christian singles scene; the story proceeds at a leisurely, episodic pace."

—*Romantic Times*

"What makes this novel so downright intriguing is how Blackston mixes doses of such trivial pursuits as picking a church for its singles rating, buying and selling stocks, and singles beach trips. He stirs in his mix of quirky characters and then weaves in poetry, fancy, and romance to produce a novel that resonates with reality and vitality. I was enthralled."

—*Christian Activities Online*

"Ray Blackston hits the market with a bang. . . . *Flabbergasted* is a light, easy read that is sure to please. This is the beginning of a great writing career for Blackston."

—www.iExalt.com

"The title says it all: You really will be flabbergasted at the fun you'll find behind the wheel of Ray Blackston's debut novel. Talk about your beach read! Full of quirky characters, including our slightly jaded hero, this book made me laugh out loud. Fasten your seat belts and get ready for a wild ride!"

—Liz Curtis Higgs, best-selling author of *Bad Girls of the Bible* and *Bookends*

"This humorous, quirky look at Christianity through the eyes of a single, non-believer is indeed an entertaining read."

—Christianbook.com

"Intelligently funny."

—Singer/songwriter Andrew Peterson, *Love & Thunder*

"Ray Blackston's debut novel is a breezy story of redemption that is perfectly charming, with characters who are utterly natural and believable—even the lovely missionary who has her human quirks and foibles. The group is filled with nice but not predictable people, and reading about their summer vacation adventures is like taking a holiday yourself."

—*The Flint Journal*

"This book is fun, entertaining, and brings you into a community that makes you want to stay and enjoy forever. It's a great way to take a vacation to South Carolina without ever leaving the comfort of your own home."

—*The Holland Sentinel*

"Blackston's got casual lit style and a sweet knack for self-aware humor."

—*The Hard Music* magazine

"My fellow single girls, all we have to do is interview all the young couples we know who have made it to marriage, figure out what they were feeling when they met, and then just go out and meet guy after guy until we all get that same feeling."

**My name is Alexis, and I am profound**

"Many people think I'm a one-color girl, a tall, independent female whose wardrobe and choice of automobile bear witness to a preoccupation with lime. Hmmm, maybe they're right."

**My name is Darcy, and like most blondes, I can be difficult**

"Roommates . . . you just never know what you're gonna get."

**My name is Steve, and I just got a new one**

"Yes, dear, the gardening club and I survived Europe."

**My name is Beatrice, I'm eighty-one, and I never slow down**

"My recurring dream has Mr. Right walking toward me between parted bodies of ocean, like Moses in Birkenstocks. Or maybe he's on a sail-boat."

**My name is Lydia, and I may have to change denominations**

"I have a feeling that mission work is going to be tougher than I thought."

**My name is Jay (and yes, of course I kissed Allie)**

"I can assure Jay that it's tougher than he thinks."

**My name is Allie (and it's been a bit warm in the jungle)**

"Welcome, reader, to a delirious summer."

**My name is Neil, and I will be your narrator**

Also by Ray Blackston

*Flabbergasted*

# A Delirious Summer

*A Novel*

Ray Blackston

Revell
Grand Rapids, Michigan

© 2004 by Ray Blackston

Published by Fleming H. Revell
a division of Baker Book House Company
P.O. Box 6287, Grand Rapids, MI 49516-6287
www.bakerbooks.com

Printed in the United States of America

Library of Congress Cataloging-in-Publication Data
Blackston, Ray.
    A delirious summer : a novel / Ray Blackston.
        p.    cm.
    ISBN 0-8007-5958-3
    1. Church attendance—Fiction. 2. Mate selection—Fiction. I. Title.
    PS3602.L3255D45 2004
    813'.6—dc22                                    2004001244

For Charles and Phoebe, my incredible parents

*It is not good to have zeal without knowledge,*
*nor to be hasty and miss the way.*

Proverbs 19:2

# Prologue

On the sea-green wall of my Ecuadorian hut hangs a small piece of plywood, scrawled with my latest earthly perspective:

> We spend vast amounts of time and
> energy crafting a thesis in our heads of
> how life should play out, then almighty
> God spends an incredibly brief amount
> of time blowing our thesis to bits

So much for perspective.

A loud knock interrupts my pondering, and I realize it's almost time to leave for the second semester of language school.

I recognize the knock—she's always had a certain rhythm about her. "C'mon in," I say.

A peanut bounces off my head. "Morning, Jay," she replies, offering her usual peck on the cheek. "Whatcha doin'?"

"Hey there. Where're the orphans?"

"Coloring."

"Turn around."

"Why?"

"Just turn around, I wanna . . ." She slowly turns in a circle, her face

9

blank, her body mocking the disengaged pose of a fashion model. "Yep, that toucan shirt is really starting to fade."

"It's all I had clean. So, what's that in your hands?"

I quickly tuck the paper in the back pocket of my jeans. "We have to turn in a piece of original writing. Just a paragraph to translate at the start of second semester."

"Can I see it?"

"Um, I really need to get going. The pickup truck taxi is waiting, just pulled into the village."

"C'mon, Jay, lemme have a peek."

"I really should get going, Allie."

She steps forward like she wants a hug, but when I try to embrace her, she reaches around and snatches the paper from my pocket. "Fooled you."

"You tore the paper, woman!"

With the paper in both hands, she turns her back and quickly skims the page. "I can't believe you . . ."

"Can't believe what?"

"Jay, you stole this. You plagiarizer!"

"I just . . . borrowed it."

"I should call your language school."

"But I was in a hurry, and now I'll have to write it all over."

"I can't believe you stole my words."

"I can't believe you tore it."

With a hug, a kiss, and a Spanish thesaurus, Allie sends me off on a sunny August morning, which is wintertime here in the rainforest. She's correct, you know. She wrote the blurb about God blowing a thesis to bits. In fact, all thirteen huts in the village have a small piece of plywood on the wall, scrawled with some snippet of her writing. She even has the orphans composing verse. Says she hopes to publish them all under the title *Allie Kyle's Deeply Philosophical Jungle Poetry for Kids.*

I can't wait.

Well, now that I've been exposed as a plagiarizer, you'll understand if I retreat to my former profession in order to make my point. And here is my point: No matter what you do with a stock, there is always someone on the other side of the trade—buying when you're selling, selling when you're buying. Same goes for traveling: Someone is always going your opposite direction—their east to your west, their zig to your zag.

So it was with Neil Rucker—the guy who helped me translate my plagiarism during first semester.

Spiritually, Neil and I were brothers. Relationally, we were single . . . though I was the one with the girlfriend, which is a bit strange because strapping, brown-eyed Neil was not only better looking than me, he was also friendlier and had been maturing in the faith ever since Algebra 1.

My buddy Neil is still all of those things—nice looking, friendly, spiritual—although as his story progresses you'll understand the unpredictable nature of maturing in the faith.

I met Neil in language school in Quito, Ecuador.

Neil taught.

I sat in the back row.

I had to go live in that sunbaked, nine-thousand-feet-above-sea-level capital city from March until June, mainly because my mission agency made me learn Spanish.

Neil's big mistake began when he befriended one of his students.

Namely me.

Neil mentioned to me that he had an eight-week furlough coming up and that he was looking for a place where he could find some good weather, a part-time job, and quick access to a beach. And since he was single and had not been on a date in forever due to his linguistic service to the mission field, a rich environment of churchgoing young women would be a nice bonus.

He would get his nice bonus.

You see, I knew of a few churchgoing women, and I told brown-eyed Neil where to find them. The rest was up to him.

If you asked Neil today, he would tell you his furlough was in 3-D:

dates, delirium, and disaster. I provided the dates, the Greenville girls provided the delirium, and Allie, well, she provided the disaster.

What I did not know at the time, given that I was four thousand miles below South Carolina, was what had gotten into those girls since I'd left Greenville.

Something to do with biological clocks, perhaps?

# *Act*
## one

*Send him to the island of misfit toys.*

—An unidentified elf

# 1

While the last of my fourteen missionary students toiled and sweated over his final examination, I remained seated at my desk, feet propped up, reading a paperback that instructs single people how to live victoriously. Only Jay Jarvis remained in my classroom. The other students had already turned in their papers and left to go celebrate, confident in their newfound ability to communicate with South America.

As always, it was hot in our stucco school-on-the-corner. Outside I could hear street vendors barking the price of oranges and bananas, hustling their fruit between bleached-white buildings, their shouts perfectly timed between the impatient blare of car horns. It was not the ideal environment in which to take an exam, but our language school was of the nonprofit variety; we were fortunate to have the ceiling fan.

Jay kept wiping his brow, rechecking his pages. Nervous, that guy. I'd glance up every few minutes, silently cheer him on, and continue reading my book. The word *purity* kept sparking on the page, as if it wanted to burn itself into my conscience, refuel, and flourish. In sizzling, equatorial Quito, I'd been pondering words like *purity* on a daily basis.

Here I'd lived alone for my twenty-eighth and twenty-ninth years while teaching Spanish to God's servants in waiting, and lately the days themselves had seemed combustible, one flaring into another below the lofty peaks of the Andes. On a good day I would go to great lengths to live a life of purity, to the point of imagining all lustful thoughts burning crisply, like some dried-up Latino newspaper. On a bad day the searing imagery would duke it out (and lose) to a scorching, black-hearted nemesis, even though I knew that all around me, in some hidden ember of circumstance, calling me back, was a raging white fire.

Singleness can be a wonderful furnace.

But enough flammable allusion. I just wanted the slowpoke to finish his test. Now that my teaching assignment was nearly over and summer furlough was coaxing me toward leisure, I wanted to get out of Quito and get back to the States. Fast. Let there be a beach, I wished. Let there be girls, I prayed.

I had not been out on a date in seven months, one week, and a day.

Now, whether or not this was my fault was a source of daily deliberation. Perhaps being the language teacher in a school for missionaries doesn't ring of long-term stability, or maybe I was too straightforward, or maybe the black-hearted nemesis was messing with my head.

Regardless, all that stood between me and furlough was my worst student, still fidgeting there in the back row, still hunched over his desk in a University of Texas T-shirt, still trying his blonde-headed best to finish the exam.

*Hurry up, Jarvis.*

I drifted in and out of my book, mostly out, my thoughts waffling between furlough and females. I didn't mind being one of the few unattached people in our school—except for when I'd catch couples holding hands while I was teaching. Those glimpses of bliss would invariably stir up the longing for companionship, reminding me that pillow talk with myself was always so lopsided.

Daily I spoke with God about these and other matters, though not in an empty classroom or a lonely church pew or while kneeling beside my bed. No, my theaters were airy, less formal, and very well lit. In a word, rooftops.

While my student continued to waffle over page 3, I left him to his exam and stepped outside. Our school had an old, pull-down fire escape, and its creak was always the same when I reached up and yanked—a high squeak groaning into a deep moan. Hand over hand at lunch hour, I climbed up rusty iron stairs, past both floors and to the flat roof of our language building. To the east a range of green mountains impaled the clouds, shadowing Quito without remorse. Within seconds—it was as if I had an appointment—a band of yellow rays broke through the clouds, splintered in their passage but still effective in their effort to roast me.

I'd been doing this ever since I'd seen a man addressing the almighty from atop an apartment building in Mexico City. The guy would go out onto the roof three or four times a week and just blather out to God whatever was on his mind.

The effect wasn't lost on me. From a rooftop my words could spew out like steam evacuating a pot—a pot, of course, being inflexible and in need of frequent washings. From a rooftop I didn't have to keep my voice down. From a rooftop I was . . . *closer*.

Here, closer smelled like river rocks and raw vegetables. Knowing that I would soon be leaving Quito, I breathed deep its aroma and savored the exhale. Soon I moved to the far corner of the building, nearest the mountains, and stood on pebbles and tar paper. After five years spanning many roofs, I had yet to fall. Now, as was my habit, I turned my back to the rays and raised my voice toward the highlands:

"Hey, before I climb down and grade Slowpoke's test, I just want to remind you that it was you who said it was not good for man to be alone. Did you mean a young man? A middle-aged man? Speak whenever you like. Pillow talk with myself . . . is this all there will be?"

Propelled into thin air, my words echoed off a mountainside and settled upon steep, slanted fields all heavy with crops. From my left a pigeon swooped down and landed on the edge of the roof. With two cocks of its head it sized me up before plunging toward the street, leaving behind a single gray feather that teetered at roof's edge until the air currents yanked it down. Birds were fleeting amigos during my rooftop soliloquies. Perhaps that feather, like a handshake from a former flame, was my consolation prize.

"You know how Latino women in tight tops affect me when I pass them

17

on the street. Do my offenses exhaust you? C'mon, surely they'll exhaust you at some point."

I took a breath and watched two clouds waltz around a mountain. Even the atmosphere had paired off.

"So would it ruin your plans to let me meet an interesting woman? I mean, even Jay seems to have found a woman. And does it tick you off to have to listen to my same request over and over? I hope not, 'cause I plan on repeating my request often, at least until you answer."

And that was all I said, only I repeated my petition in Spanish, just in case being bilingual helped.

Then I stood in that equatorial sun, listening for the voice that always seemed to tarry, hoping for some hint that I'd been heard. But invariably my thoughts became a thousand immigrants arguing in a hundred languages, and if one of the voices was God, he was lost in the static.

So I turned my back to those mountains, peered down at the bustling street, and wondered how I might insert myself into promising circumstances. Although today, as was the case most every day when I stood on the rooftop, I was certain that promising circumstances, like those waltzing clouds, would be slow afoot.

My last student was still nose-to-test when I returned to my desk and began scribbling the names of possible destinations for furlough. A married couple had asked me to hang with them in Quito, but I had eight weeks off and was in the mood to explore.

My main problem with leaving Ecuador and going home was that I had no actual home. As an only child whose parents had died before I'd reached my teens, I knew of no city within the fruited plain that I could point to and proclaim *mi casa*. Getting passed between aunts and uncles all through junior high and high school had produced no sense of family, just meals, an occasional pat on the rump, and "Keep your chin up, Neil."

Richmond was my birthplace, but it was merely my launching pad, not home. Before the Ecuador assignment, I'd spent two semesters teaching in Costa Rica and four in Mexico City. Furloughs between those jobs had been brief and uneventful, consisting mainly of sightseeing around the West Coast with my first cousin Dale, an accountant . . . who acts very much like an accountant. Mr. Detail.

I was still seated at my desk, thinking of how I did not want to tour the West Coast again with Cousin Dale, when from the back of the classroom, Jay Jarvis raised his hand.

"Yeah?" I asked, lowering my book to my lap. "You almost done?"

He leaned back in his desk and rubbed his eyes. "Kinda. But what about extra credit?"

I smiled and flipped a page of my book, the title of which could have been *Purity for Dummies*. "No one else asked for extra credit, Jay."

"C'mon, Neil! It's a religious language school. Show me some grace."

It baffled me how people used grace as a lever. But I wanted to get out of that perspiring classroom and plan my furlough, so I set the book on my desk and did something spontaneous, one of those off-the-cuff gestures that seems so innocent at the time but later proves to be life-altering.

I opened my desk drawer and found some old Ecuadorian paper money—sucres, a near worthless currency that I used in lessons. I smothered the bills with a handful of coins, and with cash in two hands walked to the back of the room.

"Here, Jay," I said, setting the money atop the desk beside him.

"What, you're bribing me to finish? Won't work, Neil, 'cause I know Ecuador uses U.S. dollars."

I stood over Slowpoke and stuffed my hands in my jeans. "Nope. I'm giving you *un minuto* to convert these sucres and coins to an exact amount of U.S. currency. Use this exchange rate." I leaned down and hastily wrote a decimal number, .035, atop his exam. "One minute, Jarvis. That's all you get."

Jay stared at the bills and the coins for no more than ten seconds and wrote $11.55 beside my decimal.

Amazing. Mesmerizing might be a better word. In ten seconds Jay had counted the coins and the bills in his head and converted them perfectly. "How did you do that?" I asked.

Not sharing my enthusiasm, he turned his attention back to his test.

"Simple, Neil. Much easier than converting this test of yours from English to Spanish. Say, does the word *grits* have a Spanish cousin?"

"Will you forget about Spanish grits and tell me how you converted those numbers so fast?"

"I was a broker before I was a missionary. Numbers are my sixth sense."

I sat in the desk to his left and nudged the paper sucres into a pile. "You're a stockbroker turned missionary?"

"Was headed for Wall Street."

Head down and concentrating, he didn't offer to elaborate. We were just two guys at a common pit stop, minutes away from going opposite directions. At least I hoped it was minutes; Jay was tapping his pencil and scrunching his eyes.

The ceiling fan was making a noise, creaking with every third revolution, out of balance but still potent enough to blow the pathetic paper sucres off my desktop. I leaned low out of the desk to gather them. "Done yet, Jarvis?"

Startled, Jay jiggled his pencil and glanced sideways at me. "So how much credit do I get?"

"Two points. But no grits."

"I might need five."

I stacked the currency on the desktop. "You'll get two."

He was still staring at his exam. "C'mon, Neil. Three? Show me some grace."

At this point I was tempted to give him twenty points just to get it over with. "Okay . . . three. But I want to request something in return."

Jay grinned as he initialed the pages of his test. "Anything, Neil. Just name it."

"Ever since you showed me that picture of your girlfriend last week, I've been wondering if she might, you know, have . . . friends."

He turned his exam facedown, then rubbed his eyes again. "Yeah. Sure, bro. Allie has friends. But not around here."

I stuffed the sucres in my shirt pocket. "Then where? Down in the village? That's only, what, a four-hour drive?"

"More like nine. Roads are very bad. But her friends aren't there."

"Then where?"

Jay looked at me and smiled. "South Carolina."

I paused for a moment. "Near the coast? Our age?"

"Not far from the beach, and about our age."

Without stopping to consider if this was an intelligent move, I pressed on. "And are any of these girls available?"

Jay leaned back in his desk and stretched his arms behind his head. "Really don't know. Haven't seen any of 'em in six months. But Allie usually mentions stuff like that in her letters. Over the last few weeks none of her letters said anything about 'em. Only that Sherbet got a new top."

"One of her friends is named Sherbet?"

"One of her friends' car. You really ought to visit Greenville during your furlough, Neil. For being the heart of the Bible Belt, it's a city of surprising complexity."

I held a silver coin on edge with my left index finger and thumped it with my right, sending it spinning like a top across the desk. "Maybe I'll go to Montana with my cousin Dale."

Jay reached over and squashed my spinning coin. "It's summertime in the U.S., Neil. Go where there's a beach nearby. Relax a little. You look stressed."

"Jarvis, I am not stressed."

"Well, you look stressed. Did you not have your daily talk with God on the roof?"

How he knew that was a Latino mystery. "Yes," I stammered. "Yes, I did. But I've also been sitting at my desk for four hours waiting for you to finish the exam. Everyone else was done in two. You've got to be the slowest student in the history of language school."

"I daydream."

"Adults shouldn't daydream in class."

"You should try it. Might relieve your stress."

I glanced down at his papers. "I hope you flunked."

Jay folded his arms, looked up at the ceiling, and exhaled. "It was a tough exam, Neil. Whew, I couldn't figure out how to translate Galapagos."

hey're islands, Jarvis. Part of Ecuador. You know . . . tortoises and all."

"I know they're islands. I meant the Spanish spelling."

"There's no Spanish spelling, goon head. Galapagos is Galapagos whether you're in Texas or Ecuador or Vancouver."

"Even Vancouver?"

"Even Vancouver."

"So I guess I missed that question, huh?"

"You do need more points."

"What about Peru?"

"It's still Galapagos in Peru."

From the look on his face I could tell he was using his math skills to try to estimate his test score. "Okay," he said, arriving at some mysterious number, "you still want me to call Steve?"

"Who is this Steve?"

"That friend in Greenville I told you about, the one who saved my life when I fell off the boat and whacked my head. He'll rent you his spare bedroom . . . if you want to visit Greenville, that is. It's a city of surprising complexity."

"You said that already." His anxiousness had me wary, as did the thought of South Carolina.

"I'm tellin' ya, Neil. It could change your life."

"I don't wanna change my life. And I'm not a Bible Belt kinda guy."

"And you thought I was?"

"I'd need to think about it. Plus, I'd need to find a part-time job."

Jay had maintained an insistent expression on his face, like he was sure he had my best interest in mind. Then he wagged his finger at me like he was the teacher and I was the student. "Thinking will stifle you, Neil. Just explore South Carolina. Besides Allie's girlfriends, there's also this eccentric ex-janitor and a preacher who owns a boat. What else would you do? Go to Disneyland again with Cousin Darrel?"

"It's Dale."

"Whatever. You really should go visit. And I'm sure there are lots of part-time jobs."

My thoughts wandered to Montana, then to the Grand Canyon, which I had yet to see. But then these weird images came of me standing there on the edge, next to honeymooning couples, next to teenagers in adolescent romance, and me sleeping alone in some rented camper. I pressed further. "These girls you mentioned . . . they're not wallflowers, are they? And don't fib, or I'll cut your extra credit."

He looked me straight in the eye and winked. "Neil, they represent a diversity of all that is female."

"Aw man, now I'm going to Montana for sure."

He grabbed the edge of my desk and shook it. "No, don't do that. Listen up, Neil, there's a hospitable redhead with lots of rules, a tall blonde with a classic convertible, and then this raven-haired girl with a tiny silver piercing who I can't really recommend . . . but she is entertaining."

I considered all the possible interpretations of the word *entertaining*, or *entretenido*. "Okay, let's just suppose I do visit this Greenville, and I move in with this guy named Steve. I still won't have any way of getting around. No car. No motorcycle."

Jay looked flustered, as if I'd admitted I owned no shoes. "You don't own wheels, Neil?"

Eyebrows raised, I shook my head.

"Not even some old clunker in a U-Lock-It?"

"I'm tellin' ya, Jarvis, I own no adult toys. For five years I've lived out of a suitcase, teaching Spanish to people much more qualified than you to serve on the mission field."

I think he knew that I was just needling him, yet he feigned shock anyway. "Well then," he said, sitting up in his desk, "you can just drive my old Blazer. It's still at Steve's, under a tarp in his backyard. You see what's happening, dontcha, Neil? God is providing for you in exchange for my extra credit."

"I can't believe God called you to be a missionary."

"I'm very giving. And I've already offered—" He suddenly stopped talking.

"What?"

He looked straight up. "Did you know that your ceiling fan creaks every fourth revolution?"

"Every third."

"Fourth, Neil. I'm the numbers guy. Now back to what I was offering—"

"I know what you're offering. It just sounds a bit . . . ominous."

Jay took one last glance at his exam and nodded his agreement. "Yeah, Neil. Ominous is a good word. North Hills Presbyterian is definitely ominous."

More than anything it was his enthusiasm that stoked my interest. My next question was intended to buffer that enthusiasm, though it did nothing of the sort. "So all these friends of yours are Presbyterian?"

"Except for when they're Baptist or Pentecostal."

"Huh?"

Jay stood and headed for the front of the classroom, exam in hand. He set his papers atop the stack on my desk. "And sometimes Lutheran."

I followed him to the front and tucked all the exams in a folder. "That fall off the boat gave you brain damage, right?"

"Just go visit, Neil. They have beach trips every summer."

"Who, the Baptists or the Pentecostals?"

"North Hills Prez. The singles love to go to the beach."

I didn't need to ponder for more than a moment. "I do love the beach."

And right there, right inside that sentence of give-in and self-persuasion, is where my innocent little gesture—currency conversion as extra credit—began my delirious summer.

That evening, under the balmy, pastel skies of Quito, Jay and I met at a downtown eatery where we celebrated, with crab legs and chocolate-chip pizza, his score of 73 on the final exam. I have never seen a grown man so proud of a 73. He even insisted on paying for my dinner. I'll never forget his glee—in the middle of the crowded restaurant, surrounded by the steamy scent of crab legs and some breakneck Spanish he could not understand, he gestured with a piece of half-eaten dessert pizza. "It's a sign, Neil. A sign that God wants me on the mission field, wants me to make a difference, wants me to spell Galapagos in every language. Next year I'm learning Portuguese. Do you teach Portuguese too?"

I laughed and shook my head no. Then I stole a bite of his chocolaty dessert and said, "I don't think Ecuador is ready for you, Jarvis."

As much as I tried to needle Jay about his inexperience, it never seemed to affect his outlook. I envied him, serving in a remote area like he did. I had always felt a bit too shielded as a missionary language teacher, what with the classroom and the order and the paperwork. Instead of being on the front lines, I'd spent five years preparing others to go to the front lines. I wanted a change, an adventure, a taste of the wild. An *almost missionary*, that's what I called myself.

Jay picked up a crab claw and wagged it at me. "I'll learn as I go, Neil. Now you gotta keep in touch. We'll exchange emails, okay?"

"Sure, man. I'll type it in English."

"That'd be best. So tell me . . . which one of those girls are you gonna ask out when you get to Greenville?"

"Yes."

He wiped his mouth. "Whadda you mean, yes?"

"Since I've been dateless for so long, maybe I'll ask 'em all out."

For the first time since I'd known him, Jay Jarvis was speechless. He let his mouth drop open, far enough that I could see melty chocolate clinging to his incisors. Then he took a swig of ice-less cola, leaned in, and told me his Greenville story—how he had been immersed in the world of Wall Street, met Allie at the beach, visited her village in the rainforest, and decided to stay. He called himself the rookie missionary and said that he and Allie were jungle dating, whatever that meant. His story made me fear I would never meet anyone that I thought so highly of that I would up and move. I didn't ask Jay what all he had given up to pursue his girlfriend. But considering his former profession, he'd probably given up a lot.

I admired Jay's courage, if not his Spanish.

Monday morning, before going our opposite directions, Jay and I shared a cab to the Mariscal International Airport, where he caught a ride in a five-passenger Cessna owned by Mission Aviation Fellowship. I was standing at a lobby window—still pondering Montana and the Grand Tetons, still unsure about where I was headed—when the Cessna taxied by.

Seated in that skinny plane, Jay looked out the window and gave me the thumbs-up sign, apparently still celebrating his 73. It was at that moment—my thumb, his thumb, raised in tandem for a fleeting second on opposing sides of lobby glass—when I realized we were brothers.

I waved just before the white-and-red plane rose and banked into clear skies. Once again, I envied Jay's journey. I knew that the pilot would drop him off in the jungle town of Coca, where his girlfriend, Allie, would be waiting in an old pickup truck to drive him back to the village. My own flight promised nothing so romantic—some guy named Steve was meeting me in South Carolina.

I had checked one suitcase and had my olive-green cap on my head when I boarded a 757 run by Tortugas Air, bound for Miami, to be followed by a two-hour jaunt to Atlanta. Then a puddle jumper to Greenville.

At takeoff I was half awake, alternating between reads of *La Hora* and *USA Today*. It was my contention that one gets a more well-rounded view of the news if it is read in two languages. Setting aside the *USA Today*—the salaries of the superstars, the price of real estate, and the audacity of the politicians were too shocking—I shifted back into Spanish mode and read Ecuadorian articles about drug traffickers in Colombia, the lack of rain in the jungle, and the growing number of large families in South America. None of that was of much interest to me—I'd nearly given up on ever finding a true family—so I stuffed the paper back in the seat rack and thanked God for furlough.

As the jet leveled off, so did my vision of what lay ahead. I pictured it all like an eager kid gazing for the first time through a telescope. In my lens, however, were not stars or planets or galaxies but things that could be just as distant and hard to fathom—Southern girls.

I wondered if they'd changed much in the years I'd been abroad.

Somewhere over the Gulf of Mexico a dark-haired flight attendant named Marlena served pretzels and drinks. "Nice cap," she said, arriving at my row. "Vacation?"

I nudged my brim higher to see her. "Feels more like adventure."

26

She handed me a napkin. "There's been lots of adventure around lately."

I figured there was no time like the present. "So, Marlena, where're you from?"

"Charlotte," she said. "Same place as my fiancé." And she flashed me her ring and moved on.

# 2

From two thousand feet, South Carolina looked harmless. We were descending over a lake, a golf course, and the manicured lawns of suburbia. U.S. Air's landing gear groaned into place, a startling sound given the fact that we'd only been in the air for forty minutes. Suits and ties dominated the 6:00 p.m. flight from Atlanta, and many of the suits were looking frazzled. A dozen hands smoothed the same haircuts as we approached the runway. I hadn't had a haircut in months. People told me I had the kind of hair that looked better with length. But just to mock the suits I pushed some locks behind my ears.

Since takeoff, no one around me had said a word. To be fair I hadn't initiated anything either—that many briefcases intimidated me. I was sure they contained lots of important briefs, maybe classified company data, maybe pics of spouses and children and loyal dogs. To my chagrin, I had no such pictures. I preferred to travel light—my carry-on bag was a harmonica, asleep in the key of G and resting snug in the pocket of a favorite blue madras shirt.

My hiking boots felt heavy on my feet, and after the suits had cleared out, I was the lone pair of jeans departing flight 229 into the gray-walled terminal of Greenville-Spartanburg. Out of the tunnel and into a main corridor, I played spectator to the many forms of reunion: kids hugging daddies; husbands kissing wives; incoming captains greeting outgoing captains. I dragged my independence past them all and made the best of a hugless arrival.

First one down the escalator, I arrived at the baggage carousel and sat on thin blue carpet, my back against a concrete column. Around me small crowds gathered and departed, pinstriped arms pulling obedient luggage. I watched the bags diminish until the carousel was circulating my tattered suitcase past an audience of one. After watching six more revolutions I got up off the floor and plucked my luggage from its lonely orbit.

If there was a Steve Cole in this airport he had not shown himself timely. I sat back down against the column and began to blow into my carry-on bag. One bar of blues proved that airport acoustics were terrible, so I hauled my suitcase outside and sat on the curb. It was still daylight and very humid, very June. Across the drop-off lane, the tame rays of a tired sun turned the security guard yellow. Like the briefcase crowd, he made no effort of welcome.

Disheartening, coming all the way from Ecuador and not having one person acknowledge my presence.

There were ways to change that.

I began a slow melody of wandering pitch, a tune whose main theme was one of exploration. Soon the guard looked over from his post and nodded, like he welcomed the distraction of music.

Within minutes, several of the briefcase crowd had gathered outside, listening in, edging closer, as if they couldn't figure out if I was waiting for a ride or if I was a curbside regular playing for tips. To keep them guessing I began playing louder, adding various head bobs and grimaces to my act. Soon the security guard saw what was happening, and he surprised me when he seized the opportunity to toy with the suits. He came strolling over and, right in front of them, dropped a quarter atop my suitcase. He winked at me, then turned and hustled back to his station. I kept playing, looking off across the parking lot as if this was routine.

That one shiny quarter resting on a tattered suitcase must have been too much pressure for the businesspeople. Out of the corner of my eye I saw one blue suit nudge another. The first leaned down, set a five on my suitcase, and stepped back beside his buddy. Not to be outdone, another suit stepped forward and contributed a ten, his Rolex flashing as he gave me a thumbs-up.

Figuring that they now deserved the full spectacle, I played even louder, adding nose scrunches and a tapping of foot to my sunset vaudeville.

Fifteen dollars for five minutes of music?

Nothing else about furlough would be so simple.

But I couldn't keep the money. After the suits left, I got up from the curb and walked across the darkened lane to speak to the guard. "Here," I said, holding out the cash, "it was your idea."

He smiled and shook his head. "No, no. You're the musician."

"But I insist."

He crossed his arms, shook his head again. "Nope. Can't take it."

"Then we'll split it." I stuffed the ten in his shirt pocket and kept the five. "Deal?"

He peeked into his pocket. "Okay. Deal." He peeked again and smiled. "We're open tomorrow night as well."

The boredom alone convinced me to practice. Since no more spectators were left, my second curbside effort was choppy and experimental. I was revising it a third time, adding more low end, when an orange Jeep came fast into the drop-off lane. It swerved into the pickup lane and screeched a tire. The security guard turned and glared as the Jeep braked quickly to my left. Through the windshield, the driver looked at me there on the curb and mouthed a one-word question. *"Neil?"*

I nodded, pointed at him with my harmonica, and mouthed, *"Steve?"*

Out of his Jeep and over to greet me came a stocky guy in khakis and a white collared shirt all sweaty at the armpits, its logo hinting at engineering. Steve was square-jawed and unshaven, although his dark hair was neatly trimmed. "Man," he said, extending his hand, "I thought you'd be skinnier from living in the wild and having to eat bugs."

I shook firmly and laughed. "Nah, Jay and I ate lots of smoked piranha."

"Really?"

I tucked the harmonica in my pocket and flung my suitcase into the back of his Jeep. I spoke over the roof. "No, not really. I lived in the city—Quito, near the equator."

His reply came back through the interior. "So that's why you're tanner than me. And sorry I was late. Was answering emails and just lost all track of time. How was the commute from Charlotte?"

"From Atlanta. And it was just lots of suits."

I climbed into the passenger seat, which held an assortment of CDs. Curious as to what was popular, I examined them for familiarity but dismissed them as alien. After relocating them to the backseat I found a rental guide for beach homes and was shocked at what a week would cost in summer.

Steve veered down the on-ramp and sped us toward the interstate. "Yeah, Neil, we got lots of suits here. Lots of BMWs too. What kinda car do you drive?"

"I don't own a car."

My admission was met with a confused silence. He eased us into the right lane. "You gotta have some kind of ride, somewhere . . . don't ya?"

"Jay said I could use his old Blazer, said it was under a tarp in your backyard."

"It's under a tarp all right. Been there ever since he left to go play missionary with Allie." Steve shifted into fifth and sped us toward the heart of Greenville. As an afterthought, he asked, "Do ya think Jay makes a good missionary?"

I'd debated that question while flying across the Gulf of Mexico. There was really no definitive answer. "Actually, I think Jay would make a great circus clown, but he does bring a certain enthusiasm to the position."

Steve laughed knowingly. "You're gonna need some enthusiasm to get that Blazer started. Hasn't been cranked since January."

He merged us onto I-385, then onto North Main, past old homes, restored homes, and a smattering of fixer-uppers. Steve's house was somewhere between restored and fixer-upper. The brown brick looked recently pressure washed, as did the sidewalk and the driveway. His carport contained an assortment of well-used sporting goods. A basketball goal—lofted

31

on a pole to the side of the driveway—appeared shorter than regulation, its rim bent forward as if suffering from too many dunks. "It's no palace," Steve said, pulling into the carport, "but you can walk to downtown from here."

My stomach growled. "Can we head for a drive-through?" I asked. "I've really missed American burgers."

Steve shook his head no before cutting the engine. "Nope. We're having a cookout. I figured that since you've been dining on all those insects, I should feed you well."

"And you invited some friends over, right? And some of them are women?"

He yanked up the parking brake. "It's just you and me, bro. Unless my friend Ransom shows up. But surfer dude has a kid now, so it'll probably be just you and me."

Disappointed at the guest list but moved by the generosity, I let pass the fact that he'd been a half hour late to pick me up. "I was hoping you might invite some girls over. I haven't been on a date in seven months, one week, and two days."

Steve left his keys in the ignition and opened his door. "You keep count?"

"Yeah, you?"

"Three months and three weeks for me."

I climbed out and spoke over the roof again. "We're pathetic."

He showed me to a sea-green bedroom. The room contained window blinds but no curtains, bookshelves with no books, and a single bed with no sheets. I'd brought sheets, but I couldn't get over the room color. "What's with the paint?" I asked.

Steve stood in the doorway and gripped the frame on both sides. "I had an extra gallon after a beach project last May."

He left to tend to dinner as I installed my sheets. From the looks of things, I'd be sharing the room with a Chicago Cubs baseball poster, five fishing rods, and two goldfish dubbed Hawk and Pig. Across their bowl—as a sort of reminder or plaque, I wasn't sure—the names were written on a piece of masking tape. Pig was the fat one.

32

I was about to unpack my suitcase when hunger got the better of me, which was not unusual. Like temptation, its strongest trait is consistency.

Steve's back deck was old and rectangular, and the setting sun seemed not to bathe it in orange but to faintly airbrush the edges. While his grill flamed behind him, Steve tore open a package of shish-kebab skewers. Before us were marinated chunks of steak, tiny tomatoes, bites of chicken, and red potatoes, all waiting patiently on his glass-topped, outdoor table. When he went back inside to get drinks, I took over preparations and soon had four kebabs fully skewered. Not that I claimed a talent for cookery, but in Quito I'd experimented with the fiery art of kebabbing—it was my regular Tuesday meal.

From the deck I scanned the backyards of middle-class neighbors before pronouncing them rich. The lack of clotheslines and the absence of iguanas reminded me of how far I'd come. The preponderance of fences confirmed that my homeland was still quite territorial.

Steve had changed into shorts and a gray softball jersey when he came out on the deck with two cold cans of Fanta Grape. He handed me one, then picked up a kebab and set it on the grill. "Neil, you're the first roommate I've had who's helped cook dinner."

I adjusted the flame and watched it rise to tickle our meal. Satisfied, I tried to size up this new roomie. He looked beat. "You look weary, señor."

Before offering comment, Steve topped off a second kebab and dunked the tip, which was weighed down with three hefty chunks of steak, back into the marination. "Deadlines, Neil. Just a steady flow of uncompromising engineering deadlines."

"More taters?" I knew nothing about engineering.

"I'm just glad tomorrow is Saturday. Engineering can be very—"

I rotated both the skewers and the conversation. "It's Friday, man. Forget work. You didn't plan any female interaction this weekend?"

Steve plucked his grape soda from the table and sat down in a lawn chair. "That's the dilemma of this town. Great job market; confusing girl market. Didn't Jarvis tell you what's happened?"

"He only mentioned that a few of your church's single women had begun wandering a bit."

"Not just wandering," Steve said. "They've become downright elusive."

After turning the skewers again, I went to the table and stabbed two potatoes and three chunks of steak, topping them off with a single tiny tomato, another raw totem pole of culinary delight. "Did ya scare 'em off? Or are they just playing hard to get?"

Steve set his drink on the deck and sunk into his chair. "Hard to find. It seems, Neil, that the women's new favorite activity is an extreme sport called denominational hopscotch. They think that's how they can meet a man."

"How 'bout yourself?"

"I have no interest in meeting a man."

I was half smiling at his wit while I tended the kebabs. "I meant have you ever hopscotched to meet women?"

He paused and thought about it. "Once or twice."

"Any luck?"

Steve sniffed the grilled air, then took a long swig of his drink. "I felt outta place. After being Presbyterian all my life, being Pentecostal was disorienting. They'd stand when I wanted to sit, then yell when I wanted to doze. Doesn't that sound disorienting?"

"Very." In the distance a train chugged away. No whistle, just the rumbling clatter of wheel on rails. "How far away is that?" I asked, up on my toes and straining to see.

But there was no answer. I turned and saw that Steve had gone inside to fetch something from his kitchen. He came back out on the deck with paper towels and an unmarked jar of something reddish.

"What is that?" I inquired.

He opened his jar and took a long, hard sniff. "El Grande Mystery Sauce."

The train faded out as we prepared to eat. I pulled a second lawn chair around his outdoor table, and with little talking we each finished off two kebabs before reloading our skewers. Steve went to the grill with a skewer in each hand and set them diagonally across the top. "Medium?" he asked.

"Medium well."

He then produced a small brush from his back pocket and began spreading his mixture on the already marinated meat. This seemed like overkill, but I let it go, still contemplating the hopscotch. Surely there had to be some value in picking one denomination and sticking with it. As with cell phone plans, I'd prefer to know the parameters in which I operated.

"Steve-o, you gotta tell me how all this got started."

"Shish kebabbing?" he asked, manning the grill again. "Probably third century BC."

"Not shish kebabbing, man. Church hopping. I don't recall much of that when I lived in Richmond."

Steve reached for his soda, and after a deep swig he suppressed a burp. "This is pure speculation, but I believe it started with emails. I have inside knowledge of an email list that circulates around Greenville. Get this, Neil—it actually ranks our largest churches as to the volume of single men. Only single women, of course, can get the updates."

Now I knew what Jay had meant when he told me he'd left one jungle for another. I'd only been in town for two hours, but already I could sense this city had an air about it, like all was not right, the Bible Belt missing a loop. Maybe two. I squashed my aluminum Fanta can, dropped it on the table, and watched it wobble to a standstill. "Jay didn't tell me this was epidemic."

Steve returned to his lawn chair and sat heavily on the nylon. "I'm tellin' ya, Neil, it's gotten worse since Jarvis left town. Much worse. Even my friend Ransom and his wife have been hopping, trying out different nurseries for their kid."

Puffs of smoke uncoiled from his grill, and after watching them fade over dark suburban skies I got up and resumed the duty of chef. "And you think women are more prone to this behavior?"

"It's biological, you can bet on it. Two weeks ago at singles class, we had only eight people—seven guys and Lydia."

"Good odds for Lydia."

"Yeah, well, the week before that we had thirty-three. How would you explain it?"

"I dunno. Everybody went to the beach?"

"Nope. Twenty-six of those thirty-three were women. I counted."

"And you still got no date this weekend? Man, you're beyond pathetic."

The air smelled hot and meaty. One by one I plucked the kebabs from the grill and served my host his seconds. After a chew and a swallow he pointed at me with his fork. "It's the hopscotch, Neil. I'd never seen most of those women before. They were all just scoping . . . I could tell."

I turned off the gas. "Maybe so, but you still gotta explain how you didn't manage one date out of all that."

Steve looked embarrassed, and his answer was slow in coming. "My ex—Darcy—was one of those girls. Sometimes it's awkward for me when she's around."

"So why'd you two break up?"

Moonlit and yawning, Steve stretched his arms high overhead before lounging back in his chair. "Darcy is two inches taller than me and ten times as complicated. As for what happened, I can hardly explain it. One day we were sitting in this Mexican restaurant, munching on a second bowl of chips and salsa, when she blurted out that dating me lacked all momentum, that it was like trying to water-ski behind a canoe."

"Ouch."

"That's what I said."

"Really? You said ouch?"

"Ouch. Right there over the chips and salsa."

Lingering scents of grilled kebabs filled the air as I leaned against his deck railing and scanned the neighborhood. I was warming to Greenville, and also to this new roommate, who seemed, well, almost normal. "So, you two weren't having fun dating?"

Steve began his answer with a shrug and a frown. "I thought we were having fun. But I still can't believe she said a canoe. She could've at least said a tugboat, something with an engine."

"So what happened to y'all?"

"Who knows. Maybe I wasn't sure where it was going. Maybe I was too busy performing high maintenance on the skis."

His comments had me wondering if all the girls in this town were high maintenance. Regardless, there was still the matter of earning money. I had little savings, certainly not enough to live on for eight weeks. The language school paid a salary during the school year, but it never went far. In fact, it went about as far as the plane ticket to Carolina. "On Monday I'll be looking for a part-time job."

Steve dropped his empty can on the deck and squashed it with his foot. "Nah, bro, don't worry about jobs. Jay's email said you'd need to find something to do, so I've got a possibility lined up for ya."

There was no further explanation; he just left me hanging like a green banana. "So you're not gonna tell me tonight?"

"Nope. Maybe next week." Having all vocational matters in control and all the remaining kebabs consumed, Steve rose from his chair. "Follow me inside, Neil. There's something you need to see." He pulled back the sliding glass door, and I followed him into his den.

"Dessert?" I asked, right on his heels.

He stopped between his sofa and his computer nook. "No, I got a little surprise for ya. Though my name really is Steve Cole, I also go by the name of Stephanie Coleman."

*What?* I froze in midstride. *What happened to almost normal?* After processing what he'd said, I thought about running out the door. But I couldn't move. Unable to form a syllable, I sifted my thoughts and questioned my faith. *Did you hear him, God? Did he just say he also goes by the name of Stephanie Coleman? The God of Abraham sends me on furlough to room with a cross-dresser?*

Stunned, I wanted to leap off the back deck and sprint to a bus station. Instead, I braced myself against the back of the sofa and left lots of room between us. "What do you mean," I said, slow and deliberate, "you're also Stephanie Coleman?"

Steve laughed and sat down at his computer. "I knew that would throw ya, Neil. Oh, man, you got all pale there for a second, lost all that tan. Come over here and educate yourself."

Still skeptical, I stood several feet behind Steve as he logged on to the Internet. If he didn't explain himself quickly, I was going back to the airport. If he asked me to call myself Neilarita, I was going to find a roof and have a long talk with the almighty. "You need to start explaining yourself quickly, Stephanie . . . I mean *Steve*."

He laughed again, in the way that hides a secret. "Relax," he said, noticing my extreme hesitation. "I only use the female name to glean information. Remember what I said about the girls and their ranking of churches? The email list?"

"That only girls can get?"

He was scrolling through a list of emails. "Yeah. At the suggestion of my friend Ransom I came up with my own feminine email name so I could learn what the girls are up to—you know, get the weekly update. Go ahead, Neil," Steve said, pushing away from his desk and nodding at his monitor. "Read this."

Comforted in no small way by his explanation, I leaned down to look at his screen, silently praising God for a return to normalcy.

But normalcy was a fleeting comrade. The email was typed in a small font, and it was baffling:

Ladies of the Quest,

Woodhaven Methodist Church has now dropped all the way to forty-seventh in church rankings. There was one, just one single guy in the entire church. And he was sixteen. Sixteen! I could not believe it. So I need to urge all women on this email list not to submit erroneous reports of various congregations. Someone must have confused Woodhaven with some other church, and this error puts us all (well, at least three of us) one week behind in finding Mr. Right.

I appreciate the enthusiasm, ladies, but let's try to be accurate in our assessments. I'll need updates from Group 1 on the Pentecostals; from Groups 2 and 3 on the Baptists; from Group 4 (Nancy's group) on Episcopalian; and my group, well, me and Darcy and Lydia were the lucky ones who volunteered to try Methodist this week.

The spreadsheet is attached, and I'll need next week's report by Monday afternoon. By the way, North Hills Presbyterian has been number nine for a month now. Is anyone scoping it? I have no recent report.

We will persevere, ladies. We will all find our bliss. Just be wise, and remember to travel in pairs.

Alexis Demoss, secretary, Ladies of the Quest

I was still staring at that email when Steve logged off and the screen went black. He'd already gone into the kitchen when I came to my senses. "So it's true?" I asked, my voice loud enough to carry across two rooms. "It's true what Jarvis said?"

Steve came back into his den and went over to the coffee table to grab the remote. "If you're hoping to meet women, Neil, you'd better pray for divine guidance. You might have better luck in Alaska." He landed on the sofa and found a baseball game on cable. Not being a big fan of baseball, I went into my sea-green bedroom and fed the Hawk and the Pig. Soon they were nibbling the surface of the water, making fish-mouths and gorging themselves on wispy flakes.

I wondered if they were male and female. My tap on the glass brought no clarity to the issue, and a harder tap failed to get the Hawk to turn upside down. No anatomy showed itself worthy of a particular gender, although if they were both female or both male, at least they seemed content in their circumstances, in no hurry to leap bowl to bowl in some desperate search for the perfect mate.

*Goldfish of the Quest* . . . maybe they ranked the pet stores.

Before going to bed I played my harmonica for them, composing a fishy lullaby while they nibbled their meal. Hawk seemed to move its fins in rhythm, as if it preferred dining to music, but Pig just gulped away in gluttony, not at all interested in being serenaded at feeding hour.

After they were done eating, I named the song "Unisex Pillow Talk for the Submerged."

That was my last coherent thought as I collapsed on the bed and brought to conclusion my first day of furlough. Tomorrow was Saturday, and in Ecuador that had always been my day for making new acquaintances.

# 3

When the lawn mower passed by my window at noon, it didn't so much wake me as add substance to my dream. I was having that one where the madman chases me in slow motion and my legs won't function. But instead of the madman swinging an axe at me, he was trying to run me down with the mower. I was straining to climb a tree when I turned and saw that the madman was Jay, telling me in bad Spanish that I'd left my camera in Ecuador.

I woke with an urge to explore—initially by digging through my suitcase for shorts and a moss-green T-shirt. Next I found some chocolate milk in Steve's fridge, frozen grapes in his icebox. But I didn't eat, just hurried down the front steps and into the brightness of Saturday.

Through the mower's whir I waved at Steve, who was pushing his Lawn Boy in tight circles around the basketball pole, trying to nip the last few blades creeping up the base. Finally, he cut off the mower and leaned down to yank up the weeds by hand.

"My WeedEater's broke," he said.

I moved to the edge of the yard and sniffed the smell of fresh-cut grass. Unsatisfied, I reached down for a handful of clippings and held the stubble to my nose, trying to inhale the South. One by one, my senses were adapting.

After tossing the clippings into no breeze at all, I asked Steve for the shortest route into downtown. He was still yanking away at those weeds.

"Walk down Buist, then right on North Main," he said without looking up. "It'll take you a good fifteen minutes."

I was already halfway down his driveway. "Anyone to watch out for?"

"If you see any suspicious-looking girls in a convertible Caddy, duck behind a building. My ex goes cruising nearly every Saturday." Then he strained to pluck the stubbornness from one last weed.

I would help him eventually, but my policy was no yard work on the first morning of furlough.

Sweat was a constant by the time the tree-lined street of North Main came into view. Besides my roommate, many Greenvillians had chosen this day to mow, and the moist aromas of fescue and zoysia escorted me all the way past the office towers anchoring the north end of downtown. Live music murmured in the distance, causing me to cringe as I considered my comparatively poor solo at the airport. Down Main and into the shopping district, I felt waylaid by the sheer volume of storefront product. People brushed past me on the street, swinging their shopping bags and rushing store to store. I quickly felt out of place, a have-not who was ill-equipped to participate. I'd been out of the United States for two years and was grasping for something familiar. Music brought that sense of familiarity.

Weekends in the South—which I had viewed as slow and meandering—were, from all the stateside evidence, just as hurried as the rest of the week, the pressure to earn transferring readily into the pressure to consume. While I understood the rush to purchase what was man-made, five years on the mission field had won me over to the leisure of observing what was created.

Into the heart of Restaurant Row, I was passed on both sides by skateboarding kids, a clattering duo weaving through pedestrians. They were reckless in the same way I could be with meeting people, sometimes too bold, almost always too eager—but to leap right in had always been my habit. So when the kids stopped, I hurried up the sidewalk and squatted down to talk eye to eye.

"Guys," I said, looking first at the little one and then his chubbier buddy, "I'm Neil Rucker, and I just got here from Ecuador and was wondering what you could tell me about Greenville . . ."

The smaller one only glanced at me and turned away, too cool to talk with adults. The chubby one lifted his skateboard with one hand and spun the front wheels with the other, a nonchalance to couple his reply. "It's whatever you want," he said.

With that they set their boards on the walk and took off again.

I caught up to them a block later, past a deli and a bookstore. They stood in front of a skateboard shop, gawking in the window at shinier versions of the same contraptions they held under their arms. I waited silently, pretending to admire the inventory. After several seconds the chubby kid eyed my reflection above his own and turned to his comrade. "Man," he moaned, "this guy followin' us."

The little one looked up at me, then back at his buddy. "Yeah, he stalkin'."

I made my best madman face and said, "Yeah, I'm just Neil the stalker, out to spook all the little skateboarders." The words had barely left my mouth when in the glass a long reflection of lime green rolled by. I spun around, but the convertible was already past us, easing down the street in a low rumble.

I hurried to a nearby bench and stood atop it. Craning my neck, I saw the backs of two girls, one blonde, one raven-haired. They were car dancing and paid no attention to the fact that sidewalk shoppers were watching with amusement.

The chubby kid tugged on the back of my shirt. "Hey, mister, you see somethin' you like?"

The car made a left and disappeared. I jumped back to the sidewalk but kept staring down Main Street. "Not sure. I've been told about some particular young ladies and thought maybe that was two of them."

Chubby bent down to tie his sneaker. "I seen that car all over. They always cruisin'."

"Yeah," the little one said, sideways on his board and rolling downhill. "Always cruisin' . . . like me."

Youth shoved off again, swerving past shoppers and scaring small dogs.

Over a rise in the road came guitar chords riding the breeze, rolling up the sides of buildings in bold waves of improvisation. I quickened my pace, and the chorus became crisp, immediate.

Sidewalk bands always drew me in—probably because I'd been in the worst one ever assembled.

For three months in Mexico City I'd been a member of a weekend band called the Resonant Tacos, which I'd named after watching our drummer try to eat his meal to a percussion rhythm. Rafael would take loud bites of his lunch—a six-taco supreme—by exposing his teeth and chomping down quickly: *crunch crunch, crunchcrunchcrunch*. He actually thought eating in this manner helped him as a drummer. Since our four-man band only lasted three months, and all six of our songs were about having the blues in Mexico City, I can't say whether or not his method helped. We broke up after an old solo guitarist told us that blues don't transfer well to the young, that the true essence only comes with age, poor health, and lots of relational baggage.

But this was Greenville, South Carolina, where maple trees lined scenic sidewalks, the music sang of youth, and the peso was but an answer on a grade school exam.

I followed the sounds to their source and stopped near the entrance to an ice cream joint known as the Marble Slab. Deep into song, three musicians sat on stools under a black awning. One young woman was singing, another clanged a tambourine, and the guitar player—the guy could not have been over nineteen—strummed shut-eyed. They were sweaty and played with great enthusiasm, each of them nodding when someone would walk up and drop some change or a dollar bill in the red-lined guitar case. A crowd of forty or so gathered around, some leaning into rails and bobbing their heads, others sitting on plastic chairs and bobbing their heads.

I stood to the side, under a red maple, and bobbed my head.

A small banner hung from the awning, proclaiming the band to be the SoulFixers. I had no idea whose soul they were trying to fix, and I wondered, with a name like that, what genre they professed, given that the singer, the guitar guy, and the tambourine girl were now into a fourth chorus of "Me and Bobby McGee."

I watched guitar guy lose himself in his strumming. He had sandy blonde hair grown out to his shoulders, bangs hanging into his eyes. The tips of his bangs were wet with sweat, sticking to his eyebrows and refusing to bounce.

The singer rocked on her stool and belted out the chorus. My hopes of meeting an available female musician were quickly squashed, however, when she lifted her mic.

Another glance at a finger, another wedding ring displayed. God was frowning on me in half-carat luster.

Tambourine girl was the youngest, checking in somewhere just below or above high school junior. She had a saxophone next to her chair, and near the end of the song she hoisted it to her lap and blew an inspired solo. The SoulFixers strummed, sang, and blew until the song itself was exhausted. As light applause diminished, the long-haired strummer announced a break. His band mates rushed into the ice cream shop.

Many quarters piled up in the case. I waited for the crowd to filter down before easing under the awning to introduce myself to the guitar player. Plastic pick in his teeth, he beat me to hello.

"Willum," he said, which I took to mean William.

"I'm Neil."

William leaned over and spit the pick into his guitar case. But before he could speak, the two skateboarders rolled past on the sidewalk, the chubby one making a face at us.

"I saw you up there talking to those kids," William said, watching them go. "You know 'em?"

"Just met. They think I'm a stalker."

William set his guitar against the storefront and shook his hair from his eyes. "The older one calls me William the Conqueror. Says I'm gonna conquer Nashville one day."

I was about to ask William the Conqueror if there were any bands needing a Spanish-speaking harmonica player when he stood on his toes and looked past me into the street. "There they go again," he said, his eyes tracking left to right.

I thought he meant the kids, but I spun around and caught a second glimpse of the convertible Caddy climbing over the rise in the road, a lime monstrosity heading back the way it came. This time the two girls weren't car dancing but sipping drinks through red straws.

"You know 'em?" I asked, wondering if I stayed on Main Street long enough that those girls would stop and be sociable.

William the Conqueror sat back on his stool, reached for his guitar, and slung the strap over his neck. "I don't know 'em. But I see 'em cruising in that car. You want to meet 'em?"

I leaned against the wall beside him, thinking of how bad I wanted to meet those girls but not wanting to appear too eager. After a short pause I muttered, "Perhaps."

William plucked his bass string and began to retune. "Can't blame you for that."

To press for more information felt pushy, but I went ahead anyway. That too had always been my habit. "So, William, you know how I can meet 'em?"

"Maybe." That was all he said, and he said it without looking up from his guitar.

"You gonna make me beg?"

He cocked his head to the side, listening to his careful tuning of the fifth string. "Throw a couple quarters in the guitar case, and I'll tell ya."

"You're bribing me?"

"I'm a poor college student, man . . . I gotta eat."

"And I'm a poor missionary from Ecuador."

He glanced up from the third string. "You're kidding."

"Just flew into town last night."

William furrowed his brow, then reconsidered his bribe. "Okay then, keep your quarters. That girl who was driving, the tall blonde, she and her friend volunteer at a little coffeehouse down on the lower end of Main. Sometimes they're both working, sometimes it's just one of 'em. You might try there on a weeknight. I got to get this second set going, so excuse me now, Curious Neil."

I tossed a quarter into his red-lined guitar case. "Thanks, Conq." Then I reclaimed my spot against the trunk of the maple tree and listened to their too-young-for-blues second set.

When the set ended, the crowd dispersed and the women in the band slipped away with friends, leaving William to pack up the equipment. I offered to help, but when I leaned down to pick up a speaker, my harmonica slid out of my pocket and clanged off the concrete.

William saw me stuffing it into my pants pocket. "Curious Neil plays? What key?"

"G."

He asked if I was any good.

I told him I'd made fifteen bucks at the airport.

He asked me if I was in any hurry.

"No hurry at all," I said, watching him unpack his guitar and point at the two remaining stools.

My first note bent into his chords, and in no time we'd found that elusive entity called chemistry. This time William not only lost himself in the strumming, he went off into some other world, his eyes shut, his head down over the guitar to where sweaty bangs tickled his bass string. I did my best to keep up, blowing and pulling, bending the high notes, stretching the low, the two of us loud enough that people began to stop and listen. Some even tossed change.

We improvised, took requests, and, yes, we played the blues. Poor-folk blues. Summertime blues.

And finally, an inspired remix of "Me and Bobby McGee," whereby Bobby, at the end of the song, wins the lottery and gets to live happily ever after with that girl who has missed him for all those years.

A half hour later we pulled twenty-six quarters and eight ones from William the Conqueror's red-lined guitar case. We split the cash, slapped high fives, and called it spontaneous.

"Pretty good?" I asked, divvying up the change.

"Not bad," William said. "But you'll make more money as a missionary."

I bought a burger and an ice cream with my half of the money and decided to lick my way back through a neighborhood of old homes, in no real hurry to get anywhere, just aiming in the general direction of Steve's.

The burger went quickly; the ice cream kept dripping onto my hiking boots. After I'd wiped them off and walked past all the mowing Greenvillians, I found the right street and turned the corner. Six houses ahead, at the fringe of Steve's yard, the Caddy convertible made a third appearance. It was backing out of his driveway.

I couldn't walk fast enough.

From five houses away I watched the Caddy and lots of wind-tossed hair coming toward me, the roar of the car's engine growing louder as it approached. With the remaining nub of my ice cream, I waved hello.

But the convertible flew past without so much as a nod from driver or passenger, just a light green blur in a warm rush to somewhere.

I turned and stared, the whoosh of it all blowing street dust into my last inch of waffle cone. Then it happened—a quick, backward wave from the passenger seat. Her straight black hair fluttered around her hand while she offered the briefest, no-look gesture of hello. It was one of those on-second-thought types of waves.

I'd gotten and given several of those in my lifetime.

I tossed my dust-riddled cone into a drain, hurried past the next four houses, and decided to confront Steve right there in his yard. Greasy stains covered his shorts. He was spraying WD-40 into the wheels of his mower and did not see me approach.

"You didn't tell 'em to wait on me?" I asked, striding up his driveway. "Why didn't you tell 'em to wait on me?"

Over the spray he said, "Didn't know when you were coming home."

"But you did mention me, right?"

"Sorry."

"Ya didn't even mention that I was staying with you?"

"I was just borrowing a WeedEater, Neil."

"From your ex? Wasn't the blonde one who was driving your ex?"

"Darcy owns a really nice WeedEater."

The long-handled contraption rested against his front steps, looking like it had never been used. "So this Darcy, the girl who said that dating you was like water-skiing behind a canoe—she lets you borrow her stuff?"

Steve scooted around to the other side of his mower and sprayed away. "Darcy moved into a second-story apartment last month. A refurbished thing on the far end of Main, so she doesn't have much use for a WeedEater. We still talk occasionally."

I stood over him, letting my shadow dim his work. "Well . . . you could have at least mentioned me to the other one, that raven-haired one. She looked kinda cute."

"She's bonkers," Steve said, pulling clumps of grass from around the blade. "Remember that email addressed to Ladies of the Quest?"

I squatted down to tilt the mower for him. "She's out on the quest?"

"She wrote the email."

"So that was Alexis?"

"Did ya see her silver piercing?"

"That Caddy flew past. I didn't see much of anything."

"She has a tiny piercing in her left eyebrow."

"I didn't see it."

"It's quite small."

"A thoughtful roommate would've mentioned me."

Steve pushed his lawn mower back into his carport, an uphill journey with a surprising lack of squeaks. Intent on finishing his project, he hurried to his front steps and picked up the WeedEater. He was about to crank the thing when he paused and said, "My advice is that you probably don't wanna date Alexis until you've scoped the city. There'll be single women at church tomorrow. Nice, normal girls."

Still put off that he didn't ask the Caddy girls to wait around, I shook my head. "There is no such thing as normal in this town."

He yanked the cord to his borrowed toolage. Over the whir of it he yelled, "Just give it a week. But if you were thoughtful, you woulda brought me a waffle cone!"

As punishment Steve had me rake up all his grass clippings. Figuring that I shouldn't complain about chores my first weekend, I loped to the

48

middle of his yard—my mind still on that car—and began stuffing gobs of clippings into a black plastic bag. I was sweaty, and the ants were marauding my boots. Soon Steve came out of his house guzzling a soft drink. He lounged on his steps, out of earshot and watching with indifference.

I squatted down to fill an already bulging bag. *Only men, God? Ya send me on furlough to meet Steve Cole, two skateboarders, and William the Conqueror?*

I tied off the bag and heaved it over my shoulder, my posture stooped as I hauled it down the driveway. Against the curb the bag landed with a thud. I stood on that hot suburban street and gazed the length of it, down to where the Caddy had blown by me just minutes ago. *Tomorrow, God, I'll be Presbyterian for the first time in my life. I know so little about the Presbytery, but would it be too much if you make a few of them female?*

Down the street, heat fumes rose from the pavement, and in the mirage I could still see that hand waving backward through all that hair.

# 4

Odder than a typical singles class would be a Presbyterian singles class with only five attendees—and all of them male.

My first Sunday in Carolina brought that very reality—five disappointed men about to gather in a semicircle reserved for the unmarried segment of North Hills Presbyterian, which met in a building across the parking lot from the church at 10:30 a.m., all by themselves.

Females were scarce, although at the snack table in the rear, powdered donuts were abundant.

Besides my new roommate—who had assumed the duty of host and was busy pouring coffee—I saw no one familiar. No tall, Caddy-driving blonde. Certainly no raven-haired, pierced girl who was bonkers. There were only other *hombres* in the room, a mingling threesome of business-types stumbling through small talk while wondering where everybody had gone.

I was wishing I'd gone to Montana.

Our teacher—a lanky, well-dressed fellow named Wade—came over in his pinstriped suit and yellow tie, shook my hand, and helped himself to one of Steve's atomic coffees. "Neil from Brazil?" he asked, reaching for the cream.

"Neil from Ecuador."

He nodded knowingly, then went to his wooden podium and motioned for us to have a seat.

Four suits and ties faced a more expensive suit and a much nicer tie. Then there was me, right in the middle of the front row, in my best pair of blue jeans. I thought the demographics were comedy enough, but then Wade folded his lesson in two, surveyed the room, and stuffed the papers in his coat pocket. "I must admit, guys, this has never happened."

"Pretty sad, huh?" Steve said, speaking for every bachelor in the room.

"Can I read you guys a verse?" Wade asked.

Steve looked left and right at all the surrounding maleness. "Wade, you're the teacher here, the appointed leader of a singles class. You're required to read us a verse."

So there we sat, girl-less and reverent and nibbling our donuts, waiting for well-dressed Wade to recite the Word.

Wade looked up from behind his wooden podium. "This is from Proverbs 18:22," he said, fingering the page. "He who finds a wife finds what is good . . . and receives *favor* from the Lord."

Vigorous head-nodding affirmed his recital.

Wade then explained to us that Jarvis himself had pointed out that very verse the previous summer, during his brief sojourn in the upstate. "According to Brother Jay," Wade said, looking up from the proverb, "for that verse to have true meaning, for it to come to fruition, requires real initiative on the part of the man. Now notice, men, that the verse says *find*, not sit on your sofa and wait for her to show up at your doorstep, delivering a large pepperoni with green peppers."

"I'd never date the pizza delivery girl," Steve said. "That'd be a mixing of priorities. Besides, I hate green peppers."

"I'm willing to take initiative, Wade," I said. "In fact, I came all the way from Quito, Ecuador, to do just that."

"Good for you," Wade said, both hands gripping the podium, "because the question before us is not whether the Lord will grant us favor. We know that in his own time he can grant every one of us some surprising favors. The real question for you guys is something far, far different."

I crossed my legs like the other men in my row, then uncrossed them when I realized I wasn't wearing socks. "How different?"

"Far, far different," Wade said, his voice frowning through the syllables. "It's a question from eras past, a question that has resounded through congregations long departed."

Steve squirmed in his seat, as if his logical, engineering brain could not handle any more allusion. "Could you please just tell us the question, Wade?"

Wade paused, looking at each of us before speaking. "Okay," he said, leaning on his podium. "To hopscotch or not to hopscotch, that is the question."

What followed was not so much laughter but a manly discussion of the pros and cons of church hopping. We discussed Hopping Man versus Waiting Man; Passive Man versus Aggressive Man; and, of course, man's history of going where the girls are.

It was no contest. We were going where the girls were.

So on the morning of June 26, and by a vote of 6 to 0 (Wade himself even raised a hand), the male-only singles class of North Hills Prez decided that in cases where there are no single females gracing pews, serving coffee, or sitting in the semicircles, the volatile game of hopscotch was entirely permissible.

Once a month, anyway.

Wade was firm in his belief that churchgoers of all genders needed a home base and a regular dollop of accountability. Most of us agreed. Then I elbowed Steve, and all of us agreed.

Now bonded as a group, the six of us gathered around the donuts, washing them down with our atomic coffees and speculating on which denominations had stolen all the single women. One guy blamed the Baptists, another the Pentecostals.

Wade, speaking with his mouth full, theorized that since contemporary music and casual dress seemed to be catching on fast, a large nondenominational church on the east side might have lured the women away. "And as far as our little attendance problem," Wade said, "my sympathies to you guys, but you better enjoy singleness while you can. I do love the married life, although I kinda miss driving an RX-7. Now I'm a daddy of two, driving a brown minivan."

Wade had to go fetch one of his kids from kindergarten, so Steve and I stuck around to clean up the snack table. A skinny refrigerator was wedged into the back of the singles building, and after I'd put away the half-and-half, I stopped to admire the photographs taped to the door. Some were faded with the years, others were fairly new. Most were pictures of men and women in various outdoor settings.

One showed ten people on a sailboat, waving as they left the dock. Another had two girls and three guys in cut-off jeans and T-shirts, sliding off a river ledge, over a waterfall, and into a mountain pool. I felt like I'd missed out.

I scanned across the freezer, then down the door. On the far right was a picture from a beach. In the foreground was a tan surfer, his thick brown hair tumbling nearly to his shoulder, a yellow and purple surfboard under one arm, a petite blonde under the other. What struck me about the picture was not the surfer couple—attractive as they were—but the people in the background. For one: Jay. Looking sunburned as he stood between two girls, Jarvis had two clumps of airless floats all squished up in his hands, one sky blue, one bright orange. I recognized the brunette to Jay's right as his girlfriend. The other girl was tall and fair, statuesque in her light green swimsuit.

I was looking for other pictures of them when Steve tapped me on the shoulder and said to hurry up, that we needed to lock up the little brick building and get going.

The vinyl seats felt hot as Steve cranked his Jeep and stared into his rearview, waiting to back out of a crowded parking lot. In less than a minute the sweat beads were forming on our foreheads. He turned the AC on high.

"That was her, right?" I asked, sheathing my seat belt into place. "In the beach picture, in the light green swimsuit . . . that was Darcy?"

Steve gunned the engine. "Yep."

"And the surfer couple, that's who you mentioned the other night?"

"Ransom and Jamie Delaney," Steve said, adjusting his mirror. "Parents of Wally Kahuna. They've all been visiting a Pentecostal church lately."

"I saw Jay and Allie in that pic too . . . So where were you?"

He shifted into reverse. "Painting with that second gallon of sea-green latex," he mumbled.

We were still in the parking lot, trying to wedge ourselves into a Presbyterian departure, when a middle-aged lady hopped out of a black Lexus and rushed over and tapped on my passenger window. I lowered it, then returned her smile. "Yes ma'am?"

She thrust a gold business card into my hand, reached across me, and handed one to Steve. "My name is Mary Ann Demoss," she said with confidence, "and I sell real estate. If either of you young men ever get the urge to buy a house, I'd appreciate your giving me a call."

A nod to each of us and she was back into her Lexus, motioning for Steve to cut in line.

"Who was that?" I asked.

Steve waved to her and cut in. "She's the mother of Alexis, who you saw yesterday in the Caddy."

"And her mom hands out cards after Sunday service?"

Steve nodded as he made a left out of North Hills Prez. "Ms. Demoss knows little about Jesus but everything about real estate."

I made no judgments. Like Jarvis said, it was a city of surprising complexity.


Not so surprising was the third item on the back page of the church bulletin. On the way home, beneath the flapping soft top of Steve's Jeep, I was considering the implications of "Last names A thru M bring a vegetable. N thru Z bring a dessert. Fried chicken and baked beans supplied by the deacons." I had heard about the popularity of Southern church picnics but had not attended one since elementary school.

Steve braked for a stoplight and frowned when he noticed me reading the bulletin. "Neil, if there were no girls at singles class, then why in the world would you want to go to the picnic?"

I countered his frown with an overconfident grin. "I have a hunch."

My hunch was that the church-hopping girls—wherever they were— might also be inclined to hop between picnics. Maybe they'd have a Jell-O salad with the Methodists, a croissant with the Episcopalians, some fried chicken here with North Hills Prez, and later, a spoonful of vanilla pudding with the Lutherans, who I understood to be connoisseurs of good pudding.

This event also provided a needed excuse to say no to my roomie, who had plans—and asked me to join him—to visit his parents in Gaffney, South Carolina, an hour away.

Steve pulled into his driveway and pressed the issue. "What's it gonna be, Neil? Home cooking or the picnic chow?"

Surely his mom's meatloaf was awe-inspiring, but I was in the midst of introducing myself to Greenville and did not care to spend a sunny Sunday afternoon looking at childhood pictures of little Stevie, or Stephanie, or Stephen, or whatever they called him in his hometown.

I climbed out of his Jeep, an N through Z who would have to buy, not make, his dessert. "Give my best to the house of Cole."

He shifted into reverse and said, "Later."

An hour later I installed a new battery in Jay's old Blazer, then changed into shorts and my madras shirt. Time to test the powers of potluck.

At 1:30 p.m. I cranked the Blazer barefooted, heading for a Presbyterian picnic with my hopes up, my cap on, and my store-bought pecan pie riding low and sugary in the passenger seat.

The lush green lawn of North Hills looked to have sprouted families instead of weeds and mushrooms. The crowd numbered at least two hundred, folks mostly seated and eating when I arrived. I saw no one familiar, not even Wade, the singles teacher, who I'd pictured seated on a quilt, surrounded by giddy kids and a comely wife.

The four tables of food set in the center of the lawn seemed friendlier than the picnickers, and soon my Chinet was filled to overflowing, the plate heavy in my left hand, a sweet tea sloshing in my right.

*Now, where to sit?*

I turned east, west, and south.

Surely someone would say, "Sit with us." But no one looked my way.

Surely someone would wave me over. But no one was waving; they were all busy eating.

Not being the recipient of a "sit with us" or a wave over, I was about to sit by myself when I received, of all things, a "yoo-hoo."

I was not expecting to be yoo-hooed, but that's the greeting a sovereign God chose to allow.

From behind me, under the shade of a tilted oak, came the high-pitched "yoo-hoo" from a twosome. Both women. Elderly women. They nearly matched with their gray hair and flower-print dresses, both of them spooning macaroni and nodding hello.

This was not the ideal single-guy-at-church-picnic scenario, but maybe they had granddaughters.

I approached with sloshing tea, timid smile, and a compliment. "Ladies, that has got to be the biggest and brightest picnic blanket I've ever seen."

The one in the pink flower-print smiled and motioned for me to sit. "It's of European fabric, dear. We recently returned from a journey." She had gauze wrapped around her left ankle, and when she reached to adjust it I could see sunspots covering her hands and wrists.

The other lady, who wore dark shades and a beaded, oversized apple-green necklace normally reserved for the young, nodded her agreement. "Yes, yes, it was quite a journey." Then she slowly rose and, for a moment, stood there tottering. "I need a dessert, young man. Can I get you a dessert?"

Already seated cross-legged, I had not even begun to eat. "No thank you, ma'am. Maybe later."

In a shuffle she made for the dessert table. After she was out of hearing range, her friend leaned forward and whispered to me. "Her name's Francine, dear, and she's been through three husbands."

This probably was not relevant information for a twenty-nine-year-old, but I made the best of my circumstances and continued to people watch. Past the big people was a horde of little people, children in designer clothing exhausting themselves in a garbled game of soccer. I tried not to laugh at them, but it was no use. Try as they might, these middle-class Presbyterian children couldn't kick a ball out the back of a pickup truck. In Ecuador I'd seen countless neighborhoods of barefooted *niños*, six-year-olds with ragged shorts and calloused toes who could whip these suburban kids two age brackets ahead. The children running around behind our picnic were all handsome and stylish and loved, but soccer players? Nope.

After two quick bites of chicken and a swig of tea, I introduced myself. "I'm Neil, ma'am, and I'm visiting from Ecuador."

My senior citizen lunch partner dabbed at her mouth with a napkin. "And I'm Beatrice. My friend Francine and I are visiting from First Baptist."

This lady had to be at least eighty, and her friend a solid seventy-five, and so I reconsidered my first impression: Elderly Baptist women at a Presbyterian picnic to meet retired men? If so, then there was something in the tap water of Greenville County, and it wasn't fluoride.

Their European blanket was fringed in gold, and its pattern was elaborate: bright red ovals crisscrossed waves of navy blue, then navy blue returned the favor. Adding symmetry to the whole was an elaborate gold weave, its luster so rich that I imagined the threads were shredded from the metal itself. I rubbed my hand over its thickness, fingered the fringes, and guessed at its cost.

With much less admiration, a black ant began a journey across a section of red.

"Flick that critter away," Beatrice said, watching me watch the ant.

"This blanket, ma'am—it looks like something from royalty."

Beatrice sipped her tea, then dabbed at her mouth again. "Roy was not his name, dear. I bought it from Pierre. Did you flick it yet? I can't have ants parading through my potato salad."

"Yes ma'am, consider it flicked." I looked around a third time at the clusters of picnickers but saw no one resembling an available, twenty-something female.

When I turned my attention back to Beatrice, she was holding a spoonful of macaroni to her mouth, confusion etched on her face. "Neil, of what were we speaking?"

"About Europe . . . your royal blanket."

"Yes, of course. Have you ever been to Europe, dear?"

"No ma'am, I've mostly taught Spanish to missionaries in Central and South America."

She swallowed the spoonful and nodded. "And just what will the missionaries do with their Spanish?"

I was about to bite into the thicker side of a chicken leg, so I gave her my condensed answer. "Well, ma'am, they use it to communicate with the citizens, and we hope they'll use it to spread the gospel."

"Oh my," Beatrice said, her eyes wide with surprise, "that sounds like so much work. Why can't the citizens just get the gospel off the television? They do have a Spanish gospel program, you know. I like the way the host dresses. Ricardo is very flashy. Do you watch Ricardo, dear?"

"No ma'am, but I'm sure he's terrific."

"Oh yes, and one time he and Julio Iglesias sang a duet of—" She stopped in midsentence, sat up straight, and looked out at the crowd.

I took a hasty bite of the chicken leg before speaking again. "What is it, Beatrice?"

"Where is that Francine? She was only going for dessert."

I stood on the royal blanket and scanned the picnic. Past the tables and the clusters of families, Francine was seated on the grass, talking with an elderly gentleman who wore one of those tweed British driving hats. From the look of things, he was entertaining her quite well.

Beatrice stood, her weight on her good ankle, and put a hand on my shoulder. "Do you see her, dear?"

"Yes," I replied, pointing across the grass. "See over there?"

Beatrice frowned hard, then sat back down. "She always does this to me. If it weren't for my ankle I could've met him first. You'd think Francine would look out for me, wouldn't you?"

"You would think, ma'am. So, how did you hurt your ankle?"

"Blackbirds, dear. One was pecking at my snapdragons, and when I went to kick him I missed and hit my wheelbarrow."

"Ouch."

Beatrice poked at her macaroni. "I just despise a blackbird."

In keeping with my policy of leaping right in, I began to question this old lady about her motives—not that my own were the essence of purity.

58

"Ma'am, I don't mean to pry, but how many times have you visited North Hills Presbyterian?"

She sipped her tea and glanced again across the lawn, visibly jealous of Francine. "Visited? Oh, I've never visited, dear. We just came for the picnic. All the good Baptist men in this town are taken."

Beyond the church a mass of gray clouds had enveloped the west. I watched them gather momentum, saw the grass lose its sheen. "So how did you know about the picnic?"

"Email," she said matter-of-factly. "Francine gets emails telling her which churches are having picnics, and then we bake our best pies, show up, and do that thing you young folks do."

"You mean scope?"

"Yes, dear. Francine and I are learning to do the scope. I think she's the quicker study, which is strange because I have the better vision. Francine can't see to drive, you know. So we always take my car. The mooch never offers gas money."

*Senior Ladies of the Quest?* Maybe they ranked the retirement homes too.

The first crackle of thunder alerted all that a storm was approaching. I helped Beatrice to her feet, then folded her pricey blanket into a thick square. "Can I escort you to your car, Beatrice?"

She glanced down at her ankle-wrapping. "Why, yes. Yes, you can. And I fully intend to tip you."

"No ma'am, no need for tipping."

We were still on the lawn but halfway to the parking lot when she squeezed my arm and stopped our progress. "Are you sure I can't tip you? Surely you can use some date money."

"No ma'am, I couldn't take it. But I could use all the part-time jobs I can get."

Together we shuffled toward her car. "Do you like working outdoors?" she asked.

"Outdoors would be fine," I said, impressed at how well she was walking on that bad ankle. "You have a job in mind?"

"It's going to rain soon."

"Yes ma'am. Um, about that outdoor thing . . ."

She looked up at the clouds. "Patience, dear."

After walking her to her Oldsmobile, I watched the tweed-hat gentleman escort Francine to the passenger side. Just another senior scoper, saving his best moves for Sunday picnics.

Dark clouds gathered quickly and the temperature took a plunge, the entire picnic now in a swirl. I said good-bye to the ladies and to the dapper gentleman, then hustled over to the dessert table. There was no real rain yet, but the wind had increased to where it blew the stack of napkins from atop the table and sent them dancing on their corners, fluttering across the lawn in an airy samba of white.

Windblown Presbyterians were grabbing up dishes and heading for cars, and since no one had yet claimed any of the desserts, I decided to take advantage of foul weather and use the opportunity to load up a paper plate. I was trying to decide what to pilfer when, from my right—with a handful of recaptured napkins in her hands—a short, redheaded young woman hurried up to the table. She set the napkins under a stack of plates and reached for a serving knife. "Here," she said, literally rubbing elbows with me, "let me help you. Which would you like?"

Thunder cleared its throat, and we both glanced over the church. "What?" I muttered, distracted by the gathering storm.

She pointed at the assortment. "Desserts. Which would you like?"

"Oh, I was thinking of sampling them all."

"Don't be a pig."

"I'm not a pig. I'm just curious."

"Maybe so, but one of the deacons set a two-dessert limit per adult."

"A two-dessert limit?"

She smiled and said, "His name is Stanley, and I hate that rule."

That's when I pointed at the one marked key lime.

The first drops of rain bounced off pie lids as the redhead served with great haste. I looked past her at all the families rushing toward the safety of minivans, wives ducking to protect their hairdos, kids trying to catch drops on their tongues. I was in no great hurry myself—watching storms was a favorite pastime.

Filled with two heaping slices, my Chinet performed as advertised. "You're getting wet," I said to the server girl.

"I'm about to bolt," she replied, setting down the serving knife and grabbing up two pies.

She seemed intent on saving the food. I found a box of plastic forks, and before I knew it I was standing with seven strangers on the top step of the North Hills Presbyterian sanctuary, watching a thunderstorm from beneath the cover of an awning.

Miss Pie Server, who I surmised was near my age and was not wearing a ring, stood beside me, round-faced and friendly, the top of her head even with my shoulder. Given how this weekend had begun, I was determined to get in at least one get-to-know-ya question. "Did you make this?" I asked, sliding my fork into the sweet, tangy dessert.

A bolt of lightning frontlit a monstrous gray cloud, drawing our attention skyward. She shook moisture from her flattened hair. "Yep," she said, "but I just got here."

With no hesitation whatsoever, I set the Chinet at my feet, wiped my hands on my shorts, and introduced myself.

# 5

A married friend from the language school once told me that he had not so much found his wife as bumped right into her, as if God just plopped her right in his path. There was (and is) truth in that, I'm sure. But it's the kind of truth that comes in hindsight, not in the midst of a seven-month dating drought, where every shared glance in a grocery store aisle, every five-second hello across the pews, every fleeting glimpse of girlish hair flayed back in a speeding convertible causes a man to think, *Ah, yes, that one, that's got to be her.*

A flash of "that's got to be her" jolted me when the redhead, still beside me under the awning, told me that her name was Lydia. Everyone else had already run for their cars, taking with them most of the desserts and leaving her and me standing on the top step, our backs to the sanctuary door.

Raindrops shrunk into a drizzle, although neither Lydia nor I were in a hurry to leave. Still damp from the run through the rain, she looked at me like we'd met before. "You've got to be the Neil who teaches Spanish and climbs on roofs to talk to God, right?"

Stunned by what she knew of me, I took a step backward—right into my empty dessert plate.

"Okay," I said, playing along, "who've you been talking to . . . Jay?"

Her burgundy blouse was dotted with raindrops, and she admired her damp khakis before answering. "I got an email from my friend Allie down in Ecuador. She's Jay's girlfriend, and he told her about you, then she told me. Information flows freely in our crowd."

"So I'm learning." My glance across the lawn revealed three cakes left out on the tables, their icing melting in the drizzle. I was trying to think of what to say next, a reason for Lydia to stick around and not bolt for her car. "I wish you hadn't given away those two pies. I'm still hungry."

She rubbed her stomach and smiled. "So you want to break Deacon Stanley's two-dessert limit, eh?"

"By multiples of three and with icing on my chin."

Lydia looked out at the parking lot, then at the ruined cakes atop the tables. "Neil, do you have any objection to wearing damp clothes to a swanky restaurant?"

"Nope. I'd even wear swanky clothes to a damp restaurant."

After a dash across the lawn, I opened the door to the Blazer for her. She climbed in, and off we went.

Lydia knew every restaurant in Greenville, and in less than a mile she'd recited the best and the worst of them. "We could try downtown," she said, pointing left as I braked for a stoplight. "But most places are closed. You like Italian desserts?"

I mashed the gas as the light changed. "Haven't had Italian in eons."

"Then turn right on Stone."

Finally, I had met one of the Greenville women. So far, so good.

She was what some guys call a double-door girl, a female who, upon arriving at a restaurant, unlatches her seat belt and sits perfectly still, hands in lap while waiting for the guy to get out and walk around and open her door again. I suppose an extra measure of class is afforded a woman if she does it correctly.

So defined, Lydia was a classy woman.

"I only do this on first dates," she said, smiling as I shut the car door behind her. "After that I've been known to open doors for the man."

Her comment made me laugh. If this was a date, it was the most spontaneous one I'd ever been on. But at least my streak was over.

We were at the south end of Greenville's Restaurant Row, seated in a booth in a softly lit corner of an Italian eatery. Rich melodies of opera piped through the ceiling, the speakers embedded in terra cotta. It was almost 3:00, and the few patrons around us looked upscale, reserved, and dry. We, on the other hand, looked lower class, uninhibited, and damp. The waiters were ghosts in white shirts—they seemed not to walk but to glide between tables. There was probably a special school for that. Glide school. A tall one with rolled-up sleeves eased over with glasses of water. He left in a wisp, then returned and set a basket of rolls on our table. He said he'd be right back.

Lydia tucked her napkin in her lap. "So you came to the picnic all by yourself?"

"Steve had a family thing," I said over the menu. "That picnic was all families. And, of course, the elderly."

"It's always families. Always too many kids, and always too much macaroni. The singles mostly avoid the picnics."

I lowered the menu to my lap. "But you managed to show up, although you were very late."

She shrugged as if not to tarry on the subject.

We dipped our bread into a dainty dish of olive oil, measuring each other between the dips, using food as camouflage. I was about to ask her where she'd been on Sunday morning—if she had fallen victim to church hopping—when she picked up the leather-bound wine list and dropped it, *smack*, beneath our booth.

"Now, that's much better," she said, grinning with pleasure. "No more temptation."

I lifted my water glass and inspected the shrinking cubes. "I've never really considered it temptation. Just an accessory."

She seemed to silently grade my responses. Next she pressed her knife into butter and admired the yellow square. "Neil, did you ever have to eat bugs in Ecuador? I think one time in her village my friend Allie had to cook bugs."

What could I say? Apparently upstate South Carolina thought that anyone remotely connected with missions lived in a hut and grubbed around for seeds and insects. "Nope," I said, playing with my fork, "no bug burgers for me."

"Oh," she said, as if my response fell short of expectations. "It's just that my girlfriends and I speculated on your living conditions."

I tore some crust from a roll and bent it in two. "I lived in a city with bleached-white buildings and lots of noisy street vendors. I could buy milk and eggs, even Rice Krispies. Plus I had a real, working commode. Hot water too."

She looked disappointed. "Oh. I just thought . . ."

I leaned in, elbows on the table, eyebrows raised in inquisition.

"Well, I knew you did the language thing, Neil," she said, reaching back to test the dampness in her hair, "but I still thought I was having dessert with a jungle missionary and that I'd get to hear about some rainforest adventures."

I hated to let Lydia down, but after my next sip of water I did just that. "I teach Spanish to people in a city so that they can communicate in the midst of adventure. *Sí?*"

She wiped her fingers on her napkin and managed a halfhearted *"Sí."* Her clothes had dried, and her questions continued. "You don't smoke, do you?"

I muttered a quick no as our stealthy waiter arrived to take our order. We ordered two spoons and a tiramisu.

As soon as the waiter left, Lydia resumed the interrogation. "What about beer, Neil?"

"Nope. Rarely drink beer."

She sipped her water, then wiped her mouth. "Rarely or never ever?"

Between my own gulp and swallow I cobbled together an answer. "Okay, six years ago at a Super Bowl party in Richmond I had a Michelob Light with my pizza. Think I'll still get in?"

"Where, Richmond?"

"No, heaven."

She plunged a wedge of lemon into her glass. "Not according to some elders I've met."

With sleek efficiency our waiter delivered dessert, the glass goblet swooping down before us, landing soft and centered. I motioned for Lydia to take the first sample, which she did.

She seemed to have a predetermined list of first-date topics to plow through, as if she would eliminate me quickly if I did not score in the ninety-eighth percentile. But maybe I could be like Jay and ask for extra credit. At this point I really just wanted to enjoy the dessert.

My first bite would have to wait. "Neil," Lydia said, scooping a second spoonful, "this may be early for such inquiries, but how do you feel about the work issue?"

This had to be the rule-obsessed girl that Jay had mentioned.

My napkin had fallen to my feet, so my answer began from the leaned-over position. "I love my work. Love teaching language. Living in foreign countries, it's—"

"Not *your* work, Neil. The woman's. Do you believe in stay-at-home moms?"

I sat there wondering what had happened to picnic personality, to twin servings of pie, the pecan and the key lime, which was marvelous. I was Neil-on-furlough, not at all prepared for a stay-at-home-mom type of date. I wanted a marvelous-key-lime-pie type of date. "Lydia, I suppose it benefits the kids greatly if moms stay at home. Unless of course the mom wants to work . . . and so I'd stay at home, teach the rug rats some Spanish."

Judging from her nod, I thought my answer scored reasonably well, so I used my small success to try to steer things back the other way. The time had arrived to ask her what I'd been waiting to ask.

"Lydia, if you're confident that God is in control, and you claim membership at North Hills Prez, then where were you this morning during singles class?"

She pushed the dessert away from her and performed closure with her spoon. "I'd rather not say."

I finished the tiramisu and set my spoon across hers to make an X. "You were Methodist, weren't you?"

"Nope."

"Pentecostal?"

"I don't have the energy."

"Baptist?"

66

Her gaze was on the table. Then she held her napkin over her face, as if to hide a blush. "Maybe."

"No kidding? You were Baptist today?"

She dropped the napkin in her lap and reached for her water. "Southern fried!" she said, just before a sip and swallow. "It was actually fun. I've only been Baptist four times this year."

I rethought the X and set the spoons in parallel. Then I crossed them with my knife to make an H. It stood for hopscotch. "Four times . . . and the other weeks you're something else?"

"It's such fun!"

She seemed to have all kinds of rules for a man but little account-ability for herself. To openly try to convict someone was not my style. However, I at least wanted to find someone who could give reasons for what she was doing, something beyond using fun as the determinant for hopscotching.

And how about a dash of faith? When I shared the gist of these thoughts, her response confirmed that the two of us were just singles who had little in common but singleness itself.

"Neil," she said, avoiding my gist altogether, "you've got to loosen up. As a visitor you'll never get far in this city if you don't play along. But maybe you can't because you're an, um, almost missionary."

There was that word again. Almost. I was almost a missionary, almost thirty, and almost amused at myself for being on this date. To my credit, I'd learned to tolerate nearly anyone, and Lydia was no exception. "Okay, Lydia, then why go out with the new guy? Have you already eliminated most of Greenville?"

With her left hand she swooshed a piece of bread into the olive oil, holding it before her and talking around it. "Maybe I wanted to check you out before you met my friends. I usually get lost in the crowd when Alexis and Darcy are around."

Curious over where this was going, I leaned back in the booth again. "Doubt that. But really? You fear losing a guy to your girlfriends?"

She licked a crumb from her lips. "Oh, I'm not worried about it.

Besides, your roommate emailed me last night. We're going out on Wednesday."

"You're going out with Steve?" In a gesture of surrender, I waved my white napkin and draped it over my water glass.

Lydia smiled the confident smile of a redhead with a dating backlog. "It's a bit strange, given that Steve's ex, Darcy, is my good friend. I guess we'll all just have to learn to share."

Right at that moment, right there in that corner booth of an Italian eatery where I could barely afford dessert, I very nearly left Greenville. I couldn't grasp it. The city was just a huge, boiling pot of relational gumbo.

The only reason I stayed was the vague feeling that I was in town for some purpose beyond searching for my soul mate. The substance of that feeling, like our dessert check, would be long in arriving.

When finally the check did arrive I reached for my wallet and set my cash on the table. "Would you like anything else, Lydia?"

She shook her head no. Then, as if she'd been waiting all afternoon to spring this on me, she said, "Neil, I know something that you don't know that I know."

I picked up the napkin and waved it overhead. "I give up. What?"

"I heard something . . . But I shouldn't say."

"Fine." Maybe she wanted me to beg her. I wasn't going to beg.

She leaned back into the leather booth and crossed her arms. The look on her face told me this was one of those stored-up, spring-it-on-him-at-end-of-date topics. "I heard you're also planning to ask out my other two friends, that you're planning on dating all of us."

That must have been one fact-filled email from Ecuador. Maybe these Greenville girls were tighter than I thought. "Okay . . . yes. Yes, I am."

"Well?" She looked downright annoyed with me.

"Well, what?" I asked.

"How can you just wander into town and ask out a whole group of good friends?"

The waiter returned to gather payment, detected the awkwardness of the moment, and with great stealth removed my twenty. But his timing had distracted me. "What were you saying, Lydia?"

She crossed her arms tighter. "I asked you how you could just wander into town and ask out a whole group of good friends."

"But you just admitted that you're going out with my roommate."

The logic in that did nothing to mute her emotion—a possessive huff preceded an unhappy puff, as if she were my wife and had a claim on me.

But this woman had nothing of the sort. She had a free dessert, two opened doors, a ride back to the church, and a future with someone else.

We were about to leave when I reached under the booth, picked up the leather-bound wine list, and set it back on the table. "Some progressive Episcopalians might need this," I said.

Whatever sound she made fell somewhere short of genuine, perhaps a muffled giggle or a first-date nicety.

I've always had trouble distinguishing genuine giggles from first-date niceties.

# 6

Over the course of nearly thee decades of singleness (the count began at birth), I'd entertained thoughts of "that's got to be her" no less than fifty times. It was true of Denise Skruggs, who sat in front of me in tenth grade world history. It was true of Carmella, in Quito, who sang alto in our twenty-person choir at the small Bible Church and eventually fell for an Argentinean tenor. And it was true of a collegiate cello player named Georgianna, who after four months of dating me proclaimed that cellos and harmonicas made for very poor duets. So I imagined she and her cello had by now plopped down in the path of a conductor, or a violinist, or, heaven forbid, a flutist.

I mean no offense to anyone who prefers the daintier instrument, but most men would have ego issues if a woman were to dump him for a flutist. Who knows, maybe Georgianna married the conductor.

With old flames dominating my thoughts, I returned home from the afternoon rule-a-thon determined to stick to the plan—to meet all of the Greenville girls, even though the city continued to baffle. I sprawled out on Steve's sofa and wondered again if I'd chosen the right destination for furlough.

Greenville, South Carolina, did not seem backwoods, redneck, or slow. It seemed yuppie, fast-track, and diverse. A junior Atlanta, perhaps. Yes, a junior, yuppie Atlanta where no one, at any age, waited for God to plop someone down in their path. In fact, it seemed that all the paths were merging, and bliss-seeking convoys of the unwed were speeding toward a collision course at an already crowded address, the intersection of Faith and Impatience.

I'd spent many nights stalled at that intersection.

Noisy there.

Lots of horns.

Confusing traffic signals.

And plenty of folks running yellows.

After turning these thoughts over for a few minutes, I pulled my harmonica from my pocket and tried to play myself into a nap. Yet composing "The Bad Date Blues" provoked not slumber but analysis, a Sunday evening comparison between the harmonica and single women: The harmonica is simple, fairly tough for its size, and can easily be stored in your pocket, backpack, or glove compartment.

Contrast this with a single woman, who is complex, fairly sensitive about everything, and cannot, under any circumstances, be stored, backburnered, or compartmentalized. If the man messes up and treats her in such manner, the relational notes will go sour, and the melody that he's tried so hard to create will end up sounding like a muffler dragging on the interstate beneath an '84 Dodge.

Sparks will fly, sure.

I'd witnessed such sparks. The Dodge had belonged to Georgianna, my college flame who thought cellos and harmonicas made for poor duets but did not think a muffler dragging on concrete was anything that required immediate attention. This is why I hoped she married the conductor, someone who has a sense of equilibrium.

My own sense of balance convinced me to stop reflecting and do something productive. Filled with triple desserts, I somehow managed to roll from the sofa, shuffle to Steve's computer desk, and log on. Not to search the classified ads but to make good on my pledge to email Brother Jay. He and his village tribe deserved an update:

**Jarvis,**

**It's Sunday evening, day three of furlough. South Carolina is even nuttier than you described it, including your buddy Steve, who has no problem posing as a woman.**

**This afternoon I drove your old Blazer to a picnic at North Hills Prez.**

You should've seen them, food-toting hordes arriving at the tables as if their Corning Ware contained the crown jewels. I've never been Presbyterian before, Jarvis. And I've never seen so many people eating so many variations of macaroni. Ecuador would invade Peru for macaroni like that.

At the dessert table I met Lydia, the redheaded one. She has about four thousand rules for any male she meets, so I've eliminated myself from her pool of prospects. The other two girls remain elusive.

As for the hopscotch, it does appear to be epidemic, having now infected the elderly.

Didn't you tell me that you met Allie in the singles class? You have no idea what a feat that was.

sogapalaG,

Neil


After cyber-sending the note into the wilds of South America, I spotted a phone list next to the keyboard, buried under some bills and a 401k statement from Steve's engineering firm. I didn't peek at his 401k, but the phone list looked interesting. The list totaled three pages, and it contained all the phone numbers for the far-flung singles of North Hills Presbyterian.

A quick flip through the alphabetized contents revealed an Alexis Demoss, the aforementioned Lydia Hutto, and at the bottom of the last page, a Darcy Yeager. My thoughts had now caught up to my surroundings, and in place of vague reflections on old flames came clear visions of fresh sparks.

*Darcy Yeager. Hmmm. No, she's Steve's ex, plus she still loans him power tools. No ex of mine ever loaned me power tools. Should probably not call her. Might cause friction with roommate—can't do friction on first week of furlough. But that other one, that black-haired Alexis Demoss who waved at me backwards from the car on Saturday. Sí!*

*What if the hopscotching women of Greenville were to get dates not from*

*their plethora of congregational scopings but from the new guy who doesn't*
*even possess a car or a suit, just a borrowed phone list?*

The obvious question was how many church phone lists those girls appeared on. From what I'd seen and heard so far, a dozen or more seemed likely.

Free advertising, I guess . . . and why not?

I wondered if the apostle Paul ever took advantage of free advertising, leaving his forwarding address while tromping around on all those missionary journeys. Probably not, as I'd always thought his thorn in the flesh (whatever it was) made him headstrong, unfazed by the opposite sex. That theory was countered once by Jay, who believed Paul's thorn was having to deal with all those Jewish and Gentile singles groups, donkey-riding legions of bachelors and bachelorettes who constantly interrupted Paul's preaching to invite him to prehistoric Putt Putt and beach retreats to the Red Sea.

Who knew, but I suspected Jay's New Testament theology was worse than his Spanish.

Perhaps it broke some unwritten, Bible Belt dating custom to call a young woman whom you've yet to meet, just because you saw her name on a church phone list. Perhaps I would get reprimanded by an elder. Or perhaps Deacon Stanley would impose a one-date limit on visiting missionaries.

Yet waiting on a formal introduction seemed so constraining. I didn't care if Jay and Steve wouldn't recommend that raven-haired Alexis. I didn't even care if she had a tiny silver piercing in her left eyebrow. At least she'd waved.

I was flipping through the phone list a second time, speculating on the sincerity of that backward wave, when Steve opened the door to his kitchen and hurried inside. Through the doorway to his den he saw me at his computer desk. He held up a Tupperware container so that I could see it. "Mom's meatloaf. You can have one slice of the three."

He shoved it into his fridge as I waved him to the den. "Guess what I did this afternoon, Steve-o."

He came up behind me and gripped the back of my chair. "Tell me you didn't use my computer to search the personal ads."

"Nope. I was just emailing Jay. This afternoon I had a dessert date."

"With who?"

I logged off the computer. "A little redhead named Lydia."

He pulled my chair backward and raised his voice. "And?"

"And I'm sorry for stepping on your toes." I rose from the chair and faced him. "She told me that the two of you were going out."

Without responding Steve walked down the hall and into his room. He came back out wearing shorts and a beige, logoed engineering shirt. I think he owned about ten of those shirts. He sat on the sofa, and I plopped back down in his desk chair, anticipating an awkward conversation.

"I do have a friendly dinner date with Lydia," he said matter-of-factly. "But remember, Neil, you and your dating agenda have to avoid my ex. No asking out Darcy. Even if she asks you to go cruising in her car, you have to decline."

"Because we're roommates, right?"

"Because we're roommates."

I pulled out my wallet and rechecked the contents. "I only have enough money left for one more date, so tonight I'm gonna call Darcy's friend, that Alexis who waved backward from the ugly lime Caddy."

"Darcy's Sherbet is not ugly," Steve said, crossing his arms.

"Sherbet? Oh, so now you're defending your ex?"

"No, I just have memories with that car."

I picked up the phone list and scanned it again. "I think you still want her."

"I think you need to forget dating and find a job."

He was joking, but he was right. "Um, about a job . . . the other day you said you had something lined up for me."

Steve reached out, took the phone list from me, and flipped it over. "Right here, Neil, on the back of this phone list, is the number for the church secretary." He handed me the list. "Call her on Tuesday morning and tell her that I sent you."

He was heading for his bedroom when I blurted out, "Do you have any idea what you're getting into by going out with rule-obsessed Lydia?"

He stood in the doorway and paused before he answered. "You go out with Alexis, I'll go out with Lydia, and then we'll compare notes. Deal?"

I reached for the phone. "Deal."

"But no hanging out with my ex." Ten seconds later he came back out of his bedroom, barefooted, and stared at me from the hall.

"What now?" I asked, about to dial the number for this mysterious Alexis.

"There're rumors of a beach trip over July 4th," Steve said, grinning. And without another word he shut his door, leaving me to imagine the sandy details.

# 7

At the kitchen table on Tuesday, I was doing math on a napkin. The facts were not encouraging: I had $373 in cash, no checking account, and no credit card. I'd agreed to pay Steve $250 per month in rent for June and July; I still owed for June. And the Blazer needed gas. I didn't need Jay to tell me this wasn't adding up. When the figuring was done and I'd stared numbly at the facts, the blue numbers on the napkin took on a wavy appearance, as if their sinewy shapes and lamp-lit sheen were mocking me, letting me know I'd never be able to afford a beach trip.

Unless, of course, there really was a job waiting for me at the church.

I dialed the number. Elaine, the secretary, answered on the first ring, like she was expecting me. In a surprise move she asked if I would be willing to help a professional gardener, as North Hills Presbyterian was in the middle of a church beautification project. She even told me that the deacons had requested a theme—"Purity of White."

I knew little about gardening, but the three-day job would pay nine dollars an hour, so I put on my worst clothes, grabbed my cap, and drove the Blazer to the church.

When I arrived, the professional gardener was working midway down the side of the brick sanctuary, hunched over and digging in the dirt. She seemed very experienced. She appeared quite knowledgeable. And she looked older than flora itself.

Why Baptist Beatrice was planting Presbyterian petunias one can only

76

guess. Whether divinely nudged or of her own choosing, there she was, on her knees and rearranging the earth. Her hands were covered in brown dirt, and her straw hat cast a circular shadow across the petunias. Behind her was a pull-along toolbox that held every gardening tool imaginable.

I approached from behind, and when my shadow fell across her she turned from her digging and squinted. "Hello there, young man. You must be the helper?"

"Yes ma'am, I'm Neil from the picnic. I was hired to come and help with—"

"Oh yes, dear, I remember well. You did the scope with me and Francine. I hope you had better luck than me." She began digging again, talking to the dirt. "That Francine, she got a bingo date and a ride in an Austin Healey. Lucky dog. Now, put on those gloves and grab a trowel."

I put on the gloves and grabbed a trowel. "Now what?"

"That's not a trowel, dear. That's a dibble."

I exchanged the pointy-nosed dibble for the trowel and assumed the position of digger. The sun warmed our backs as we planted, and soon there were six ferns, countless white petunias, and many white periwinkles lounging in earthen beds along the red brick architecture of North Hills Presbyterian.

Beatrice would go long stretches without saying anything, immersed in her work and the leafy details. Like a chef who needs no recipe, she knew instinctively which plant liked living next to which, how deep to dig, and how much space to allow between all things botanical.

I took her instruction and used my trowel like a ruler, setting it horizontally on the ground and using its metal point to mark the next spot for digging. Gardener Neil was slow, precise, and good at packing dirt.

After securing a periwinkle in its hole, Beatrice brushed off her knees. "Neil, do I recall you saying you lived in Ecuador?"

"Yes ma'am, for the last two years."

"Good for you. But you've planted your geraniums too deep. Uncover some of that."

"*Mucha tierra?*" I asked, using my hand as a grader.

"In Carolina, dear, it's mucho dirt-o."

We moved slowly along the sanctuary, scooping holes with our trowels and moistening the dirt with our sweat. In a kind of landscaper's leapfrog, we'd scoot around each other to speed the progress.

In no time Beatrice was down on all fours and inspecting her handiwork. I thought she was going to comment on our labors. Her mind, however, was elsewhere. "Geography has gone the way of my late husband. Can you refresh me on the whereabouts of Ecuador?"

I scooted two feet to the east, below a stained-glass window, and dug a new hole. "It's in the northwestern corner of South America, bordering Peru."

She leaned low and sniffed the dirt. "And you like both Ecuador and Purdue?"

"Like Ecuador a lot," I said, chopping through a root. "Hard to get a date, though."

She sat up on her knees and brushed her hands on her pants. "It's not any easier at age eighty-one, believe you me. I had no better luck touring Europe than I had at last Sunday's picnic. Did you know that older European men prefer to marry women thirty years younger than themselves? I had no chance. No chance at all."

"That's, uh, too bad, Beatrice."

She swatted a grasshopper off her pants, those halfway-to-the-ankle pants that men can never remember the name of. "Just think, Neil, if they want a woman 30 years younger . . . why, for me to have appeal the man would have to be 101!"

With great mental effort I did the math. "I think it would be 111, ma'am."

She began another hole, muttering as she dug. "Math and geography . . . such tedium. Francine says facts and math are the husks of old age, and so I should just relax and let them peel off as they please."

I packed the soil around another white geranium and scooted farther along the sanctuary. "That's a good line, Beatrice . . . about the husks of old age."

"Thank you, dear. Francine composed it one night when we were discussing the Alzheimer's. Neither of us have it, praise the Lord, but we're prepared for the worst."

After a mistimed swat at a bee, she spotted a spigot protruding from the brick wall and went to fill her bucket with water. Not wanting to discuss the ailments of the elderly, I moved a few feet farther down, to a fresh spot of earth, and tried changing subjects. "Beatrice, Jay Jarvis told me that he used to be your stockbroker."

She came over with her watering bucket and soaked my latest plantings. "That Jay was an adventurer. Shame he left his job for that jungle girl."

"From the picture he showed me, she's one attractive jungle girl."

Beatrice shook her head. "I must confess, dear, my new broker is dumber than dirt. That goober tried to get me to invest in a Turkish soap maker."

Below the spout of her bucket, I packed around green stems and sniffed the Presbyterian dirt. It smelled no different than any other dirt—wormy, with a dash of decay.

"So you didn't buy into Turkey, Beatrice?"

"I've got to find me another Jay," she said, absentmindedly dripping water down my neck. "Did he mention that he convinced me to sell my stocks just days before the market crash?"

"No ma'am, we mostly talked about women and Spanish."

She watered two geraniums and my left foot. "Jay got me to sell all the Ford, all the Ma Bell, even the Proctor and Gamble that I thought was Piedmont Gas. Did y'all discuss Piedmont Gas, dear?"

"Nope. We mostly talked about Spanish and dating."

"Piedmont Gas is doing well, I hear."

I began a new hole and changed the subject. "Beatrice, do you have any advice about the Greenville girls?"

"Don't bury the leaves in the dirt, Neil," she said, pausing to gauge our progress. "The plants must be allowed to breeeathe."

"Yes ma'am."

Apparently she was lost somewhere between the floral world, her watering bucket, and her retirement funds. She never even heard my question. After pacing the length and breadth of our labors, she stepped back to get the grand view. With hands on hips and eyes wide with excitement, she said, "Neil, I have an idea."

"I'm all ears, Beatrice."

She stared at the side of my head. "Dear, your ears are hidden by your hair. You could use a trim."

"I meant that I'm willing to listen to your idea."

Her many blinks helped her thoughts unclutter. "Now, about my idea. To attract more singles to this church, both the old and the young, we should spiff up this garden. A more colorful theme will dazzle the Presbyterians."

Sweat dripped off my forehead as I stood and considered her plan. "Do Presbyterians like being dazzled?"

She shook her head in frustration. "I'm much too old for arguments, dear."

I looked behind me and saw that we only had three small clusters of white geraniums left. The whole side of the sanctuary was covered in white petunias, white periwinkles, white geraniums, and droopy ferns. "Add color or redo the whole thing?" I asked.

Beatrice swatted at a fly with her trowel. "You're not hearing me, Neil. We must upgrade. Look at the row we just planted, all white and so, so . . ."

"Boring?"

She dropped her trowel and frowned. "Yes, dear. Boring. So let's modify." She pursed her lips and stared into the dirt, as if imagining something wild.

"Señora Beatrice, for nine bucks an hour I'll modify till midnight."

She began turning in a slow circle, occasionally stopping and pointing at a patch of mulch, using her hands to summon imaginary plants into particular plots. "I'm feeling so creative today, Neil. Like a muddy Van Gogh." She gazed across three hours of work, then nodded at the long line of white flowers. "Yes, I can see it all in my head, it's coming now . . . a psychedelic oasis."

I wiped my hands on my shorts and tried to imagine her imaginings.

But the only things psychedelic stirring in my head were vague images of the Greenville girls, hopscotching the city in a quest for bliss. "Nope. I can't see it."

Beatrice seemed not to hear me, preferring instead to finger the extremities of a limber fern. Then she began turning again, only this time she was waving her trowel in swoopy, fluid gestures. I stepped back so she wouldn't hit me. "Neil, I'm renaming this project. Let's call it 'Tribes of Many Nations.'"

"But I thought the Presbyterians already requested a theme—Purity of White."

"No, dear. It's a certainty; we're going with Tribes of Many Nations. We'll use every color of every nation." She reached into her pocket and pulled out a wad of twenties. "Here, now you get everything I'm about to tell you. These gardens will look like an Olympic ceremony . . . well, except for those Nordic people. They always look so pale."

With dirty fingers I took her cash and stuffed it in my pocket. "Sí. Color, not pale. Sounds like Ecuador."

"Oh yes, Neil," Beatrice said, "it's all a vision now." Disgusted with the original plan, she pulled up three white petunias and dropped them back in their containers.

Like a dentist gone mad, I yanked five from muddy soil and cast them aside. She plucked two more. In a hasty, stooped-over game of how fast can you yank them, we worked down the side of the sanctuary until Purity of White was uprooted and prostrate. I had enough issues with purity already, so I rather enjoyed the extractions.

Soon as we were finished, I counted the cash and came up with $240. "Beatrice, there is no way I can know all the colors of all the nations."

She frowned at me and pointed over my shoulder. "The Home Depot is just down the road. Go left on Woodruff, and you can't miss it. They have a special running on coleus, cannas, and daylilies. I just adore the colorful coleus. And the zinnias and cosmos too. Get them all, dear."

I found a pencil stub in her toolbox and began writing the flower names on an old business card.

"I've been to the Depot exactly twice in my life."

Beatrice began turning again. "It's no matter, Neil. Just ask for a Mrs. Gould. She's very helpful."

As a loyal apprentice trying to catch on, I was writing furiously and nodding frequently but had no feel for what it all might cost. "Beatrice, are you sure you want *me* to buy all this stuff?"

She switched to a counterclockwise rotation. "My count is off. Yes, we'll need much more if we're to cover both sides of the sanctuary." Then she stopped, pulled more twenties from her pocket, and handed them to me. Restraint was not in her vocabulary.

I now had $440 in cash. A strange feeling, having more to spend on flowers than you have to your name. "Maybe we can find some coupons in the paper," I offered.

"Coupons are a nuisance," Beatrice said. She stopped turning and teetered on the grass.

"Are you okay, ma'am?" I asked, reaching to steady her.

"I think I'm dizzy."

Beatrice took a moment to recover from her excitement. She blinked rapidly, pinched her nose, blinked some more. Then she took the pencil stub and card from me and added to the shopping list.

When she was done she thrust the card into my hand, then clutched my hand in her own. She squeezed hard. "If there's any brown at all, dear, reject it. You hear me, now? Reject a flower if there's even a hint of decay."

"Sure thing, ma'am, not a hint." I looked at the cash in my hands and tried to picture myself in the Depot's gardening department. "Beatrice, I don't mean to be a bug in your tomato, but don't you think we should get approval before spending the church's money on such a, um, colorful plan?"

Shock nudged the happy from her wrinkled face. "It's not their money, dear. The Presbyterians have only a small budget for flowers. A pity and a shame. I found that out at the picnic when their pastor said I could donate all I wanted. So I'm here to do them a favor."

Maybe personal preferences were allowed with great charity, but I had no way of knowing, given the lifestyle to which I was accustomed. I side-stepped toward the Blazer. "See ya in an hour, señora."

Beatrice walked toward me, shaking her finger to make one last point. "Get all the colors, Neil. Asian hues. African hues. And throw in some of those gaudy colors you people wear in South America."

"We people? Gaudy?"

She frowned and put her hands on her hips. "Those kicker people all running around and ruining the grass."

I backed up against the door of the Blazer. "You mean soccer teams? World-class soccer teams like Brazil?"

"I rarely watch games, dear. Too many rules and ugly mascots. But oh my, the radiant colors when they do the homecoming strut!"

On the way out of the parking lot I drove past her Oldsmobile, which I nicknamed the Beatrice-mobile, due to the Gardening Club stickers plastered across its rear window.

After I'd handed her the list, pushed two carts, and let her do all the shopping, the knowledgeable Mrs. Gould helped me load the Blazer with Home Depot's finest offerings. I thanked her twice and climbed behind the wheel.

At the first stoplight, irony pulled up beside me, reminding me that I was a guy who couldn't afford to give a girl flowers but who was driving across town with a truckload. Somehow, this fit furlough perfectly.

When I returned with seventeen flats of flowers and a hatchback full of taller plants, Beatrice was seated in a lawn chair, lounging on the grass at the rear corner of the sanctuary. Her chair had its own blue-striped umbrella, and it was cocked at a steep angle. On the edge of the pavement, in a long line, lay all the white flowers she'd pulled up and repotted. She was shaded and covered in grime, sipping from a glass bottle of lemonade. "I have a drink for you too, Neil," she said in between sips. "Did you get some of everything?"

I told her yes, that I had done my best and was quite thirsty after loading into the Blazer seventeen flats of purple zinnias, pink zinnias, deep red dahlias, yellow marigolds, lime-green zinnias, orange daylilies, every color of coleus, and finally, the bronze foliage of big-leafed cannas. For twenty minutes I unloaded them as Beatrice pointed here and there, the plants lining up on the grassy sideline like an all-star team in mismatched jerseys. Then I remembered her change was in my pocket. Over lemonade I pulled out the bills. "The total was $419," I said, handing her the cash. "Here's your balance."

She waved me off. "Keep it, dear. Consider it your tip."

"I can't.

"Nonsense. Keep it."

"I really can't."

She flicked her hand at me as if the matter was trivial. "Then bury it. I'm starting with the cannas, in a diamond pattern." She was gesturing wildly across the church property, talking of coleus and cannas and the height of their blossoms. "Can't you just see them?"

"Oh, I can see 'em, ma'am. But now that it's already 3:00, will we have time to plant 'em?"

As if to hurry me, she clinked her thumbnail on the steel of her trowel. "You start at the far corner with zinnias and dahlias. Stagger them nicely, you hear me? And do some of those soccer colors you're so fond of."

Sunlit and sweaty, we planted till 5:00 p.m. Like tubas behind a choir of flutes, majestic cannas and limber daylilies towered over their shorter brethren. The order of plantings went from largest to smallest and from back to front. At the end of the afternoon, there were seven flats still in waiting, and Tribes of Many Nations had engulfed the entire east side of the sanctuary. I had no idea if such arrangement would lure more singles to North Hills Prez, but it was certainly an improvement over boring white petunias and those sad, droopy ferns that looked like stage props from a Shakespearean tragedy.

Beatrice asked me if I would meet her again on Thursday, the second scheduled day of the project. I said okay and pulled her tool contraption to the trunk of her Oldsmobile. She wadded a towel into a dirty ball and tossed it on the spare tire. With a handkerchief she dabbed at the sweat on her face, then finally got around to the subject I'd been on hours earlier. "Tell me, Neil, did you get any prospects from the picnic?"

"Girls, ma'am?"

"Of course, girls. You were doing the scope, were you not?"

"Yes, and I did get a dessert date with the short, redheaded one who served dessert. Broke my dateless streak at seven months."

She knocked the dirt from her trowel and set it in her bucket. "You should praise God for such a short streak, dear. Mine is three years and counting."

I banged my trowel against her rear tire and tossed it in with its mate. "You keep count too?"

"Guesstimates, Neil. At my age, one must guesstimate everything." She moved closer to me, stood on her toes, and looked me in the eye. "Now, is there going to be a second date with the redhead?"

"No way. That girl has more rules than you have money. Besides, I have a new opportunity with somebody I've yet to meet; I just called this girl named Alexis off the church phone list."

Beatrice smiled as she emptied the dirt from her gloves and threw them in among the clutter.

"A phone list? Why, I never thought of such a strategy."

"It's not much, but it's all I could think of. I—"

She reached over and poked me in the ribs. "Neil, do you think the Presbyterians would give me a phone list?"

I tossed my borrowed gloves in atop hers and shut the trunk. "Don't know. You could ask at the front desk."

As I drove away in Jay's Blazer, I saw Beatrice Dean pulling around to the church office. She got out of her Oldsmobile, preened herself for a moment, then hurried toward the office door.

Eighty-one . . . maybe that's when all our husks of inhibition just peel off and flutter away.

# 8

If any former flames interviewed me, they'd likely all ask the same question: Neil, if you've tried this hard to meet women, then why oh why are you still single at age twenty-nine?

A fair question, sure, and the answer involves many tangents, a tan gentleman, and a tangelo.

During my four semesters in Mexico City, the language school let out every weekday at 3:00. Afterwards I would sometimes volunteer at a soup kitchen at the corner of a lower-class commercial district.

The soup kitchen had been run by a fiftyish couple who'd established similar forms of charity in Houston, Brownsville, and El Paso. The wife was of Guatemalan descent. He was a mixture, a true Tex-Mex with a preference for huge belt buckles and pointy-toed boots.

This servant-in-an-apron was named José, and he was the tan gentleman for whom I volunteered at the kitchen. José had mentored me in many things, including the value of time, the importance of character, and the ways of women. A father figure with convoluted English was how I described him.

The month was April. I forget the day of the week.

I had just spooned out the last of our seven-bean surprise to a group of unemployed construction workers and was wiping down the steel counter when José came up and looked at me as if he were inspecting for cataracts. "You look downcast, young Neil. Is something wrong?"

"Nope," I replied, spraying degreaser on the counter. "It's just that today marked the dreaded three-month mark without a date."

José had a piece of fruit in his hand. He rubbed it and said, "This fact depresses you, no?"

"Only if I dwell on it."

He held the dark orange fruit to my face. "Neil, if I were not married, if I were not wed to my lovely Maria, I could use only this tangelo to find myself a wife."

This pronouncement struck me as odd and just a little bit cocky. I took a step back and leaned against the counter. "Why, oh great José, would you employ the lowly tangelo and not an orange or a mango?"

He sniffed his ripened fruit and drew it slowly across his mustache. "This is your error, young Neil—considering too many possibilities. The secret is not in a particular fruit, it is in using what is available. You think way too much."

"That's what Georgianna said."

At the mention of a feminine name, José grinned and scuffed his pointy-toed boot on the floor. With curiosity, he looked at me sideways. "You will tell José about this Georgianna, yes?"

I went back to wiping the counter, talking over my shoulder. "She's my college flame who played the cello and let her muffler drag on the concrete beneath her Dodge."

He moved closer to me, invading my personal space. "Ah, and this car you speak of, it was a Coronado?"

"Yeah," I replied, moving farther down the counter. "Dodge Coronado. How'd you know?"

He followed me as I cleaned. "The model is famous for the looseness of muffler. Piece of junk, that car."

"So what about the tangelo and finding a wife?"

Beside me now, José leaned against the shiny counter and folded his arms, his right hand caressing the fruit. "José knows your consideration, young Neil. You think, 'Ah, José will tell me that the tangelo is to be shared, to be used as an ice cracker with the woman. Or José is going to make some sensual reference about tangelos and females.' Both are incorrect. And both are the product of a warty mind."

"You mean a warped mind?" I asked, reaching up to clean a light fixture.

"Warped, warty, is all the same for the gutter dweller."

"Maybe so, but I still wanna know how the great José would use a tangelo to find a wife."

He said nothing, just looked at me with raised eyebrows. Then he tossed the tangelo overhead and caught it left-handed. "You must pretend."

"C'mon, José. Stop playing with my head. If you have a useful strategy, then it is your duty as a God-fearing man to share knowledge with the wifeless."

He moved to where he was directly in front of me. Then he made a throwing motion with the fruit. "You must pretend, young Neil . . . Like this." He did it again, in slow motion.

I balled up the rag in my hands. "That's it? What, you try to knock her out with the fruit and then drag her away like a Neanderthal?"

He shook his head in frustration. "You must pretend to pitch."

"That's the whole strategy?" I asked, gripping the rag like a baseball. "To lure a woman you would just grab a tangelo and act like you're Nolan Ryan?"

José gently pushed me aside. Right there behind the soup counter, he assumed a pitcher's stance and said, "Now you do not think enough."

"Evidently not."

He made the throwing motion again, this time holding his follow-through as if he'd just struck out the New York Yankees. "Picture the drama, young Neil. The attractive woman is walking toward you on a busy sidewalk. All the other interested men are frozen with fear. They are fearing the rejection and the humiliation. They wonder how to steal her attention without looking stupid in front of all the men. But you, young Neil, do the opposite. You are brave. So you stand ahead of her on the busy sidewalk, ready with your bright tangelo. You wind up and pretend to pitch. You do not think she pays attention, but truly she is watching. You concentrate on your form, for the pitching motion does many things to a woman. First, she sees you as uninhibited, and is less scared of hurting you should you begin to date her. This is a good thing for you. Yes, a very good thing.

"Second, she sees you not just pitching a tangelo on a sidewalk, but pitching a baseball to her sons, the sons she has yet to have but yearns to have. So this pitching motion also signals to her that you have fatherly tendencies. This too is a good thing, and may serve to warm her heart. Third, she may think you a famous player of baseball, and so she desires to meet you for your money. In the long term this is not a good thing, but any of these dramas can boost the conversation. And that is your only goal—to create one chance to talk with her. So, young Neil, my wish is for you to leave here tonight with this tangelo . . . free of charge." He was grinning when he finished.

I took the fruit, inspected the thick, orange skin, and said, "This is a soup kitchen, José. Everything's free of charge."

José gripped me by the shoulders. "Still, if my method works, you will thank me, no?"

"*Sí.*"

"Yes, of course you will thank me."

I left the soup kitchen at 7:30, still daylight in Mexico City. As always, the sidewalks were dusty and crowded. But as I walked home, the way began to clear. Far ahead of me I saw a young woman in a long, teal skirt, hems swaying at her ankles. She was walking toward me, thin-waisted and wearing a wide-brimmed hat that shielded her from complete viewing by oglers like me. Her stride told me that she was in a hurry.

I needed to act fast. The tangelo felt warm in my hand. I tried to summon confidence. I even tried gripping the fruit across the seams. But there were no seams. Here she came, looking distant and rushed. When she was some thirty feet from me I moved to the center of the sidewalk and assumed the position of pitcher. After winding in slow motion, I pretended to throw the tangelo directly over her head. Then, just like José, I held my follow-through and gritted my teeth like a major leaguer.

In mock celebration, I clenched my left hand in a fist.

She brushed past me in a flurry. "Grow up," she muttered, dress hems swaying at her feet.

So if any former flames ever ask me why I was still single at age twenty-nine, I'll have an answer. Mostly it was lack of chemistry, numbskull advice from José, lack of chemistry, the inability of cellos to play duets with harmonicas, and lack of chemistry.

I may not have brought many possessions into the upstate of South Carolina, but at least I brought honesty.

# 9

At first she seemed skeptical of my calling. But after I'd mentioned that I was rooming with Steve, that I'd worked on the mission field for five years, and that I was the guy she'd waved at during the on-second-thought, drive-by hello of Saturday, Alexis quelled her fear of being phoned by a total stranger. Could I visit her Wednesday night at the coffeehouse, she asked. Her night to volunteer. A convenient time for a visit, she explained, a night when customers were scarce due to Greenville's propensity for midweek services.

The sun was low when I left home at 7:45. Past the manicured lawns and up the long hill of North Main, I strode into downtown and saw that she'd been right—the sidewalk crowd was nearly nonexistent.

With only one more block to cover, I kept trying to picture Alexis in my head. Yet the vision was but a vague rendering, one in which only two or three qualities showed themselves prominent. All I had to go on was the brief description offered by Jay and that one fleeting glimpse. *Straight dark hair and a little silver piercing in the left eyebrow. The emailer for Ladies of the Quest.*

On the south end of downtown, hanging from a brick building, was a round, scripted sign glowing in four shades of neon. Carpenter's Cellar advertised itself as a coffeehouse run by volunteers from the Greenville church community. I opened its glass door and peered down a skinny concrete stairwell. At its end was an open doorway, through which soft illumination filtered to the bottom step and lingered, a bashful lighting worthy of long visits.

The aromas were less timid; I had only smelled richer blends in the cafes of Quito. As was my habit since childhood, I counted the steps. At the bottom of the fourteenth, well below street level on the south end of Main, I stopped to read the drink menu hanging at the end of the stairwell. The chalkboard was square, and its precise, yellow-chalked lettering looked to be the work of a female hand:

> Patrons, the beverage menu at the Cellar is always a surprise. It depends on three factors: which church happens to send a volunteer, if the volunteer happens to go to church, and if several denominations are represented by one volunteer. Since our opening last fall, we've served Methodist Mocha; Jumpin' Java (made and served with vigor by the Pentecostals); Lutheran Latte; Episcopalian Espresso (powerful, that); a strawberry/banana concoction called Back Row Baptist Blitz; and my home church favorite, a milkshake called Predestined Pralines 'n Cream, mixed in secrecy by volunteers from North Hills Presbyterian.

After reading the words twice, I concluded that this place was just a percolating tangent of the hopscotch. The sign said it all.

I stepped from the stairwell into a long rectangular room, where the motif affirmed the drink menu—the walls a broad spectrum of glazed primary colors, seeping into one another like an impressionist mural on steroids. To my left was a stage. To my right, an L-shaped bar. Across the sitting area two teenage boys lounged at an olive-green table, sipping on smoothies and making failed attempts to look cool. Behind them, doing a much better job, two skateboards were propped against the wall. I moved through a maze of colorful tables and approached a bar that boasted no attendant.

I checked my watch: 8:02 p.m.

Two pots of coffee turned me optimistic—behind the bar they were perking in tandem, their steams mingling. I moved closer. The bar stools gleamed of cobalt blue, the bar itself was black, and four cone lights beamed a richer blueness down upon the stools. With no volunteer in sight, I glanced first at the stairs, then at the teenagers, who still refused to make eye contact. So I simply knocked on the countertop.

A young woman as tall as I was rose from behind the bar, balancing in her hands a stack of ceramic mugs, alternating in yellow and light green. She set the stack carefully on the far end, watching the mugs until they stopped teetering. This girl had no pierced eyebrow and nothing at all resembling raven hair—hers was cut neatly at the shoulders and was the very definition of blonde.

She arranged the mugs into two lines by color, then met my stare across three stacks of take-out cups. "Can I help you?"

I was distracted by the string of wooden beads draped across her T-shirt; they looked so Ecuadorian. I had already guessed who she was but played dumb anyway. "Are you Alexis?"

"I'm Darcy," she said, bringing up a stack of saucers that matched the mugs. "So you must be the guy who's asking out all my friends?"

"Only two. And you . . . you're the girl who drives the old Cadillac and sent dust flying into my waffle cone?"

She smiled in remembrance. "Sorry we zoomed past. Steve didn't tell me he'd gotten a roommate. Have a seat. It's Neil, right?"

"Right." I sat on a bar stool, which forced me to look slightly up at this statuesque volunteer. Her green eyes seemed to greet me and study me all at once, an intimidating look that brought to mind the fact that she had once told my roommate that dating him was like water-skiing behind a canoe. Perplexed as to the whereabouts of my date, I sniffed the Colombian aromas and said the first thing that came to mind. "Steve said you have a great WeedEater."

She reached below the counter and produced a tip jar. "My parents gave me three power tools for my birthday . . . as if I know how to use any of them."

For a moment I watched her rearrange the counter clutter. "So, where is Alexis?"

Darcy stuffed a lone dollar bill into the tip jar and shoved it to the end of the bar. "Can't say for sure. She called thirty minutes ago and said she was showing a house."

In a decade of dating I'd been stood up for flat tires, stomach viruses, and once for plain old lack of interest, but I'd never been stood up for a house showing. "So she sells real estate by day, coffee by night?"

Darcy added a quarter to the tip jar and said, "Well, she tries. Her mom's the local expert. Mrs. Demoss seems overwhelmed by the real estate market taking off, so Alexis helps her out. I think that's how she's going to pay for her 280z."

Darcy ducked into the supply room. I plucked a packet of Sweet'n Low from the container and converted the moniker to Spanish before wedging it back in with its siblings. Translating sweetener, however, did nothing to help me understand what had happened to my date. I raised my voice so Darcy could hear me. "So Alexis is late because she's using a sports car to show a house. Does she have to make multiple trips to pick everyone up?"

Darcy emerged from the supply room, turned to the back bar, and began pouring coffee beans into a chrome-plated grinder. She spoke over her shoulder. "Alexis just got herself a silver 280z. Totally restored. Not a great auto for showing real estate, but she never thinks in terms of practicality. We're kinda alike in that respect."

I glanced over at the stairwell and saw no one descending. "So lemme get this straight. You, Darcy, drive the huge car and don't use it for business, but Alexis shows real estate in a two-seater?"

"Right. I work at an ad firm."

"Ever consider switching cars with her?"

"Never ever. Lex drives worse than I do." Coffee grounds spilled from the machine, and Darcy quickly brushed them into the sink. "Anyway, her Z is a '77. Two years younger than my Caddy. Lex wanted something classic but has no room to park a big car. You sure I can't make you a coffee?"

I turned sideways on my stool and leaned against the bar. "I'll wait on my date."

After waiting another ten minutes I walked back up the stairs and stood on the sidewalk. I looked to see if Alexis might be coming, but the only thing approaching was dusk. Across the street and above the Performing Arts Center, the sun drained away in a lazy smudge of orange. Not the best sunset ever, but a solid, first-date sunset. Except, of course, if you're first-dateless.

Flustered, I walked back down the fourteen stairs and plopped on the bar stool. Darcy served a second batch of smoothies to the two teenagers, hurried back behind the bar, and switched on the espresso machine. She filled the bottom of a light green mug. "I'm making myself a mocha, Neil," she said, now busy with the milk steamer contraption, "and since Alexis might be awhile . . ."

"Okay, then make me a mocha too."

She grabbed a second mug and said, "It's our Methodist drink. Ever been Methodist?"

"Can't say that I have. You?"

She thought about this a second, shrugged, and said, "Yeah, two weeks ago I was Methodist. I make a pretty good Methodist Mocha." She reached for a brown plastic bottle and began pouring chocolate syrup into a shot glass. Then she doubled the dose. "Extra chocolate, twice the caffeine?" she asked.

I looked around and saw no Alexis coming down the stairs. "Why not."

For the next couple of minutes Darcy manufactured two turbo-charged mochas. Meanwhile I scanned the back of the Cellar, amused by the tacked-up drawings and short stories hanging like children's homework on the cobalt blue wall. "Those from local kids?" I asked, pointing at the papers.

She served my drink in a yellow mug, then speared the froth with a tiny straw. "Actually, most of those papers are from adults. Occasionally some teenagers will lose their inhibitions and pitch in. We're trying to foster creativity in our patrons. Allie and I came up with the idea when she worked here two years ago. Wanna try?"

"Drawing?"

She leaned down and sipped her drink. "Coloring, verse, whatever. You'll be limited to just one crayon and a sheet of paper."

"Maybe later," I said, trying to stay detached and do the right thing. At this point the possibility of being completely stood up was not even on my radar screen.

Darcy leaned against the business end of the bar, took a long, slow sip of her drink, and glanced at her watch. "You may not know this yet, Neil, but Alexis tends to be tardy."

From opposite sides of the L-shaped bar, we drank deeply from our mochas. I glanced at the stairwell once and then again, but each time, and with increasing dominance, reality squashed hope.

Darcy's hospitality made for good ballast, and soon I'd forgotten about hoping and grew increasingly amused by the cone lighting and how it tinted her hair a pale shade of blueberry as she played with her mug. I tried once more to make sense of what was happening. "So a few minutes ago, were you hinting that Alexis might not show up at all?"

Darcy's sympathetic shrug foreshadowed her response. "Neil, she might not even remember."

My pride gasped for respect, and my question appeased my pride. "When she called thirty minutes ago, she didn't even mention me?"

As if inspecting for cracks, Darcy held her mug up against the lighting. "She mentioned you yesterday at lunch. But that was yesterday. Tonight she was really in a hurry to go show that house. It's a four hundred thousand dollar house."

Like being yoo-hooed at a picnic, this was neither the company nor the conversation I'd envisioned. It was as if Jay and his missionary girlfriend had set me up in a revolving practical joke. But maybe these circumstances reflected the true Greenville. Maybe at the intersection of Faith and Impatience was not a traffic light but a strobe light, where between the dazzling flickers everything—and everyone—was hard to interpret.

I looked into my yellow mug and saw that the liquid, like my date, was nonexistent.

Darcy smiled briefly, then plucked her straw from her own mug and tossed it in the trash.

"Hungry?" she asked. "We serve cheesecakes too. It's free to all visiting missionaries."

Though she was being extra friendly, I told myself not to admit attraction to Steve's ex. I told myself to smile politely and wait on Alexis. I told myself to listen to the little voice that was urging me to be responsible. But then a second voice muted the first, not asking me to do anything bold but simply to acknowledge that I hadn't engineered this on my own, that this was just one of those chance meetings that God arranges.

We agreed to split a dessert. I was into my third or fourth bite when, for no apparent reason, Darcy began ringing the rim of her mug with her finger, glancing from the mug to me with every revolution. I tried to avoid her eyes, but only the two of us were at the bar, and now she was rimming so slowly, so . . . femininely.

"Neil?" she said. My name oozed from her lips; in two long syllables it oozed, dripping off her perfect chin in a syrupy, Southern form of name spillage that could entrance the most devoted man of faith, much less a vulnerable single man on furlough.

"Darcy?"

Until now I hadn't noticed her springlike perfume. Until now I'd stayed neutral. Until now she'd been rimming clockwise, not counterclockwise. Not with her pinkie.

"How long are you in town?" she asked.

I tried hard to avoid her eyes, concentrating instead on the silver ring below the soft knuckle of her pinkie, the one with the green stone set in a dainty oval. Around and around went the little stone, circling the mug in slow, girlish arcs, a marvelous little gem rotating under my gaze, moving smoothly around the warm surface; what a fascinating little stone.

She didn't wait for my answer. Instead she glanced into my mug and said, "If you want a second mocha for free, you could go up on our little stage and sing or mime or play an instrument."

Her sentence must have taken a half hour to travel from her lips to my ear; what a fascinating little sentence. In slow motion she pointed across the coffeehouse to the wooden stage, raised no more than a foot off the floor. Two microphones stood at the ready, blurring in and out as coffee-mug hypnosis began all over again.

"We have an old guitar in back" is what I think she said next.

"Sorry, I don't play guitar" was my delayed response.

She began rimming clockwise again. With her thumb.

"Me either," she said. Her words lagged the movement of her lips. "Do you sing?"

*How would a guy sing when he's hypnotized?* "Nope."

"Play anything at all?"

*Oh, that lucky mug.* "The harmonica," I mumbled.

In slow motion again, she raised her thumb from the mug to her mouth, and then carefully, almost unconsciously, licked away the mocha residue. What a fascinating little thumb.

"Well," she said, "did you bring it?"

"Um . . . yeah." I patted my front pocket.

"You carry your harmonica on dates?" she asked, her eyes wide with surprise. "How sweet!"

The word *sweet* may have contained as many as three syllables, although in my hypnotic state I could not be sure. I could only mutter, "Good cheesecake."

With a confused shake of her head, Darcy pointed at my shirt pocket. "And I suppose when you're on the mission field, playing music keeps you from being lonely?"

"Sometimes," I replied, gathering my senses. "But don't ask me to play. I'm not that good, and it would look really bad if Alexis walked in and thought I was serenading her friend."

Darcy laughed as she stopped rimming the mug. Then she propped her elbows on the glossy surface of the bar to study me more closely. "Then why do you carry it around?"

I gave her the answer I gave everyone else. "It's private. I have a hard time talking about it . . . but it isn't to perform."

She raised her hands around her face and wiggled her fingers. "A big secret. Wooo."

That was not quite the reply I expected. We were alone at the bar, however, so expected replies were of little consequence. With the help of the caffeine, I just sat there and kept the conversation going, subjects often changing for no reason whatsoever.

At 9:45 the two teenagers at the olive-green table left with their skateboards. Darcy frowned when she noticed their empty cups still on the table. "Those skateboarders never tip," she grumbled, walking over to clean up the mess. "They must think that I get the money, when really it all goes to the house."

Still perched on the blue bar stool, I turned to face her, remembering well my own nontipping teenage years in Richmond. "Well, your sign said this place is nonprofit."

"Even if we tried to make a profit it would be nonprofit," she said, stuffing used napkins into a cup. "Look around. No one in the place on Wednesday night. And we have a plumbing problem. We should really just be open on Fridays and Saturdays. But this is my service to God—I can't sing in the choir or keep a nursery, ya know." Then, to make her point, she looked me in the eye. "Alexis and I both avoid the nurseries."

I imagined that nurseries avoided both Tardy Alexis and Displaced Darcy. I mean, what parent would want to leave their toddler in the care of church hoppers, only to come back after the sermon to find that Junior had been taken across town because the Lutherans had fresher apple juice?

Yes, it was better for the kingdom if Darcy and Alexis served coffee.

Darcy threw away the trash and eased back behind the bar. "Would you like a second mocha?" she asked, pointing at the espresso machine. "I'm in a double-double mood."

"Sure, but these two are on me." The Cellar sold the drinks for $2.50 each, which, according to what I'd seen upon my return to the States, was cheap. I pulled a scrunchy five from my pants pocket and handed it to her.

After closing the cash drawer Darcy turned to the back bar and began steaming milk again. She tilted her head and watched it froth, moving the stainless steel container around in a manner that allowed her dainty green stone to orbit in the steam. Not wanting to be hypnotized again, I played with my yellow saucer and tried to make it roll on its edge.

She poured chocolate syrup into my mug, followed by the espresso and frothy milk. She slid the mug to me. I took a sip as she opened the cash box, studied its meager contents, and shut the lid. "Looks like the Cellar is going to make a grand total of twelve dollars tonight," she complained.

I clinked my mug against hers. "Well, at least the Cellar kept a stood-up guy from drinking alone."

Darcy drank deep and set her mug aside, as if she'd just thought of something more entertaining. From behind the counter she pulled out a forest green crayon and a sheet of white construction paper. "Okay, Mr. Neil, let's add a page of creativity to that back wall. Would you like to contribute a drawing or a short story or a poem?" She tapped the crayon on the paper, as if enthused over the prospect of seeing what would develop.

I didn't feel particularly creative, though I did feel hyper. "Let's make up a short story . . . together."

Darcy leaned over into the middle of the bar and set the paper between us. She gripped the crayon near its point and gestured with it as she spoke. "I only do think-fast short stories. Can you think fast?"

"I've had to think fast ever since I arrived in this city."

From her posture it was evident that Darcy was going to do all the writing. "What's that noise?" she asked. "Are you nervous, Neil?"

"No, it's these double-double mochas. My foot won't stop tapping."

She pointed at the paper with her crayon. "You start or I start?"

"I'll start. You write."

"Okay," she said. "What happens?"

"Guy meets girl."

She scribbled the words. "Okay, where?"

"Coffee shop."

"Then what?"

"She's just been dumped."

"Ooh, good." She was deft with that crayon.

"And she's on the rebound."

"Perfect. What's she wearing?"

"Jeans and T-shirt."

"Then what?"

"He buys her an *el grande* coffee."

"Slow down; I can't write that fast."

"Then she spills it on him."

"Good."

"Then he laughs and spills it back?"

"Yeah. He's a flirt."

"Yeah, then he calls her his coffee-stained babe?"

A tap-the-crayon pause. "Too corny, Neil. Try something else."

"She calls him a klutz?"

"Mmm, okay. Then they walk hand in hand down Main Street in their coffee-stained jeans." Her crayon was flying across the page now.

"Hand in hand already?" I asked.

"It's a great date."

"Oh. Okay. Then what?"

"It's a starry night."

"Now you're being corny."

"No, Neil, starry nights are good. Trust me. Now, quick, what's next?"

"Do ya think Alexis will ever show up?"

"Probably not. What's next?" She tapped on the paper to hurry me.

"My head is spinning from the caffeine."

"Mine too. But then what?" She kept tapping the crayon until the tip was a dull blob. "C'mon, Neil. Then what?"

"I dunno."

"Think!"

"They catch a flight to Ecuador."

"Sounds too much like Jay and Allie. Gimme something else."

"They go for a ride in a convertible."

"Cool. What kind?"

"Old Cadillac."

"Even better."

"Then she lets him drive."

Suddenly she stopped writing and looked me in the eye. "You want to?"

"I'm willing if you are."

"Really?"

"It's a starry night."

"I'll lock up."

Then it dawned on me that the caffeinated creativity had gotten me all out of sorts. Flirtation had masqueraded as mocha, and I had swallowed hard. I pushed my stool under the bar, and in a halfhearted effort at common sense, said, "But what about your customers who might come by?"

"Don't worry," Darcy said, already pouring the second pot of coffee down the drain. "No one ever shows up on Wednesdays. We're closing early."

"But what about Alexis?"

"Don't sweat it. My friend Lex stood you up."

I went around the bar and put the cheesecake back in the fridge. Then I pulled a rag from the door handle. "Okay," I said, wiping down the bar, "but you're sure Steve won't mind if the two of us go . . ."

She stopped and rolled her eyes. "He has my WeedEater, Neil, not my heart."

With that, Darcy cut off the stage lights. When I cut the ones in the bathrooms, only a yellow bulb was left to illumine the paper-studded back wall. "So can we cruise the mountains, Darcy? How far are the Blue Ridge Mountains? You know I've never driven a convertible in any mountains."

She had already made for the stairwell. "You wreck Sherbet and I'll ring your neck," she said over her shoulder.

So on the sixth night of furlough I hurried up the fourteen steps from the Carpenter's Cellar coffeehouse, right behind the green-eyed, statuesque Darcy Yeager. We were just two double mocha storytellers looking forward to a top-down cruise into blue-ridged mountains, on a starry night in June.

The night felt youthful, and much like our think-fast short story, its conclusion was but blank space, an unfinished narrative demanding to be lived, as opposed to merely imagined.

102

# 10

There were only lap belts in her Caddy, and standing below the rearview mirror was a four-inch plastic Elvis. As I steered us past the storefronts and out of downtown, a renegade feel came over our impromptu cruise—I'd given up on my date; Darcy had given up on the coffeehouse; and Mr. Presley, well, he'd given up on fame and had gone into hiding way back in August of '77.

Darcy still had the original radio in her car, and at the sound of the engine cranking she'd reached over and fine-tuned a station. Out of the back speakers came sounds resembling those from an old jukebox, fifties music, the rhythms muted but still charming if you strained your ear.

"Go left at the next light," Darcy said, pointing up Main before tying her hair back. "Then just drive."

"Anywhere I want?" I asked, still feeling awkward over cruising with Steve's ex.

"As long as it's north."

I drove north, then north some more, beyond Greenville and onto desolate Highway 11. Dark masses of mountains shaped the horizon, a spooky Southern sierra urging me to drive all night. I settled on forty miles per hour and used the foot switch to brighten the headlights.

When the song ended she turned off the radio, as if she preferred the engine's purr. All that was left was a low rumble of forward momentum, the Caddy's big V-8 chasing the headlights into curve after curve. Warm and swirly, the air rushed around her windshield and tapped us on the back, a teasing gesture reserved for older convertibles and all but forgotten by more modern, plastic-bodied cars that tend to subdue teases for the sake of aerodynamics.

I glanced at Darcy and saw her frowning. "You cold?" I asked.

She shrugged. "No, not at all."

I steered left-handed and leaned toward her to talk over the wind. "So why were you frowning?"

"Well, I'm trying to be patient, Neil."

"What . . . you're still afraid I'm gonna wreck?"

"No. Just the opposite. You drive too slow."

Self-conscious now, I accelerated to forty-five. "I was only trying to be careful with your—"

She turned to face me. "Be honest, Neil. Since you don't own a car and you've lived in Latin America for the past five years, do you even have a driver's license?"

I decelerated back to thirty. "It, uh, expired in January. My birthday . . . it's in January."

"So that explains it."

"My leisurely pace? Yeah, that mostly explains it. You mad that I drove without a license?"

She sat up in her seat and looked behind us at the highway. "Not really, but it does dilute the fun. Go ahead and pull over."

Either side—the left or right profile of Steve's ex—was fine with me. I wasn't picky. We passed each other at the back bumper, where I handed off the keys in the soft red glow of the parking brakes.

Back in the saddle, Darcy said she'd drive us toward a lookout point called Caesar's Head. According to her, we were halfway there, although at this late hour I could not tell if the head of the mountain resembled Caesar; it mostly resembled a giant black blob with trees.

At the base of the blob, she stopped in the road, where the steep angle had us looking square into the middle of a lime green hood. Before us was only a high, twisting road that curved left into blackness, then disappeared around a corner of limbs growing at odd angles to their trunks.

Darcy revved the engine. I looked above us at the dark, empty road, then up at the starry night, then back at the tall, elegant woman and her overconfident smirk.

"You've done this before?" I asked. The word *ominous* strutted into my conscience, duking it out with *anticipation*.

"Many times," she said, both hands on the wheel.

*Ominous* was the word Jay had used to describe Greenville's single scene, the word that had swayed me to come to South Carolina in the first place, and the word I was using to describe the second half of this late-night cruise with a moonlit blonde.

Before putting the car in gear Darcy reached over the dash and flicked plastic Elvis with her finger. "Pull your lap belt tight," she said.

"Already tight."

To my astonishment, she then reached under the seat and produced a pair of leather driving gloves. "I know what you're gonna say," she said, tugging the left one into place.

"That no other Caddy owners use driving gloves?" I ventured, having no idea what she was talking about.

She tugged on her right glove and flexed her fingers. "No, I thought you were going to say that these look like men's gloves—which they are. My fingers don't fit well in women's gloves."

"Mine either. So, just how fast are we going to go?"

"Oh, don't worry," she said, using her southern accent to stretch *worry*. "This uphill part is just to memorize the turns."

I tightened my seat belt even farther. "You mean you don't have 'em already memorized?"

"Used to. But it's over two miles of turns, and that's a bit much to remember, even for a woman."

"This might not be such a great idea."

"Don't worry, Neil."

The weight of the car kept her from accelerating too quickly, which was a good thing, given the way the turns grew ever more hair-pinned and curvaceous, twisting beneath tunnels of limbs now heavy with the moist leaves of midnight. I felt as if at any minute a snake would drop from those limbs and land in the backseat, anxious to take its first, slithery ride in a classic.

Instead, on our rumbling drive up the mountain, where twin yellow lines coaxed us ever higher, nothing dropped into the car except dew, and even that went unnoticed until we'd reached the top and felt the interior.

We'd arrived at Caesar's Head. I saw no other cars, and to the right of the Caddy's hood ornament were four empty parking spaces inviting us to stop and look out across the valley.

But Darcy showed no sign of wanting to park her car. She turned the Caddy back the way we'd come before shifting into neutral, gunning the engine, and tugging on her gloves again.

"Darcy?" I said, using my best this-could-be-fun voice.

"Yes, Neil?"

"I wanna look out across the valley."

With only the dash lights to illuminate her, the second frown was hard to perceive, but it was there. She put both hands on the steering wheel and gave me one of those "let's be honest" kind of looks. "Neil, I asked you to come enjoy a late-night jaunt in my car, but the invite did not include parking at a romantic, mountaintop vista and gazing out over a valley while you contemplate your move and try to get me to make out with you. That is simply not going to happen."

In my best defensive posture, I sat up straight and gripped the door handle. "No, Darcy, really. I just wanna look over the ledge. I'll keep my hands in my pockets. And you . . . you cover your lips with those men's driving gloves if you're worried. Can't you join me for one brief look?"

She stopped revving the engine and let the car recoil into an idle. "Tell you what, Neil. You walk over to the ledge and look. And here's a quarter for the viewing scope." She reached over and handed me a coin. "I'll be right here, making small talk with Elvis, who by the way has much smoother moves than you."

"Right. He'd be singing 'Blue Hawaii' in your ear." I got out of the car and walked over to the ledge, which was skirted with guardrails, two viewing scopes, and a metal sign that referenced bird-watching. But it was too dark for ornithology. Elevation was king tonight, though neither cool air, lofty peaks, nor a midnight setting were as fun by myself. Under better circumstances, such horizons would appear scenic and memorable and romantic. Standing there on that ledge alone, however, I thought the horizon appeared as just six more giant black blobs with trees.

After a minute of looking south at the distant lights of a small town, I let my thoughts drift back toward Greenville's boggling assortment of females.

I remained at the railing, five thousand feet up, and imagined myself here on a real date. First I inserted Darcy into the date, but she kept roaring off with her blonde hair flying and her lime-o-licious car flying, and everything in the thought kept flying until Darcy herself flew right out of my head. Then I inserted Lydia into the date, but she began firing off questions of financial concern before asking me if I'd allow kids out on a lofty bluff, did I always but always wear a life preserver at the lake, and did I really have a Michelob Light with my pizza at that Super Bowl party in Richmond.

After another minute I tried to insert the mysterious, unpunctual Alexis-who-sells-real-estate into the date, but I had no clear rendering of her. Like bird-watching at night, the imagery lacked all vivid feature.

Maybe furlough would lack all romance. Maybe it would fill itself with picnics and gardening by day, car rides and mochas by night, and I would leave Greenville the way I'd found it—loony and friendly but devoid of meaningful relations.

I figured the thing to do was work on the one relation who was consistent. Behind the railing was a huge slab of rock, so I sat down, pretended it was a roof, and addressed the heavens. "You had one girl accept a date but another show up. I aimed for dark hair; you sent blonde. I aimed for a coffeehouse; you drove me up a mountain. In a Caddy. Moses himself had fewer surprises. And now the blonde thinks I'm trying to get her on the ledge so I can make a move. God, when a guy combines a lack of chemistry with a lack of moves, there's no wonder he's not married. That's one reason I play the harmonica. Whether I'm any good at it or not, it does keep me from getting lonely on the—"

Sherbet's horn sounded twice, echoing off the mountain and down into the valley, waking all classes of bird and taking with it my befuddled attempt to make sense of furlough.

The short walk back was edgeless and cool, although the sight of Darcy sitting in her car with the engine at low idle and the moonlight giving shine to her hair had me wondering how she would look trying to water-ski behind a canoe, Steve paddling for all he was worth.

Tall and poised, Darcy Yeager had none of the appearance associated with hot-rodders or daredevils. But there on that mountaintop, she was about to show off.

I opened the passenger door and climbed back in. "That was quite a breathtaking view, Darcy."

She put the car in drive. "I'm sure it was. But it pales against breathtaking descents."

We were rolling forward, to the edge of the twisty, darkened road, when I set her quarter on the dash and pulled my lap belt gut-tight. Then, for no reason at all, I reached up and flicked four-inch Mr. Presley in the knee. "So you like Elvis, huh?"

Darcy glanced up at the heavens, and I couldn't tell if she was about to pray before she drove or if she was seeking a blink of confirmation from the stars. After a long moment of staring skyward, she said, "I think he's still alive."

"God?"

"Elvis."

I laughed nervously. "He's deader than Lincoln."

"That's not very nice."

"No, Darcy, that's not what I meant. I love Abe. Really I do. But he's very dead. So why'd you buy the Elvis with the white suit and the big hair? I've always preferred younger Elvis."

"He's really not mine."

"You mean you stole plastic Elvis?"

She shook her head. "Belonged to Steve. It's the lone remnant from our dating."

The moment struck me as odd—in the dark, Sherbet's engine was idling and we were about to descend the mountain, and instead of getting on with it, we were discussing the ownership of a plastic doll. "Some would find it interesting that you'd display a gift from your ex-boyfriend."

"I'm not discussing him." She clicked her brights and sat up straight. "You ready for this?"

Filled with the same trepidation I had about coming to Greenville, I nodded.

Darcy nodded back and revved the engine. It was stunning to see that over her hood ornament, in the brightness of the headlights, were tree-tops. The road was so steep that the tops of maples and oaks were mere feet from the front bumper. Below us were blacktop, road stripes, and an endless maze of trouble, all posing as hairpin turns.

She took her foot off the brake, and sheer gravity pulled us into turn one.

High beams sliced through tree limbs. Tires strained for grip. My stomach wedged in my throat, and a whoosh of wind tried to scalp us.

She cut the wheel left, then right. "Fun, isn't it?"

*"Muchacha loca,"* I gasped, gripping the door handle.

She mashed the gas, tapped the brakes. "First mile down's the steepest." We skidded into a loopy left turn.

Steep was an understatement; it felt like the rear end would topple over the hood. "We're doomed."

"Isn't it fun?"

Gravity gripped us, pulled us lower, slung us through turns. Her steering was precise; my prayers were intense. A Caddy was not built for this. Beneath the limb tunnels at breakneck speed, I braced for the worst.

"Isn't it fun?"

Glove over glove, Darcy cut left and tapped the brakes, then reversed her hands and punched the gas. Sherbet slid left, then across the bench seat went her purse, me, and the quarter on the dash. "I got your purse," I said quickly. "Your quarter's under your feet."

"S-turn coming up, Neil. Hold on."

I couldn't breathe. My hands braced against the glove compartment.

A rush of wind jolted my head back as a wandering leaf, out of sync with our downhill dash, bounced off my nose. Weightless one instant, I was slung against the car door the next. "Mercy, woman."

"Just hold on."

I did just that as she screeched her tires and swerved through a left-right-left.

We were straddling the line of faith and stupidity, when, slung against the door a second time, I considered us firmly in the camp of stupidity.

Darcy cut left, tapped the brakes. Below us in the beams curved more downhill pretzels of tar and stripes. She was pure concentration. "This is the worst part. Hold on."

"How could it get any worse?"

She slung us right, left, then right again, lime-green tonnage screeching through dewy air. "Just hold on."

Another jolt of wind. Whiffs of brake dust.

"Just hold my purse," she said, manic and methodic. "Do you have my purse?"

"Yep, but your quarter—"

"Just don't lose my purse."

Scared Spanishless, I nearly pressed holes in the leather. Darcy slung Sherbet into a steep hairpin, jabbed the brakes, jabbed them again, cut right, and slung us downhill. I tried to breathe but inhaled a gnat. Down and around a third hairpin, Darcy tapped the brakes, flung us left and up, then right and down. Then, to my amazement, she braked with both feet and stopped us halfway down the mountain.

My elbow hurt from crashing into the door handle. I coughed up the gnat and took a long breath of cool air. Then I took a deeper breath—a gasp really—as beneath black tree limbs, in the beams of the headlights, were more turns, more tar, and the broad yellow line of caution. Darcy leaned over and, squinting in the night air, looked me in the eye. "You okay? It's very dark here, but I'm guessing you're pale."

I could only manage a weak smile. "Pale and exhilarated."

I must have leaned too close—she straightened up and gripped the steering wheel. I thought she was about to plunge us down the mountain again. But instead she cast another glance skyward. "Say it for me in Spanish, Neil."

"Pale and exhilarated?"

"Yeah . . . say it."

I rubbed my elbow. *"Pálido y alborozado."*

She paused and absorbed the language while Sherbet's engine idled over a distant chirping, the high-pitched annoyance of long-departed birds ticked off by our recklessness. "Okay, Mr. Missionary," Darcy said, tugging on her driving gloves again, "are you ready to *pálido y . . .* now, what was the rest of that?"

*"Alborozado."*

"Yeah, let's go *pálido y alborozado* down the rest of this mountain."

Before she pulled the gearshift down into drive I tried to rationalize being out at this hour on a Wednesday by convincing myself that this was furlough, that I had come to Greenville to taste the social life, and that riding shotgun in a convertible on the treacherous downhill of Caesar's Head would somehow square up perfectly with God's will for my life.

High beams sliced through treetops, and Darcy mashed the accelerator.

I was sitting on her purse.

# 11

Darcy's hair was now bandless and free, bouncing gently to our slow cruise home. Though we'd left tread marks on Caesar, our jaunt was sealed away—unknown to others, unforgettable to me, and most importantly, unrecorded by cops. Able to breathe again, I filed the descent as memory and allowed my thoughts on the Greenville girls to level with the landscape.

*Independent* was the word that kept coming to mind as I pondered Darcy. She seemed to crave momentum, whether it be swerving down mountains, bouncing between churches, or being towed behind a canoe. She was fun, sure. She was attractive without dilution. And she made a mean double mocha. But when I considered what I was looking for—a loyal woman who could detach herself from the trappings of North America and serve with me on a mission field—there had not been enough time, or depth of conversation, to be making any kind of decisions apart from asking her for a ride home. Tonight was only a ride.

Plus, I'd almost forgotten she was Steve's ex.

From the mountain's base, she turned us back onto desolate Highway 11. She dimmed her headlights as a truck approached, and in the backwash of his pass resumed our mountaintop conversation. "You were telling me about your visit to North Hills Prez."

I loosened my seat belt and hung my arm out the door. "Yeah. Only guys showed up. So we all speculated on where you females might be."

"And?"

"And so where were you females?"

"Us females?" she asked, feigning innocence. "You mean as in Alexis, Lydia, and me?"

"Yeah. What flavor are y'all going to be this Sunday?"

We entered a small town, and Darcy coasted toward a stop sign. "Probably Pentecostal. How about you?"

I fingered the passenger-side mirror and watched the streetlight glint off the chrome. "Not sure yet."

When we were fully stopped she said, "Wanna come along?"

"Do I get to drive?"

"Wait. No."

"No, I don't get to drive?"

She shook her head as if I'd missed the point. "I meant no, this weekend the gang is going to the beach. Monday's July 4th, ya know."

"Yeah . . . Steve kinda invited me."

*Probably not the wisest thing to say*, I thought at the sight of Darcy's frown. No one else was approaching the intersection, so she put the car in park. "Neil, all that was available was one tiny beach house, and I don't know if I can take being around my ex all weekend. I mean, we still talk and all, but vacation is, well—"

"Vacation?"

"Exactly."

There was something else I probably shouldn't have said, but the words just spilled out. "You may not have to worry much about Steve. He and Lydia are starting to, um, hang out."

Darcy rolled her eyes and slowly shook her head, as if she knew all there was to know. "He's just on the rebound. I'm sure of that." Then, as if to affirm herself, she nodded several times. "Yeah, Steve and Lydia would never work out."

Cautious of saying anything else wrong, I retreated to a safer subject and inquired about the coastal scenery. "Okay, Darcy, tell me about this beach we're all going to. Jay said your gang had a wild time last year."

This topic seemed to excite her. While her car idled away at the intersection, she tossed her hair back and turned to face me. "Last year the group was so big that I hardly got to see my friends. This year, because everyone is so scattered due to the hopscotch, it's just us—me, Alexis, you, and I guess Steve and Lydia. Did I mention that they'll never work out?"

"Twice now."

"Yeah, well, this place we're staying—oh my word—it sounds like a dump. We waited too long to reserve a place, and after a jillion busy signals Alexis and I finally got through to the rental lady. The lady said North Litchfield was full, South Litchfield was full, and don't even think about Pawleys Island because it's been full since April, except for a skinny two-bedroom that's still under renovation, but we need the money and if you only use the hall bath and remember to hold the handle on the toilet then we can rent it to you. That's how she talked—all the facts just spewed out as if she had forty more customers panting on hold. She said, 'It's six hundred dollars for three nights,' and I went, 'Even with having to hold the handle?' Then she said, 'Okay . . . five fifty.' So I said, 'Fine.' And then she said, 'But no house parties.'"

Darcy leaned into the wheel and pulled through the intersection. At the next stop sign the screech of her brakes was beyond piercing. It was the kind of sound that embarrasses you regardless if you're riding or driving, a sound to make dogs howl and babies cry. Come to think of it, even dogs might cry.

"Sounds awful," I said, glancing at Darcy for a hint of reaction.

She said nothing. She kept staring at the dash, her hands wrenching the steering wheel as if trying to extract juice.

The stench of hot, metallic brakes rolled up over the doors. And just to test her countenance, I rubbed it in. "I'm no mechanic, Darcy, but your brakes not only sound horrible, they smell really bad too. *Comprendes?*"

"Just hush a minute, Neil. I need to vent." In silence she shut her eyes, pursed her lips, and wrenched the steering wheel again.

Another screech, another stench. My guess was that her knuckles were white. I considered the sound and smell as adding texture to the memory of our ride, in case I never again rode shotgun while a speed-lovin' blonde hurled a Caddy down a mountain at midnight.

Finally she rolled forward and pulled into a grocery store parking lot. The dash clock showed 12:04 a.m. Without another word, we both got out and stooped for a peek. As a nonmechanical male, I wasn't sure what to look for but figured the maroon glow smoldering around the brake housing was probably not a good thing.

"A gaggle of late-night curses," Darcy muttered, standing now, hands on hips and leaning against the car. "That's the third set of brakes I've ruined."

"Third set this year?"

"This summer."

We decided it would be good for Sherbet if we let her sit for a few minutes and allow the maroon glow to fade to black. But it was a very stubborn maroon.

So with screechy brakes we entered downtown Greenville and turned onto North Main. After easing us up a hill and down the other side, Darcy offered to drop me off at Steve's driveway. "You'll understand if I don't come in," she said, turning left onto his street.

"Steve's probably asleep anyway."

She was two houses away when she surprised me by pulling over. "Oops," she said.

"What?" I asked, wincing, as her brakes were certainly waking neighbors. "Now you've decided to make your move? It's kinda late, Darcy. Plus you have noisy, smelly brakes."

She shook her head in mild frustration, as if this night had gotten the best of her. "No, Neil. I left my cell phone in the coffeehouse. Can you go with me to get it? It's only a mile."

Through a yawn I nodded okay.

Past the darkened storefronts, Darcy parked slow and crooked on South Main. She slung open her door. "I can't believe we left the lights on at the Cellar," she said, hurrying around the hood. "Didn't we turn them off?"

I shut my door as confusion settled in. "I'm sure we turned them off. Maybe you—"

She looked left, and her mouth dropped open. "Oh no."

"Oh no, what?"

"Alexis . . . she's here."

I'm not sure what my own mouth did, other than mutter, "No way."

Darcy pointed across the street. A silver 280z, complete with chrome bumpers and a USC sticker on the hatchback, was parked beside a delivery truck. "Only Alexis would have the coffeehouse open at this hour."

Feeling somewhat decaffeinated, I remained planted by the passenger door. "You're sure that's her car?"

Darcy laughed and went to push open the Cellar door. She found it locked. Then she swooshed her mane like only girls can do and reached in her pocket for a key. "This should be interesting, Neil. Get ready to meet your Wednesday night date."

There was a right thing to do here, though it was not taught in language school. The larger part of me was not wanting to go back down in the Cellar. The smaller part said *Be a man*. But before I allowed the smaller part to win, there was an issue that needed clarifying. "Darcy, with the circumstances and all, I thought that you were my Wednesday night date."

She stuck the key in the slot and turned it a complete revolution. "I was your Wednesday night thrill. That's much different than a date."

Figuring that my best move was to confront this situation head-on, I pushed open the glass door and motioned her inside. Halfway down the stairs, Darcy signaled our entrance by reaching out and knocking on the inner wall.

Alexis was sitting on the short end of the L-shaped coffee bar, reading the incomplete short story I'd dictated to Darcy. In jeans and a loose-fitting black top, she was holding a milkshake in her left hand, the construction paper in her right. She was a bit smaller than I'd figured. From her partial profile and straight black hair she looked like a pale Italian, never mind the cheap sandals.

Despite my intentionally heavy footsteps, she had not yet acknowledged us.

Darcy and I stopped ten feet away, surrounded by colorful tables and the most awkward silence since Adam hid in the bush. Darcy then moved several steps away from me, to my left, distancing herself. We both looked anxiously for a reaction. But Alexis only glanced at us, then looked slowly back down at the construction paper. "Well, well," she said, dark eyes focused on the top of the page. "Guy meets girl, eh?"

We nodded in unison.

Alexis read the next line. "Then girl spills coffee on boy, and boy spills it back? He spilled it back?"

We nodded again.

"And you, Darce, are you the wearer of coffee-stained jeans?" Alexis peered over the paper to check her friend's clothing. "I don't see any coffee stains on your jeans. Did Darcy go home and change clothes?"

Braced against a wooden chair, Darcy quickly shook her head.

"And then, oh lemme see . . . then girl and guy hold hands on Main Street. How very Hallmarkish. Insta-chemistry! Did this happen as well?"

I shook my head no. Darcy appeared frozen.

Unmoved by our denials, Alexis scanned the page. "Well now, let's read a bit further . . . Girl who has old Cadillac invites guy for cruise? She takes him on a cruise? And then she lets him drive?"

"Uh-huh."

Alexis flipped the paper over and saw no more words. "Okay, you two, so after the starry night part, what happens? You left the story right there? That's a terrrrible place to leave a story." She hopped down off the bar and walked over with her hand extended.

I stepped forward to meet this slender girl of mystery. She wasn't smiling; but then she wasn't frowning either. Not nearly as tall as Darcy, she looked intriguingly pretty. "Hello, Neil," she said, "I'm Alexis, and I was almost your date tonight. I'll explain in a sec."

Her hand was strong for her size. I shook it gently and stole a glance at the tiny silver piercing in her left eyebrow. I'd never been a fan of piercings, but on her, coupled with creamy, pale skin and those dark eyes that not only captured but improved the cone lighting above the bar, the miniature circle looked halfway between edgy and cute. "I'm Neil, and I was almost your date tonight. But you never showed up. So I just figured—"

She let go my hand and motioned to the bar stools. "Let's all have a seat, shall we?"

First Darcy, then Alexis, then I took up residence near the cobalt blue wall, the three of us forming a crude triangle of awkward visitation—a triangle, and yet I felt oddly in the middle.

Alexis reached behind her to the bar and grabbed her drink. "I'm having a celebratory milkshake. I would make y'all one, but generosity seems to have gone the way of my date tonight—fled the premises." She smiled, slurped her shake, licked her lips. "So, you two, I'd really like to hear about this spontaneous evening. Where'd you go . . . movie? Dinner?" She was talking straight to Darcy, with only an occasional glance at me.

Darcy drew her feet up onto the bottom rail of the stool and put her hands in her lap, looking as innocent as possible. "I took Neil on a steep descent."

Alexis gently bit into her straw. "Not Caesar's Head again?"

"Yep," Darcy said, doing her best to look humbled. I didn't feel humbled, just baffled. Maybe she had a good excuse. And maybe it was best to let the two of them talk.

With the straw now resting on her humorous bottom lip—humorous because it looked ready to burst into a grin at any moment—Alexis winked at Darcy. "That makes three guys this month, Darce. Did you drive him all the way to the top?"

Darcy nodded in the affirmative. "Yes. Well, no. Actually Neil drove to the base. Then we switched." She looked at me for confirmation. "Didn't we switch, Neil?"

"We did indeed switch."

Alexis stared over the top of her drink at Darcy, playful accusation seeping from dark pupils. "You did that midnight dash thing, didn't you?"

"Scared Neil to death," Darcy said.

"Burned up your brakes again?"

"It's getting expensive."

Alexis took another slurp of her shake. At this point I was sure the two of them were in cahoots, just toying with me. Then Alexis looked sympathetically at me and studied my face. I studied her back, impressed with her directness, her eyes, and the near comical way she was handling all of this. Maybe she was as curious about me as I was about her. After a good ten seconds of dual absorption, the slightest trace of a smile formed at the corner of her mouth. "Darcy can't beat my time down the mountain, Neil, 'cause her car's too big and bulky."

Caught in the middle, I just said the first thing that popped into my head. "I thought she did pretty well, especially with all the dew on the road and her purse flying around in the—"

Palm up, Alexis gave the halt gesture, cutting short my reply. I was used to such stoppages—José used to halt me with his tangelo.

Despite being the shortest person on a stool—she was five-feet-five, at most—Alexis did a great job of holding her head high, leading the conversation, and forgetting that she owed me an explanation. "Neil, you've been in town, what . . . four days? First you go out with Lydia, then you call me, then you leave our arranged meeting place and go night-racing in the mountains with my best friend, Darcy. Do you ever sleep?"

I was pretty sure she was kidding. To appear in control I tried rocking on my stool, but the stool was uncooperative. So instead I sat still and went on the offensive. "Well, Alexis, you didn't call and were very late." I tapped on my watch for emphasis.

Confronted with fact, she twirled her straw inside her cup and said, "Sorry, I was trying to close my first deal and I got nervous and forgot to call Darcy. Plus when you said you'd drop by for a visit I didn't know you were coming right when we opened."

My reply was half nod, half "hmm."

Darcy seized this chance to change subjects. In an effort at peace, she smiled at her friend. "So you sold that country club house?"

Alexis slurped again. "I think so. If I buy three light fixtures."

"Shouldn't the seller of the house do that?" Darcy asked.

Conversation had entered the realm of realty, of which I knew about as much as I did about brake housings, engineering, and Greenville's dating scene.

"No one would give in," Alexis said, gesturing with her milkshake. "I hate the negotiating part. I don't know how my mom stands it. Buyers want the curtains, sellers want the curtains. Buyers want sellers to pay for matching light fixtures that are ugly, like those white stone things the

Romans used. Or maybe it was the Scots . . . I can't ever remember. And so there was the contract laying on the table and 3 percent of $394,000 just waiting to be split between my mom and me, and nobody but nobody will give in and pay for the ugly white Roman light fixtures. So I said, 'Fine, I'll go to Lowe's or Home Depot and buy the light fixtures myself so we can make the deal.' But when I said 'fine' I hit the table with my fist and spilled the buyer's water all over the contract. So then we had to write out a whole new contract because the ink had smeared and the words *light fixture* looked like *tight mixture*. Then, after another thirty minutes of writing out a new contract and having to endure this gross stomach growl from the buyer's grandfather who had skipped dinner, everyone agreed that I, Alexis the rookie realtor, should buy the light fixtures out of my own commission. So everyone signed the papers, and then the buyer-couple shook hands with the seller-couple and then everyone gave each other fake smiles. Then my mom pinched me on the ear and whispered, 'I wanted you to buy the light fixtures, Alexis, so that you could learn the art of closing a deal.' So I show up at the Cellar at 10:05 but it's closed. And now here I am at midnight, just me and my chocolate shake, celebrating the closing of my first deal . . . alone! Y'all just left me to the dogs."

Darcy reached out, poked her friend in the ribs, and said, "Woof!"

"Stop. I'm not finished."

"So finish," Darcy said.

Alexis took a breath and glanced into her cup. "Okay," she said, "so I arrive here at the coffeehouse at 10:05 p.m., pumped up over the deal and thinking I would have a nice, celebratory drink with this new guy who'd called me." She winked at me, the new guy who'd called her. "And where is he? He's out cruising the romantic Blue Ridge Parkway in my best friend's Caddy, and Darcy is just playing along like nothing at all has happened. Now, oh Neil from the mission field, who do you think is most at fault?"

"The starry night?"

Alexis bit into her straw and grinned.

For a moment we were all just jeans and sandals and fresh-brewed confession. But then it all unwound. Over the next five minutes Alexis did her best to accuse Darcy; Darcy did her best to defend herself; and I reminded Alexis that she was very, very late. The sum of it all was mutual embarrassment, for there is rarely a winner in triangular venting, especially when the triangle is obtuse, though I can never be sure, because geometry was not a required course for missionaries.

Finally Darcy yawned, rose from her stool, and fetched her cell phone from behind the bar. "Well, friends, it's been interesting," she said. "Some of us have to be up early tomorrow. Can you give Neil a ride home, Lex? After all, he's really your date tonight."

Alexis looked at me sideways and shrugged.

Shoulder shrugs must mean yes in girlspeak, because Darcy plucked our short story from the bar, quickly taped it to the wall with all the others, and made for the stairs. "I'll see ya around, Neil," she said over her shoulder. "You too, Lex. Remember to cut the lights."

It was 12:25 a.m., and lead-footed Cinderella waved good-bye.

# 12

On the B-side of midnight there is minimal time in which to salvage something from an almost-date. But seated next to each other on the cobalt-blue bar stools, Alexis and I were going to try.

She spun on her stool to face the bar, and when I did likewise, she pushed a sheet of paper in front of me. With a purple crayon she tapped on the paper, securing my attention.

"Before you came in, Neil, I'd started to do my own paper for the creativity wall. But I got all sidetracked by that awe-inspiring short story from you and Darcy . . . You didn't really hold her hand on Main Street, did you?"

She was close enough that I detected berry scent in her shampoo. "No, I didn't."

"Honest?"

"Honest."

She studied me for a moment. "I think I believe you."

Before either of us put crayon to paper, she went to the freezer and pulled out a carton of vanilla ice cream. Then she reached behind her for the chocolate syrup and promptly made another milkshake. She poured it into a take-out cup, installed a lid, and handed the cup across the bar to me. Then a straw.

"I really didn't want a shake, Alexis. I've already had—"

"It's not for you. I'd just like for you to go up the stairs and set it on the brick ledge at the entrance to the coffeehouse."

"What for?"

"It's for Roger. He's a homeless guy, and he'll take it if I leave one out for him. You see, Neily, I'm a community missionary . . . with a blender."

I couldn't believe she called me Neily, and on the way up the fourteen stairs I kept thinking of how Jay and Steve had warned me about this girl. Yet she was already showing some heart, a nod to the less fortunate. Maybe those guys never really got to know her.

Back in the Cellar I sat on the stool and scanned the wall of drawings, poems, and verses taped over and around each other, all of them composed from the colorful hues of a sixty-four-pack of Crayolas. "I suppose that short story was pretty lame. But it was a think-fast story."

Alexis pulled the paper toward her and examined her crayon. "I was going to contribute a drawing, but I never got started. North Hills Prez is gonna give the drawings to their elementary kids. Sorta like the opposite of when kids bring stuff home to adults."

"Sounds like the exact opposite."

"That's what I meant. So I have here an exact purple crayon, just for this drawing." To gain a better point, she began peeling back the lavender paper.

I scooted my bar stool closer to hers, trying to be extra-friendly and make up for my half of the evening's error. My thoughts kept bouncing between the scent of her berry shampoo and how God arranged all the relational tangents, how, at his own discretion, he'd employ tardiness, tangelos, and even tan gentlemen to get Guy Y to meet Girl X. Of greatest curiosity to me was how he redirected traffic at the intersection of Faith and Impatience. I wondered if at the end of this night I'd be honking my horn, running a yellow, or calling a tow truck.

Then it occurred to me that all this thinking was counterproductive; that before me was a young woman, a blank sheet of paper, a purple crayon, and a chance to get to know someone. So I buried my heavy thoughts and said, "What's the deal with all the creative single females in this city?"

Without looking up Alexis centered the paper and prepared to write. "I think it has something to do with abstinence," she said. "Anyway, go ahead. Gimme a subject to draw."

I thought of her Ladies of the Quest email. "An enraged pastor."

"No, Neil. Something more fun. I've enraged enough pastors without sticking them in my art."

"Okay then, since you're in real estate, draw a house."

"Too boring."

"Then try the obvious option—draw the churches that host all you hopscotchers."

She stared at her paper. "That I can do."

Purple crayon in hand, she sat perfectly still, imagining a masterpiece. Then she drew, in each quadrant of the paper, a purple church with a purple steeple. Then she drew purple highways connecting purple denominations. After she added three girls in purple dresses striding toward church No. 1, she handed me the crayon. "Neil, I think this drawing needs some male input."

In the bottom right corner, in church No. 4, I drew five purple men seated in a purple semicircle, eating purple powdered donuts while listening to purple Wade read a proverb.

Alexis picked up the paper and stared at my handiwork. "Where are all the girls?"

"There weren't any girls last Sunday."

"Well, there should have been. According to the schedule, Nancy's group was supposed to be scoping North Hills Prez." Alexis took back the crayon. "But maybe they got sidetracked at Pentecostal, met some guys."

Beside church No. 2 she drew a new building and labeled it "RR." Inside the addition she drew a purple girl, upside down, doing a cartwheel. "Neil, I think the Bible's right about there being many rooms in God's house. I just like hanging out in Romper Room." And without further comment she labeled church No. 2 Baptist. It was now 12:45 a.m.

When we were done—she insisted on titling our drawing "A Hopscotch in Purple"—she set the paper in the middle of the bar and wrote our initials on the bottom. "You should keep that," I said. "It's quite original."

Already distracted, she rose up on her toes to where her hair was centered an inch below the first blue cone light. "Look, Neil, my electric beanie."

I laughed. "How very angelic." She motioned for me to join her, so I leaned over the bar and raised my head until the heat from the next cone light warmed my scalp.

"Don't you feel like a biology experiment?" she asked, turning under the light.

"Yeah," I said, feeling silly but very alive. "I'm a rare lizard."

Still under the light, Alexis raised her shoulders to her ears and flicked her tongue like a toad. "In ninth-grade biology I cut open my frog and found a Dentyne gum wrapper. The next day Mr. Duke read my dissection report to the class. It said, 'Specimen appears cold, stiff, and green, but has very fresh breath for a frog.'"

Before I could respond, she spun around to begin cleaning up around the sink. A whirl of motion, that girl. In contrast to Lydia, who was full of rules, and Darcy, who had more empathy for her car than for a man, Alexis seemed accessible, a what-you-see-is-what-you-get type of girl.

I went to the men's room and returned to find her washing out her blender. "You sure you don't wanna keep the drawing?" I asked.

She turned off the tap and said, "Nah, maybe some bar hoppers will come in and see it, then they'll discover a new alternative."

There was much to learn about Alexis Demoss, and I looked forward to that chance amid sandy shores and beach houses.

I was wiping down the bar, helping to close down the Carpenter's Cellar, when she went over to the cobalt blue wall and taped our drawing right over the top of the think-fast short story. She stepped back and considered our effort. "Opinion, Neil?"

Before we turned off the stage lights, I admired the drawing one last time. "Add a jug of grape Kool-Aid for the Romper Room, and it'll be perfect."

We turned off the lights and made for the stairs. At the top, she pulled a key from her pocket and locked the door to the Cellar. Even in the act of turning a lock she was different—she just turned the key and never shook the door handle. I always shook the handle.

Then she pointed behind me at the brick ledge. "See, Neil. Milkshake's gone. Roger lives on the streets of Greenville, and he's very shy. But he'll come by and take whatever I leave out."

I reached behind her and shook the door handle. "So, how long have you been in charge of milkshake missions?"

"For six months now," she said, motioning at her car across a darkened Main Street. "Most of the churches are so formal about their missions. But I don't like meetings and committees, so I invented my own project."

Further impressed, I stooped low and got into her silver 280z. "This car would fit in Sherbet's trunk," I said, shoehorning myself into place.

A copy of a real estate contract occupied my seat, and just before I sat down she snatched it up and tossed it in the hatchback. "Excuse the mess, Neil, but this is my office." She flashed a grin and shifted into first. "My two-hundred-horsepower office. Did you say you were staying with Steve?"

"In his sea-green room. With his mismatched fish."

Quickly into third gear, she zipped us up a long grade on North Main. "He told me about those goldfish. One is big and fat, right?"

I wondered how much she knew of my roommate. "Yeah, the Pig. So, you and Steve know each other too, huh?"

We both lurched forward when she jammed the brakes and hung a left. "Sorry, almost went right past his street. Steve took me to lunch one Sunday. It was last winter when we both happened to be Methodist on the same weekend."

This was relational overload. "Okay, hold it. Has everybody in this town dated everybody else?"

"Don't worry. Steve's not my type."

There was much I wanted to ask this wacky young woman, though I had less than a mile to do it. "Before I go, Alexis, I wanted to ask you about all the hopscotch. You girls aren't embarrassed that people know?"

126

"Not at all," she said, slowing down as if to give herself more time to answer. "Listen, Neil, if you were a single woman and your social circle was your local church, and the guys were either passive or nonexistent, what would you do? I don't wanna be fifty-seven and sitting in the same pew all alone. So if it takes a new strategy, then so be it. And by the way, Steve is not fooling any of us girls with his Stephanie Coleman imitation."

I had to laugh. "So you know about his feminine email address?"

She turned into the driveway. "Oh, we'll let him play along. If he wants to know what the Ladies of the Quest are up to, we don't mind."

I almost didn't press her any further—the mere pondering of her pros and cons was quite enough, and the pros were winning handedly. I admired her spunk, her honesty, and especially her waiting around at the coffeehouse. Her energetic eyes—dark pupils beaming adventure with every blink—were also a plus. And how could I judge her for going to church for the wrong reason when my own reason for being on the mission field was less than pure?

To question her further seemed inappropriate, but I couldn't help myself. "Okay, Alexis, all that church hopping . . . what about trusting God?"

The light atop Steve's carport had cast an eerie lighting into her coupe. She cut her headlights but left her Z idling. "I trust God, Neil. I tell him that all the time, but rarely does anything happen."

"Nothing at all? What about the real estate sale?"

"Okay. Yeah, that."

"And there's got to be more."

She pulled a few strands of her hair behind an ear. "Okay, last month when my checking account was overdrawn, I prayed hard, and then an hour later I found a scrunched-up ten-dollar bill in the bottom of my purse."

"Manna?"

"Actually, I spent it on a movie ticket."

Her unpredictability intrigued me; there was an innocence among her variables. I literally had no idea what she might say. She was the one I'd been warned about, yet she was the one I wanted to see again.

Right there in her car I could hear both Jay and Steve taunting me. *Neil, Neil, Neil.*

Not wanting to get out of the car just yet, I pulled the sun visor down to block the carport light. "You don't think there should be a sense of membership in a church? A sense of belonging?"

She pulled her own visor down and answered within its shadow. "Oh, I do belong to God, Neil. I'm certain of that. But what difference does it make which church a single attends?"

"Lots of people think it makes a huge difference."

"Well I don't."

"No?"

"Nope. I mean, at Methodist you get a sermon and some hymns and some protocol. At Baptist you get a sermon and some hymns and an altar call; at Pentecostal you get a sermon and some hymns and some aerobics; and at Presbyterian you get a sermon and some hymns and then more sermon. And besides, belonging to one of these churches when they treat the singles like stale oyster crackers, well, I just think—"

"Hold it, Alexis. Oyster crackers?"

"Sorry, I was thinking of the beach. We're driving down this Friday morning." She paused for a moment, then pushed up her visor. "You're coming with us, aren't ya?"

I raised both my visor and my eyebrows. "You're the third person to invite me today. But Darcy told me that Lydia won't let guys stay in the same beach house with her."

Alexis shifted her Z into reverse. "Pay no attention to Lydia. Sometimes she can be a real party poop. We'll find a place for ya. You can even tell ol' Stevie to come too."

I stepped out of the car and held the door open, stooping down to see in. "Thanks for being my almost-date tonight."

She leaned across to the passenger seat and peered up at me. "Hey, a girlfriend told me that there's a place in town that serves grilled ostrich meat, and that it's delicious. Are you experimental with your dining?"

"I live in Ecuador, remember?"

She grinned like she was embarrassed. "Forgot about that. So, I was

128

thinking if we ever do go out on a regular date, we could try grilled ostrich."

I nodded okay and gently shut her door, wondering how she'd behave on a so-called regular date.

When she rolled her car back a few feet and then forward again, the long, silver nose of her 280z seemed to me a wayward arrow that could not make up its mind as to direction. I put my right foot on her front bumper and pretended to push. Her car rolled down the driveway, she facing backward but waving forward, a posture that reflected well this bewilderment of a city.

Before going to bed I found a note Steve had left for me in the kitchen. It said to listen to a phone message. So I went over to the recorder, turned down the volume so as not to wake him, and listened to a very formal, stern introduction from a deacon at North Hills Prez.

And while all the happenings were fresh and visceral, I felt an urge to log on to the Net and relay it all to Jay in Ecuador.

Jarvis,

It's 1:22 a.m. Day Seven of furlough.

By some strange quirk of God's providence, and in the span of the last four days, I've been out (sorta) with all three of the churchgoing prospects you mentioned . . . a kind of dating trifecta, I suppose.

Do you know an old lady named Beatrice Dean? We were in the middle of a gardening project together at North Hills Prez. We were halfway done when she decided to get creative with the colors. We were both fired tonight. I just now listened to the phone message from the church. A deacon by the name of Stanley informs me that I am welcome to continue attending Sunday services but asked that I not be involved anymore with landscaping. So I'm now looking for new employment.

As for the Greenville girls . . . oh, man. Perhaps a relaxing weekend at the beach will bring perspective?

stirG,

Neil

After I'd sent the note I went to my in-box and saw that Jay had already written me earlier in the day:

Neil-in-Looneyville

I'm not gonna press you for how things are going in South Carolina. I reckon you'll tell me when you get ready. But when I drove into Coca with Allie this afternoon I realized that I'd forgotten to tell you something about the three Greenville girls: They are all good friends, Neil, so if you're in a dating mood, it would probably be best to pursue just one of them. (And probably not Darcy, since she's Steve's ex and you're rooming with him.)

I'm surviving the dry season and trying to find quality time with my girlfriend. Allie tries to do everything herself, and I think it's wearing her out. She even tries to do most of the cooking. I try to help, but the natives turn up their noses to my grilled-cheese sandwiches. Ministry is tougher than I thought, as is the Spanish. Today I translated a phrase, just for you: Hopscotcho denominacional. Pretty good, huh?

Behave yourself,

Jay

Sleepy but amused, I logged off and went into my rented room and fed Hawk and Pig. In the pastel glow of their fishbowl lay a shipwreck, sunken in red gravel. Perhaps the crew had not taken direction well, and all had perished. Then again, perhaps the crew had been rescued by some gregarious mermaids and were enjoying themselves immensely.

I could almost smell the seawater, and I wondered if mermaids hopscotched between sunken ships.

*Mermaids of the Quest . . . a maritime romance.*

# 13

Already the day felt beige. There sat Steve in his beige engineering shirt with the engineering logo on the pocket. He was folding laundry, eating a turkey sandwich, and talking about love languages. It was noon on Thursday, and he'd rushed home for lunch. After three yawns and a stretch, I'd rolled out of bed to tell him all about my coffeehouse adventures. In an effort at peacemaking, I sat on the opposite side of his kitchen table and first told him that I hoped his date with Lydia had proven promising.

Steve pushed his sandwich to the side of the table and began folding T-shirts. "Your problem, Neil, was that you didn't speak her love language. Every woman has one, a way for a man to best woo her. Some women have more than one. Lydia's two main love languages are small gifts and hugs of affection, but all you offered was Italian dessert and chitchat."

I had no reply. I'd always done well with Italian dessert and chitchat. At least it had worked with Georgianna . . . at the start, anyway.

Steve folded clothes with precision, just like you'd expect of an engineer. "Neil, I thought you missionaries would know all about the love languages, given that your job requires you to sit around in huts and read books while waiting for the natives to repent."

I studied him long enough to see that he was probably joking. Steve was a hard one to figure, and the vagueness of his smirk only muddled my head. "You aren't serious, are ya?"

"No, I'm not serious, but it's all in a book."

"About missionaries?"

"About love languages."

"Well then . . . maybe I'm discovering new forms of love language."

"Like?"

"Like purple art and midnight dashes down a steep black blob called Caesar's Head."

He stopped folding a pair of brown socks and glared at me. "You didn't go racing up there with my ex?"

It was time to repay him for his slam. "Not only did I go racing with your ex, but I even got to drive. At least a little. And the moonlight was shining on her hair and—"

"I can't believe you went out with my ex."

"I was supposed to meet Alexis, and then it got all messed up because she was showing a house to some finicky buyers and had to buy ugly Roman light fixtures because the—"

"Neil, whatever the circumstances, you went out with my ex after I told you that exes are off-limits while you're staying with me."

"I didn't go out with her, Steve. We just went for a ride."

Flustered, he matched a blue and a green. "Was it just you and her, in the mountains, late at night?"

"Yes."

"Then it was a date."

"She called it a thrill."

"I'd call it a date."

While Steve pouted, I helped fold laundry. In midfold I thought of my financial situation, the cheap rent that Steve was charging me, and decided to change the subject. "Did you know that the girls extended us an invitation to the beach this weekend?"

Mentioning *beach* changed the tone of everything, as if the word itself had liquefied and washed the silt from our dialogue. Steve actually smiled. "Lydia is sharing a ride with me."

"So she has no problem going out with Darcy's ex?"

"It's different with girls. They're more understanding."

"Lydia never told me about any beach trip."

132

"That's 'cause you didn't know her love language."

I refuse to fold another guy's underwear, so I grabbed the last two towels. "Alexis said I could ride down with her and Darcy. So I guess you can honk from your Jeep when you and Lydia pass your ex in her Caddy."

Steve unfolded my triangular efforts and refolded the two towels into perfect squares. "Well, fine then. We'll just be one big happy singles group. All five of us."

"Happy—sure. Oh, I have a confession."

Steve held up his hand to stop me. "Before any confessions, I gotta show you something so you'll realize who you're hanging out with."

We went over to his computer, and he logged on under the name of Stephanie Coleman. This new note was shorter than the first yet still baffling:

Ladies of the Quest,

Our thorns remain embedded, snug and secure, burrowing deeper with each passing week. They are, of course, two-sided thorns, labeled *single* on one side, *not married* on the other.

Who can know in which congregation our masculine tweezers reside? Impaled on prickly stakes of singleness, we continue our quest while refusing to bar hop. I'll need this week's reports by noon on Monday.

In perseverance,

Nancy (substituting for Alexis, who is busy selling real estate this week)

Steve shut down his computer before he turned and stared at me, restraining a smile. "There ya go, Neil . . . proof. The Ladies of the Quest are all crazy."

I backed against his sofa and shook my head. "I won't even ask who Nancy is."

"Charter member with about a dozen others." Steve got up and went back into the kitchen and gobbled up the rest of his sandwich. "Now what was that confession?" he asked with full mouth, so that his words came out as "Nawhut wuzatunfeshun?"

I opened his fridge but remembered I hadn't bought any groceries. "Is this take-out box from your date with Lydia?"

"Yep."

"May I eat the contents?"

"Nope."

"Please. I'm a poor missionary."

"Only if you first tell me your confession."

"Deal." I reached for the Styrofoam box, pleased to discover a filet mignon and baked potato inside.

"C'mon, Neil, I gotta get back to work. You went out with my ex? Is that it? You already told me that."

"Well, yeah, I did, but that's not the confession. I don't think I can pay all the rent for July."

"But you're going to the beach anyway? How financially responsible of you, Neil."

"I was fired."

"From gardening? Nobody gets fired from gardening."

I dumped the food onto a plate and set it in his microwave. "The Presbyterians didn't like all the color."

"Maybe not in Sunday services, but—"

"Apparently not in their dirt either. Or so says Deacon Stanley."

Steve rolled his eyes. "Stanley fired you?"

"Both me and Beatrice."

"Oh, man. Ever since he got back from seminary, he's been worse than ever—Mr. Iron Fist."

"Must be a white geranium fist, 'cause he sure hates color."

"Stanley hates anything he can't understand."

"But it was just flowers, arranged like Tribes of Many Nations."

"He probably sees it as many hues of sin."

"I can't believe you just used the word *hue*."

"That did sound feminine, didn't it?"

"Kinda."

A frightened look came over him. "Must be all this laundry—it's making me soft. And don't worry about the rent yet. I've got another job lead brewing."

"Will I be digging in dirt?"

"Nope. But you'll be outside."

Without even a good-bye, Steve left folded stacks of towels, underwear, and T-shirts on the kitchen table and rushed out the door, off to do an afternoon of engineering in his beige logoed shirt. I was convinced that all vocations had their merit—and from what I'd gathered, Steve was good at his job—but if I had to wear the same logoed shirt as my coworkers, I'd go berserk. It'd be like McDonalds . . . with blueprints instead of burgers. *McBlueprint?*

I removed the plate from his microwave, and the food I did not pay for reminded me of my humble station. No matter the attire—blue jeans, dress clothes, or company-issued shirts—I needed some income, not a dependence on charity.

After lunch I went out into Steve's front yard and scanned his roof. A steep one for sure, but atop the air-conditioning unit I saw a way to the top. There had to be a reason for my being in this city, and I was climbing up to discuss it with the Head Honcho of Reasons.

# *Act*
## two

*Carolina girls . . . best in the world.*

—Chairmen of the Board

# 14

Truckers are the epitome of flirts, claimed Darcy. She, Alexis, and I were only twenty minutes into the four-hour beach jaunt—so I was told—when the third trucker of the day honked his horn.

Reclined in the backseat, receiving the brunt of Caddy-induced, gale-force winds, I had not been asked to drive.

"Usually I never honk back, Neil," Darcy said, explaining loudly between her shoulder and wind-whipped hair. "But he's driving a Bed, Bath and Beyond truck, so I gave 'im a little toot."

Alexis nodded her agreement. She had the passenger seat at half-tilt, her feet braced against the dash. "Toot all you want, Darcy," she said. "It's July 4th weekend. No better time for tooting."

All three of us were wearing baseball caps; mine was turned backwards, advertising Ecuador to the flirtatious trucker; Darcy's was garnet with her hair pulled through the back; and Alexis, well, hers was a black cap that, coupled with her black shades and Rand McNally road atlas, made her look like an amateur sleuth.

It was Friday morning, July 1, and half the state of South Carolina was on I-385, southbound. Even the truckers looked headed for the beach. In a life-threatening, lane-weaving game of anything goes, the good citizens of the Palmetto State were racing for the shore, having rented every condo, beach house, and hotel room on the coast.

Or so claimed our driver. After she blew by a red Camaro, Darcy spoke over her shoulder again. "It's like this every Independence Day weekend, Neil . . . NASCAR for dummies."

"So we're passing the dummies?"

"We're the pace car," Alexis said, tugging her cap down low. "The lead dummies."

At 9:00 a.m. I'd met Alexis and Darcy in the parking lot of North Hills Presbyterian, the two of them loading too much of everything into Sherbet's trunk. Her air conditioner wasn't working, but that was no matter—the convertible top folded perfectly. I tossed my tattered suitcase atop their heap, although where I'd be staying had not been revealed. All I knew was that one of Lydia's rules (she and Steve were leaving later in his Jeep) was that no men would be staying in the women's two-bedroom rental house, regardless of moral character, relational intent, or spiritual service to South America.

Fine. Think the worst.

Darcy drove for miles without saying much, weaving in and out of heavy traffic while her passengers anticipated the sea. Actually, I think we were anticipating much more than the Atlantic. I had visions of going on a normal date. From the evidence, I concluded that Darcy's vision was to win the race to the coast. And tardy Alexis? Well, who could predict her visions? She was doing well just to have shown up at the church this morning. Such were my eighty-mile-per-hour thoughts as we rumbled through the tree-lined county of Laurens.

While the wind stayed steady and Darcy held the lead, I shut my eyes and tried to take a nap. But we'd only traveled another mile or so when the girl talk in the front seat had me straining to overhear.

I opened one eye and saw Alexis leaning over to speak to our driver. "I need to ask you something about Allie, your friend who serves in the jungle."

Darcy spoke quickly. "Sure. What ya wanna know?"

"God gave her a boyfriend, right?"

Through the humidity, I could nearly hear her mind turning. "So what are you getting at, Lex?"

"She became a missionary, right? And then, boom! She got a boyfriend."

Darcy weaved right. "It doesn't quite work that way," she said, back to the left lane.

"Well, it worked for her," Alexis countered. "So maybe we should try it, just go serve somewhere."

"Serve where?" asked Darcy. "Rural China? I'll just keep serving coffee once a week, thank you very much."

Alexis plucked plastic Elvis from the dash and stroked his head. "Um, well, maybe rural China is too far away. Neither of us speaks rural Chinese. Or even regular Chinese."

Darcy laughed out loud and adjusted her mirror. "What about our passenger?" she asked, tilting her head my way.

There was a short pause, a lowered voice. "He may have potential."

"Are we gonna fight over him?"

Alexis thought about it a moment. "Nah, let's just adopt him for the weekend."

Officially adopted, I was pondering the ramifications when conversation ceased and momentum slowed. I sat up and saw a convoy braking in unison. Darcy slowed to thirty-five on a congested interstate.

Then twenty-five.

Then ten.

Then two.

Alexis tuned in the radio—I thought to get a traffic report—but she was resolved to music. A beach band was singing "Hey Baby" when we came upon the wreck, if you can call being a mile back a "came upon." One of the truckers—we were too far away to tell if it was the Bed, Bath and Beyond guy—had spilled his load all over I-385.

We were stalled on sweltering asphalt, and the stall left Darcy frustrated, me horizontal, and Alexis studying her atlas. "I have an idea, you two," she said, talking into the topography. Then, "Wake up, Neil. I have an idea."

Right there is when sunblock began to replace wisdom.

"I heard you," I said, rubbing dabs of Hawaiian Tropic on my arms and face. I inhaled some hovering exhaust fumes and coughed them back.

Darcy took a swig of her bottled water and, as if she'd heard it all before, said, "Okay, Lex, let's hear the idea."

Alexis turned in her seat and looked at both of us, excitement in her eyes. "We play Road Trip."

Darcy frowned, shook her head, and in her deepest, most exaggerated Southern accent, said, "Frankly, Scarlett, I'm not fameelya with Road Trip."

"Then I'll explain."

Changing the tone and pace of our journey, Alexis opened the Caddy's monstrous passenger door, climbed out, and stood on her toes. There, on the shoulder of I-385, she looked behind us at the stalled traffic, then ahead of us at more stalled traffic. "Okay, Neil, you and I gotta switch places."

For a second I didn't budge, remaining sprawled in the spacious backseat while Alexis, for whatever reason, perused the interstate. I turned my cap back around. "Do males get to drive in this game?"

"Not a chance," Darcy said. "Go ahead and switch places with her, Neil. If history is any indication, this should be interesting." She glanced into her rearview and gave a brief wave to a 7 UP trucker idling inches from our back bumper.

Alexis reached over the door, grabbed my hand, and gently pulled me from the backseat. I would have climbed out by myself but was hoping she'd offer help—so I'd get to hold her hand, if ever so briefly.

I was now out onto the shoulder and stretching my back. The trucker looked down upon all this with great amusement. He gazed longingly at the two girls, then gave me the thumbs-up. I shrugged and thumbed him back.

Twin lines of annoyed traffic continued to pile up behind us. Alexis climbed into the backseat, and after digging through her purse—which was really just a rope-tied bag of beige weavings—she produced a pen and a scratch pad.

Sweaty and curious, I got into the passenger seat beside Darcy and tried to imagine what we were about to do. She looked at me and shrugged, as if to say, "Humor her, Neil, just play along."

"Face the front, Neil and Darcy," Alexis said, scrawling in haste. "No peeking."

"What for?" I asked.

"Just face the front, ladies. I'll be with you in five minutes."

"I'm not a lady."

"Hush, Neil."

For five minutes Darcy and I sat facing the rear of a Dodge pickup and a red bass boat. I admired the chrome propeller and saw in its blades an abstract reflection of lime.

Then Darcy reached down and pressed a button beside the bench seat. "Any guesses?" she asked, easing backwards.

Slowly, my legs grew longer. "No clue."

She lowered her voice. "Hope I didn't scare you too bad the other night."

"Not too badly," I replied, lying. "But at the top of Caesar's Head, when I asked you to get out and look over the ledge with me, did you really think I was—"

"Y'all are all the same."

"Who?"

"Men."

There was no way to know the basis for her put-down. And I didn't care to be lumped in with the entirety of the male gender. I mean, think of with whom a guy would get lumped. "I just wanted to share a look, Darcy. Just a look."

The front-seat confessional ended as Alexis revealed her idea. "Okay," she said, leaning up between the seats, "we'll need to get off the interstate."

In hindsight, we should have stayed between the bass boat and the ogling 7 UP trucker. We should have waited the hour and a half that the newscaster later told us was the total length of the wait on I-385 due to the poultry truck turning over.

But we were young. We were single. And three out of the three of us were impatient.

So Darcy cut the wheel as far as she could, pulled onto the right shoulder, and drove a quarter mile past all the patient people. Up the ramp we went—to the exit toward regret.

When we reached the top of the ramp, Alexis thrust her black cap out between Darcy and me. "Pick one, Neil," she said.

"Pick what?" I replied.

"A letter. All twenty-six are in my cap."

I reached over and picked one. "W," I said, waving the yellow scrap under her nose. "So? You're gonna scope for guys at a Wesleyan church?"

Alexis grabbed the paper from me, balled it up, and threw it on the floorboard. "No, silly. In Road Trip you have to drive through a town whose name contains the letter you picked. The very first town has to start with that letter."

"What about the second town?"

"Um, I'm not sure. Wait, yeah, you have to ask someone in that town to pick the next letter." She sat back and studied her atlas. "Go left here, Darcy."

Hesitant, Darcy looked to her left, down at the traffic still bumpered and shiny and stagnant. I craned my neck to look. "Maybe we should get back in line on the sweltering interstate," I said.

As if to flash warning at our detour, a midmorning sun reflected off a thousand bug-stained windshields. It was so humid that you could hug the steam—and then the steam, in a rare display of affection, would hug you right back.

"Just go left," Alexis said. "This'll be fun."

There is an odd feeling to pulling out of miles of stalled traffic to strike out on your own, asserting your independence. I used to shake my head at such people. Now, to my amusement, I had become such people. But it was still only 11:00 a.m., the air conditioner was broken, and the girls couldn't check into their beach house until 3:30. Why not take a detour?

Darcy looked at me as if reading my thoughts, and motioned toward the backseat. "You buying gas, Lex?"

Alexis peered over her road atlas. "I'll pitch in. We can't sit back there in that traffic and roast. Just go left."

We went left. In the rearview I admired Alexis without her cap—her pale and nearly flawless skin, her dark shades, and all that straight black hair blowing every whichaway, as if each wandering strand was an extension of her thought life.

Back over the interstate bridge the three of us looked down at the long metallic line of frustrated travelers. To the south were blue lights flashing and red lights flashing and the upturned wheels of a poultry truck.

"All the wasted *pollo*," I muttered.

"I bet Colonel Sanders is ticked," Alexis said, now sitting on her knees for a better view.

In the distance people scrambled up the banks of the highway, presumably chasing gaggles of liberated hens. I was cheering for the birds.

Our two-lane journey down Highway 72 led us to the tiny town of Whitmire. Population *us*.

At slow pace we passed trailer parks, cornfields, rows and rows of pecan trees, and an antebellum home with a flock of fake geese posing beside dead azaleas.

"Yard art," said Darcy.

"Less mess," said Alexis.

Whitmire was not just a sleepy town; it was on anesthetics. There were two stoplights (both red), three dogs (none barking), one convenience store (no customers), a curbside water hose (ever dripping), and a single orange gas pump that looked left over from *Happy Days*. I could almost picture Ralph Malph bounding out and asking, "Fillerup?"

The store was called Jerry Jean's, and in this neck of Carolina there was no way to tell if such a moniker denoted one person or two, male or female.

"It could go either way," Darcy said, reading my mind. She parked on gravel in front of the store's weathered screen door, which was propped open with a fire extinguisher. "But I'd lean toward female."

"Male," I said, opening the passenger door. I held it wide as Alexis scrambled from the backseat.

"Husband and wife," Alexis said, leading the way. "Jerry and Jean have gotta be hitched."

Whichever it was—Jerry or Jean or both—they possessed no organizational skills. The only items in any kind of order were two ceiling fans blowing hot air into warm air and circulating it past the clutter. Actually, the store was charming, in a three-minute-visit sort of way. Pathetic hardwood floors were crowded with wooden drums topped with cookies and coffee and cheap cigars. The first shelf to my right had Cheerios next to Oreos, peanuts next to pantyhose, and some poorly stacked cans of Beanie Weenies.

"Look," Alexis said, stooping to check out the bottom shelf, "original Jolly Ranchers!"

She reached into the glass bowl and drew out a fistful of grape.

Darcy returned from the ladies' room, and we joined Alexis in picking out snacks, fully aware that our trip was being stretched and that seafood platters would be long in coming.

At first he was just a voice, scratchy and Southern. "Hep you, folks?" He was seated behind the counter, hidden by the lottery ticket display, and I could only see one side of his gray-brown beard.

With her hair in her eyes, Alexis walked over and dumped her candy on the counter. "Sir, are you Jerry or are you Jean or are you Jerry Jean?"

"Name's Earl. Jerry died in '99."

Darcy and I came up behind Alexis and reached around her to set our stash on the counter. Earl was still seated, and in his lap he held a paper sack around something undeterminable. The text on his T-shirt referenced watermelons and a South Georgia tractor pull.

"Well then," Darcy said, digging money from her purse, "what about Jean?"

"She buried Jerry."

Alexis leaned into the counter. "So . . . now you run the store?"

With great pain in the effort, Earl stood and began ringing up our purchase. "I fill in around holidays. I'm in horses."

We were now three abreast at the counter. Darcy pushed up the brim of her garnet cap and looked slightly downward at Earl. She had him by a good three inches. "You raise horses?"

"Well, I feed 'em."

While Earl sacked our candies, Alexis scooted out to the car and came back in with her black cap still full of paper scraps. Earl handed me the sack of candy. Alexis showed her cap to Earl.

"Pick a letter, Earl, " she said, dangling the cap under his nose.

He took a step back. "What for?"

"It'll determine where we're going next."

He stepped up to the counter and studied us for a moment. "Looks to me like you all headin' for the beach."

"We are," Darcy said. "In a roundabout way."

"Then why you askin' me to pick a letter?"

"To see what town we go through."

Earl shut the register and propped himself against the counter only a couple feet from Darcy. "Listen here, blondie. I know all the towns, all the shortcuts too. So why don't I close the store and ride along? That'd make two and two, ya know." He glanced at me and winked.

I did not wink back. In the role of protector, I nudged Darcy toward the screen door, then tapped Alexis on the back and pointed outside. "No, Earl," I said over the candy. "The car is filled with luggage, and it's all girl talk, and believe me, you just wouldn't enjoy it."

For some reason Alexis stubbornly remained there at the counter. "He's right, you wouldn't enjoy it."

Earl drank from his paper sack and disagreed. "I seen that car y'all got, so I know I'd enjoy it. A lot." He pointed out the door. "'Specially if we could cruise by Jean's house real slow so she could see me."

From the doorway, I motioned for Alexis to come on. Darcy was already sprawled in the driver's seat, studying the road atlas. I motioned to Alexis again. She waved me off and leaned into the counter like it was her regular watering hole. "Why Jean's house, Earl?"

"She's my ex."

Alexis crossed her arms and frowned. "I thought you just told us that Jean was married to Jerry and that she buried him."

Earl sat back down and scratched his beard. "She was, and she did. But she needed some consolin' from her grief, so me and her ended up a thing."

"A thing?"

"Married three years. Well, close to three."

By now Earl appeared harmless, so it seemed the thing to do to simply let conversation run its course. In the doorway I ate my Reese's and watched Alexis begin her cross-examination.

"Did you do her wrong?" she asked.

147

"Nope," Earl said, shaking his head between swigs of whatever. "We just parted ways."

Alexis was now face to face with Earl the Magnificent. "Did you ever take her anywhere nice?"

"Mostly horse auctions."

"You never took her to a steakhouse?"

"She prefers fried chicken."

"Ever send flowers?"

"I grew some stuff out back. Mostly cabbage."

Alexis took a breath, then pushed away from the counter. "Earl, did you ever take her to church?"

Earl looked stunned. "I bowed my head at Jerry's funeral. Paid my respects. Him and me hunted together."

"So," Alexis said, crossing her arms again, "Jean still owns the store and lets you work?"

"We have an arrangement."

Cross-examination over, Alexis held out her black cap and shook it in front of Earl. He stood and set his disguised beverage on the counter. Then he slowly reached into the cap and held up a slip of paper. He started to read it, but then he reconsidered and turned it upside down. "Wanna guess what it is?" he asked.

Alexis set the cap on the counter and pointed at his drink. "First I wanna know what's in your sack."

"This here paper sack?" he asked, flicking it with his thumb. The sound rang of buffered aluminum. "I bet you think it's somethin' strong, dontcha?"

Alexis straightened up and shook her finger at him. "If it is, you shouldn't be serving the public."

Earl pulled a bright red can of tomato juice from the sack. He set it—bang—on the counter. "You and blondie done gone and judged me, dintya?"

An embarrassed Alexis picked up her cap. "Sorry, Earl. Just tell me what you drew."

"We drew a *P*."

"Not *we*, Earl."

"Okay then . . . y'all drew a *P*. No town around here with peas, though. Just lots of corn and cabbage. Hoo-wee! You like my joke?"

Alexis turned for the door. "Jean must be a patient woman."

Darcy looked miffed at being hit on by Earl. Gravel sprayed from her rear tires and pinged off the orange gas pump as we departed Whitmire in a flurry.

From the backseat, I didn't say what I was thinking: *Feminine aggression expressed vehicularly.*

Then I thought it again. In Spanish: *Agresión femenina expresada vehicularmente.*


Traffic was still sardined on the interstate when we passed back over the bridge. There were vans and pickups and SUVs—half of them towing boats and Jet Skis—as far as you could see. Darcy made a U-turn, drove a third time over the bridge, and turned us south onto Highway 121. At least we were now going in the general direction of the coast.

Pomaria was the closest *P* town according to Alexis and McNally. After just two letters, I was already tiring of top-down alphabet soup. However, there was no way any of us were going back and sitting in that July traffic. We still had two-thirds of a tank, and according to Darcy, that was good for at least ninety miles.

Alexis requested a Dr Pepper, so for the second time in thirty minutes we searched out and found a convenience store. In contrast to Jerry Jean's, Pomaria's version looked modern, crowded, and so very neon. But by this time dozens of other holiday motorists had detoured off the interstate, and many were stopping off at the Spinx station for drinks and restroom breaks. Darcy parked in the back, and the three of us got out and walked around to the front.

A line of twenty people was waiting to pay. We made selections and joined them. I stood behind my unpredictable but attractive new friends, holding a cold bottle of strawberry-mango juice that reminded me of how far I'd come from my bleached-white apartment in Quito. There I used to drink a similar concoction after language class. Soothed the throat.

But this was South Carolina, a state that could both soothe and baffle in the same instant.

The line had barely moved when Alexis went back to the cooler and exchanged her Dr Pepper for a colder Dr Pepper. She was also buying a roll of string. "I'm going crabbing when we get to the coast," she said, wiping condensation from her bottle.

"If we ever get to the coast," Darcy said, holding a Canada Dry by the neck. "That cashier guy is slower than Earl."

I stood between them. "Do you think we could get back on the interstate and at least progress toward the coast?"

"Patience," Alexis said.

"Yeah. Patience, Neil," Darcy added. At the counter she paid the cashier with my five. When she got a meager amount of change, Darcy handed Alexis a quarter, then dropped two pennies in the shortage tray.

We were only seconds away from identifying strongly with shortages.

The blacktop felt spongy as we made our way around the back of the store. The sun was straight overhead now, Carolina on broil.

Alexis was the first to gasp.

Then Darcy.

I was too shocked to gasp. My instinct was to hurry past them and find the crooks.

But the crooks had fled.

Darcy stopped ten feet short of the car. She looked like she wanted to yell "thief" or "fire" or "I've been robbed." But what she did was go blank, lose all expression. Her plastic bottle of Canada Dry dropped from her fingers and rolled backward toward a dumpster. She blinked twice and tried to come to grips with Sherbet without hubcaps. She'd had them when we parked, but now the passenger side had none.

"Quick," I said, looking rapidly left and right. "Call the police on your cell phone."

"The thieves are gone," Alexis said, one foot on the front bumper. With her Dr Pepper she pointed toward the highway. "Long gone."

I hurried over to the driver's side and felt a small victory when I saw that two of Darcy's hubcaps were present and accounted for.

In her open-mouthed version of shock, Darcy shed no tears. There was not even a curse or a stomping of feet. Okay, maybe there was a muttered curse.

Atop steamy asphalt, in a convenience store parking lot, Darcy took two steps toward her car, then stopped again, as if the Caddy were contaminated. She stepped slowly, trying to gather herself, trying to form words. "I feel so violated," she said, now with her back against the passenger door, head down and sulking. "Like someone just molested me in broad daylight . . . Why would this happen?"

Neither Alexis or myself could give an answer.

Darcy clenched her fists at her side. "Why, y'all?" She kept pounding her fists into her thighs as if to beat the frustration from her body. "I only took a whimsical holiday detour."

Sometimes the best thing to do in the presence of an emotional female is not offer an instant solution. So I just remained there beside her, silent, wondering how she could think up words like *whimsical* at such a moment. If it were my car and my stolen hubcaps, the chosen words would alternate between English and *español* and be much clearer of meaning.

Alexis set her drink on the hood and came over to put an arm around her friend. Her consolation first appeared as a loving, gentle gesture. But then she said, "It's just fate, Darce. Simple fate. If ol' Earl had picked a letter like *C* instead of a *P*, we could be halfway to Charleston by now."

You could see it coming. Darcy pulled away from Alexis, leaned over into the backseat, and grabbed the black cap that still contained twenty-four of the twenty-six scraps.

Fuming, she held the cap under Alexis's nose and waved it. "Let's play Road Trip, eh? Lots of fun and adventure, eh?" Voice raised, Darcy was chiding Alexis in a manner permissible only between good friends. Next she pointed at her partially naked car. "Now look what you caused, Lex! Do you see what you caused? My car looks redneck, and my hubcaps have gone to the dogs."

Alexis took a step back. With her hair again in her eyes, she grinned at Darcy and said, "Woof."

Darcy almost laughed. Instead she reached out and dumped the contents of the cap over Alexis's head, scraps of paper raining down on her friend, herself, and the hot, spongy blacktop. "You and your twenty-six letters. Me giving in to your moronic games. Why can't we be normal, Lex? Why can't we just stay on the interstate like normal people?"

Alexis stared at the letter N resting on her left sandal. "None of us are normal, Darcy. Not you. Not me. Not even Neil here, who at age twenty-nine doesn't even have a driver's license."

"I used to have a driver's license."

"Hush, Neil."

Darcy backed up against her passenger door. She looked pale. "I might just throw up, y'all. I'm sick to my stomach."

"I'm really sorry," Alexis repeated, now beside Darcy and holding her hand. "I just noticed that they stole my sack of Jolly Ranchers too."

Darcy quickly pulled away and glared at her friend. "Lex, that does not make me feel any better! A grown woman cannot compare grape Jolly Ranchers to stolen hubcaps. It does not compute, it will never compute, and I'm still probably gonna throw up . . . so watch your feet."

That was all she could say. Propped against the car, looking paler by the second, Darcy showed all the preludes to a vomit. With one hand on the door for balance, she leaned over and faced the blacktop. But it never came.

I retrieved her well-shaken bottle of Canada Dry, unscrewed the top, let the fizz diminish. Then I made Darcy take a drink. She swallowed hard but pushed the bottle away. "Neil, can you just go tell the store manager what happened?"

I left them there and ran to the front of the store.

When I returned without a manager—a cashier said he'd gone to the bank—Alexis was squatted at the back wheel, staring into the lug nuts as if to replay the crime in her head. She swiped her index finger across a rim of brake dust and said, "Hmmm."

The sight of Alexis Demoss trying to solve a crime was the comic relief we needed. Darcy stood over her, arms crossed. "Hmmm?" she parroted. "All you can say is 'hmmm'?"

Wheel-high on the asphalt, Alexis kept glancing from the tire to the

152

highway and back again. Then she raised her head, sniffed the air, and said, "I wonder what Spiderman would do . . ."

After she stopped pulling Alexis's hair, Darcy flipped open her cell phone and called the police.

We were three abreast again, all with our backs to Sherbet's side door, Darcy in the middle. She had the phone to her ear. "Thank you, Officer," she said before tossing her phone into the front seat.

"They're coming?" Alexis asked, her voice now soft and sympathetic.

"Yeah," Darcy said, staring at the dumpster. "Five minutes."

"Did the officer sound young?"

"I don't know."

"Single?"

"I'm gonna punch you, Lex."

We were waiting for the cop to show up when Darcy had a relapse of emotion. This time there was a scream and the emphatic stomping of feet, but no curses. "All I want is my hubcaps back. I don't care who did it. I really don't. I just want my hubcaps. I wanna rewind the clock and get back in line on the sweltering interstate behind the Dodge pickup and his ugly bass boat and wait out the poultry debacle like the rest of the patient people."

Alexis leaned into Darcy. "None of us are patient people, Darce."

"Of course not. We just give in to your idiotic pick-a-letter-and-drive games because we're hot and sweaty and my air conditioner isn't working. No one will find my hubcaps, I know that. My hubcaps are already loaded with other, less attractive hubcaps in a black truck owned by a crime ring and they're on the way to some back-alley pawnshop in northern New Jersey where they'll get traded for a handgun by some Mafia man who loves '75 Caddies—can't y'all just see it?"

We nodded like we could see it.

She concluded her spiel with a backward fist to the door.

Alexis knelt down to inspect the wheels again. I tried to comfort Darcy by telling her that she'd done the right thing to stay there and wait on the cops, that it was surely the Mafia's fault, and that such crimes were probably rare in the sleepy town of Pomaria.

Darcy would have none of it. "Neil, I don't care if Pomaria is low on crime or if it's lost in slumber; I just want my hubcaps back."

It was right then that I saw, for the first time, the humbler, generous side of Alexis. She rose from staring at the lug nuts, stepped forward, and hugged Darcy long and hard. "I'm so sorry," she said. "I get paid next Friday, and I'll buy you two hubcaps then. It's all my fault."

I really thought Darcy would agree with her, that she'd say, "Pay up," take her money, go on eBay, order herself two hubcaps for a '75 Cadillac, and be done with it.

But Darcy hugged her back and said that insurance would cover it. Then she reached out and pulled Alexis's hair again.

After a minute of silent contemplation and no sign of the officer, Darcy elbowed me. "Neil, we could all get a ticket for littering, so would you mind picking up all those scraps of paper that I dumped on Alexis?"

My first instinct was to tell her to pick them up herself. Being the victim of crime, however, did bring on Darcy a certain degree of charity, however temporal. So I motioned for Alexis to help out.

"C'mon, Lex," I said, "your fingerprints are on the scraps."

We squatted out of earshot of Darcy and gathered the litter.

"Neil?" Alexis whispered, stuffing the scraps in her pocket.

"Yeah?"

"You think we're nuts, don't you?"

"Mixed and heavily salted."

She picked up the *O*, stared at it, and said, "So are you still gonna take me out to experience grilled ostrich?"

I wasn't expecting her to bring that up, especially now that they'd agreed to adopt me. "Yeah, but I'm really short of cash."

"We have that covered."

"Who is we?"

"Me and Darcy."

"You two are taking me out?"

She scooted closer, still whispering. "No, not our ostrich date. This news is supposed to be a surprise, but me and Darcy know of a great job for you."

154

"Where?"

"Can't say."

"C'mon, Lex. Tell me."

"Shhh. Darcy might hear you."

"Just tell me."

"I can't. It's a surprise."

"You can't leave me hanging."

After plucking the last scrap from under her sandal, she glanced at Darcy, who was leaning shut-eyed against her Cadillac. "You get sea-sick?"

"I don't remember. It's been years since—"

"Stand up, Neil. Here comes the officer."

The police cruiser pulled in next to us with lights flashing but no siren. The officer got out and surveyed the scene, wiping his brow as if he too would rather be at the beach. He was stocky in the tradition of Southern law enforcement, and when he approached he looked at Darcy like he'd seen her before.

She must have been thinking the same thing, because she tugged her garnet cap down low on her head and stared at the ground. As if to protect her friend, Alexis moved quickly in front of the officer and began explaining our theory on the Mafia, pawnshops in northern New Jersey, and the crime world's fixation with '75 Cadillacs.

The officer clasped his hands together like he was trying to appear sympathetic. "Ma'am, I do believe the Mafia prefers black Mercuries."

Alexis went blank, pulled her hair behind her ears. Darcy would not look up.

After pulling a notepad from his shirt pocket, the officer asked for a name and address. Darcy raised her head only slightly and dispensed her Greenville info. Alexis could not restrain herself. She squeezed in between them, smiling politely. "And you can write down my name and address too," she said to the officer. "Just in case you recover five suspicious-looking grape Jolly Ranchers."

After hasty jotting, the officer tucked his notepad in his pocket and admired the car. "I'd love to have me one of these some day." He ran a finger across the lime paint, then squeezed into his squad car and pulled away. Darcy climbed back into the driver's seat of her Caddy, but before starting the engine she picked up plastic Elvis and whopped him on the head with her fist. "Elvis, I don't care if you prefer Caddies and the Mafia prefers Mercuries; I just want my hubcaps back." Then she tossed him, somersaulting, into the backseat beside me.

Ten minutes later—with ugly, barren wheels on the passenger side—Darcy Yeager ramped back onto I-385. Traffic was now moving swiftly, yet from the look on drivers' faces, the entire upstate of South Carolina was in a foul mood, hundreds of seaside vacations delayed by liberated chickens. Shimmering seas were not yet shimmering. Wavy sea oats were not yet waving. Every motorist, every trucker, appeared ticked off.

Still, nobody was as ticked as Darcy. She was Queen Ticked. She got us into the fast lane, and with her five-hundred-cubic-inch V-8 sucking gas, she weaved and honked and goosed it until we were the lead car in a diverse convoy, a high-speed line of Carolinians trying to make up for lost time.

In the fast lane she passed a yellow Audi full of teenagers, the whole lot of them bouncing a tennis ball around the interior. The kid driving tried to pass us back, but the big block engine of the Caddy was too much for whatever toils under the hood of yellow Audis.

Darcy yelled to me over the wind, "Neil, ordinarily I am stylish and poised, but you're going to get a bit windblown."

Alexis had withdrawn into the quiet contemplation that comes over friends of the victim. I lay across the backseat and tried to guess our speed. My estimate rose when Darcy's garnet cap blew off and hit me in the ear.

Since no one could hear me, I decided to experiment with some mood music. I pulled out my harmonica and, at ninety miles per hour, composed "The Stolen Hubcap Blues."

# 15

Arriving at a swanky marina with two of four hubcaps on your car is like arriving at a resort with one of two sandals on your feet.

A road sign had said only nine miles to Pawleys Island, but the port city of Georgetown was my first gander at the South Carolina coast. More importantly, the salt air had emerged as a balmy tonic, and the freshness of its scent and the constancy of its source seemed to pull Darcy out of her pity party. She was actually humming to the radio, though she had not spoken for miles. Her last words had been that she just wanted to get to her rented beach house, unpack, and take a long, leisurely walk on the sand, hoping that by some miracle of God her hubcaps, like a pair of chrome starfish, would wash up on the shore.

"Good drivin', Darce," Alexis muttered, waking from her afternoon nap. The compliment was followed by a clear-the-head pause, then a glance around at slender palm trees girdling the parking lot and rattling in the breeze. "Did we stop for gas?"

"An hour ago," Darcy said. She eased the Caddy into reverse and parallel parked between the marina and a seafood restaurant. "You owe twelve bucks."

To the south and over a marsh, scavenger birds were circling in loose clusters of white and gray, a dizzying squadron that Alexis watched with great delight. I scanned the coastline, where over the hood ornament and across the marsh were several hundred boats, their shapes similar, their length varied, and all rocking gently in their moorings. From the buoyant evidence, Georgetown Landing and Marina had few vacancies.

"Okay, ladies," I said, wondering why no one had gotten out of the car. "Why stop here?"

Alexis turned from watching the birds. "This is our surprise for you, Neil." She then put a dab of sunblock on her nose and that of plastic Elvis before propping him back on the dash.

"Yep," Darcy said, undoing her lap belt. "This is where a poor missionary can get ahead. Just follow us. They'll want to interview you."

With reluctance I climbed out of the backseat and onto hot blacktop. "Who are they?"

"Follow us, please," Alexis said. Ahead of me they sauntered toward the docks, shoulder to shoulder.

Behind the restaurant, the dark flow of the Intracoastal Waterway coursed seaward, moving slow and southerly beneath a concrete bridge. It was clear why the Georgetonians had named the cedar-framed restaurant "Lands End"—at the banks of the waterway, the land just disappeared.

My best guess was that the girls wanted to stroll past all the boats and perform some version of nautical scopage, looking for Lutheran sailboaters, Pentecostal yachters, perhaps a Methodist speedboat owner. There on that dock, they'd dump me for the upwardly mobile.

Luring us onward were four long rows of seaworthy vessels, some large, some medium-large, but all bigger than I'd ever afford on a language teacher's wage.

"Pretty nice, huh?" Darcy said, leading the way.

"I'm not commenting until one of you tells me what I'm here for."

They only looked at each other and winked.

By now the marsh appeared tide-washed and supple, a lithe peninsula swaying in three shades of green. Extending across it to the marina was a hundred feet of access ramp, slatted with wood and bordered with rails spaced close and precise. I followed the women onto the ramp and felt a rambunctious breeze jerk the hug out of the humidity.

A subtle contrast struck me as we made our way across—the way my new women friends walked: Darcy, tall and postured, was somewhere between Southern belle and runway model. Alexis, on the other hand, moved in what can only be described as a free-spirited tromp. And since I'd detected Steve-feelings lingering with Darcy, I paused to envision a late-night tromp down the beach with Alexis, who might be hard to keep up with, given how she was now ten steps ahead.

"Hurry up, Neil," she said, motioning for me to catch up.

"Just a second." I paused on the ramp to watch tiny crabs feeding on a muddy bank. Sideways they moved together in short bursts of paranoia, claws raised in harmony.

Before continuing on I looked past the girls at a vast fleet of boats, figuring that washing them down with a hose was the most likely job scenario. Anything to pay the rent. Although earning some money during furlough was a top priority, my pride had me convinced that I'd find my own way and not need any more favors. Alexis, however, was adamant about this favor.

"Will you hurry up?" she said, hands on hips, her hair flapping across her eyes.

Backdropped by the boats, she and Darcy looked like miniature, wind-blown dolls. They both waved me onward.

I leaned farther over the railing. "I'm admiring nature."

"That's nothing. I'll show you some nature." Alexis pointed at a tackle shop all sunlit in the distance. "There . . . that's some nature for ya."

"Gross," said Darcy.

To the side of the tackle shop, hanging from a scale at a weigh station, was something long and pointy-nosed. Two sunburned teenagers and a fisherwoman were having their picture taken with the catch. They had already gone inside the shop when we arrived. Above the vertical fish was a tote board scrawled with blue chalk, proclaiming the catch as a wahoo, its weight at sixty-four pounds.

With her nose scrunched in disapproval, Darcy walked a wide circle around the fish.

Alexis, however, hurried right up to its dorsal fin. She leaned in and sniffed. "Smells quite wahooey."

It was the briefest comment, yet a thing of which I took notice. There on that windswept dock, after my own sniff of that impressive fish, Alexis's zany manner began to trump Darcy's classy independence. This feeling was startling for me since over the entire six-hour drive, through stalled traffic, the chitchat with Earl, and the emotional ordeal of the hubcap debacle, I'd considered the two women equally desirable. The relational scales had definitely tilted toward Alexis, although I was aware that my scales and God's scales were rarely calibrated.

Confused, nearly broke, and out of my element, I decided the only thing to do was what I always did—leap right in. "All right, girls, what am I gonna do, clean fish and get a nickel per pound?"

Darcy gazed longingly at a white yacht. "Neil, you are so impatient. Just look around. Isn't this the most wonderful office?"

"Yeah," Alexis said, testing the wahoo's dorsal fin for rigidity. "It's the kind of office where a person can get adventurous. Hasn't today been adventurous?"

"My brain can't hold it all." I turned to see the entire marina spread out before me, the occupants polished, masted, graceful. "Somebody better tell me what we're doing here or I'm gonna steal the other two hubcaps."

As if they knew I was bluffing, they gazed out at the boats, paying me no mind, just giggling with girlish indifference. I removed my cap and used it to swat a horsefly.

Centered on the main dock, Darcy swept her hand across the breadth of the marina. "Out of all these magnificent boats, Neil, we have to find a particular one. And that will begin your surprise."

The sky was clear, but their agenda was pure fog—almost as foggy as the eye of that dead wahoo. "Don't you two at least know the name of the boat? Surely it has a name."

Alexis elbowed Darcy. "Yeah, Darce. What's the name?"

Darcy shrugged. "I don't know the whole name, y'all. But Maurice said it has the word *Asbury* in it."

Now we were getting somewhere. "And just who is this Maurice person?"

"An ex-janitor."

160

"So I'm gonna help a dock janitor clean the boat that has the word *Asbury* on it?"

Alexis reached out and gripped my shirt. "No, Neil. No. You're jumping to conclusions again. Maurice used to be the janitor of North Hills Prez."

"Yes," Darcy said. "But he quit."

"Why? 'Cause there weren't any single women?"

Darcy took a tentative step toward the wahoo and leaned down to look for teeth. "Maurice left to co-captain the boat with Asbury, who is sometimes a Baptist preacher and sometimes out to sea."

For some reason Alexis was now making faces at the fish. "Some say he's out to sea even when he preaches."

From what I knew of Alexis and Darcy, they were not about to go inside the tackle shop and ask which row we were supposed to walk down. And they didn't. They just glanced east and west, then randomly selected row C. When I volunteered to search row D, Darcy insisted I stay with them, whispering that Alexis was not much of a swimmer and was prone to falling in the drink during her more animated moments.

We zigzagged down the long and wealthy dock, reading off the names and coming up empty. All the teakwood and brass had me comparing this coast to the waterways of Ecuador, where in many communities a dugout canoe was considered a sign of wealth. Here, I felt like an imposter. "Tell me again what I'll be doing?" I asked.

"Nice try, Neil," Darcy said, standing on her toes and making like a tall, blonde periscope. "We haven't told you what you'll be doing."

"I'll tell you, Neil," Alexis said, edging beside me on the dock. "You'll be going on night patrols in the Atlantic, searching for five missing Jolly Ranchers."

"I should push you in."

Down row C, in search of the boat with *Asbury* in the name, I saw a yellow-and-white sailboat called *The Ponderosa*. A dark-haired man with legs tanner than mine was rigging a sail. I was slightly envious of his legs, maniacally envious of his boat.

Some rich lawyer guy, I figured.

At the end of row C we did not find the boat of Asbury, just the vast southerly flow of the Intracoastal. Before reversing course Darcy removed her sunglasses and wiped them with her T-shirt. "Okay, Neil. Here's the deal: Steve is in on this too. He called down here from Greenville yesterday and spoke to Maurice—Maurice is the full-time co-captain. Asbury is part-time, 'cause he still preaches. But it's his boat. Actually, he inherited the boat, or traded for it with some land . . . I forget exactly how it all came about. Anyway, they said they could use a first mate for a few days."

They might as well have asked me to be a petroleum engineer for a few days. While the breeze stiffened across the end of the dock, I leaned against a post and prepared to tell them they were nuts. "Darcy?"

"Yes, Neil?"

"Alexis?"

"Yes, dear?"

"Both of you are off your rockers if you think I'm qualified to be a first mate. I've been to sea exactly once in my entire life. I mean, thanks for the effort and all, but I can find my own part-time job."

As if to tempt her sense of balance, Alexis dangled one leg off the dock, and the reflection of her pale and slender leg shimmered on the water. "Neily, you've already told us that you have no computer skills, no sense of business, and that off the mission field you and your harmonica are virtually unemployable."

"Did I say that?"

"In a manner of speaking." She propped herself against a light pole and folded her arms. "Now, please don't ask me or Darcy what a first mate does, 'cause we have no idea. We just brought you here to interview."

"With the Maurice guy or the Asbury guy?"

"Whichever one we can find. Aren't we your bestest buddies?"

"I'm getting really close to pushing you in."

Leading the way back past *The Ponderosa*, Darcy was once again the runway model and Alexis the free-spirited tromper, her sandals flopping against the dock. She slowed down enough to whisper to me that if the interview went well then maybe one day soon I could afford to take her out on a real date. This was my first experience with nautical flirtation, and before I could respond the subject had already changed. Alexis bolted ahead of Darcy and spoke over her shoulder. "Neil, you do have a fishing license, don't you?"

I quickened my pace. "For Ecuador, *sí*. For Carolina, no."

"I hate fishing," Darcy said, scrunching her nose again.

After seeking but not finding, we made our way back toward the tackle shop and the frowning wahoo still hanging upside down from a rope. There on the main walkway, with the entirety of the marina in front of her, Alexis held up one hand to stop us. She then began a closed-eye version of eenie meenie minie moe.

"No," she said, stopping in mid-rhyme. "Won't work. I think marinas park the boats alphabetical."

Darcy put her left arm around Alexis and hugged her tight. "You must get this straight, Lex—boats are not parked, they're docked."

Alexis faced the wavy horizon and went blank, allowing new data to fully process. "Okay, then maybe they dock them alphabetical." With her finger she motioned for me to follow her. "C'mon, Neil, Darcy is way too busy with grammar to be any help at boat-searching."

I could not believe their lack of sense. "Hold it. Both of you just stop a second. Didn't this Maurice guy or this Asbury give you a hint at which row?"

Darcy tugged her cap down near her eyebrows. "All we know, Neil, is that Maurice said the boat would be near the end. Now, don't ask us if he meant the end of the marina or the end of a particular row, 'cause we're not sure."

"Yeah," Alexis said, leading the way again. "We're girls, and we always reserve the right to be not sure."

Row A was hardly alphabetized. It began with a charter called *Merritt's Bluewater Mansion* and ended with a catamaran called *Wes's Monsoon*. In the middle were three matching yachts, the *Matt 1*, the *Matt 2*, and the *Matt 3*. Those Matts must have been having a good year—and now I was hoping I could go work for them. Maybe they'd be sympathetic to missionaries.

Regardless of the time spent searching for the right boat, it felt good to be off the highway and onto a marina—the water lapping, gulls squawking, all of coastal creation oblivious to the distant whir of traffic rushing over the bridge toward Pawleys Island. The next sound convinced me that whatever the duties, a job here might have enormous fringe benefits. In a low, gurgling rumble, a yacht left the marina, its wake an ever-expanding V rippling against the marsh.

"Maybe that's them," I said, pointing beneath a 4:00 sun.

Darcy shook her head. "Nope, the preacher doesn't own a yacht. A yacht like that is probably heading for a romantic dinner in Bermuda . . . Right, Lex?"

Alexis stood on her toes and watched the majestic boat melt into the Atlantic. "Yep. They'll be dining on lobster tails in the Caribbean. I have to go."

"To the Caribbean?" I asked.

Alexis rolled her eyes. "No, to the bathroom. Darcy, can you go with me?"

Darcy shrugged her agreement, and they hurried back toward the tackle shop, leaving me standing there like a moron.

In an effort at efficiency I decided to scout out row B all by myself.

Two minutes later, at the very last slip, I hit pay water.

*The Asbury Raspberry Strawberry Lemon 'n Lime* was a longish name, yes, but an impressive vessel. There were two levels above the main cabin. The second level housed the captain's seat and a myriad of electronic equipment. The top level was smaller and railed with chrome, a mere lookout.

Just below me on the deck was a chair for fish-fighting, padded and swiveled and surrounded by four sturdy-looking rods and reels. The deck boards looked damp, like someone had recently hosed them off.

I stepped off the dock onto the gunwale of the boat, then jumped the final two feet onto the deck. "Anyone home?" I said loudly.

There was not a sound other than the mingled squawks of shorebirds.

"*Hola,*" I said, propping myself against the chair. "Your interviewee is here."

164

Again, nothing.

After standing there awkwardly for a minute or so, I heard a creak from behind the skinny cabin door. Its brass knob began to turn. Out poked the head of a lanky fellow in a soiled Fishing Rodeo T-shirt. He had gray in his stubble and wore the sleepy look of the just-woken. "What you yellin' about?" he asked, standing in the doorway.

"I'm Neil," I said. "The one they called you about . . . you know, for some sorta boat job?"

He rubbed his eyes. "Neil from Peru?"

"From Ecuador."

In navy shorts he stepped out onto the deck and sat on a long, built-in cooler. He squinted into the glare and took his time before speaking. "Okay, awright. I know who you are, and I know why you're here. But where are those Presbyterian gals who were supposed to have brung you?"

I sat in the fish-fighting chair and swiveled it around to face him. "They wandered off to find a ladies' room . . . and I'm not sure if they're purely Presbyterian. You're Asbury, right?"

He shook his head no, then pointed at his left forearm. "Maurice black. Asbury white."

I reached out and shook his hand. "Got it."

Maurice rose from the cooler, leaned over the gunwale, and looked out across the stillness of the waterway. "Awright, Mr. Neil. Now that you botched the first part of the interview, just gimme a minute to put on a clean shirt and I'll go introduce you to Preacher Smoak." He turned and stepped down into the cabin.

He had just shut the cabin door when I tried to make conversation. "Hey, Captain Maurice, does the preacher live on the boat with you?"

From below deck, his voice was muffled. "Neither one of us lives on the boat. I was just takin' myself a nap. Preacher Smoak is up at the restaurant, having his afternoon root beer. Now you wait right there."

To amuse myself I swiveled in the fishing chair, facing the rear and trying to imagine being strapped in, fighting something large. Then I looked up and out at the arching bridge, at all the afternoon traffic flowing toward the coast, and wondered if Lydia and Steve had beat us to the beach.

Steve had been strangely aloof when I'd left the house. Maybe he and Lydia were in that early stage where two people don't want to be bothered about the status of things.

Maurice emerged wearing his captain's hat and a light blue Charleston T-shirt, the pastels of Rainbow Row emblazoned across the front. "Okay, Maurice fresher now," he said, motioning for me to be first off the boat. Down the dock we went, me wondering what I was getting into, him writing quickly in a well-used Day-Timer. I snuck two looks as we strolled. Scribbles of client bookings occupied one column, recordings of catch sizes filled another. He had blue circles around shark catches and green around tuna. When we passed the vertical wahoo, Maurice surprised me by reaching out and, almost without looking, thumping the fish hard on the nose. "I love my job," he said to no one in particular.

Then he stuffed the Day-Timer in his pocket and knocked on the window of the tackle shop, telling some teenager to get out there and clean the fish before the meat spoiled. He waved a twenty at the youngster before pointing me toward the restaurant.

Just to fit in, I too thumped the fish hard on the nose. I must not have done it right, 'cause it hurt bad. "You caught the wahoo, Maurice? Because I saw some people with a camera and they were—"

He took two steps backward and ran his finger across the dorsal fin. "Them folks were our clients, Neil. Preacher Smoak and I lured that fish with a blue'n yellow teaser bait. By now Asbury has already sold the fish to the kitchen. Big bucks for a wahoo. Now you remember that one detail—if Asbury ask you about tackle, mention a blue'n yellow teaser. He'll be impressed if you speak the lingo."

"Thanks for the tip."

He walked ahead of me, mumbling. "Figured you need help after botching both my name and my race."

I didn't bother to rap on the bathroom door to see what was keeping the girls; they'd catch up eventually. Instead I followed Maurice over the long and wooden ramp, back across the marsh, past the paranoid crabs, and all the way to the entrance of Lands End Restaurant.

Huge windows overlooked the marina. Between the panes and the dining area, a black-tiled bar sat long, cool, and inviting. Its glossy finish reflected the coastal motif: sea oats drawn on menus, shrimp nets hung on walls, and at the bar's end, a pudgy, red-capped preacher sipping his root beer and reading a tide chart. Past his drink lay the remnants of a shrimp cocktail, at his waist the evidence of a seafood belly. There was no one else at the bar, and he seemed all to himself and unaware of our entrance.

Maurice coughed loudly, but it did no good. So we pulled two bar stools near, and the screeching sound of their legs on the hardwoods caused the preacher to look up and nod.

Without rising from his stool, he extended his hand. "Asbury."

I shook it with vigor. "Neil Rucker."

"Pleasure, son. I saw you admiring my fish."

I sat next to him and praised God for air conditioning. "But Maurice just told me he caught it."

The two of them looked at each other with the amused faces of old friends. "Maurice steered the boat," Asbury said. "But I set the hook. Fridays and Tuesdays are my days for catchin'."

"We rotate," Maurice said, pulling his stool around so that the three of us sat in a kind of triangle, he facing the windows, the preacher and me with our backs to the bar. "And if you'd have been on board, Neil, you coulda gaffed that wahoo in the head."

I was trying to think of what to say to impress them, yet all that came to mind was the Spanish word for mackerel. *Caballa.* I forewent the *español* in favor of flattering myself. "So, without me there on board to help, you guys were shorthanded?"

"Oh no, son," Asbury said, "I gaff 'em myself . . . right in the skull." He made a swiping motion with his arm. "Blip! Just like that."

Maurice nearly jumped off his stool to disagree. "No, Smoak, that ain't how you do it. Hand me that straw, Neil." He pointed at the preacher's glass, so I plucked the straw from Asbury's root beer and handed it to Maurice. Standing before us in the role of teacher, Maurice gripped the

167

straw in both hands, bent at the waist, and made a hard, tugging motion. "There, that's how you gaff a fish."

When the impromptu lesson concluded, I sat back on my stool. "You wouldn't be the same guy who gaffed Jay in the, um . . . booty?"

Maurice plunged the straw back into the preacher's drink. Asbury seemed not at all disturbed by such invasions of privacy; he just seemed humored by his partner's enthusiasm. "Okay," Maurice said. "I'll admit it. Jay was my first gaffing, and I botched it. When he fell off the boat, I missed his belt loop, but he healed up good. No scar to speak of, from what I hear."

If this was an interview, they weren't asking too much. I kept waiting for the hard questions, the probing inquiries into my boating expertise. Asbury was the first to look halfway serious. He set his tide chart on the bar and studied me in a way that was unreadable, first appearing to give me the benefit of the doubt, then, with a narrowing of his eyes, looking like doubt was all he possessed. Maurice was no relief either; he was tapping his foot against the bar stool with no rhythm whatsoever.

The preacher leaned back against the bar, raising an eyebrow but still not speaking.

I tried to smile at him, but it was the sort of strained smile that says "I'm nervous and would appreciate it if you would just say something."

"Guys, I'd really appreciate it if one of you would say something."

The preacher pulled a strand of fishing line from his shirt pocket and began coiling and uncoiling it around his thumb. He looked at the line, then at Maurice, then back at me. Finally he tied it in a complex knot and dangled the loop in front of his nose. I figured he was about to ask me if I could tie knots.

Wrong again.

Asbury tucked the knotted line in his palm and said, "Son, can you make ambidextrous pancakes?"

I raised my chin and stared around my nose, as if higher altitude would bring clarity. "Sir?"

He untied the line, then rewrapped it around his pinkie. "I'm gonna give it to you straight. Shouldn't we give it to him straight, Maurice?"

"We should give it straight," his co-captain said.

The preacher leaned forward on his stool, commanding my attention. "Neil, we need somebody who can make breakfast and make it fast. Captain Maurice here prefers the blueberry; I take to the plain. We eat big because the ocean requires a man to be strong. There's just way too much to do on that boat for either myself or Maurice to concern ourselves with meals."

Maurice affirmed Asbury with hearty nods. "Yep, what we need is a deck hand who can cook."

Though this job was likely little more than charity, it sounded much more suitable than flowery tribes of many nations. "Well, I can definitely make pancakes."

Asbury reached over and took me gently by the arm. "But Neil, can you flip 'em with both hands?"

"Preacher Smoak, if the money's good I'll stand on one leg and flip 'em behind my back."

There was a smile and a nod from Asbury, then a low "hmm" from Maurice. They whispered to each other before Asbury took a swig from his root beer. "It would really help us if you knew a little bit about fishing," he said. "Ever been out on a charter boat before?"

I nodded as if I were a veteran of the seas. "Yessir, I've been to sea . . . off the coast of Ecuador. In the Pacific I seem to remember the bigger fish preferring a blue'n yellow teaser bait."

The preacher's eyes widened. He slapped himself on the knee. "I knew it, Maurice. God has sent us a man who knows the lingo."

Maurice was trying not to laugh. He turned to stare out at the marina. "Yep, Smoak, gotta flip the pancakes and speak the lingo." He pointed at the docks. "Looka there . . . Neil's lady friends are all lost and confused."

Sunlit and searching, Alexis and Darcy were halfway down row D, walking fast but unaware that they'd chosen every wooden path but the right one.

"I better go get 'em," I said, rising from the stool. "Can I be excused from the interview a sec?"

Asbury stirred the ice cubes in his glass. "Interview's over, son. Better fetch 'em. But before you go, you haven't told us anything about your female relations. Captain Maurice and I don't mean to pry, but since we'll all be at sea together, we figured—"

I was almost to the door. "Those two on the dock? Um, not sure yet."

Maurice had the tide chart in his hands. He spoke from behind it. "One other warning, Neil. Tomorrow we'll be taking my sister-in-law to sea. Her name's Quilla, and she's rather . . . flamboyant."

I paused in the doorway. "This whole state is flamboyant."

Across the marsh a third time, I caught up to the girls mid-dock and told them about my interview. Though frustrated that I hadn't knocked on the bathroom door, Darcy seemed genuinely pleased for me. Alexis, however, was already running back across the ramp, far ahead of us, saying that she had an important question for the preacher and Maurice.

In the rambunctious air of the marina parking lot, young ladies greeted co-captains, and co-captains greeted young ladies. "Maybe we can all go out to sea on July 4th," said Asbury, opening the car door for Darcy. "But you, Neil, you be here tomorrow, 7:00 a.m. sharp."

"Yep," Maurice said, checking out the car. "By then Neil might know what happened to those two hubcaps." He pointed at the barren wheels and shook his head.

After I'd climbed into the backseat, Alexis remained outside the passenger door, first pulling her hair from her eyes and then standing there with hands on hips. "Okay, Mr. Asbury and Mr. Maurice, we're all excited about Monday's boat ride, but why in the name of Orca do you dock your boat in row B and not in A or C or D?"

Preacher Smoak smiled and put one foot on Sherbet's front bumper. He fingered the hood ornament and said, "Go ahead and tell her, Maurice."

Darcy was about to crank the engine but paused until Maurice could answer. He walked around to the passenger side, opened the door, and motioned for Alexis to sit. She sat.

Then he leaned down at the door, face to face with his raven-haired questioner. "Young lady, the reason the preacher and I picked row B isn't complicated. We pick it because the word *boat* starts with *B*."

Alexis smiled knowingly, shook his hand, and turned to her driver. "Shoulda thought of that, Darce."

The two co-captains waved heartily as we left the marina. Wind-whipped and nearly senseless over what the day had wrought, we crested the bridge in the rarest of manner—the slow lane. At the apex of the bridge Darcy honked twice, and the echoes resounded across the waterway and faded into the boating establishment.

Not an hour of this weekend was unfolding as I imagined, and I still had no clue about the sleeping arrangements.

Daylight was far from depleted, however, and from the way Alexis was bouncing to the music, she had plenty of energy left.

Oh, man.

# 16

Even plastic Elvis looked relieved when we turned toward the sandy paradise of Pawleys Island.

Darcy made a left onto a two-lane blacktop and rumbled slowly past a row of beach homes. Our four-hour jaunt to the coast had become seven, and not even the feathered white ascent of a heron's neck, rising through a canvas of green marshland, prompted any comment.

Beyond the stilts and to the west, an inlet curved behind the island, rippling waters drawn shallow within the unrelenting suck of a falling tide. I watched the current etch its signature in wet sand, a silent *adios* exposing what was formerly submerged.

"This is all very scenic, y'all," Darcy said, braking for a wooden stop sign. "But I still want my hubcaps back."

This obsession with pilfered car parts was too much for Alexis. Lounged in the passenger seat, bare feet on the dash, she reached over and poked Darcy in the ribs. "You are not going to do this, girlfriend."

"Do what?"

"You're not going to mope around all weekend longing for two stupid pieces of chrome that would never appreciate being at the beach . . . even the two you have left won't appreciate the beach."

I thought there was going to be a fight, right there on that scenic island road. Darcy, however, controlled herself—a slow wrenching of the steering wheel was her only sign of frustration. "Lex," she said, driving even slower as we neared the far reaches of the island, "my set of original hubcaps happens to be very important to me."

Alexis leaned forward and inspected her toes. "They're just shiny pieces of metal that turn."

I avoided their disagreement, preferring instead to dwell on weightier issues, thoughts of submerged things that eventually get exposed.

At the northern tip of Pawleys, where the dunes grew larger and the houses more weathered, Darcy turned us between two prodigious homes and into the sandy driveway of one far less impressive. Initially she didn't pull all the way in, allowing Sherbet to idle between two clumps of pampas grass while we stared up at the tiny two-bedroom with half a paint job. Faded taupe was partially covered in a warm pastel, somewhere between pumpkin and coral. Whoever had been working had painted just under the second story windows before heading for the beach, tiring of the color or running out of paint. Further down the front of the dwelling, centered on the front deck, a conch shell held open the screen door to the humble rental house dubbed "Point o' View."

Darcy eased forward and parked us beneath the house. The cool of the afternoon shade joined the tonic in the salt air to ratify furlough, and when she cut the Caddy's engine, the only sound was of flitting gulls welcoming us to their habitat. "What do you think it means?" she asked.

"That sorry paint job?" I replied.

"No, the name of the house."

Alexis got out and went around the car and waited for the trunk to release. "Since we're not on the oceanfront, I think it means that your own point of view determines if the house is worth the price."

Darcy said, "Hmm . . . five hundred fifty," before popping the trunk lid.

Up the wooden steps with armfuls of female luggage, I found a note wedged beneath the conch shell. The words were written on the back of a bank deposit slip:

Neil, what kept y'all?
We've gone sailing with a bunch of Pentecostals. They've invaded Litchfield this year. Must be eighty of 'em on the beach.

*I'll find us a place to stay. A certain female still insists that it looks bad for church guys to stay in a rental house with church girls.*

*Later,*
*Steve (and Lydia)*

*P.S. Only one bathroom, and you have to hold the handle.*

Lydia and her rules.

Go ahead, Lydia. Think the worst. I would have been fine with sleeping on the floor, although the anticipation of discovering what Steve had arranged was worth the insult.

Light wood paneling and glass-encased seashells walled the foyer to Point o' View. Upon entering the house we concluded that such decor must be a bargain in Carolina—it dominated the interior.

While the girls unpacked their suitcases in the bedrooms, I opened the refrigerator but found only a six pack of Diet Coke and a lone banana. Disappointed, I shut the door and moved into the well-lit living room, which offered backyard views of an inlet and marsh grass through an abundance of floor-to-ceiling windows. Though small and narrow, this was a typical beach house—the kitchen, the see-through bar, and the living room holding no secrets from each other, sharing all conversations and the slanted, wood-beamed ceiling. "Girls," I said, "what do you think about guys staying here with you?"

From back in the second bedroom, Alexis raised her voice. "I wouldn't mind at all if you and Steve stayed here," she said. "I think you're . . . probably trustable."

Darcy strolled into the kitchen and draped a light green beach towel across the counter. From driving all day she had a long wrinkle on the back of her khaki shorts, more jagged ones on her T-shirt. "I'd probably lock my door if you stayed here," she said, inspecting the fridge for herself. She was kidding. I think.

For a moment I sprawled out on a wicker sofa, my feet propped up on nautical blue pillows that only a beach house could love. "Is it awkward for you, Darcy, reading that note from Steve?"

"I'm not talking about him," she said, plopping down on a bar stool. Then, "I forgot to stop for groceries, Neil. I'd rather not go get groceries."

"Man has to have food, woman," I said through a gap in the wickers.

Alexis came out of the back bedroom in navy gym shorts and a pink Bahamas T-shirt. She hurried over and tugged me from the sofa, then Darcy from the bar stool. The three of us went out on the front deck, discussed briefly the issue of groceries, then stood on our toes and tried to get a glimpse of ocean.

We were second row, however, blocked from clear views of the Atlantic, although not from feeling its charitable breeze. July's blue horizon had no discernable edge. Low, distant sky could have been water; or high, distant water could have been sky.

Not yet satisfied, Alexis stood on the conch shell, teetered for a moment, and put a hand on my shoulder for balance. After straining to see the shore she frowned and stepped off. Then she picked up the yellowed conch with both hands and held it to her ear. "Whoa."

"Is it saying anything?" I inquired, instantly regretting that I'd asked.

Her eyes narrowed and her head tilted, like the conch was whispering to her. "Yes. Oh yes. The conch is saying that Darcy should take that long stroll on the beach, and there she'll find her hubcaps near the stand of a handsome lifeguard, who will reinstall them, marry her, and ask her to live happily with him in his . . . single-wide trailer."

Darcy could only shake her head. She flung her beach towel over her shoulder and pulled her sunglasses down. "Lex, can you get me some granola bars and some low-fat milk at the store? And maybe a bottle of sedatives for yourself?"

"I know what it is, Darcy," Alexis said, "and I can sympathize."

Having no idea what they were talking about, I borrowed the conch, held it to my ear, and let the sea's incessant harmony join the gulls in welcoming me to the coast.

Darcy moved to the top stair and turned her face toward the dunes. "I really don't need your sympathy."

Alexis went over and stood on the step with her friend. She put her arm around Darcy, which was a bit awkward given that she was a good five inches shorter. "I've been there, sister," Alexis said, left shoulder raised high. "Your ex, Steve, is hanging out with a good friend of yours, so now you're trying to decide if you care."

Darcy pursed her lips and stared into blue skies. "I don't care at all."

"Not even a little bit of care?"

Darcy hesitated a moment. "Lex, can you and Neil just get me some granola bars and low-fat milk? My keys are on the kitchen counter."

I was already in the passenger seat when Alexis bounded down the stairs of the beach house, her sandals flopping, her hair in windy chaos. In a flurry she was behind the wheel, adjusting the mirror and pressing a button to move the seat forward.

"She cares," said Alexis. After tuning in and rejecting five radio stations, she backed us from under the house and into the island road. "Darcy never lets me drive. Only when she's sad."

I turned in the seat and saw Darcy walking toward the northern tip of the island. Between high dunes and low dunes and sea oats she walked, a blonde nomad wandering among shorebirds. Ahead of her lay tidal pools and the wet glimmer of seashells. The victim of a theft, the victim of too much Alexis, and the victim of having to endure her ex hanging out with Lydia, Darcy was the tall, elegant picture of discontent. Maybe Steve had more than just her WeedEater.

I said a silent prayer for her, then scribbled my grocery list on the back of the rental form. I was glad to be alone with Alexis, even if it was just for groceries.

But as we left the island and the wind tried to lift our caps from our heads, I reminded myself that I had no moves, no real sense of how to nudge things forward. Being tenacious without knowledge is an odd way to approach the opposite sex.

Alexis drove without incident between the marsh and a feeder creek, where four women with straw hats and cane poles sat dawdling away summer. At the first stoplight we totaled our cash and found we had fifty-seven dollars between us. "Which way to a grocery store?" she asked, watching an endless stream of traffic roll north toward Myrtle Beach.

"No idea. You?"

"Nope." Her expression changed to something between mischievous and flirty. "Wanna skip the groceries and have some fun?"

"We oughta at least get Darcy her granola bars."

"Yeah, and some chicken necks too."

"For Darcy?"

"For crabbing. I'm gonna make she-crab soup tonight. It's her favorite, and it'll cheer her up."

She-crab soup sounded rather sexist, but I kept the thought to myself. After driving two miles down the highway and one mile back, we found the island grocery store. By this time we were both bobbing our heads to the music, and I couldn't figure out if this was chemistry or just beach fever.

Perhaps a little of both.

Across a parking lot full of scavenger gulls, we hurried into the store. Alexis went straight for aisle 3, where a 6-pack of granola bars sold for $5.29. She inspected the box, shrugged her disbelief, and without looking, tossed it overhead.

Startled, I managed to catch the box.

"For that price I'd grow my own granolas," she said, hurrying toward the back of the store.

Her simple act of tossing the box blindly overhead reminded me of José—José of tangelo fame—and how his wife, Maria, would be working in the soup kitchen and toss things to him without looking, as if the two of them knew instinctively where the other one was. I had never known instinctively where any of my former girlfriends were, mentally or physically.

How did Alexis know I was right there, paying attention, and that her overhead toss would be caught? Perhaps this was a test thought up by the Ladies of the Quest, whereby prospects are taken to a store and the girl grabs a box of granola bars and tosses it backward. I supposed the worst that could happen was that the bars break into pieces on the tile floor and cost her three bucks, twice that if she was on vacation. But a girl had to figure that either price was worth discovering that she and Mr. Clumsy didn't share the instinct. *Sí?*

I decided that chicken necks might be the one true bargain of island grocers. At the meat department, Alexis was inspecting frozen packages when the butcher—who, like all good butchers, looked to have dined on lots of meats—came over and smiled politely. "Help you, young lady?"

Alexis held up the chicken necks to his bloody apron. "Sir, your store sells both turkey necks and chicken necks. If you needed to catch six crabs in only one hour, which would you buy?"

The butcher rubbed his chin before leaning down to see for himself. He held one end of the package and stared at the grainy, pink skin of a plucked chicken. "I'm not much of a crabber, ma'am, but I hear turkey necks tend to stay together longer, though we sell more of the chicken."

"Then we'll go with the chicken."

"Very well."

"But we'll need extra blood."

"Chicken blood?"

"Any kind of blood, sir. We only have an hour to catch six blue crabs, and then I've got to clean them myself 'cause Neil here has no experience. So we're gonna need something smelly."

The butcher signaled with one finger that we should follow him. Around the back of his meat department he led us to the chopping station. "I just sliced up some mahimahi and two big salmon," he said, pointing at the remains. He removed the chicken necks from the package and dipped them in fish blood. Then he rewrapped them twice with cellophane. "How's that look?"

"Juicy," Alexis said, smiling with pleasure.

He held the package out to her, but when she grasped the other end he didn't let go. "Miss, I need to warn you. These are now very potent, so don't get any of it on you, especially around your eyes. A crab grabs hold of that little piercing there on your eyebrow . . . ooh-wee, that could get painful." The butcher winked first at her, then at me.

Apparently Alexis didn't know whether to laugh or be offended. Blank-faced, she accepted the double-wrapped package of chicken necks and promptly tossed it overhead.

Once again, I caught it.

We arrived back at sandswept Pawleys with all but the main ingredient for she-crab soup. Alexis parked Sherbet under the beach house, and I lugged all the groceries, except the bait, up the stairs.

She remained below, measuring off two twenty-foot sections of string before tying to their ends the potent necks of humbled chickens.

When I entered the beach house, Darcy was standing on the wicker sofa, barefooted, a rolled-up magazine in her hand. She cocked it behind her head and looked up. "It's a spider . . . a big one. I just hate bugs."

I shoved the low-fat milk in the fridge but left the other groceries on the floor. "I'll do that for ya," I said, hurrying over to the sofa.

She glanced down, shook her head no, and refocused on the spider.

Death came quick and glossy—she squashed it with the April issue of *Southern Living*.

She handed me the magazine, and I helped her from the sofa. Her fingers felt warm and longish, but I quickly let go. "I'm in a bad mood, Neil," Darcy said. "First the hubcaps, then ex-boyfriends, and now spiders. I might just make a sign and picket my own vacation."

"So, how was the beach walk?" I asked, having no clue what to say. "You looked a bit dejected when we left."

Darcy stooped down and looked beneath the furniture, searching for more spiders. "I just needed some alone time . . . time to think." Satisfied that no other arachnids were lurking, she sat on the sofa and held the nautical pillow to her chest. "Don't guys ever need alone time?"

Not expecting to be engaged in long conversation, I sat on the edge of a bar stool in my best half there/half not posture. "Sure we do, but it's kinda hard considering the present company."

She nodded knowingly. "Has Alexis not calmed down at all?"

I tried fitting *calm* and *Alexis* into the same sentence, although neither proper grammar nor meaningful logic would come of it. "You shoulda been there, Darcy. She had the butcher unwrap a pack of chicken necks and—"

Darcy held up her hand to stop me. "Don't even tell me what she did, Neil. It'll gross me out."

"Probably. She does have a heart, though. Said she's making you your favorite vacation soup."

Darcy rested her chin on the pillow, then raised her eyebrows in a gesture of hope. "She-crab?"

"We're about to go catch some out back . . . off the dock."

She pushed her chin further into the pillow, blonde hair folding under as it found support. "Lex is such a sweetie. Out of her mind, but still a sweetie."

I rose from the bar stool. "Since you hate bugs, I don't suppose you'll want to join us in catching dinner?"

"I'm taking a nap," Darcy said, poking her head above the back of the sofa. "But do you think . . ."

I stopped in mid-stride. "Think what?"

A long pause preceded her question. "Do you think Steve really likes Lydia?"

I hated being the middle person, although if God had me in the role, I might as well leap right in. "To be quite frank, Darcy, he may just be in a rebound. But who knows. He did mention that you said dating him was like water-skiing behind a canoe."

She slid down into the sofa, the pillow still clutched to her chest. "That may have been a bit strong," she said, pausing in reflection. "I almost said a pontoon boat, but actually I've seen people ski behind a pontoon boat, and so I went with canoe."

I stepped forward and looked down at her. "You want me to tell Steve that you're revising your comment?"

She clutched the pillow tight and scrunched her eyes. "No, don't do that. Since our social circle is so small, I guess stuff like this is inevitable."

"Yeah, suppose so."

"I just don't like being on the downside of inevitable."

Darcy settled into her nap, and on my way out I stopped in the kitchen to wipe the spider guts from the cover of *Southern Living*.

# 17

Behind Point o' View the inlet curved gracefully to the north, bordered on each side by a hundred feet of marsh grass, photosynthesis gone hog wild. It was nearly 6:00 p.m., the hour of angled sunlight. A long, skinny dock extended from beside the house, out across the marsh, and into the water. A cocktail of fish blood dripped from two decapitated necks tied to white strings. Alexis strode ahead of me, swinging a thrice-tied neck like an uncooperative yo-yo.

I held mine at arm's length, much like I'd seen new dads do with dirty diapers. In my other hand was a Styrofoam bucket, lightweight at the moment but optimistic of a heavier future.

Just steps from the end of the dock, Alexis stopped and said, "Shhh."

I looked around at all the surrounding marsh, at a dozen skinny docks all sunlit and weathered. The only sounds were a faint whistle of wind and the distant caw of sea birds. "Why the shhh? Aren't these crabs under the water?"

"I like to sneak up on 'em."

Imitating the careful steps of a cat burglar, Alexis moved slowly toward the end of the dock, the back of her pink Bahamas shirt fluttering in the breeze, our chicken necks dripping on the boards. She looked very much at home.

"Alexis?"

"Shhh."

"You've done this before?"

"Twice . . . Stop pounding your feet, Neil. You'll scare 'em."

Ever the quick study, I heel-toed it till we were just a step from the end of the dock. "What now?" I whispered.

"Kneel down."

"Here?"

"Beside me."

"This bait really stinks."

"Scoot over. You're too close to me."

"That was intentional."

She moved to her right, kneeling again. "We need room to fling the necks in the water, silly. I don't want you hittin' me upside the head with that thing."

On my knees, facing the slow-moving inlet, I watched Alexis rear back and twirl her bait like a sling. We were a good six feet above the water line—and still not to the edge of the dock—so we didn't see the splash, only heard it. The rippling evidence expanded from below, only to be absorbed in the current.

"Go ahead, Neil," Alexis said, peeking over the edge to watch the water flow over her bait. "Fling yours to the left of mine."

I twirled the neck and flung it high but forgot to hold on to the other end of the string.

With all the grace of a downed kite tugging its tail, both neck and twine joined whatever lurked in the bowels of low tide. My fleeting white string floated partially on the surface before the inlet slurped it, like a dangling spaghetti noodle, down into the dregs of gone forever.

Behind windblown hair, Alexis's lips parted in shock. "Oh my word, Neil, you're worse than Darcy . . . and she absolutely hates crabbing."

Baitless and embarrassed, I rose to my feet. "Any more necks left?"

She was on her stomach now, peering over the edge of the dock to spy on the sea life. "Three more in the cooler. Now hurry back to the house and cut off some string. You're gonna work on a charter boat this weekend? God help Maurice and Preacher Smoak."

"You didn't remind me to hold on to the end," I mumbled, already striding back across the marsh.

Fifteen minutes later I returned with thirty feet of string tied to a fresh neck, the opposite end fashioned in a loop and tethered to my wrist.

Alexis was sitting on the dock, her feet dangling over the edge, her attention focused firmly on the business end of her string. "Have a seat, rookie."

I sat beside her, this time on her right. "Any bites yet?"

"Look in the bucket."

"You've got to be kidding . . ."

"Just lift the lid and look."

After flinging my bait successfully into the water, I leaned back on the dock and pulled the Styrofoam bucket close. The weight of it told me that something—I was guessing just water—occupied its innards.

I pulled off the top and saw three blue crabs, bigger than my hand and very agitated, clawing up at their captors. "Not bad for a realtor."

Alexis was back on her stomach, her hair swishing across the back of her shirt with every gust of wind. She didn't look up from her work. "While you were gone I figured out a new technique."

"What's this gonna cost me?" I asked, drawing my string taut.

"Nothing," she said. "I'm in a generous mood."

What followed was a short but informative lesson from Alexis, the Raven-Haired Crabber.

Her method was simplistic and came not from out of the blue but from somewhere within the vast playground of her psyche. She explained that the tendency in crabbing is to tug the string too fast, to get in a hurry and cause the crab to let go as you inch it, pinchers gnawing, up to your dock. So the secret, according to Alexis, was to put yourself and your quarry in a relaxed mood through the art of humming. Just hum something slow and methodic—she suggested a Frank Sinatra ballad. How this girl picked Sinatra music was beyond me. But next thing I knew she leaned over the dock, stared into the shallow current, and began humming the melody to "I Did It My Way."

Odd thing is, it worked.

Five minutes later I watched a crab scurry to my bait. After letting it chew for a minute I too began to hum, pulling the crab slowly from the water. Above the ripples came its left pincher, then its head, its body, right pincher, back legs, a whole crustacean dangling midair, me humming, inching string, feeling the weight, sensing Alexis watching me, hearing her whispering instruction, me still humming, inching the crab closer, closer still, afraid to breathe, afraid to move, afraid of being out-crabbed by a girl, until it was close enough to the dock for her to scoop it with the bucket.

"Got 'im!" she said, proudly setting the bucket between us. I mashed the lid into place, and a crab fight ensued.

"Well?" I asked, nodding at my noisy catch.

"Well, what?"

"You said *him*. Is it a he or is it a she?"

She lifted the lid and peered into Styrofoam. "I'm not that savvy."

"But we'll use it, right?"

Alexis raised her feet to the dock, set her chin on her knees. "Yeah, we'll use it. Lots of meat in those claws."

From our left, being pulled along by the current, a pair of kayakers paddled toward the curve in the inlet. Ocean bound, the orange and yellow hulls slid between the marshes, their plastic colors nearly aglow against the picturesque seaboard of Pawleys.

Behind and above them, in further proof that the coastal diner was always open, three pelicans circled over a school of minnows. The feathered kamikazes drew themselves into tight formation before plunging, wings folded, into the water.

Minutes passed. The sun dropped anchor. But no other crabs showed up. We watched our bait sway in the current, where tiny minnows kept nibbling at the chicken. My butt grew sore from sitting on the boards, so I turned on my stomach. Alexis did likewise. It was peaceful on that dock—beside her at early evening, the marsh tinted orange, random gusts blowing hair across her back, brushing my arm, a soft reminder that the person beside me, though bonkers, was very female indeed.

"Neil?"

"Yeah?"

"This is so much better than Tolstoy."

Our faces were flushed from peering under the dock, so I raised my head to reverse the flow. "Just how is it that you slide so easily from chicken necks to classic literature?"

She was entranced by some tiny creature at water's edge, and she spoke as if it had asked the question. "On last year's beach trip there were all these girls reading on the beach. I didn't have a book, and so this girl named Nancy loaned me one of hers."

"And?" ·

"And I'd rather dip chicken necks in fish blood than read Tolstoy."

The tide was now dead low, and the barnacled posts below us had grown muddy and elongated, giving the illusion that we'd ascended three feet whenever we looked under the dock. Perhaps the setting reminded her of a childhood vacation, for she began telling me about her family.

"So . . . your parents split when?" I asked. "When you were six?"

"When I was five," she said, pulling her string taut. "I was six when Dad remarried. What about your parents?"

"They've both passed away." I pulled my string to match hers, to where the breeze flexed our lines in tandem. "At his funeral I just kept telling myself that Dad's greatest love was his family."

Alexis pulled in her chicken neck, retied it, and dropped it softly back in the shallows. "Well, my dad's greatest loves are bimbo former models from the Fleeting Discretion Agency."

There was a sting in her voice when she said this, so I let her comment fade into salt air. Coastal winds, however, produce no tonic strong enough to make up for wandering fathers.

"Any brothers or sisters?" I asked.

"Nope. You?"

"Nope."

We raised our heads and caught a whiff of low tide, the smell of mud and roots and dead plankton, a warm tango of a scent that rose from the marsh in muggy waves, the ecosystem passing gas.

There were things I wanted to ask Alexis—and surely she had inquiries of me—but if all submerged things eventually get exposed, the dead calm of a tidal marsh was the perfect setting. "So your parents didn't want any other children?"

She shifted uncomfortably on the dock. "At first they didn't even want me, or so claimed my dad."

"That's horrible."

"Dad let it slip one day when he got mad at me for scratching his car. I was ten." She tugged her bait, frowned, pulled hair behind her ears. "You're crabbing with an accident today, Neil."

The weight of her words settled over the inlet, and I didn't have to search long for a like response. "I know all about accidents, Lex. One claimed my mom at the ripe old age of forty-two."

Alexis looped the twine around her thumb. "Car wreck?"

"I was in the backseat, nursing a stomachache."

She stared across the ripples for a moment. "Oh wow."

"A truck came over a hill in the wrong lane. Mom yelled, 'Duck, Ne—.' And that was it. She didn't even get my name out. They carried me away with minor injuries, but Mom was pronounced dead at the scene."

Alexis stared down into still water, fingered her string. "I have no idea how to respond to that."

I nudged her arm and said, "You don't have to. I have better memories of her."

"Like?"

"Like the harmonica she gave me for my twelfth birthday. Her note inside the little box read, 'Neil, live your life in the key of G' . . . Took me awhile to figure out what she meant by that."

"Do you mind sharing?"

"Well, finally she told me that it stood for the key of grace. She'd had to live in that key herself after my dad's stroke—I was nine when he died. And then to lose Mom, well, I just drifted between aunts and uncles."

Alexis reached over and patted the back of my hand. "I knew there had to be a reason why you carry that harmonica around like a pet rock."

I nodded twice and tugged my string. "And what about you? Any good times with your parents?"

She paused, scrunched her nose. "My mom and I do the real estate thing together, but outside of that I've never been quite sure where I fit in." She looked off into the curve of the inlet, as if her thoughts were about to shift with the tide. "Hey, you know what, Neily, this is like the two of us are bonding or something. If only we had some saltwater taffy."

How quickly she could lighten a moment. "Bonding . . . yeah," I said, swatting at a fly, "but first we need to catch a couple more crabs."

Quiet and without warning, inbound waters from the Atlantic began flowing back into the inlet and between the marshes. Alexis turned on the dock to face me. "Before we get serious about dinner, Neil, I'd like to reintroduce myself." She reached out to shake my hand. "I'm Accidental Alexis, coffeehouse volunteer in need of a father figure."

I shook back, glad to have shared with her the low tide of my life, a thing fully exposed. "I'm Neil Rucker, orphaned clay in need of a potter."

With the sun low and our allotted hour expiring, the prospect for more crabs looked dim. We'd tried everything: We switched places on the dock—me on her left, and then back. I dragged our baits into shallow water. Lex flung them into deep. We hummed "My Way" more times than I could count. To Alexis's credit, the technique had produced four of our needed six. But now, like Darcy contesting her vacation, the crabs were picketing.

Finally the biggest crab of the day showed up and grabbed my bait.

It fled at my first tug, never to be seen again.

"I think I know what it is, Neil," Alexis said, pulling her well-soaked chicken neck in for inspection.

"Our baits have been out there too long and they've lost their scent, right?"

"Bingo. Wanna go get the last two necks?"

Alexis stayed on the dock while I hurried back to the beach house to fetch bait. This time I returned with the secret weapon. After tying our baits we dropped them in shallow water, among oyster shells and tiny minnows fighting the current, the oysters doing a much better job than the minnows.

We sat together and dangled our feet. Then I pulled out my harmonica and began serenading the caught and the uncaught, playing once again that slow tune of wandering pitch, the nameless melody begun on the airport curb, the one with the main theme of exploration.

At the second verse Alexis leaned into me and said she liked my music, that it was a nice change of pace from Frankie Sinatra, who was probably too Hollywood to appreciate lowcountry traditions like crabbing.

At the third verse she put her head on my shoulder. The breeze whipped her hair across my chin.

At the fourth, two blue crabs arrived at our baits and ruined whatever moment had just up and fled.

Initially the crabs fought only over her bait, but soon one of them grew tired of undersea combat and noticed a second smorgasbord oozing its scent downstream. It scurried left and pounced.

"Slow," Alexis whispered, on her stomach again, fingering her string. "Play the tune real slow, Neil, while I inch in mine."

I immediately ceased playing. "And just why do you get to go first?"

"'Cause I'm a girl."

I played something akin to lullaby as she drew her string over the edge of the dock, delicate fingers gathering wet twine. I would never have guessed that she, of all people, could show such patience.

At one point she stopped completely and just let the crab eat; the unwary crustacean gnawed away even while suspended two feet above water. *Just how stupid are those things?*

"Slower, Neil," she whispered. "Now put down the harmonica and grab the bucket."

I did, and in a blink, a fifth crab was clawing at Styrofoam.

Surprising, what Alexis did next. While the sixth crab nipped and chewed at my chicken neck, she pulled strands of black hair behind her left ear, then reached over and gently took the harmonica from my pocket. Ordinarily I allowed no one to play my instrument, but in efforts to further chemistry I did not protest.

She couldn't play at all, but she could find a note and hold it, play it soft. This apparently was enough to soothe the nerves of the sixth and final crab. When I had it halfway out of the water, I concluded that the critter was not only stupid but tone deaf, and that it likely would not have let go even if Alexis had played Scottish bagpipes to a disco beat. That crab was intent on devouring the rare luxury of blood-soaked chicken.

The butcher had done it.

Doesn't the butcher always do it?

I hadn't yet done it—kiss Alexis, that is.

But at least I'd held on to the string.

# 18

The sun was setting in a splash of orange when we returned via the narrow dock. Between the stilts of the humble beach house lay nothing but air—Darcy and her car had disappeared.

After walking up the stairs with dinner's main ingredient, I saw that the groceries I'd left on the floor had been set on the counter. A half-eaten granola bar sat crumbly on the wicker sofa.

"Find the biggest pot in the house, Neil," Alexis said, rinsing out a plastic mixing bowl. "Fill it two-thirds with water, dump in some salt, and bring it to a boil."

"*Sí.*"

Pans clanged together as I dug deep under the counter for a pot. In partial darkness, and without telling her, I used a skillet to squish the second spider of the day.

When I rose from the search she was mixing together heavy cream and a spice called mace. She stirred left-handed and added more cream. "Neil?"

"Yes ma'am?"

"Did you just squash a bug?"

I began filling the pot with water. "How'd you know?"

She sniffed her mixture, then sampled it with her pinkie finger. "I just know. Now stoop back down there and wipe the bug from the bottom of whatever you used to kill it."

Alexis was both an individual and a multitude, and I kept wondering how any guy could ever keep up with her. What would an average week be like? Or Christmas morning?

At the first eruption of boiling water, she added butter, pepper, and another dash of salt. Still alive, the crabs in the Styrofoam bucket scratched at the sides and shifted their weight around.

"Is it time?" I asked, lifting the bucket from the kitchen floor.

"Don't think about the suffering, Neil," Alexis said, removing the top. "Just dump 'em in."

Death came slow and bubbly. In an act of defiance, the sixth and final crab raised a claw above the boil, waving in desperation before it sank, lifeless, down into the pot.

Dominion over nature . . . easier for some of us than others.

Six blue crabs had turned steamy red when I heard a car door shut beneath the beach house.

"No tellin' what kind of mood she'll be in," Alexis said, putting ice in tumblers and setting them on the counter.

With a wooden spoon I checked the crustaceans and decided they needed more time. "And you're sure this concoction will cheer up Darcy?"

"Never failed me before."

The front door opened, and into the paneled foyer walked Steve Cole. He was by himself, just him and an uneven sunburn, like he'd been sitting on one side of a sailboat all afternoon. His hair was wind-whipped, and his engineering T-shirt had a tear under the right armpit. "Howdy, beach bums."

"Hey, Steve," Alexis said, not looking up from her preparations.

I pointed to the boiling water. "We caught dinner, bro. Off the dock."

Steve came into the kitchen, saw steam rising above the stove, and took a long gander into the pot. "You guys making she-crab soup?" He borrowed the wooden spoon and poked at the crabs. "Darcy used to order this all the time . . . back when we were an item."

Alexis said nothing, silent in the way girls are when the ex of a friend says something already known as fact.

"And where's Lydia?" I asked, nonchalant as I reached high for bowls.

Steve was fascinated with those boiling crabs. "Oh, it's a long story," he said, his back turned, still spooning at dinner.

"Lydia didn't come back with you from sailing?" I asked.

"Nope. Say, can I join ya for soup?"

Alexis turned off the stove, took the wooden spoon from Steve, and pointed it at him. "Will you stop being vague and tell us what happened to Lydia?"

I leaned against the sink, enjoying the sight of someone else getting interrogated. At spoon-point Steve backed against the refrigerator. "She, um, met someone."

"We thought she was with you," Alexis said, holding the spoon to his belly.

"Didn't stop her from meeting someone," Steve said, sucking in his gut. "Lydia said a ride to the beach didn't qualify as a date, and so her field was wide open this weekend."

"So who'd she meet?"

"A Pentecostal sailor guy."

"And?" Alexis raised the spoon to Steve's nose.

"And so after seven of us had sailed for a couple hours, Lydia and he took the catamaran out by themselves. Just before they launched she said to tell y'all that she'd be staying with a houseful of Pentecostal girls. Said you two would understand."

"So they just left you on the shore?" Alexis asked, taking a step backward. "Left you with a bunch of strangers?"

"Not exactly."

"No?"

"No. Guess who else has gone Pentecostal."

Alexis rolled her eyes, set the spoon on the counter. "Oh lemme see. Nancy? Some of the Ladies of the Quest?"

"Well, yeah, them too. And their books. But that's not who I was talking about. Ransom and Jamie are switching as well. They told me on the beach that the Pentecostals have better nurseries in Greenville, plus they splurge on oceanfront houses for their beach trips, not the third-row stuff that North Hills Prez always rented." Steve snooped around the kitchen for a minute and finally asked if he could help make soup.

Alexis pointed at the pot. "First, one of you guys needs to scoop out four cups of broth and mix it in with my other stuff . . . Neil?"

"I can do that," I replied, spying a ladle hanging over the stove.

"And you, Steve, you fish out the crabs and we'll all peel 'em. This is gonna take a while."

Scooping broth from a pot of boiled crabs seemed strange, a bit gross even, but it was her recipe.

"Now what?"

Alexis peered into her mixing bowl, the contents of which kept increasing as she added two egg yolks, three dashes of mace, and an ounce of cooking sherry. Satisfied, she covered the bowl with a paper towel. "There," she said, "we'll get back to that in a minute."

In the kitchen of Point o' View, the three of us stood facing the counter, each squared off against a pair of boiled crabs. Even in the steam of their death they proved frustrating. From the drawers we plucked ice picks, crusher tools, steak knives, and three-pronged forks. What ensued were shell fragments flying at weird angles, popping us in the face and careening off kitchen cabinets. Let me just say that extracting the meat from the armature of a crab is like extracting the truth from an impeached president—concentrated effort on the part of the extractor may not yield the desired result.

Fragments of crab shell clung to Alexis's pink Bahamas shirt as she dissected her quarry. She finished peeling her second crab before me and Steve were done with our first. My fingers were already pricked and complaining.

Alexis reached across me with her knife and tapped Steve's crab on the crown. "So when Lydia left you there on the shore and went sailing with Joe Pentecostal . . . just how does a guy respond to that?"

Steve glanced at me for support.

My support was a shrug.

Steve picked up his crab and spoke into its face. "He gets into his Jeep and retreats to his friends."

When we were done Alexis methodically sifted through half a bowl of crab meat to remove pieces of shell. She spooned the meat into her mixing bowl, added butter and another dash of cream, and shooed us from the kitchen. From the see-through bar I watched her dump the mixture into a pot and set it on the stove.

This aroma was noticeably sweeter than the ecosystem passing gas.

Her facility in the kitchen, added to her zany manner, pale skin, and Italian eyes, had me summing her traits, the totality of her. I summed it up as potential. Then I gave bonus points when Alexis pointed at us with the wooden spoon and told us to bow our heads—that she not only prepared dinner but would ask a blessing over it. "God of wonders, salt marshes, and chicken necks, I thank you for the crabs that bit our baits so that I could make the soup to cheer up Darcy, who is sad. And also for Steve here, who can't keep a girl, and for Neil, who tossed both his bait and his string into your inlet."

At *amen* I looked over at Steve, who was seated on a bar stool, nursing half a sunburn and his two-day stubble. I wondered about the events of the day, his avoiding Darcy by riding with Lydia, then getting dumped by Lydia for a ruddered Pentecostal, then arriving here at the beach house where his ex was sure to return. It seemed that this was—like my coffeehouse adventures—just another one of those meetings that God arranges, a meeting of flickering flames and blurred edges, one in which the almighty was leaving it up to Steve and Darcy whether or not to nudge things forward.

I didn't voice these thoughts to him. I just sat there beside him on a bar stool, like most guys would, thinking but not speaking, knowing yet not knowing, sifting the possibilities while hoping Steve would gather his thoughts and take some initiative.

Guys and their initiative—sometimes that too is like extracting meat from the armature of a crab.

She-crab soup danced the jitterbug on our tastebuds. We were three spoonfuls into dinner when Darcy bounded into the beach house, two shopping bags in her hands, light green flip-flops on her feet. She set her bags on the floor and sniffed the air. Shopping seemed to have rejuvenated her.

"Oh, look," she said, acting not at all surprised to see Steve seated at the dining table. "Mama Bear comes home and finds her ex-boyfriend eating all the porridge."

Alexis nearly spewed soup. "On the stove, Darce," she said, wiping her chin. "There's half a pot."

"Oyster crackers on the counter," Steve said, hunched over his bowl like he hadn't eaten in days.

Darcy ladled a bowl full then sat down facing Steve. I faced Alexis. Every few spoonfuls Alexis would look up, first at Darcy, then at Steve, then me. She'd crack a smile, then quickly glance down at her bowl when Darcy would look around and mouth "What?" A comical tension, camouflaged by soup-slurping, had replaced normal, adult conversation.

Steve, being the only left-brained person at the table, seemed oblivious to the girls' smirks, smiles, and shared glances. His only comment was to ask if anyone wanted seconds. No one was done yet, so he got up to help himself. We were just four singles surrounded by beach, marsh, and that obscure feeling known as potential. In that skinny beach house, on that warm July night, there seemed not a care other than what was right in front of us—tasty soup and the opposite sex. What might be going on outside of Pawleys Island didn't matter, as our coastal paradise had become a shield to outside news, be it good, bad, or indifferent.

Not much else was said over dinner, other than a host of piggybacking comments like "Great soup, Lex," "Dee-lish, girlfriend," and "Gimme your recipe."

Coerced into a Grammylike moment, Alexis stood on her chair and took a bow.

When we'd all reached the point of tilted bowls and tiny spoonings, Steve and Darcy began a new series of shared glances, as if they were not exactly glad that the other was there but at the same time were ecstatic that the other was not with someone else. Who knew what those glances contained.

All I knew was that our bowls contained no more soup, so I collected dishes and rinsed them in the sink. Through the kitchen window an unexplored beach summoned me to its shore. Though I could see no surf from our second row house, I knew it was there, knew it could likely make or break potential, and knew, upon a long gaze skyward, that God had sent the South yet another starry night.

Irresistible, those Southern starry nights.

Alexis had followed me into the kitchen. She put the first two rinsed plates in the dishwasher, then stopped and said, "Cleanup can wait, Neil. You wanna . . . ?" She pointed out the window.

"Yeah," I said, reading her mind. "Lemme brush my teeth."

At 10:00 p.m. all four of us walked down the island road, two by two, coupled off, sandals swishing on thin layers of sand. Into a balmy night of possibility we walked, escorted by moonlight and the ever-present scent of salt air. An access sign directed us to the oceanfront. It was there—where soft sand met firm—that the pounding surf and relational tangles caused us to do what foursomes usually do in the midst of potential.

We split up.

Alexis and I strolled south toward the pier, where in the distance of night the structure looked like the black skeleton of something massive. Steve and Darcy went north. I turned once to check on them and saw that they were walking several feet apart, their posture confirming that the feelings between them, however powerful, remained unresolved.

We had not been walking two minutes when Alexis stopped me and pointed at wet sand. Some literate soul had carved a whole sentence in the shore, the bottom of the letters fading as the tide rose.

We took off our sandals and held them, backing to the edge of the surf, where moonlight angled across the words. Carved on the shore of Pawleys Island was not a love note or a poem or an autograph but something from two decades past: *Her name is Rio, and she dances on the sand.*

"Who would name a girl Rio?" Alexis asked, looking up and down the beach.

"It's from the eighties," I said. "From the song."

Alexis sloshed her way to dry land, dragging a toe through the wet words. "I was just a kid during the eighties."

196

"You're still a kid," I said. "A crab-catching, twenty-five-year-old kid."

"Then we're two of a kind." Alexis kept urging me to walk crooked, saying that our tracks would confuse whoever might later walk the shore behind us, including Miss Rio, whoever she was. "Neil?"

"Yes, Chef Lex?" Though I had no moves, I at least recognized that we'd spent enough time together to start using the abbreviated version of her name.

"Why do you think God sent you to South Carolina for the summer?"

I considered the question loaded, a probing for chemistry. And though our steps may have been crooked, my answer was dead straight. "I could be here just for furlough, or for more important reasons. But right now I'm here and you're here and we're getting to know each other. Ask me that question when it's time for me to leave South Carolina."

We were approaching the pier, and she said nothing for three more loopy turns afoot. But when I began walking normal again she nudged my arm. "Neil?"

I stopped near the water, feeling lunar in the night air. "Yep?"

"I'm glad you didn't say something corny like 'Oh, Alexis, I was sent here to meet you.'"

"Never considered it."

"I woulda barfed," she said, watching a wave fracture against the pier. "Right here on this beach."

That was plenty of chemistry, especially for a missionary who'd endured one year, five months, and two weeks without kissing anyone. I'd kept count of last kisses too.

Moonlight shone the way to her lips. Then I forgot about moonlight and shut my eyes. In the midst of kissing her I almost made the unspeakable error of bursting into a grin. But not because of anything she was doing, or me. I just couldn't get a vision to leave my head. I kept picturing moonlight in the shape of a canoe—a canoe stuck in wet sand—with Steve inside, scooping mud with his paddle. Behind the canoe, moonlit Darcy was on skis, holding a silver rope but going nowhere.

At the instant of parted lips I was able to keep a straight face. After waiting all I could of two more seconds, I went ahead and burst into a grin.

"Was it that good?" Alexis asked, eyes wide with surprise.

"Well, yeah, but I was just thinking of what Steve said . . . about Darcy breaking up with him."

Alexis took my hands in hers, softly squeezing. "Do ya mean when Darcy told Steve that dating him was like playing tennis with a bowling ball?"

"No, Lex. That's not what Darcy said."

"Whatever." She pulled me to her. "Kiss me again."

"Just a sec."

"Why?"

"There's a piece of crab shell in your hair." I reached up and brushed it into the night, remembering, for a split second, more numbskull advice from my mentor, José: *Young Neil, to properly kiss the woman you must place one hand behind her head, cradling her hair as if you held a gerbil. Such technique is of importance, no?*

Then I pulled Alexis close and kissed her again, lost in the moment, vaguely aware that inside my head clanged dueling tambourines of warning and pleasure. *At what point will I have to ask God to forgive me?* One more kiss, softly. *Am I to that point?* Bottom lip, top lip, back to the bottom. *How close am I to that point?* Top lip, top lip again. Her hand in my hair, my hand in hers. Waves crashing behind me, pulse quickening inside me. Top lip, bottom lip—she had a great bottom lip.

*When did I set a point?* Top lip. Bottom lip. Bottom lip longer. *Now just where is that point?*

The point itself disappeared on the warmth of her lips, and all thoughts of having something to confess beyond kissing got lost inside the romance of having someone to kiss.

We were seated in the soft sand, near the dunes, when I brushed her hair from her eyes and took her by both shoulders.

# 19

The marsh was so close to our tent that we were certain we'd heard a gator snore. Only ten feet of yard lay behind Point o' View, just crab grass and sandspurs and patches of weeds. Yep, we were spending the night in a tent.

Not me and a girl.

Me and Steve Cole.

His great idea for a place to stay—actually, our only option since all the beach houses and hotels around Pawleys Island were booked over the holiday weekend—was his tiny A-frame of green canvas. He'd brought the pup tent that he'd owned since junior high, and the musty odors and frayed seams attested to its age. We'd asked the girls to let us set up the tent out back. They claimed that even though Lydia was off with the Pentecostals and not on site with her bag of rules and regulations, they still didn't want us staying in the house.

Darcy—the Rhapsody in Lime, as Steve privately referred to her—had explained on the front deck, at midnight, that it would be too weird to get up for a glass of water during the wee hours and see her ex-boyfriend sleeping on the living room floor. No can do, she said. Alexis had stood behind Darcy, nodding and grinning as if the two of them were going to stay up late, sipping coffee and pondering men.

So there we were, in a tent so small that our shoulders touched if we rolled an inch toward the middle. Steve and I folded two blankets in half for padding and lay on our backs, the musical missionary squished on the right, the enterprising engineer crammed on the left, harmonica and furlough laying down with blueprints and logic.

"You lost Lydia to a Pentecostal?" I chided him in darkness.

"I didn't lose her. I just saw that she was getting along with sailor boy, and so I—"

"Couldn't remember her love language?"

"Well, I couldn't exactly compete with a sailboat. So I hung out on the beach with Ransom and his wife. They now have his 'n her surfboards. Hot pink for her. Same old purple for him."

"Did ya try surfing?"

"I got up."

"How long?"

"Five seconds. Maybe six."

"I don't believe you."

"Okay, three seconds. Now what about you?"

"I've never surfed."

"I meant about you and Alexis."

"What about it?"

"Any smoochie?"

"Maybe."

"Here we go again. Vague Neil."

"Okay . . . a little."

"On the beach?"

"Of course on the beach . . . and then near the dunes."

On the island road, a motorcycle purred into the night. Steve waited for it to fade before he pounced on my confession. "Did you behave yourself?"

"I'm proud to say that I did. But it wasn't easy. I had to take her by the shoulders and explain that if—"

"Hold it, Neilandra. You had her by the shoulders, in the dunes, and what?"

"I had to shake her a bit to get her mind settled. You know how Alexis can be scatterbrained and all, well . . ."

"Well, what?"

"It's like everybody thinks the guy is always the aggressor, but some-times it's tough when the girl is, um, you know . . . encouraging."

"Been there," Steve said. "I'm hip."

"Whadda you mean, you're hip? You're white and you're an engineer with a closet full of logoed shirts. How can you ever be hip?"

"I just am."

The cicadas were humming without direction, and the pounding surf lent an odd percussion to their one-note chorus. "So tell me what you and Darcy did."

"Well, there wasn't any smoochie, that's for sure."

"Details, man."

"Why do you need details?"

"'Cause it was a starry night."

"Aw man, now you sound all romancey."

"Not romancey. Curious. You just know the girls are up there in that beach house, going over every detail."

"Worse. They're probably journaling every detail."

"Yeah. Journaling."

"Yeah."

"So, give me some details before I get sleepy and start rambling about Mexico City."

"Oh, man, not another Mexico story. You've already told me about your blues band, Rafael the taco drummer, plus José and his magic grapefruit."

"It was a tangelo."

"Whatever. So do ya want the details?"

"Gimme 'em."

Steve shifted in the tent, and our shoulders touched. I quickly scooted right. He scooted farther left. "Darcy and I walked all the way to the north tip of the island, near the jetties. When the talk got serious, Darcy stood on a rock with her arms crossed. She was towering over me like some blonde goddess of dating. Said she felt like we'd lost our momentum, that I was too worried about whether or not I was going to get transferred

201

with my job and that I'd taken the easy way out and let things sit idle. I had no idea how flustered a woman can get when a relationship sits idle . . . I was fine on idle."

"I've idled before."

"Yeah, idling is nice. No pressure."

"Pressure bad. Idle good."

"For a missionary, Neil, you have a bizarre sense of humor."

Still rustling, the marsh grass was a poor opponent for the cicadas, who must have gotten caffeinated before bursting into song. It was getting late, although I didn't want to go to sleep yet. So I reverted to two of my favorite subjects. "Did you know that Alexis knows nothing about eighties music?"

"Nothing at all?"

"Nope. On the beach someone had scrawled that old lyric about Rio dancing on the sand. Lex was totally lost."

"Weird."

"Alexis?"

"No, finding those lyrics. When Darcy and I were walking back from the north end we found two of those."

"No way."

"Yes way. Someone had scratched 'Tainted Love' in wet sand, then another hundred feet down the shore we found 'Come on Eileen.'"

"That was one of my favorites."

"Mine too. So who do you think—"

"Wrote the song?"

"No, scratched it in the sand."

"Some kid."

"Nah. Some adult. The beach brings out the nostalgia in people."

"Yeah, nostalgia."

"Yeah. So any advice from you about me and Darcy?"

"Not really . . . maybe you should buy an outboard motor for your canoe."

I'd chided him enough and was about to turn over and go to sleep when, in the swift 180-degree manner of engineers, Steve turned the conversation. "So, Neil, when you drove up the mountain Wednesday night, did you try to kiss my ex?"

"Darcy?"

"That would be my ex."

"Nope, she had smelly brakes."

"So that ruined the moment?"

"There was not going to be any moment. She just had hot, stinky brakes."

"Darcy's very classy . . . except for her driving."

"Seems that way."

"So what about Alexis?"

"We'll be up all night."

"I wanna know."

"It'll take hours, man."

"Who cares. I wanna know."

Where to start was my dilemma. And on second thought, I didn't have the energy, especially from inside a musty pup tent. "The drive down to the coast earlier today was insane, but I can't tell it all tonight, bro. Sorry. It's late."

"You can't just stop there, Neil. I gotta know. Also, can I go fishing with you and Maurice and Asbury tomorrow? I wanna see you flub your first day as first mate."

"No way. Besides, we have a client to take out tomorrow."

"Who? Some big shot?"

"Her name's Quilla."

"Quilla like . . . manila?"

"Or like vanilla."

"Know anything about her?"

"Only that she's Maurice's sister-in-law and she's flamboyant."

Steve paused, shifted farther into his side of the tent. "What kinda flamboyant?"

"Gimme a break, man. Flamboyant is flamboyant. Maybe she dresses funny . . . or maybe she talks funny. All I know is that it's my first day on the job, I have to cook breakfast, and you cannot tag along and mess me up."

"Well then, I'll tag along on Sunday."

"They don't fish on Sunday. Preacher Smoak is against it."

"Then I'll go on Monday."

"That's July Fourth."

"So what? You think the forefathers were against fishing on Independence Day?"

"Who knows. But did you ever hear the story of John Adams catching the swordfish on the day he signed the Declaration?"

"No."

"I rest my case."

Steve paused, and before the marsh grass could rustle again he produced a flashlight and beamed me in the face. "You're kiddin' with me, aren't ya?"

"Duh," I said, squinting. "On July Fourth there's some kinda dinner cruise that Asbury is putting together. You may get an invite."

Steve turned off his beam. "Cool."

"Do ya still wanna know what Alexis did?"

"On the trip down?"

"Yeah."

"Okay, but she didn't do anything off-color, did she? 'Cause I don't need to hear it if she did. I'm trying to protect my ears from impurities."

"Oh, right . . . Puritanical Steve. Anyway, I've never seen Alexis do anything off-color. In fact, she credits abstinence for the art that goes on the wall of the coffeehouse."

"What are you talking about?"

"Do you wanna hear what she did or not?"

Steve lay flat on his back, arms crossed on his chest. "About the trip down, yeah. Not about the art."

"Okay, then stop talking a minute and listen."

"I'm listening."

The moon had risen to where faint light squeezed through the canvas, an eerie glow that blurred the specifics of my storytelling. So I began reciting with closed eyes. "First, Alexis had us turn off the stalled interstate to avoid the traffic caused by six thousand liberated chickens."

"Why were they liberated?"

"Because their truck flipped over."

"Oh . . . then what?"

"Then she invented a game called Road Trip, and I had to pick a letter from her cap. I picked a *W*, and so we drove to Whitmire and—"

"Why not Wilmington?"

"Will you stop with the questions and listen? Wilmington is in North Carolina and Whitmire was only fifteen miles down the road."

"Proceed."

"Yeah. So we made it to Whitmire, and after Lazy Earl swigged the tomato juice that we thought was malt liquor, he sold us some Jolly Ranchers and tried to hit on Darcy. So Darcy fled to her car while Alexis interrogated Earl about Jean, the woman he had a thing for after she buried Jerry. Then we drove to Pomaria because Lazy Earl picked a *P*. We had to park around back because the convenience store was crowded. Then when we came back out, two of Sherbet's hubcaps had been stolen. Alexis gasped, then Darcy gasped, but I stayed calm 'cause I'm a guy."

Steve sighed and put his hands behind his head. "You're starting to lose me. But I gotta hear the rest of this."

I took a breath and continued. "So Darcy almost barfed, but she held it, then she blamed Alexis for leading us astray. Lex tried to comfort Darcy, but then she compared stolen hubcaps to stolen Jolly Ranchers, and that enraged Darcy so much that she dumped the letters on Alexis's head, even though Alexis had tried to solve the crime by looking for fingerprints in the brake dust."

"Find any?"

"No, she just got her finger all greasy. So then Darcy blamed it all on the Mafia and gave the cop her forwarding address. I think the cop knew her. Then Darcy turned her cap around backward and drove ninety all the way to the marina."

"She drives like that even when she's not enraged."

"Yeah, anyway, at the marina I caught up to Maurice, who was napping in the cabin of the boat. He introduced me to the preacher, who asked me if I could make ambidextrous pancakes. So I said yeah, just to get the job. And then later he told me that it only means flippin' 'em with both hands when you're in a hurry. So tomorrow is my first day. Pretty cool, huh?"

"More fun than my trip down."

"Aw, c'mon. I thought you were looking forward to riding down with Lydia."

"You won't believe what she did to me."

"Tell me."

"She made me listen to a taped sermon—'Sixty Instructions for Becoming a Godly Man.'"

"No way."

"She even rewound it and played it again."

"My sympathies."

"I'd have much rather been there to see Darcy get her hubcaps stolen."

I let his comment settle for a moment, the silence broken only by our whistling companions of surf and marsh grass. "You're not wishing Darcy ill, are ya?"

"Not at all. It's just so entertaining to see her get mad. When tall girls get mad they're like, um . . ."

"Volcanoes?"

"Yeah. Blonde volcanoes. Watch out for the lava."

"Yeah, the lava."

"Yeah."

I pulled out my harmonica and blew a low G. "Ready?" I asked.

"Oh, man. If you play a lullaby, I'm gonna croak."

"Not a lullaby, bro. After the hubcap debacle I wrote a song."

"You get inspired by crime?"

"It's called 'The Stolen Hubcap Blues.'"

"Okay then, let's hear it."

"I forgot the first line."

"Just make one up."

"Gimme a second."

"I thought you were inspired."

I brought the harmonica to my lips and blew the low G again. "You'll have to do the echo."

"What's the echo?"

"When I sing a line, you repeat it. I'll play the blues notes, then sing a line, then you repeat what I sing."

"I'm not a singer, especially at this hour. Especially in a pup tent."

"Just fake it."

I heard him take a deep breath. "Okay, Neil, play the blues."

I did, and when I sang the first line, Steve did his best to echo.

"Lazy Earl is not my friend."

*"Lazy Earl is not my friend."*

"We thought his tomato juice was gin."

*"We thought his tomato juice was gin."*

"Then Earl went and picked a P."

*"Earl done gone and picked a P."*

"Not black-eyed, y'all, the letter P."

*"Not black-eyed, y'all, the letter P."*

"So Darcy parked around the back."

*"Darcy parked around the back."*

"Unsuspecting, that's a fact."

*"Unsuspecting, that a fact."*

"Her hubcaps gone, it made her blue."

*"Hubcaps gone, made her blue."*

"Thieves took Lex's Jolly Ranchers too."

*"Thieves like Jolly Ranchers too."*

"Brake dust held no ev-i-dence."

*"Brake dust got no ev-i-dence."*

"Thieves must have some common sense."

*"Thieves must have more common sense . . . than Darcy."*

"Yeah, Darcy."

*"Yeah, Darcy."*

"'Cause she got distracted by Alexis and now her hubcaps gone to live in Mafiaville . . . oh yeahhhh."

At the end of my bass-voiced last line Steve clapped loud and exaggerated. In the pale light of our pup tent, his hands looked ashen. "Good playin', Neil."

"Man, I'm really sleepy."

"If you roll over tonight, I'll punch you in the nose."

"Same here."

Our tiny *casa* was humid, and slumber proved elusive. Occasionally a shorebird would squawk from out in the marsh, but mostly it was thoughts of women that kept me awake—one that I'd kissed, and one that I'd be escorting to sea.

"Steve?"

"What now?"

"Say a silent prayer for me."

"At 1:00 a.m.?"

"Yeah."

"What for?"

"I'm nervous."

"About kissing Zany Alexis?"

"No, about going to sea with Flamboyant Quilla."

"You haven't even met her."

"I have a premonition."

"How can you think up words like *premonition* at 1:00 a.m.?"

"I'm a language guy."

Another silence, another car easing down the island road. "Okay," Steve said. "Done. Now I need to tell you something about Darcy."

"Tell me."

"Well, for one thing, you don't know about her parents. They're very successful and very atheist. They have a bunch of money set aside for her if she ever wants to start her own business, but they keep telling her that she can't have it if she continues pursuing religiosity."

"Religiosity?"

"They're so atheist, Neil, that they won't even use the phrase Christianity."

"Well?"

"Well, what?"

"What is Darcy gonna do about it?"

"Darcy could use the money, no doubt. So who knows what she'll do. Her folks have always tried to manipulate her with money—even gave her that car and the money to have it painted lime green. No tellin' what will come of all this. Like I said, those tall blondes can be like volcanoes."

Ever since I'd met Darcy Yeager, there had been something not quite cumulative. I would never have guessed the nature of her struggle, or its depth. But now that Steve had shared her family story, it made sense—a girl with the appearance of independence but the reality of dependence. In the idle chatter of our tent, another submerged thing had become exposed.

"Be honest, Steve," I said, turning on my side. "What do you really want?"

"I wanna go fishing with you and Flamboyant Quilla."

"Go to sleep . . . no, don't go to sleep yet. You know what's strange?"

"What?"

"That Alexis is known for all that hopscotch among the churches, but this entire day she never mentioned it."

"Maybe she's just been lonely, and with you around she stops looking."

"Oh . . . ya think?"

"She must really like you."

"How would a guy even tell?"

"I dunno. Like always, I guess. She holds the eye contact a bit longer than normal. She offers to bring you things, offers to cook with you, she kisses you on the beach. All that romantic stuff is pretty much embedded in female DNA."

"Yeah, the DNA."

"Yeah."

"I'm goin' to sleep, Steve."

"Me too."

"G'night, el dumpo."

"I can't believe you kissed Alexis your first night at the beach."

"I can't believe you let Lydia turn Pentecostal."

Though Steve was snoring within minutes, I was eons from sleep. There in the moonlit backyard of a humble beach house, I kept thinking of why I was in Carolina, with no real reason other than curiosity. I thought about my need for belonging, and I wondered if when furlough was over any of these friends would stay in touch. I thought about Alexis and our crabbing adventures, about kissing her bottom lip, and about not allowing months of no-date frustration to sling me into its opposing galaxy, a world of hasty physicality and a residue of regret.

Then I lay there wondering if Steve and Darcy would make it as a couple. I had not figured on such an intimate little beach trip, the four of us—*quatro* singles, *dos* intertwinings.

I was rapidly sifting these thoughts when the first pebble hit the tent. At first I thought it was an acorn falling from an oak tree, but then I remembered that outside the pup tent was only marsh grass and sand dunes. Pawleys Island contained no trees to speak of.

A second pebble thudded off green canvas. Then a third.

"Alexis?" I whispered, trying not to wake Steve.

There was no answer.

A fourth pebble. Then another and another. *Thud. Thud. Thud.*

Without moving I tried to shout my whisper. "Darcy?"

Steve rolled over, snoring against my shoulder. I pushed him back to his side.

*Thud. Thud.*

"Who's out there?"

"Dude, it's me . . . Ransom. Open up."

With my foot I pulled back the skinny fold of tent just as Steve stirred from slumber. A stranger with hair to his shoulders came crawling into our already tight space and wedged himself, face up, between Steve and me. "Guys," he announced, "I gotta crash here tonight." He shoved his pillow to the back of the tent.

"Who are you?" I asked, scrunched into the canvas.

Steve shouldered up against the opposite side, stressing a seam. "Neil, this is my friend Ransom, the surfer I hung out with this afternoon. He's married."

A knee pummeled my leg into the ground. "Then get off my ankle, Ransom who is married."

"Scootch to the right, dude."

"I can't scootch any further," I said, wriggling away. "Why are you even here? Your wife kick you out?"

Steve shoved the intruder toward me. "Now off my leg, Ransom," he said, sounding miffed at being woken. "This is a two-person pup tent, bro. You can't stay."

"You're on my arm," I said, squirming to the far edge. For a moment we all got situated, lying face up, shoulders overlapping shoulders, my right side bulging into canvas.

Ransom seemed unaware of how minimal our accommodations were. After a glance left at Steve, then a glance right at me, he stared up at the A-frame above us. "Dudes, the Pentecostals ruined my plan. Jamie and I had hired a babysitter in Greenville to keep Wally for the whole weekend, and we hoped to finally have some time to ourselves. So what happens?"

"Go ahead," Steve mumbled, highlighting our guest with his flashlight. "Tell us what happens."

Ransom ran a hand through his unkempt hair, his elbow passing in front of my face. I couldn't help but think that—except for his nose, which was not as straight as mine—the two of us could have been cousins. He breathed deep and folded his arms. "Fourteen extra girls is what happened—some blonde named Nancy brought all her friends from that email list. The original plan had twenty Pentecostal couples and forty singles on this trip, and all the houses were reserved, and every couple, we thought, would have their own room. So the Ladies of the Quest show up, and the overcrowding forces all the dudes, hitched or unhitched, to crowd into two houses, and all the dudettes to jam into the other three, meaning no bedroom for the Delaneys. No privacy. No joys of marriage."

"Join the crowd, bro," Steve said, switching off his flashlight.

"It's just like last year with the Presbyterians," Ransom complained. "Except that the Pentecostals rent houses on the oceanfront."

"Bummer," I said, wondering how we were going to sleep three in a kid's pup tent, especially considering that we were all touching shoulders, not to mention the fact that the breathing was getting suffocatingly humid. I folded back the tent flaps, and the rush of cool air brought needed relief. "Ransom, why can't you just go sleep in Darcy's Cadillac? It's over there under the beach house."

"Tried that. But she's got the top up and the windows up and the doors are locked." He paused, sniffed the air. "Man, you dudes smell a lot different than my wife."

"You still coulda stayed in the house with the Pentecostal men," Steve argued. "At least you'd have room to stretch out."

Ransom shook his head. "No way. There were nineteen Pentecostal men in that house, and they were all staying up to talk about the anointing of the Holy Spirit. No telling what my poor wife is having to endure from their motor-mouthed wives."

"Poor Jamie," Steve muttered.

"Amen to that," Ransom said. "I couldn't sleep in my little pickup, so I tried sleeping on the deck, but I could still hear 'em inside, men arguing about anointing this and anointing that. This one lanky guy came outside and wanted to anoint my surfboard. I'm not kidding, dudes, he had a bottle of cooking oil. He came out on the deck, waving it in the air, hollering about how surfing could become a true ministry to the lost youth of America. That's when I said 'enough already' and drove over here to find you guys."

"I gotta get to sleep, Ransom," I said, squirming to get comfortable. "I'm working on a charter boat tomorrow."

He wouldn't let me sleep yet. "Neil-dude, I hear that you climb on roofs and talk to God." He sat up and smiled at me. "That's so gnarly, man."

"Okay, how'd you know that I climb on roofs?"

"Jay. He and Allie send us emails from the jungle."

"Figures. But didn't *gnarly* go out decades ago?"

"Yeah, but I'm bringing it back. I offer lingo classes for kids who want to be old school."

"And you charge for this?"

"Only two bucks. You should come by my store on a Wednesday night. Class only lasts ten minutes, then we all go skateboarding. 'Cept if it rains.

Then we rent *Endless Summer* and eat pineapple." He reached into his back pocket. "Wanna see a picture of my kid?"

I had no choice—he already had the picture out of his wallet, and Steve was quick with the flashlight. At the sight of little Wally I gave the obligatory nod, and just as quickly, the light went out.

The breezes coming in over the salt marsh had dropped several degrees, and they did their best to provide lullaby. All three of us were on our backs now, arms folded at our chests.

"Thanks for letting me crash, dudes."

Steve wriggled again and lay still. "Welcome to paradise, bro."

# 20

When I arrived at Georgetown Marina at 7:00 a.m., wisps of fog were floating over the water, buffering the sunrise and blurring its reflection. At the far end of row B, Captain Maurice Evans was pumping diesel fuel into the boat.

I walked softly on the dock, stopping once to stretch my back and to sniff the scents drifting past solemn yachts and naked sailboats. I'd always looked upon docked sailboats—their masts standing tall and undraped—as being naked. At the end of row D, three charter boats left in single file, a buoyant parade gurgling toward blue seas. From one knee Maurice watched the departure, his captain's hat low on his head, his well-used Day-Timer protruding from his back pocket.

I came up behind him on the dock and said "Good mornin'" in a voice that was much too loud for the dawn.

Maurice tipped the brim of his hat and, still kneeling, pointed at the top level of their boat. Preacher Smoak was standing up there, watching the sunrise from his chromed perch. He had a Bible resting on the railing, his left hand holding it in balance. I did not greet him, just watched with envy, figuring he was communing with God, the weather, maybe even the gulls.

"He's working on a sermon," Maurice whispered, screwing the fuel cap in place on the intake. "If he don't write 'em on his boat, he'll write 'em on the beach. Smoak claims that sermons written outdoors are far superior to ones written indoors."

"Something to do with creation, huh?"

"Naw, just salt air."

Squatted beside him, I was about to ask Maurice to clarify how salt air and creation differed, but since this was my first day as first mate, the only thing I was going to stir was pancake mix. "Guess I'd better go below and make breakfast, Captain M."

"Reckon you should."

When he stood, I saw for the first time the wording on his T-shirt: MAURICE—NAUTICAL 007, MAN WITH THE GOLDEN GAFF.

Whatever his qualifications, this was not a guy who lacked confidence.

The fog diminished, the gulls increased, and a red sun rose over the Atlantic. We were waiting for Quilla, so the preacher stayed up on the top level, rubbing sunblock on his arms and looking very much like he was ready to set his sermon aside and commence with fishing.

I scanned the breadth and width of row B and saw other captains loading gear and checking fuel levels. Here on the dock the preparations were numerous and calculated. A sense of anticipation hovered over the marina, and for that reason I wanted to stay topside a while longer.

Maurice stepped down into the boat and began rigging the first of four poles. I followed him aboard, nervous that I might flub something even before the day began. At the skinny door to the cabin, I turned the brass knob but did not go in. "Maurice?"

"Yeah, Neil?"

"I tie good knots too . . . in case you need me for more than making breakfast."

He sat down on the metal cooler and threaded his fishing line through the eye of a teaser bait. "Yeah, well, first you better go see about them pancakes. Now make 'em big, and don't forget to mix in my blueberries. All the ingredients are waitin' on you. Shape mine nice and round. The preacher likes his plain and oval, like a flounder."

"You've got to be kidding."

Maurice didn't look up from his riggings. "We're the captains, son. You the first mate."

Below deck was a small kitchen, the sink at an odd angle to the tiny refrigerator—a triangle of a sink, situated in such a way that you couldn't get to it if the cabin door were open. Paired with the rocking sensation, the kitchen required a certain coordination of the first mate—or first cook—aboard the good ship *Asbury*.

When I came from below with two heaping plates of breakfast, the preacher was seated in the captain's chair, checking the forecast on a tiny screen. Maurice, still fiddling with the fishing gear, reached out and accepted his blueberry pancakes without comment. Then I handed the preacher his plain ones and set the syrup bottle on the cooler.

"Good technique, Neil," Asbury said, inspecting his meal. "Looks almost like a flounder. You made seconds?"

"I ate the seconds."

After he'd eaten five of his seven pancakes Asbury showed me the electronics, including the depth finder and the GPS system, concluding his tutorial with the fact that he and his co-captain could even receive email in their boat. Jay had told me about these guys, but he never mentioned that they were so . . . wired.

The twin engines were idling when I turned and saw pure flamboyance clomping toward us.

Down the dock she came in a sort of overloaded waddle, wearing black Lycra shorts and a red Aretha Franklin T-shirt. Shiny orange beads were strung into her hair. She held two paper grocery sacks and a suitcase in one arm, an aluminum softball bat in the other. Maybe five-feet-six, she was big-boned, wide-eyed, and garnished with the type of dark, flip-down sunglasses worn by athletes.

Quilla was coming aboard.

She was still three boats away when I gathered the empty plates and whispered to Maurice, "Why's she bringing all of that stuff?"

He stuck the last rod into its brass holster and smiled at his sister-in-law. "She never been to sea. Last night she told my wife that she's afraid of having a Gilligan's Island experience." He lowered his voice as she neared us. "Me and the preacher may toy with her head a bit today, so just play along."

Maurice stepped up onto the dock, extended his hand, and helped Quilla climb down onto the deck.

She waved at Preacher Smoak up in the captain's chair, flipped down her shades, then glanced at me standing there by the cooler.

"I'm Quilla," she said. With no warning at all she handed me her suitcase. The weight of it pulled my arm down to where I looked deformed. "You the bellboy, right?"

"Actually, ma'am, I'm Neil from Ecuador, and I make pancakes." I lugged the suitcase down into the cabin and slung it across one of the single beds. The sleeping quarters of *The Asbury Raspberry Strawberry Lemon 'n Lime* were set forward in the hull so that the beds were arranged like two sides of a triangle, the heads meeting at the tip—not quite bunk beds, but V-beds.

"I'll take some of them pancakes," Quilla said from above. "I like mine with pecans."

I peeked out of the cabin door. "We have only blueberries, Miss Quilla."

Hearing that, she grinned and turned to face Maurice. "You hear 'im, Maurice? He calls me Miss Quilla. You got yourself a mannerly bellboy. Uh-huh."

According to Maurice, Quilla was always doing that. *Uh-huh*. Like she preferred to answer her own questions, or she couldn't come up with a new thought so she'd just affirm whatever sounded good. Made her very popular at church.

Maurice took the grocery sacks from Quilla and followed me down into the cabin. Out of sight and out of hearing range, we set the sacks on the bed beside her suitcase, our postures stooped because of the low ceiling. "Take a peek inside, Neil," he said, pointing at the luggage.

Though the cramped quarters were private, my instincts told me to back off, that this might be a test from my bosses. "I'm not going through her stuff, Maurice."

Apparently it was not a test. With great haste he opened her suitcase and read off the contents. "Yep, 'bout what I figured. Three change o' clothes, Coleman lantern, case of matches, four bottles shampoo, case of Butterfingers, some feminine products, fingernail polish, and the last two issues of *Ebony*."

I peeked into the grocery sacks and saw one filled with boxes of grits and Chex Mix, the other with Hawaiian Punch, Tylenol, and oil for the lantern.

As we were leaving the docks Quilla told me that going to sea was a rare opportunity in her family. Then she downed her Dramamine with a can of Mountain Dew and sat beside me on the cooler. At once she proclaimed herself ready for adventure. "Preacher Smoak," she called out, "my only previous water excursion happened on a paddleboat at Disney World with my cousin Nora. We somehow flip that paddleboat upside-down, uh-huh, and Mickey himself was watching and waving from a sidewalk. So don't you go flippin' us over today, preacher. I like my voyages nice and smooth."

It took us two hours to reach the fishing waters, and when we did Quilla brought out a pink sun visor that caused her hair to mushroom out below the band. It was midmorning, Quilla's turn in the fighting chair, and she was anxious to battle anything with fins.

"I can smell fish," Maurice said, sniffing the air. "Can't you smell fish, Preacher Smoak?"

"I can smell 'em," Asbury said, steering us eastward and whistling a tune.

Quilla raised her head high and sniffed. "I don't smell no fishes, y'all . . . not even a whiff. And why did y'all have to name the boat like it's some kind of fruity poem? Why can't y'all call it something more plain, like *Fishing Boat*?"

"*Fishing Boat?*" Asbury said, tugging on his cap. "Why don't you name your children *children*?"

"That's different," Quilla said. "Uh-huh. Much different."

I sat back on the cooler and sipped Hawaiian Punch from a cup. The wavy journey out beyond the sighting of land had made me dizzy, and the juice combined with the pills had me almost ready to stand again. But not quite. I still had jelly legs, not to mention a Jell-O head.

We trolled for an hour, but nothing struck our baits. We turned into the sun, reversed course, made a second pass. Again, nothing. We stopped, ate lunch. Changed the color of the baits. Trolled some more. Another hour passed without a strike. Ever optimistic, Maurice stepped up into the cockpit beside the preacher. "Smoak, it's time to mix up the mojo."

"Yep," Asbury said. "Mojo needs mixin'." They had obviously employed this technique many times and switched places without further comment. Maurice slid into the captain's chair as if it were a favorite La-Z-Boy recliner. He altered our course to a wide arc, and I wondered if he ever dreamed he'd be doing this back when his daily duty was pushing a mop down a church hallway.

Quilla's hands were in her lap, fingers interlocked, and her black shades sat low on her nose. She had the wide leather fish-fighting belt still looped around her waist. A gust of wind nearly blew her visor from her head. She held it in place and said, "Men, what do we do when somethin' bites?"

Asbury leaned against the stern, rocking at the mercy of the waves while watching four lines tail behind the boat. He spoke over his shoulder. "I'll grab the pole from its mount and hand it to you. Then Neil and I will reel in the other three lines so they won't interfere. The butt end of your rod goes in that belt around your waist."

"This is one ugly belt," Quilla said, adjusting herself in the chair. "No fashion at all."

Asbury shook his head, then turned to face the sea. "Just do what we tell you."

"It's a bit tight. Uh-huh."

"It's supposed to be tight."

Feeling slightly less wobbly, I stood at the helm, fingering the chrome knobs and watching Maurice steer us around the edge of a reef he'd found on the electronics. Maurice claimed a genuine love for the electronics—said they made him feel like a spy. Thus the T-shirt.

The bite came—as they all do—unexpectedly. Quilla was staring off into the horizon, gently rocking in the fighting chair, fingers still interlocked in her lap like she was cradling a small bird. Maurice seemed to sense what was coming. He slowed the engines and dialed in the GPS, which guided us over the man-made reef, a structure built from discarded naval vessels and, according to my bosses, known to house an abundance of game fish.

"There!" Asbury shouted, grabbing a starboard rod and setting the hook. In a split second, all boredom vanished, replaced with the rollicking sight of a taut line slicing through the ocean.

"What?" Quilla shouted, looking left and right. "What do we do? Y'all tell me what to do!" She was bouncing in the fighting chair like she was about to explode.

Asbury lifted the rod high. In one motion he reset the hook and stuck the butt end into the receptacle of the belt around Quilla's waist. She had a death grip on that rod.

"Pull, and pull hard," said the preacher.

"I can't get no crank," Quilla complained, trying her best to turn the handle.

"Let it run," Asbury said.

"Let what run?"

"The fish, Quilla. Let it peel off some line."

With the boat steadily rocking, Quilla pointed the pole straight out, and in less than a minute half of the line was stripped off the reel. Maurice stopped the boat and set it to idle—Quilla-with-a-fish was a happening he had to view from up close.

"What you think it is, Maurice?" she asked, noticing him standing beside her.

He could only shrug. The wind blew her visor up, so he pressed it back down on her head.

She arched her back and pulled. "One of you men please tell me what it is . . . I gotta know."

Asbury was busy reeling in the second of the three remaining baits, so I rushed over to the port side and reeled in the last limp line, a blue teaser scooting across the surface.

"Quilla," Maurice said, leaning down to talk into her right ear, "what you have on that rod might very well be a great white shark."

"No!"

"Yeah. See the way the line is running to the west?"

She gritted her teeth and pulled hard on the rod. "Uh-huh. I see it, I see it!"

"Well, only the great white shark swims to the west. All other hooked fish go east. It's a strange quirk of nature. Right, Smoak?"

Asbury opened the cooler and spread the ice. "Quirk of nature indeed."

The 3:00 sun was behind us now, and its angle gave clarity to the fight. For ten minutes we watched Quilla pull hard on the rod, then lean forward and reel in the slack—only there wasn't much slack. None at all. Whatever was attached had turned ornery, dove deep.

"What's the world record for great white shark, Asbury?" Quilla asked, sweating profusely but refusing to give up.

Asbury sat down on the cooler. "I believe it's well over two thousand pounds."

"Might be over three thousand," Maurice added. He was standing behind her, cheering her on between bouts of detailed instruction. I watched from the port side, impressed that our extroverted client already had the basic technique down pat.

Quilla cranked the reel, grinning as she turned the handle and grimacing as she pulled backward on the rod. "I think I just might beat the record."

"Ya reckon?" Asbury asked.

"It'll be close," she said, lips pursed. "But why is the line now going . . . which way is it going now, Maurice?"

"To the north," he said.

She tugged again, cranked the reel. "I thought you said great whites only goes to the west."

Still behind her, Maurice gripped both sides of her chair and spoke into her other ear. "When they get really mad for being hooked, Quilla, they'll occasionally turn north. But only if they're really, really mad." He turned to face his co-captain. "It's a rare occurrence, right, Smoak?"

"Very rare indeed."

As if in on the joke, the creature turned back to the west again. Quilla mumbled, "Uh-huh, there it goes . . . gotta be a great white."

Twenty minutes later, with Quilla tugging and cranking for all she was worth, Maurice—Nautical 007—leaned over the stern and gaffed through the head something thick, gray, and yellow-finned.

He heaved it up on the gunwale, grunting with the effort.

Asbury killed the fatted tuna. With Quilla's softball bat he whopped it once on the noggin, and the fish immediately went comatose. Observing this sea-based circus—Maurice's enthusiasm, Quilla's spastic cranking of the reel, and the preacher's country-boy dominion over the ocean world—I considered this just the break I'd needed from the structure and sameness of language school. And I wanted to keep these friends.

"That ain't no shark, Maurice!" Quilla shouted, admiring her catch, "That's a . . . what, a catfish?"

The preacher smiled and said, "A yellow-finned tuna."

The fact that Quilla landed the fish was a miracle in itself. At one point during the fight, she'd removed both hands from the pole and checked for blisters, the line zinging off the reel in a fury worthy of top-fuel dragsters. But now her fish was subdued, laid out on the deck in an expression of stupor.

The preacher grabbed the fish by the tail and pulled it across the deck. Quilla, exhausted in the fighting chair, raised her feet and looked in disbelief at what she'd accomplished. She breathed deep, then exhaled in a low whistle. "So, gentlemens, what happened to the shark that only goes to the west?"

Maurice dipped the gaff in the ocean to clean it off. "The yellow-finned tuna is perhaps the smartest of game fish. It's a great impersonator, and it will sometimes impersonate a great white so that the fisherman, or fisherwoman, will cut the line in order not to have to deal with a shark."

Quilla's eyes got big as she unbuckled the fighting belt and stepped out of the chair. "No! They're that smart?"

"A smart fish indeed," Asbury said, his thick, pale legs and St. Louis Cardinals cap looking out of place on a seaman. He still had the tuna by the tail, and the veins in his arms protruded as he hoisted the fish with both hands and hung it on a weigh scale. Eighty-seven pounds. I opened the long metal cooler, and Asbury flung the fish inside. Then there were a lot of high-fives between the crew before Maurice urged us to get serious and cast the baits back into the ocean.

A persistent man, that Maurice.

I was allowed a brief turn in the fighting chair myself, hooking and landing a six-pound jack that Asbury and Maurice called a junk fish. Maurice frowned at my fish before tossing it back in the Atlantic and declaring that we were headed home. His silver watch, with its array of buttons around the perimeter, had beeped three times, so he began reeling in the baits.

All the way home, for two rolling, sea-sprayed hours, Quilla contrasted her catch with my own—eighty-seven pounds versus six. We were seated beside each other on the metal cooler, her tuna inside, tossed upon ice. Maurice and Asbury huddled in the cockpit, the preacher talking on and on about bait colors and proper trolling speeds, Maurice jotting notes in his Day-Timer. The tuna flopped several times after we thought it was dead, then less frequently, then not at all.

Halfway home, Quilla jumped to her feet. "Get up off the cooler, Neil."

"What for?"

"I wanna look at my fish again." I stood, and she opened the lid. She reached in and thumped the tuna's belly. "My fish woulda swallowed your fish like an aspirin. Uh-huh."

After shutting the lid, we sat again. She crossed her legs to the left; I crossed mine to the right and egged her on. "You just got lucky. No woman should ever get that lucky. You even cranked the reel the wrong way, then you took both hands off the reel and let it free-spool into the Atlantic. I'm surprised you even landed that tuna."

Quilla tugged her black shades low and peered over them like she was checking to see if I was serious. Unsatisfied, she pushed her shades back on her nose and folded her arms, nodding in the way a person does when they're trying to think of a good comeback.

"Neil, what you caught was a minnow in diapers. A fish stick at best," she said, flicking a slimy scale off her Aretha Franklin T-shirt. "You'd have got two, maybe three little nibbles off your catch. I seen bigger fish sticks in the little boxes at Piggly Wiggly. Uh-huh."

This continued for most of the journey home—the waves slapping the hull, the spray cooling our ride, and her constant badgering reminding me that I had lost, and lost badly. She looked for any excuse to raise the lid and admire her fish. "Y'all care for a Mountain Dew?" she asked, shooing me off the cooler again. "There's three of 'em behind my froze-up tuna."

"I could sure use one," Asbury said.

He climbed up to the second level to find a catch-flag for tuna. Then he let Quilla run it up the pole. After the flag was fully raised, she held the brim of her visor and watched the flag flutter.

"Letting the world know we almost had a great white," she said.

Maurice took a swig of his Dew, then sounded the boat horn in three blasts of celebration. "Almost," he said.

Before we could see land, Quilla opened the cooler four more times to look at her fish. But then her bladder betrayed her—she said she had to go to the ladies' room.

"It's unisex," Asbury said, pointing to the cabin below. "Just be sure and get your balance."

Quilla frowned hard and went below. But soon she was back on deck, shaking her head. "No, aw no, fellas. I can't go at all in that tiny room. Way too much motion . . . and way too small."

Maurice had set the boat on automatic pilot and was now storing away their baits and leaders. "Quilla, that bathroom is not too small."

She put her hands on her hips and glared at him. "It's too small, Maurice. And the room rolls 'round like a beach ball. Now y'all speed up and get me to the dock."

Preacher Smoak took the helm and sped up. Quilla, having used up a week's worth of energy, sprawled out on the cooler with her eyes shut, her head resting on a towel.

In the quiet of our journey I moved to the rear of the boat and leaned against the stern next to Maurice. He impressed me as the sort who had an opinion about most everything, and with thirty minutes of ocean left to traverse, this seemed a fine time to solicit wisdom. I normally limited all solicitations of wisdom to talks with my mentor, José, but he and his tangelos were in Mexico City, so I used what was available. Over the next mile of ocean spray and breezy chop, I told Maurice all about Alexis and me, then about Darcy and Steve, whom he admitted to knowing from his janitorial days at North Hills Prez.

But mostly he wanted to know about Alexis and me. So I relayed the late night at the coffeehouse, her community missions to the homeless, our wild, detouring drive to the beach, and the beginnings of romance on a crabbing dock.

Maurice stared out over the wavy horizon, squinting into the glare before he spoke. "Neil, there are two kinds of women. Some women are like fields of yellow flowers—easy to sway along with. Others are more like a tornado, and you gotta rotate in the same direction or they'll drive you mad. Now, from what you've just told me, this girl you hangin' with is probably not a field of yellow flowers."

"Nope, Captain M., Alexis is definitely some form of twister."

Elbow to elbow at the stern, Maurice and I looked off together the way men do when they're discussing something serious. Women would probably be clutching each other's hands and looking eye to eye. But not men.

"The way I see it is just the opposite of last year, back when I was giving your friend Jay his own relational advice. Back then it was a free-spirit guy chasing a poised young lady. Now it's a free-spirit young lady and a poised young man. All kinds of strange mixtures in the relational world, Neil. Kinda like the ocean, I reckon."

"Yeah, a tornado on the ocean."

"No, now that would be a typhoon."

Staring out from the stern, lost in thought, I saw not the rolling sea but the mirage of a female typhoon spinning at incredible speed, me trying to tiptoe into the vortex but getting hurled off, again and again, somersaulted by the ferocity of its winds. "Nobody could rotate that fast, Maurice. At the end of two hours with Alexis, you don't remember raven hair or pale skin or Italian eyes, you only remember a blur."

He took off his captain's hat and wiped the salt spray from his brow. "A blur, huh?"

I nodded in the affirmative.

Another wave splashed us from the port side, but Maurice ignored it. He just rubbed his chin as if he'd never before encountered a blurry female typhoon.

"If I were you, Neil, I'd ask God to present me with an opportunity to see her in true light."

*What is he talking about? I've seen her lure crabs on a dock, seen her in a convertible Caddy at ninety miles per hour, and seen her all moonlit and kissy-faced beside the Pawleys Island pier.*

"True light?"

Maurice cleared his throat, wiped his brow again. "Right now you're seeing each other on neutral ground, testing your compatibility. Next, if you're both still interested, she's going to need to see how you handle a predicament. Catching a crab and kissing on the beach, well, anybody can do that."

"How did you know I kissed her on the beach?"

"I seen you flippin' them pancakes behind your back this morning. Surely you didn't get that enthused over the sight of me or Preacher Smoak?"

"No, you two aren't exactly *muy guapos*."

His wedding ring was glowing in the sunlight. I pointed at the band. "So, you and your wife have true compatibility?"

"Very true. Don't get me wrong, now, we've disagreed many times. Just never disrespected. She don't like fishin', so she never comes on the boat. I don't know nothin' about hair, so I never hang out at her salon."

I moved into the fighting chair and plopped down, facing Maurice, who was still leaned against the stern, his back to our wake. "So, you just give lots of slack, huh?"

"You're catching on."

In the waning minutes of our voyage, we entered the mouth of Winyah

Bay, where the Intracoastal spills into the Atlantic. We were tired, thirsty, and craving a nap. When we were a mile from the marina, the preacher summoned me to the cockpit. He had the boat on automatic pilot as he watched his gauges and plotted our course.

I took the seat next to the captain's chair and swiveled it around to face Asbury. "What's up, boss? I flubbed something?"

Asbury took his time to speak. We both glanced down at Quilla, who was sleeping on the cooler. The preacher checked the depth on his screen, then turned to face me. "Neil, you did just fine, except for that one bait you dropped overboard. But that's not what I had in mind."

"No?"

He switched off the automatic pilot, slowed our speed, and began steering one-handed. "Son, this won't take long, not long at all. You work on the mission field, right?"

"For the last five years."

In a gesture of honesty and forthrightness, he put his hand on my arm and looked at me without expression. I felt his fingers squeeze my forearm. "Neil, a missionary is never really on furlough. I know you're having a good time and all, hanging out with those girls, coming down here to the beach, working on the boat. But it would be my guess that God has you here for a deeper reason."

I had no idea how to respond to that, and no clue as to why he picked that particular moment to say what he did. Given how furlough was going, I was no longer digging for reasons; South Carolina and its inhabitants were way too unpredictable to concern oneself with anything as cumbersome as reasons.

Asbury turned his attention back to steering, not speaking another word until he'd guided us into Georgetown Marina and eased us into the last watery slip of row B, which, according to Maurice, stood for *boat*.

Uh-huh.

# 21

Above the dunes of Pawleys Island a choir of sea oats bent westward, tickling the sunset and waving g'night. The beach smelled as if a thousand vacationers had spent the day dripping sunblock on the shore. Neither Alexis nor I had spoken for a long while; the last rays of Saturday were shushing all conversation. Seated on the sand in shorts and T-shirts, we had our backs to the Atlantic, our toes in white sand, and our brains on disengage. Dinner had been quick, and we'd rushed back to the island for just this moment.

I pointed to a streak of lavender cloud. "Doesn't that look like—"

"Shh, Neil. We said we weren't gonna talk."

As if it were a guest of honor bowing out prematurely, the sun sank wide-eyed and mischievous, to where staring was permissible and admiration was the only option, a pastel departure as wondrous and unique as fingerprint. *Never again. Never quite like that.* Monet on his best day could not capture dusk at Pawleys Island.

With her thumb and forefinger Alexis formed a circle, peering through the hole like a telescope, imperceptibly lowering her lens with each lingering minute. When nothing but a coral residue was left to admire, she sat up on the sand and leaned into me. "Was it as pretty as I predicted?" she asked softly.

"Um, yeah." I could only manage the brief reply; my thoughts were consumed with what was going to happen tonight, especially given what had happened the previous night. The issue for me was whether I would stay in control or be passive and let circumstances do the steering.

Tempting circumstances . . . always ready to take the wheel.

Alexis seemed oblivious to it all. Her head rested against my shoulder, her hair teasing my forearm, her eyes locked on a temporal sky. "Bet you don't get sunsets like this in Ecuador."

At the mercy of my own teetering will, I was already contemplating serious bouts of rooftop confession. I didn't move closer, but then I didn't move away either. "Down in Ecuador the sunsets are, I dunno . . . swirlier."

"Swirlier?"

"And lazier."

Across the dunes, twilight condensed itself into a wedge of pink haze, its girth shoved below the horizon by dusk's dark belly. Alexis reached over and poked me in the ribs. "Neil?"

*"Sí, señorita?"*

"I think Darcy and Steve are back together."

Not totally surprising, that news. After contemplating them for a moment, we both turned in the sand to face the sea. Now Alexis had her chin against my shoulder.

*Control, Neil.* "I was gonna ask about those two. Where'd he take her tonight?"

"Some swanky seafood place in Murrells Inlet," she said, her voice low and comfortable. "Darcy likes to admire the presentation of her seafood."

"Oh please. The presentation?"

More hair, more tingles. Do girls not know what all that loose hair does to a guy? I began to put my arm around her but drew it back and grabbed a handful of sand. I squeezed the grains hard as she spoke. "That's how swanky places get swanky," she said. "If the shrimp and mahimahi are arranged fancy and the chef does that zigzag pattern with the sauce, then they get to charge more."

"Guys would never notice that."

She patted her stomach like she was full. "Thanks for taking me for grilled ostrich. Even if it was just an ostrich burger."

229

"Well, there was a two-hour wait at the waterfront place, plus we'd have missed the sunset."

A breeze off the ocean swept her hair across her eyes. After she'd brushed it away, she sat up and wrapped her arms around her knees. "I suppose if I had to choose between the nicer restaurant or the island sunset, I'd go with the sunset."

I sat up and mimicked her posture, still fighting the urge to get physical. "So I did good?"

"Better watch out, señor, or we might develop some chemistry."

"Um, sure."

"When I think about chemistry I just want to load it into a squirt gun and soak all my dateless friends."

Soak my dateless friends? What an awkward subject for a man. "Wanna hear about the size of Quilla's fish?" I asked.

Alexis rested her chin on her knees. "Not right now. I was gonna tell you all about Steve and Darcy."

"What . . . that you soaked them with your high-powered chemistry gun?"

"Today they rented innertubes together."

"So?"

"So, a girl would never rent innertubes with her ex if she wasn't thinking they'd get back together."

With her toe Alexis flicked sand on my foot. I flicked back. "A guy would rent innertubes with his ex just because he wanted to float in the ocean."

"So there ya go."

"There I go where?"

"Jumping to a male conclusion. The conversation slants toward romance, and you start talking about innertubes and the ocean."

"It was you who brought up the tubes."

"As props, Neil. They're just background for the budding romance. They're not the subject."

*Stop talking, put your arm around her, and kiss her. It's simple. Just do*

*it. No, don't do it. Yes, do it. No, don't. Yes. No. Aw man, just flick some*
*more sand at her foot.*

She returned the foot flirt and leaned into my shoulder again. "Well, you still wanna hear what I think about Darcy and Steve?"

"I can't wait."

Darkness had snuck up on the island, and Alexis spoke toward the moon. "Well, I knew the two of them were getting along again when they didn't go floating out in the ocean but stayed near the shore, in the shallows between two sandbars."

"That's no fun." *Now. Go ahead and do it. No, let her tell the story, then kiss her.*

"Looked fun to me," she said, briefly clutching herself like she had a chill. "A tidal pool formed that was only two feet deep, and so they just stayed in there and pushed each other around on their tubes. A buncha children were playing in the far end, but when they came over with a dead minnow, Darcy freaked out."

"I'd loved to have seen that."

"Yeah, well, she stood up in her bikini and held her innertube between herself and the kids. One of the little boys said, 'Wow, lady, are you a fashion model?' Steve cracked up before talking the kid into throwing away the minnow. When she plopped back down in her tube, Darcy had turned two shades of red. She and Steve and I ended up getting in a mudball battle with those kids."

"And that was the highlight of your day?"

"That and learning to surf," she said, rubbing her calves in a manner that caused me no shortage of impure thought. "Ransom and Jamie taught me how."

"Don't tell me you actually stood up on the board?"

"Jamie said I was a natural. Did you know that she and Ransom had to sleep in different houses last night?"

"I heard something about that."

I leaned back in the sand on my elbows, and it was as if the sharp grains were urging me to make my move. Then Alexis rubbed her chin on my shoulder in a manner that led me to believe she might purr. "Neil, I think I like surfing."

"But I thought you went crabbing off the back dock today."

"I did, after I'd hung out with Darcy long enough to make sure it was safe."

By this time even the curve of the waves looked sensual. "The ocean?"

She shook her head. "Another wrong conclusion, Neil. I had to make sure it was safe for Darcy, to see if she was having a good time or if she'd need me to do the bathroom excuse thing."

"It's all so very complicated, isn't it?"

"Thanks again for the grilled ostrich burger," she said, using her finger to draw a circle in the sand. "I just have one more question."

"Praise God."

"Are we gonna kiss again tonight?"

# 22

All I could do was get up and start walking. Accompanied only by the rolling whoosh of late-night surf, we strolled the shoreline toward the Pawleys pier.

"Nope," I said, looking ahead into darkness. "The answer is nope."

We walked another twenty feet before she took hold of my hand. "I can't tell if you're teasing."

"I'm not teasing at all. Out on the boat today with Asbury and Maurice, I was thinking about last night and how I let circumstances—warm beach, night air, waves breaking against the pier—bring on a moment that was hard to resist."

She squeezed my hand. "So you think it was wrong for us to kiss last night?"

"Not necessarily wrong. It's just that I'd rather get to know *you* before I get to know your lips."

She stopped in wet sand, her face blank. "That's a first."

"Are you shocked?"

She gazed out over the ocean, then up at the stars. "No guy has ever said anything like that to me. Ever. No Baptist. No Methodist. Not even my old boyfriend, T.J., who tried to get me to join the Lutherans."

"Turn this way," I said. She turned from the surf and faced me. "Yep, you look shocked."

After several unreadable blinks, she spun around as if to avoid more eye contact. "I think I just lost my ability to be aloof."

"Just like that?"

"I need an aspirin."

I moved around her, to where moonlight angled across her face. To see an expression of relief and confusion looking back made me glad that I'd said what I did.

I sat on a firm shore—Alexis to my left, the pier to my right. She scooted closer. "Neil," she said, a smidgen of worry on her face, "I'm going to say this quick and get it over with, so listen up. I don't have the most glowing past when it comes to relationships and my behavior, so with you being a missionary and probably wanting someone who's led a more responsible life, I'd understand if you don't want to pursue anything serious with me."

Like everything else about furlough, this came without warning. She had no clue that I had grown from a similar vine, and that I too had sampled regrettable grapes. I reached over and took her hand. "Lex, I'm not going to give you some spiritualized monologue about forgiveness, 'cause from what you told me earlier, you seem to know about that. Just know that there aren't any posters of pure white nuns on my bedroom wall."

She swung my hand up before plopping it back in the sand. "Then tell me, oh Neil from the mission field, what is on your bedroom wall?"

"A Chicago Cubs baseball poster . . . right above Steve's fishbowl."

Alexis just nodded to herself and stared out at the barnacled posts of the pier's underbelly. She started to speak but hesitated. When finally she did speak, her words were measured, nothing at all like her normal, spontaneous word-dump. "I'm glad you want to know me before you know my lips, but another question is boggling me."

"Go ahead. Shoot."

"Did you run away to the mission field after college because you had no parents or siblings?"

The next wave rose slowly, its forehead slick and widening. "How in the world did you know that, Lex?"

She plunged her hands under the sand. "Women can tell. So lemme see here—what nobody knows is that you've hopped between language schools just like I've hopped between churches, *sí*?"

Yet another submerged thing exposed. I might as well have strapped big chunks of cork to my belt loops—all of Rucker was rising to the surface. "*Sí*," I said, feeling vulnerable. "I met my mentor, José, on the mission field. Until now, José and his wife were as close as I've come to having so-called family."

Alexis plucked a shell from the sand and flipped it back over her head. "See, Neily, we do have a certain chemistry."

"A bizarre chemistry." I stretched forward and touched my toes. "Do you know that every time I try to predict what you're going to do or say, you do something totally off the radar?"

"Drove my junior high drama teacher nuts."

At this I fell back in the sand and laughed. Staring straight up at the heavens, I could not control myself. "No way. You actually . . . acted?"

"I was Tinkerbell." She remained in her seated posture and looked down at me, feigning shock at my being tickled.

Warm sand pressed through my hair and warmed my scalp. "Alexis-who-hums-Frank-Sinatra starred in *Peter Pan*? Don't tell me you got rave reviews."

"Hardly. When Peter came skipping across the stage I moved the wrong way and tripped him. My mom was seated in the front row, and she thought the accident was part of the play. When she started clapping I had to shush her."

"I woulda clapped."

For a moment Alexis said nothing, content to sit Indian style and sift sand through her fingers. "Neil?"

I sat up straight and brushed grains from my hair. "Yep?"

"I have a question about missionary work."

There it was again—in one breath she'd gone from Peter Pan to serving the Lord. Okay, maybe in the female psyche lies a direct connection from Peter Pan to serving the Lord.

"Go ahead," I replied. *She's gonna ask what missionaries eat. Or if we ever get lonely.*

She sifted another handful. "My question is, do you think mission work is more important than regular jobs?"

Oh, man. Now I needed an aspirin. Like the undersea world, there was a complexity beneath her that wasn't visible from the surface. "That's why I like you, Lex. I thought you were gonna ask if missionaries ever get to catch blue crabs with a string."

"There you go again."

"Where?"

"Trying to predict a woman."

"Tinkerbell and moonlight . . . such a dangerous combination."

"So, what's your answer to my question?"

I stood and brushed the sand from my fanny. "You mean is there some administrative angel up there ranking all of us like the college football polls?"

"Yeah."

"I sure hope not."

"Me either, 'cause I don't think real estate agents would rank very high."

I reached for her hand and pulled her to her feet. "You'll rank highest by doing what you're supposed to be doing."

Before leaving the beach we strolled below the Pawleys pier and looked down its center. A youthful energy powered the incoming waves, the whole slosh of them trying to squeeze between the posts, some staying within the parameters, and some not.

Alexis and I held hands as we passed between the dunes. I was tired of talking; she was in no hurry to stop. Incredibly, in the space of four dunes she covered three disjointed issues: that she had the right personality for selling real estate, that she was cheering for Steve and Darcy, and that she was glad Lydia had turned Pentecostal because on last year's beach trip Lydia snored. All those rules, and she snores too? José once told me that a snoring woman is like a constantly dripping radiator in a '65 Buick. Later I found out he was trying to quote a proverb.

Surrounded by sea oats and the manic buzz of cicadas, I led Alexis along a path of sandswept boards. No way was I going to let her lead;

she might have taken us on another detour till we were stranded again in Whitmire, sipping bagged cans of tomato juice while Earl told sad tales of relations gone bad. Ol' Earl—he said he was in horses, when actually he just fed 'em.

Halfway home I squeezed her fingers. "Okay, Lex, tell me about your afternoon on the crabbing dock."

"Caught eight today," she said in a tone that conveyed you-could-never-do-it.

"And you turned 'em loose?"

"Half. Gave the other half to an old man who wandered over from the mainland. I'm a crab tither." She was swinging our arms higher and higher, totally in the moment, and we glided through the dunes like happy wind.

When we reached the northern tip of the island she pointed to a short-cut to the main road. We emerged from scrub brush and sand to see only the porch light on at Point o' View. There was no Darcy, no Steve, and beneath the beach house, no Lime Sherbet. "Ya think Steve and Darcy are out walking a shoreline?" I asked.

She tossed her sandals on the steps and brushed sand from her legs. "Nope. Darcy wanted to go to a beach-music club. She's teaching Steve to dance the shag."

I was worn out from a long day at sea, not to mention the beach talk, the shore walk, and the unpredictable chemistry with Alexis, my new friend/girlfriend/zany female companion. Guys never know what to call a relationship at this stage. We just sorta . . . show up.

I walked her up the outside stairs to the porch, hugged her long, and said good night. She began to close the door, smiling her good-bye. Then she held the door ajar and peeked, one-eyed, through the narrow crack. "Neil?"

"Yes ma'am?"

"Thanks for respecting me."

# 23

I collapsed in the pup tent at 11:30 p.m., resolved to not even ask about sleeping on the floor of the girls' beach house, surrounded by their scents and nocturnal temptation.

Too tired to look for a rooftop—even though across the street, on the oceanfront, was a house with a crow's nest—I lay flat on my back but did not address the heavens. I just kept wondering what Asbury meant by a missionary never really being on furlough, wondering if that chubby preacher was trying to warn me, scare me, or prepare me. Somebody was going to have to be more clear, because I was too preoccupied with fighting temptation on the moonlit beach where chemistry was turbocharged and every atom screamed for a couple to do the thing that was quite the cure for *not good for man to be alone*.

I was sprawled out in the tent, listening to shorebirds recite their own adventures of the day, when I heard Darcy's car pull in beneath the beach house. Gravel popped under steel-belted radials. The engine shut off, its rumble dissipating across marsh grass.

Two doors opened and two doors shut.

Steve and Darcy talking. Steve and Darcy giggling.

For the longest time there was talking and laughing, giggling and more talking. Then silence.

Then "good night" and one set of footsteps tromping up the steps to the beach house.

The tent flaps flew open. Hunched over, he and his stocky silhouette peered inside. "Just another night in paradise," Steve said, on his knees and squeezing in. "Ever tried dancing with a tall girl?"

I scooted left and gave him room. "Once in Mexico City."

"They have tall girls in Mexico City?"

"She was from Texas," I said, watching him squirm to get comfortable. "Okay, fess up. Are you and Darcy and her WeedEater a happy threesome now?"

Steve wadded a beach towel into a pillow and stuffed it beneath his head. "We saved some big bucks with this tent, didn't we?"

"Oh here we go . . . Vague Steve."

In the ghostly green confines of the tent, he slid his right arm across his eyes, as if to hide himself from interrogation. "Sorta maybe. Yeah, I think."

"Sorta maybe what?"

"She's all confused because her parents are threatening to cut her off from those funds they'd offered her to start her own business. Darcy wants to renovate that coffeehouse. But Mr. and Mrs. Yeager don't approve, just because of the spiritual content of the Cellar's music and the fact that the place is run by church volunteers."

"That's so politically correct."

Steve sat up, adjusted his pillow, lay back down again. "I don't wanna talk about her parents anymore," he muttered. "Ticks me off. This tent okay with you for a second night?"

"Cooler tonight. And no Ransom squashing us."

"Yeah, no squashing. Say, did you behave yourself with Alexis?"

Overhead, between the frayed seams of our tent, I saw not canvas but sloshing waves fracturing themselves against rocks and crumbling sand-castles. Therein lay the battle, whether to be the rock or the crumbling sandcastle. "I did, bro. But it wasn't easy."

Steve took a deep breath and exaggerated his exhale. "It's never easy, Neil. We're guys. We think about sex while changing a flat tire."

"Or brushing our teeth."

"Or trimming a shrub."

"Or, or . . . while jogging."

"Or watching golf."

"You watch golf?"

"Only the women."

"But they walk like men."

"Not the Swedish ones."

"Oh, man. I can't believe you watch golf."

Steve kicked off his sandals, then lay still on his back. "I bet Ransom and Jamie got all ticked off at the Pentecostals for not having their own bedroom. They probably drove home to Greenville."

I eased my hands behind my head and interlocked my fingers. "Yeah, home."

"There's still no hotel vacancies . . . I checked."

"I thought of another option while you were gone."

Ever the engineer, Steve sat up and refolded his towel-pillow into a perfect square, as if he couldn't sleep on anything but the truest form of a right angle. "What's the option?"

"We could go sleep on Asbury's boat. It has beds in the cabin, and I have a key."

On his back, arms crossed at his chest, Steve lay silent for several breaths. "Ever slept in a marina, Neil?"

"No. You?"

"Nope."

"Want to?"

He was already crawling out into night air. "Gotta be better than this musty pup tent."

Georgetown Marina was unequally lit, the middle by rows of yellow lights, the perimeter only by the long-traveled illumination of moon and stars. Its scent, however, was distributed without restraint; a stagnant blend of salt air and fish engulfed the entire complex.

In no particular hurry, Steve and I made our way across the ramp, where a rising tide lapped against resistant marsh.

Sleeping in a marina . . . this too would be a lingering memory of furlough.

Paranoid as we reached the main dock, we looked left, right, and behind us. Steve even peeked into the tackle shop. No one was around, so between the vessels we walked soft and stealthlike until we'd reached the end of row B.

Which, for tonight, could have stood for *burglar*.

*The Asbury Raspberry Strawberry Lemon 'n Lime* lay solemn in the water, tethered to the dock by the very ropes I'd helped Maurice tie. I eased down off the dock and onto the deck of the boat. Steve was right behind me, trying his best to stay quiet. Past the fish-fighting chair, I moved carefully to the cabin door and reached in my pocket for the key.

But when I went to insert it in the lock, I noticed a crude piece of cardboard stuck across the knob. The words looked hastily written:

### Do NOT DISTURB!! per Ransom (and Jamie).

We held our breath and stifled our snickers. There was nothing to do but sneak quietly off the boat, tiptoe across the marina, drive back to the island, and resolve ourselves to the tent.

Or so we thought.

# 24

A tall girl crying is a pitiful sight. At midnight the effect is magnified.

Red-eyed and sobbing beneath the beach house, Darcy stood at the driver's door of her Caddy, lifting a hand to shield herself from the bright lights of Steve's Jeep. She had the convertible top raised. Alexis was busy behind the car, looking stiff-lipped and determined, trying to fit their suitcases into the trunk.

Steve left his lights on, and without asking any questions he hurried over to hold Darcy, who wept all over his shoulder. Apparently he knew how to handle her, because after a minute she hadn't moved. "You wanna tell me about it?" he said softly.

She whispered something to him that I couldn't hear.

I hustled back behind the Caddy and took Alexis by the hand. "What's happened? Why are you packing up?"

"There's been an accident," Alexis said, in that way people do when they aren't sure what to say but simply need to relay the gist. "And just where have you two been?"

"Out cruising. But where's this accident?" I let go of her to shove their last piece of luggage into the trunk.

Alexis shut the lid. "Back in your corner of the world."

Darcy raised her head from Steve's shoulder and looked at me across the shiny green paint of her Cadillac. "I just got a call on my cell from Elder Kyle of North Hills Prez. He's Allie's father." Unable to complete her thought, she lowered her head again and sobbed into Steve's T-shirt. "There's been an accident and—"

"And what?"

Darcy gathered herself and wiped her eyes. "He just said that there had been a fire, that Allie and Jay both had survived it, and that the details would be given at a meeting tomorrow at church. Doesn't he know that it's worse to leave us imagining the details? Sometimes I hate the way men think."

"I've never understood them either," Alexis said.

Then Darcy began crying again. Steve held her and patted her back. Finally she composed herself, pushed away from Steve, and dug her car keys from her purse. "If there's going to be a meeting at North Hills Prez tomorrow morning, then I'm gonna be there. Allie is one of my best friends."

"I met her on last year's beach trip," Alexis said, tossing her flip-flops in the backseat. "She's one of the few girls who didn't look at me funny over having my brow pierced." Alexis hustled up the stairs to retrieve some last items.

"Jay and I are like this," Steve said, extending two fingers. He and I hurried to the backyard of the beach house and began pulling up the stakes to his tent.

I stopped in mid-pull and glanced at Steve. "After what happened with Deacon Stanley and the gardening project, I don't exactly look forward to any meetings at your church, bro. But Jay and his girlfriend are two of my heroes—jungle servants."

While the marsh grass waved good-bye, Steve and I quickly folded his green canvas into a shapeless blob. We gathered towels and clothing and shoved it all into his Jeep.

Darcy wiped at her eyes and motioned for us to hurry. "Let's go."

"What about Lydia?" Steve asked. "She rode down to the beach with me, ya know."

"We called Lydia," said Darcy, who opened Sherbet's hood and began checking the oil level. "She'll ride home Monday with the Pentecostal sailor boy. Let's go." She dropped the hood, and it shut heavily, resounding in the night air and echoing across the inlet.

A four-hour trip lay ahead, and in the flurry of our packing Darcy began asking what I thought could have caused the fire. I sat in the front seat of her Caddy for a moment and told her there were so many things that could go wrong in a jungle village. My guess was no better than her own.

Alexis came flying down the stairs from the beach house kitchen, a grocery bag of snacks and drinks in her arms. She saw me sitting in the front seat of the Caddy, Darcy wiping off the windshield with a paper towel, and Steve behind his Jeep, squirting himself in the face with the water hose just to make sure he was alert.

"What are we doing, Neil?" Alexis asked, puzzled at the riding arrangements. "Playing girlfriend switcharoonie?"

Just to tease her and to lighten the mood, I nodded yes and blew her a kiss. Darcy wadded the paper towel and threw it across the hood at her. "Just ride back with Steve, will you, Lex?" Darcy said. "He gets sleepy during night drives. And you know that Neil here has—"

"I know, Darce . . . no driver's license." Alexis came over and made a sad face before patting me twice on the head. I took her by the hand and kissed her on the knuckles.

Over loose gravel, Jeep and Caddy backed out into the stillness of a gracious sea island. In our wake were the very things we'd enjoyed only hours before: inlets and sand dunes and walks beneath piers. All the remnants of paradise.

At 12:10 a.m., Darcy put her blinker on and made a right onto the north causeway.

Pawleys in the rearview, a disaster to the fore.


A lime-green blur in a warm rush to Greenville, Sherbet sped past Columbia, South Carolina. Darcy's pattern was by now established—she would drive in silence for a few miles, catch her breath, and resume with speculating on what had happened. I'd never heard a woman spout so many guesses, much less spout them in triplicate. "I think an orphan played with matches, Neil. Or maybe Jay built a bonfire and fell asleep . . . Or maybe lightning struck."

From the passenger seat I glanced in the side mirror and saw Lex chatting away, the Jeep right on our tail. Then I too got caught up in speculation, mostly to keep my driver awake. "What we haven't considered is arson. Maybe from drug-runners spilling down into the jungle from Colombia."

Blank-faced, she glanced first at the speedometer, then me, then locked her eyes on the interstate. "That's too much for me, Neil. Don't even think that. Don't even . . . can we change the subject?"

"To what?"

"Oh . . . how about you and Alexis?"

I turned to look at the Jeep again. "Seems we've hit it off."

"She talks about you day and night."

"I can just imagine. Now what about you and Steve?"

"Um, I need to concentrate on my driving right now."

"All I wanna know is if the two of you are now skiing in tandem behind a motorboat with twin engines and lots of gas."

Darcy hesitated, checked her speed again. "In tandem, maybe. But we'll have to see about the gas level."

Forty miles from Greenville, and in an effort to keep our minds off the fire, I asked Darcy about the obvious bond between her and Allie, and also about her bond with Alexis. I was curious how girls decide who is simply a good friend, and who is a best.

In a moment of late-night deliberation, Darcy slowed to the speed limit and steered left-handed. She was gesturing with her right. "It's like this, Neil. I have my spiritual best friend, Allie, who I've prayed with many times, who lives in the jungle, and who I rarely get to see; and then I have my bonkers best friend, Alexis, who I've hopscotched churches with many times, who lives close by, and who I probably see too much. One is like a sister, one is like a wacky third cousin. But I need them both. They're . . . I dunno. My ballast."

I leaned back into the headrest. "So what about Lydia?"

Darcy reached for and sipped from a water bottle. Then she screwed the cap back on and set it under her seat. "Lydia's my shopping best friend."

It seemed a strange conversation to be having at 3:30 a.m. on a dark interstate, but then furlough had been strange ever since I'd stepped off the U.S. Air connection from Atlanta.

At 4:05 a.m. Darcy pulled into Steve's driveway. A minute later his Jeep pulled in behind us, and in the quiet of our suburban neighborhood the dividing of luggage was quick and whispered.

When Steve gave Darcy a peck good night, I had no doubt they were back together. When Alexis looked at me across the lime-green trunk and shrugged, I knew we were thinking alike—we'd get to the lip-locking in its time. We were combustible, Alexis and I.

The four of us promised to meet up at the church for the Sunday meeting. After a wave but no honk, Lex and Darcy drove away, the raven-haired crabber riding shotgun with the blonde who hates bugs.

Steve and I dropped our sand-strewn luggage and his pitiful pup tent into his carport and left them there. Then we dropped ourselves on his front steps, our first chance, in four-plus hours, to compare notes. "What did Alexis speculate about the fire?" I asked.

Steve glanced up into the night sky looming above suburbia. "She thinks it's one of three things: a comet, lava, or Panamanian terrorists."

I could think of no other response except, "Interesting."

"So, what were Darcy's guesses?"

"Two of those you mentioned, plus bonfires, lightning, and orphans playing with matches."

His yawn covered mine, and that was all the talking we could stand. Steve opened his front door and spoke over his shoulder. "That was one interesting weekend, wasn't it?"

It was not so much a question as his way of saying good night, a fact confirmed when he moseyed into his room and shut the door.

Interesting? Drowsy in his den, I stood there for a minute, lost in reflection at a ridiculous hour.

Steve drove down with Lydia but ended up reconciling with Darcy. Darcy lost two hubcaps but gained back her old boyfriend.

I fought temptation, sprang for ostrich burgers, and got out-fished by Flamboyant Quilla.

Alexis caught umpteen blue crabs and . . . me.

And something horrible happened in Ecuador.

I stepped exhausted into my sea-green room and fed the Hawk and the Pig. They looked like they'd missed me, so my first instinct was to play them a tune. In the glow of their fishbowl I pulled out my harmonica. But the music would not come. Only thoughts of jungle and flames and Jay and flames and Allie and more flames.

Like singleness, missions had become its very own furnace.

# 25

The noon meeting to discuss the missionary disaster in Ecuador had yet to begin when Alexis returned from the ladies' room. Her sleeveless red dress had caused me no shortage of distraction during the morning service, and I imagined that Darcy—seated with us in the third pew and donning light green linen—had likely done a similar number on Steve, who was still in the men's room, trying to clean a coffee stain from his tie. Teetering on two hours sleep, I fought the yawns and watched a horde of Presbyterians gather in the sanctuary.

Alexis tapped me on the knee with the edge of her bulletin. "Neil?" she whispered.

"Hmmm?" I said, my mind elsewhere, anxious for the meeting to start.

"The reason I was late this morning was because I was reading Song of Solomon."

Oh, man. We were at church to find out details of an Ecuadorian disaster, and she wanted to discuss biblical sensuality. "Can this wait, Lex?"

"No, it was eye-opening."

"I'm glad."

She tapped me again. "It said that I wasn't supposed to arouse or awaken love before its time."

"And that's eye-opening?"

"Yes! I've been setting the alarm clock for love ever since high school."

I had yet to recover when Steve came bounding in from the men's room, wiping his hands on his khakis before plopping down on the far side of Darcy. A young deacon by the name of Stanley—the same guy who'd fired me over Tribes of Many Nations—was our black-suited host, alone now on the wooden stage. He began the meeting with two coughs and a gavel-pounding. The sanctuary went quiet.

"When we initiated our international missions program some two and a half years ago," Stanley said, his voice echoing between stained glass, "we envisioned several of our people stepping out to serve in foreign countries. To this day, we've had two: Miss Allie Kyle, who has served in rural Ecuador for the past couple of years, and Jay Jarvis, who left the corporate world last November and now serves along with her."

Stanley then introduced Elder Kyle, Allie's father, who walked somberly up to the stage and stood at the microphone. A deeper silence fell over the sanctuary. "Friends, Allie's side of the village burned to the ground yesterday afternoon."

Around the sanctuary came hushed gasps, and some not so hushed.

"She's currently in the town of Coca, caring for the orphans in an emergency shelter. Jay Jarvis is back in the village, digging through the rubble. Eight of thirteen huts were destroyed." Elder Kyle looked in control, but you could tell he was fighting emotion. "I have always considered my daughter to be a servant among servants, dedicated to her calling. She and Jay need our prayers and possibly our physical assistance. But first I'd like to read to you the email she sent me late last night."

He reached into his jacket pocket and unfolded a sheet of paper.

Dad, I fear that Jay and I could lose our ministry. I mean, what do the natives think? Who wants a missionary who can't even make spaghetti without torching her own village? I feel worse than the ashes of awful. I know I caused this fire. I know I did. Praise God that no one died. When the fire began Jay had all the kids except one, Isabel, a quarter mile away, playing soccer on our field cut into the jungle. I had walked from the village kitchen to the craft hut, anxious to clean up the mess after a morning of beading with the kids. I'd also volunteered to cook lunch on our stove, which is crude, although we've used it for two years without any major problems. I don't always cook, but I was giving the native women a rare day off to go enjoy the river.

In the kitchen I'd been writing in my journal, revising a poem and using a candle for extra light. The kitchen has open-air windows, so a gust of wind or a small critter inviting itself in must have tipped the candle onto my journal. The resulting flame was enough to ignite the dry, wooden walls of the kitchen hut, which were enough to ignite the next hut, and the next . . . and the one after that.

Amazonian matchsticks—that's the image I took to bed last night.

I saw the flames shooting through the roof of the kitchen hut. They leapt to the roof of the next one, the long hut in which most of the orphans live, including the sleeping six-year-old, Isabel, whom you know I've all but adopted as my own. You saw the pictures I sent over Christmas. Isabel had stepped on a sharp bead earlier in the day and had fallen asleep while waiting for the call to lunch, unaware that flames were eating at the wall of her hut. Panicked, I rushed in and plucked her from her bed. She was screaming and gasping for breath, holding her arm. I carried her across the dirt road, calmed her, and wrapped a cloth around her forearm. The skin was blistered in about a three-inch oval. I had to leave her to fight the fire so I told her to stay put. She was rolled over on her side and crying.

Dad, I fought the fire with all I had—one skinny water hose. I squirted flaming roofs and blazing doorways. I felt so helpless but tried to soak the unburned huts, and I was yelling for help but no one was around, so I gave up the fight and ran a quarter mile to the soccer field. I arrived at roughly the same moment as Jay and the other children looked above the banana trees and saw curls of gray smoke rising into the sky. It was the saddest thing I've ever seen—all the children and missionaries together watching eight huts out of thirteen total, including the craft hut, burn into late afternoon. Our peaceful corner of the rainforest was lit up like a torched oil field.

Jay and I drove Isabel into Coca (that jungle town I've told you about) for treatment of her burn. She'll be fine, they say. I slept maybe an hour last night. Jay has returned to the village to see what he can recover.

You know the strange thing, Dad? I've always so valued my poems, filing them away and keeping scrapbooks and thinking of getting them published. A year's worth of original poetry burned up in my journals and I don't even care. I lost my Bible, nearly all my clothes, my binoculars for bird-watching, and even my photo album of all those beach trips. None of that matters tonight. Nobody died, but many could have—and that scares me the most. I'm trying to see God's grace in this disaster, but it's hard when I feel like an arsonist. Tell those at the church who support me that I ask their forgiveness. I am weary tonight. Tell Mom and my brothers that I love them all.

Elder Kyle folded the paper and stood there blinking rapidly, fighting emotion. After a private moment with his handkerchief, he leaned into the mic and explained the thinking of the church leadership. "We're considering asking for volunteers to go and help rebuild. We might even buy the airline tickets—but only if we find enough people willing to go. And, of course, we'd need to find a team leader." He scanned the room, eyebrows raised. Then he asked for a show of hands from those who had previously led short-term missions teams.

Not a hand rose.

"This is, of course, short notice," Elder Kyle said, looking out at all the sympathetic faces. Faces that looked, to me, like they were broadcasting a mixture of compassion and fear—compassion for the victims but fear of traveling to a foreign land. "We would need a strong team," continued Elder Kyle, "because the scope of this project is more than what two or three can accomplish. Our other option would be to hire a construction crew from Ecuador to rebuild."

Finally, from behind us, a middle-aged man stood and waved his bulletin in the air. "But can a third-world country be trusted with our monies?" he asked, allowing his question to linger before he sat.

Darcy turned and glared at Bulletin-waver. Then she stood and faced the front. "I say we do everything we can, whether it be going ourselves or hiring the construction crew. Allie is the only person from this church who ever stepped out and took a risk."

Darcy promptly sat.

But then Steve stood. "Jay took a risk too," he reminded us, sitting again.

This protocol of stand/speak/sit was quite amusing. Kinda like Jack-in-the-Box for Presbyterians.

Elder Kyle was holding the mic, thinking but not speaking, when Alexis stood and waved her arm. One hundred heads turned toward her.

Once in the spotlight, Lex stuck her arms straight down by her side like she was reciting the pledge of allegiance. "Y'all probably don't know me 'cause I tend to visit lots of churches, but my new boyfriend taught Spanish in Ecuador for the past two years, and I think he would be just the guy to lead a team." She looked down at me cringing in the seat beside her. "Couldn't you, Neil?"

*Me, lead a team of Presbyterians into the Ecuadorian jungle?*

The congregation was staring at me like kids at the candy man.

"Is this factual, sir?" Stanley asked. He stood tall beside the front pew, arms crossed, looking as formal as the white gardenias decorating the outside of the sanctuary.

Alexis tugged on my arm, and I stood. She sat back down.

"Yes, it's factual," I said, nervous in front of all the Bible Belters—not just from being put on the spot but also because I was the only person wearing jeans. "I taught Jay Jarvis in my language class, and I do know the whereabouts of the village."

"You've been there?"

I turned and saw all the unfamiliar faces looking at me. I tried to look composed, but again my thoughts were jumbled and jittery, anticipating where this might lead. "I only know the whereabouts. I lived in the capital city of Quito, but Jay and Allie are deep in the rainforest."

Stanley frowned. Then he scuffed his shoe on the burgundy carpet and frowned again. "You're fluent in Spanish, but do you have any experience at all in short-term missions?"

"No, I do not. I just teach missionaries in a language school." I sat back down.

Murmurs of doubt seeped between the stained-glass windows of the sanctuary. Lex whispered that I'd done good. Steve and Darcy smiled in sympathy.

Deacon Stanley crossed his arms and recoiled into himself, blinking his eyes as if his mind couldn't hold all of the churchy responsibilities. And I couldn't blame him—who could relax their mind while overseeing church beautification, two-dessert limits, and Presbyterians in Ecuador?

Elder Kyle remained on the stage, nodding at me, a trace of a smile now etched on his face, as if to say "You might be just the guy to go help my daughter."

Then Bulletin-waver stood again, reiterating his cautionary stance about Ecuador and its much-maligned government. While he, Stanley, and Elder Kyle were going back and forth over whether North Hills Prez should be involved directly, Alexis turned to whisper in my ear again. "Neil, does Ecuador even have a government? I thought its people were fighting for independence from Chile."

"Did you not take world history?"

"I was Tinkerbell."

When everyone got seated again, Elder Kyle gripped the mic with both hands and addressed the congregation. "Here's our dilemma, folks," he said. "Our short-term missions people are away for the summer. Team Europe is serving in the mountains of France, and Team Caribbean is running a sports camp in Jamaica. That begs the obvious question—if we were to sponsor a mission team to do construction in Ecuador, could any of you take off from work and volunteer to go?"

I raised a hand and nudged Alexis, who raised a hand and nudged Darcy, who raised a hand and elbowed Steve in the ribs. Steve raised both hands, then dropped one and rubbed his side.

"Four, eh?" Elder Kyle said, looking to and fro. "Well, that's a good start. Neil, can you stay over after we adjourn? I'd like to meet with you in private."

I nodded my okay. Alexis reached over and squeezed my hand, like I'd just gotten promoted.

I didn't hear anything for the next few minutes. Steve would later tell me that there was frank discussion and much doubt cast by Bulletin-waver. But in that moment, as I sat frozen in the pew, a new thought rose to the fore. It was as if someone were standing behind me, holding two conch shells over my ears. But instead of hearing a breezy ocean, all I could hear were the words of Asbury as we motored in from sea: "Neil, a missionary is never really on furlough."

# 26

I left the private meeting with Elder Kyle in a furlough-shattering daze, my head still spinning from his requests. He was a gentle man, intent on sending help to his daughter, and from all he had implied, help began with me.

Alexis was waiting for me in front of the church in her silver 280z and knew just what I needed—a tea-slurping, salsa-dunking, just-try-to-calm-down Mexican lunch. At Corona's we plopped down at a table for two and ordered drinks and chips.

A minute later she slurped from her glass of sweet tea and began debriefing me. "So after Elder Kyle asked you to recruit a team, what did you say?"

I rubbed my eyes and tried to remember the details. "I told him okay, that I'd ask you to help, and that I still couldn't believe Stanley would fire me over flowers but recommend me for missions."

Alexis pulled a pen from her purse and wrote "team" across the top of a napkin. "You're not mad at me for nominating you, are ya, Neily?"

I took two matching chips, made a salsa sandwich, and handed it to her. "At first I was stunned. But then I realized that if you hadn't spoken up, Steve would have. Regardless, the singles have been asked to recruit. Elder Kyle told me that he would go himself but that he suffers from vertigo, especially after air travel."

She chewed the Mexican morsel and smiled. "So then, let's recruit."

For all of her wacky ways, Alexis had a heart for the hurting. I'd seen it first at the coffeehouse when she left the milkshake out for the homeless man, then again at Pawleys Island when I got home from the fishing trip and she'd tithed half of her blue crabs to the old guy who'd wandered over from the mainland. Today, in this noisy restaurant, it dawned on me what was happening—Alexis, who church-hopped, recruiting for a mission trip; me, the visitor, being asked to lead the team; Darcy, who hates bugs, volunteering to go; and Jay, he of lousy Spanish, serving in the jungle. Everywhere I looked, God was using the least qualified.

On the napkin Alexis wrote the names of three construction people she knew through her real estate dealings. I wrote the names "Steve" and "Darcy," who were already signed up. Then she wrote down our mutual friends, everyone from surfers to hopscotchers to fishermen. She stopped writing and looked at me across the salsa. "What about Stanley? Would he go?"

"Elder Kyle says Stanley is a big chicken. Scared of the jungle."

Alexis started to write down another name but stopped again. "What about Bulletin-waver?"

"Apparently he's an even bigger chicken than Stanley," I replied, sampling Corona's very sweet tea. "From what I've gathered, most of the members are gray-hairs and scaredy-cats."

Alexis frowned and tapped her pen on the table. "Neil?"

"Yeah?"

"I'm not sure what we've gotten ourselves into, but this is gonna be a lot tougher than milkshake missions."

Over tacos and tamales, we split the list of names and agreed to spend Monday making phone calls to all possible recruits. Elder Kyle wanted a minimum total of six people, preferably eight to ten.

In line to pay the bill, Alexis tucked her pen back in her purse. "Neil, did you ever ask Deacon Stanley why he insisted on all white flowers?"

I put my arm around her and spoke into her ear. "According to Stanley, white represents purity, the colors represented chaos."

She pulled out some cash, and we stepped forward in the line. "So what did the Presbyterians do with all those plants they dug up?"

"Donated 'em."

"To?"

"The Pentecostals."

I arrived home exhausted, my brain juggling three pertinent issues: God's will, Zany Alexis, and the ramifications of escorting Presbyterians into a rainforest. A numbing trifecta, to say the least.

After one of the greatest Sunday afternoon naps in Southern history, I woke to find a long and unexpected email from South America. At Steve's computer desk, with a serious case of bed-head, I read the words attentively.

Neil,

We've never met, but this past spring you taught my coworker (and boyfriend), Jay, in your language school. Jay gave me your email yesterday and said to contact you. I'm on a borrowed computer at an emergency shelter in Coca, Ecuador. Officially, I'm a missionary, although I now feel like an arsonist. Perhaps by now you've heard the news—that I burnt down half of the village. The only lingering injury is the burn to little Isabel's arm. She's only six, almost seven. She'll remain in Coca while she heals up. I feel awful about her arm.

My pride usually won't allow me to beg for help, but this mess is more than I or Jay can overcome on our own. There were several native Indian adults who lived in the village. Two had never seen anything of value burn before, so they fled downriver to another village. Three others have stuck around to help me here at the shelter, including my woman friend "Plaid over Stripes" as Jay calls her. I'm not good at calculations, Neil, but if six to eight people can come down, then much of the frames and most of the walls could be rebuilt in a week or so. There is plenty of food. Anyone who comes can crowd into the remaining five huts. One man who has some construction skills is the ex-janitor of North Hills Presbyterian, Maurice Evans. I believe he is now a boat captain. You might call him if you can find his number. If you've never met him, I can tell you that he's a good man . . . but don't let him start throwing Fig Newtons.

257

I need to go now—too many children to care for. I would appreciate anything you can do, and also your prayers. We fear looters in the village. As for me, I would much rather be walking on a Carolina beach right now. I've never felt so burdened.

If you've met Darcy Yeager during your furlough, please tell her hello for me, but I doubt she would come since she fears bugs and rodents, of which we have many. Please let me know if you can help. If so, I can arrange for a van to meet your team in Coca and transport you to the village. Professional carpenters are welcome!

Blessings from a humbled missionary,
Allie Kyle, Missions for the World, S.A.

I could feel the pressure mounting on me. And I wanted to toss pressure over my shoulder like a box of granola bars and hope someone else would catch it and have their fill. I wanted to help Jay, but I didn't want to be leading an entire mission team. I wanted long siestas and short schedules, warm sand and cold drinks, big piers and little moonlit excursions at low tide. I wanted to walk a beach with Alexis and catch dinner with a string. I wanted leisure. And I wanted a second chance to out-fish Flamboyant Quilla.

But here I was, a renter, a visitor, a non–Bible Belt guy being asked—by elders, deacons, the missionary girl who caused the disaster, and God himself—to recruit a team from the heart of the Bible Belt.

I needed to find me a roof.

Sometimes the doing takes precedence over the talking, so I postponed my rooftop petitions and spent Monday leaving messages with everyone I'd met in South Carolina. I even walked downtown to look for William the Conqueror.

No luck.

Back at Steve's kitchen table, I picked up the phone and called one last person about the trip: José in Mexico City. I figured any man who would suggest wooing a girl with a tangelo would be a bonus to have along for the journey. Plus, I knew José had built his own house, and I desperately needed to recruit a carpenter.

But he wasn't in either. So I left José a message, giving him the dates of the trip, the details of the disaster, and the fact that his flight from Mexico City to Ecuador would be paid for.

The first person I heard back from, however, was a boat captain. When Maurice returned my call, all he wanted to know was why I wasn't down at the marina making his pancakes. When I told him of our midnight drive back from the island and of the fire in the village, he didn't speak for nearly a minute. Finally he asked if anyone was hurt, and what he could do.

I held the receiver close. "You could go with us, Maurice. I hear you're good with a hammer."

"Better than I am with a gaff," he replied. "But just how much this little trip gonna cost me? It's not like the preacher and I are making a killing at this fishing gig."

"Flights are paid for by the Presbyterians. We just need bodies."

A long pause. "Bodies, eh?"

"Live bodies."

Another pause. "Can you hold on a sec, Neil?"

"What for?"

"I gotta go find Smoak. He's out wandering the marina, trying to convert the yachting community to saving knowledge."

In the receiver I could hear the sound of boat engines, then the muffled voice of Maurice explaining the events to the preacher. I heard the word *inferno*, then *Bolivia*.

First Asbury told me that he had to take care of his own church. Then he told me he spoke no Spanish, just a few words of Gullah. Then he paused and mumbled "Oh, Lordy" about nineteen times, as if his decision lurked somewhere between *Oh* and *Lordy,* and he was trying to scare it out into the open. Finally—after I'd said "please" more times than he'd said "Oh, Lordy"—he said that he couldn't let Maurice be the only adventurous co-captain at Georgetown Marina.

Asbury finally caved. "I'll pack my bags," he said, "but I ain't eating no piranha."

Still on the call, I was going over with Maurice what we should take to the jungle when a loud noise rattled through the line. It was like their cell phone had hit concrete.

A female voice boomed. "Hey, Fish Stick, that you?"

"Quilla?"

"Just where you all goin'? Ethiopia?"

"Ecuador. To the jungle."

"And you not invitin' no people of color?" I could hear her snickering.

"Maurice got color. Preacher Smoak even has a tan. We're gonna be rebuilding huts in the rainforest."

A short pause preceded a long exhale. "My cousin is a cabinetmaker, Neil, and I spent many an hour watching. Uh-huh, shaw did. I never seen no foreign countries. Never flown. You got somethin' against women going on your trip?"

"Not at all." I tried to imagine what a week with her would entail. "But it's wild there. Really wild. Don't expect any safety belts like when you fought that tuna."

"That belt was no fashion at all. You go ahead and sign me up."

"*Qué?* Are you serious?"

She raised her voice to a startling level. "Of course I'm serious, Neil. This summer I'm all about risk. Yesterday I even learned to surf."

"Who taught you?"

She paused a moment. "I thought he said his name was Rasputin. Anyway, I caught him and his wife sleepin' on Preacher Smoak's boat. They'd snuck on for some . . . you know, some private time, uh-huh. I made him give me surf lessons else I'd have to turn 'em in. The secret is you gotta squat down and hold out your arms."

"I can't believe you rode a wave."

"We buddies now, me'n surfer boy."

Reason burst through the small talk, reminding me that there were instructions from the elders about my recruiting efforts. "Quilla, the Presbyterians will only allow people to go who are already involved in their own church. So I have to ask, are you—"

"Involved? I sing in the choir. Me and the choir girls love to affirm our preacher, the Reverend Tyrus Williams. I affirm Tyrus a lot, uh-huh. And we clap in our church, Neil. It ain't like Asbury and his subdued Pawleys Island church. Naw, ain't like that at all."

Before we hung up Quilla told me of all the helpful household items she could bring on the trip, including a case of tacks, four cans of Pringles, and her softball bat.

The team had grown to seven. An unpredictable, gregarious seven.

God had thrust me into a leadership role. Yet in my head I was both Moses and Pharaoh, half of me struggling to lead, the other half tossing out obstacles. And who wouldn't be double minded? Look at the vision I had before me—Carolinians wandering in the rainforest for forty years because Alexis and Darcy took a detour to play Road Trip.

*You picked a B, Maurice? Let's head for Brazil.*

Oh, man.

# 27

At the end of her Wednesday workday, Alexis called me to say that she was full of good news, that she'd had a fine day of recruiting and a fine day in the real estate world, and that she just had to make herself another celebratory milkshake. For the second time in two weeks, and in much different circumstances, we agreed to meet at the Carpenter's Cellar coffeehouse.

I walked up North Main at twilight, entered downtown, and found on the coffeehouse door a posting from a building inspector. In too much of a hurry to read the details, I hustled down the stairs and saw Alexis sitting on the L-shaped bar, sipping her shake and mocking the pose she'd employed on the night we'd met. She was wearing her jeans and black top again, and she had a sheet of construction paper in her hands. I stopped just feet from her, wondering why she hadn't greeted me yet.

She peered over the paper. "Boy meets girl, eh?"

I nodded. "Yep."

"And girl teaches boy how to catch a crab at low tide?"

"While humming Sinatra."

"Then boy walks with girl on the scenic shore at sunset?"

"Absolutely."

She glanced again at the paper, which I could now see was blank. "So what happens after boy and girl drive hastily away from the beach at midnight? That's a terrible place to leave a story."

I applauded her narration as I spotted a second shake waiting beside her. Chocolate, in a clear plastic cup, red straw. She hopped down, and we sat knee-to-knee on bar stools, slurping in tandem, our backs to the drawings and stories taped unevenly to the cobalt blue wall.

I could tell she was excited about seeing the jungle. "I can't wait, Neil," she said over her straw. "I'm gonna hammer for God and talk to monkeys."

"Lex, this is going to be all about work, and very little about play. The posts and the plywood will be waiting on us. Jay used the last of his savings to buy it all."

She slurped hard then licked the excess from her bottom lip. "Well, what if a monkey comes up and watches while we hammer? Can I at least make monkey sounds, O Strictest Leader?"

I laughed at her voice inflection and reached for her hand. "Of course you can. But our team is just a ragtag assortment. That's why I'm hoping you had some luck today in recruiting. Please tell me you got somebody."

She let go of my hand and got down off the stool and went around behind the bar. She leaned over it and smiled at me. "Neily, I'm happy to report that I did get someone to sign up."

In a gesture of thanks, I lifted my shake high in the air. "I knew you could do it, Lex. Who is it . . . a carpenter? Construction manager?"

Below the blue cone lighting, she was looking at me in the way that said "My answer is not exactly your expected answer." "Well . . ."

"Well, what?" I asked.

"All the home builders and carpenters that my mom and I work with are very busy because the real estate market has gone mad, and so no one wants to go to South America to build huts for free."

I feared what was coming. "You asked your mom to go?"

"Oh, not Mom. She has no interest in Ecuador either. One of the carpenters had this friend—"

"So you did get a carpenter?"

"You must let me finish my sentences, Neily. One of the carpenters had a friend, and that friend just happened to be Ransom."

My straw rested on my lip as I stared at the floor and totaled our talent.

There was no way we would get the work done. "Lex, that surfer guy owns a skateboard shop. We really need—"

"No, he's not going either. Even though he makes his own surfboards and would be great to have along, his wife told him no way was she staying home with a four-month-old while her husband got to tour the rainforest. So I lost out on him, which led to plan C."

I gripped my cup with both hands and held it out in a gesture of pleading. "Please, please tell me you got somebody who can handle power tools."

She propped her elbows on the bar and shook her head. "I doubt it. My mom was showing a house to this lady and just casually mentioned that I was going to Ecuador on a mission trip, and then this lady started asking all kinds of questions, and so Mom drove her over to the office to meet me."

"We'll be building huts in a remote village, Lex. Did you tell the lady that?"

"Yes, and I told her there were lots of monkeys and birds and that you were the team leader."

"Does this lady at least go to church and know something about carpentry?"

"She doesn't hear too well, Neil. My mom and I ended up driving Mrs. Dean around in Mom's Lexus to look at more houses. Mrs. Dean wanted lots of yard and was very particular about the quality of the soil. After we'd shown a dozen houses she finally fell for a Charleston style that had its own underground sprinkler system. She's paying cash. Anyway, she volunteered to buy her own ticket and go with us. Isn't that the greatest thing ever!"

I bit my straw and spoke with it in my mouth. "You're not talking about the elderly Mrs. Dean, are you? . . . Beatrice?"

"That's the one."

"Tell me you didn't invite a fruity, eighty-one-year-old gardener to Ecuador."

"She already has her passport—from her Europe trip. She's donating all kinds of gardening tools to the village and even has her own straw hat."

Moses had Aaron. I had Alexis and Beatrice. My shake tilted, and a drop of light brown liquid ran down off the bar stool and onto the tile floor. Speechless, I chewed my straw and retotaled our talent. I could picture Maurice, Asbury, and myself building a hut. I could picture Steve and Darcy wandering off in the jungle to rediscover their volatile romance. I could even picture Jay sitting on a stump and practicing his Spanish. But what of the others? What of Alexis, Beatrice, and Quilla? What would that threesome be like? How could anyone keep up with them in the wilds of Ecuador?

I set my cup on the bar and shook my head. "Alexis, this work involves constructing huts—building foundations and erecting plywood walls. What is she going to do?"

Still leaning over the bar, Lex opened a packet of Sweet'n Low, dumped out the contents, and scribbled in the grains. "Neil, every quaint little village needs landscaping. Just let her come. Pleeease. I'll make you she-crab soup again."

"She's eighty-one. What if she wanders off into the jungle and gets lost?"

"I'll chain her to one wrist and Darcy to the other."

"You have lost your mind, woman."

"Maybe, but guess what I ordered today after my mom and I sold that house."

"Your very own ostrich?"

"No, silly . . . a trampoline! I ordered it off eBay, and so when we get back from Ecuador you can come over and jump with me."

Then Alexis changed subjects so fast that even her countenance could not keep up. "I'm worried about Darcy," she said. Her voice rang with discontent but came from lips that were still smiling. "She's talking of bowing out of the trip."

I swept the grains of Sweet'n Low into my palm. "Does the jungle scare her that bad?"

Now Lex looked serious. "No, her parents scare her that bad. All this year Darcy has been told of some money that her parents had put away for her. Darcy makes a living at the ad firm, but she was counting on her parents' money to fix up this coffeehouse. The city has given us one month to fix the plumbing. Darcy and Steve are talking about renovating the Cellar together, and I'm gonna help too. But Darcy's parents are using the money to bribe her because they don't want her going on mission trips to help Christian missionaries."

"Steve told me about them."

Alexis came around from the bar with a plastic cup, and I dumped the grains in it. "What he didn't tell you is that Darcy has no savings of her own. She just looks well-to-do."

"Somehow I think she and Steve are just full of secrets."

Alexis nodded her agreement then went behind the bar and made a third milkshake. Once again in the role of courier to the homeless, I put a plastic lid on the cup, grabbed a straw, and carried the shake up the stairs to set it on the brick ledge. A tiny mission to precede a bigger one.

Alexis was already cutting off the lights. She locked up the coffeehouse, I shook the door handle, and she drove me back to Steve's in her 280z.

Back home, seated at Steve's computer desk, I read the itinerary sent from Stanley and Elder Kyle. The irony was not lost on me—the same church from which Beatrice and I had been fired for jazzing up the gardens was now buying us round-trip plane tickets to South America. I logged on and sent an email to Ecuador, confirming our arrival.

> J & A,
>
> I've done my best to recruit a professional construction crew. The eight of us will arrive, no doubt, in something of a flurry, or maybe a whirl-wind, or perhaps we'll become our very own El Niño and cause undue panic in Ecuador. I will not even try to predict what will happen once we get there, as this crew is something beyond extroverted. We're scheduled to land in Coca on July 16th, at 6:20 p.m.
>
> With grace, hammers, and trepidation,
> Neil Rucker, Missions of Spontaneity

At 11:00 p.m. on the night before the trip, I went outside of Steve's house and climbed atop his air-conditioning unit. Steepness notwithstanding,

I grabbed for grainy shingles and pushed off of a drainpipe with my feet. I scratched my knuckles during the climb but scrambled my way to the top and straddled the center. Moonlit and elevated, I cast my gaze at the heavens.

"God, this roof is pointed and sharp, but there are things that need to be said. You knew there was going to be a fire. You knew that North Hills Presbyterian would ask me to lead the team. You even used Jay to get me here. So this is the reason I'm in South Carolina instead of Montana? To be entrusted with leading a foreign mission trip is one thing, but to be entrusted with the assortment you've given me . . . I mean, look who you've given me: Darcy, who hates bugs; Flamboyant Quilla; a preacher who demands that his pancakes be shaped like a flounder; Beatrice, who will landscape Ecuador with who knows what. And you almost gave me a married surfer who's trying to bring back words like *gnarly*. Out of eight people, I have but two who know anything about construction: Captain Maurice, who's an ex-janitor, and Steve, who can at least read blueprints in his beige, logoed shirts. That leaves Neil the Spanish teacher and Alexis the raven-haired crabber to organize this mess. Would it have been too much to have given me one professional carpenter? Perhaps one fluent in *español*? I dare not ask for anything beyond survival. But are you sure you want me to do this?"

With my legs splayed out to each side of the roof, I waited for an answer, some twinkling of a star or perhaps a comet in whose tail was written words of wisdom, divinely shot across the sky for just this moment.

But all I saw was a jet approaching at a shallow angle, bringing more gullible souls into this bewildering city. After minutes of silence, I still felt afraid, unqualified to lead. Cowardly even. I had not asked to be in such a position of responsibility. And I couldn't help but think of how comfortable was my language school, my padded chair, my handing out exams and assigning grades, not to mention the shish kebabs I grilled every Tuesday night in the warm air of Quito.

Beside me a blackbird landed on Steve's roof, and when I turned, it looked surprised to see me. It squawked once and made for the trees.

I listened again for a voice.

But there was no voice tonight, just my obedience.

No professional carpenters, just willing bodies.

No last-minute detours off the interstate, just eight seats reserved in economy class.

After I'd sat up there awhile and the night air had taken on a dewy complexion, it occurred to me that I had no business being on a roof and asking questions of God.

God had already spoken—Team Looney Tune was headed for the jungle.

# *Act*
## three

*Everybody's nuts, some of us just see it more clearly.*

—Elvis

# 28

After their luggage had been sucked into Delta's magical mystery tunnel, Alexis and Quilla cajoled the bag-check guy into snapping a team photo. Inside the terminal of the Greenville-Spartanburg Airport, the eight of us had backed up against a fake potted plant: Darcy, Lex, Beatrice, and Quilla kneeling in front, Asbury, myself, Maurice, and Steve across the back—arms around shoulders, everyone grinning with the wild-eyed excitement that precedes a shared adventure.

I framed the picture in my mind: the shades of olive green on Lex's and Darcy's T-shirts. The camouflage shirts on the preacher and Maurice. Beatrice in her gardening pants and flower-print blouse. Quilla in her same Aretha Franklin T-shirt and the orange beads strung into her braids. Steve in contrast to everyone else in his beige golf shirt with the engineering logo on the pocket.

After the second flash had faded, Maurice kept his arm around Steve and spoke into his ear. "Son, I'd probably not wear a logoed shirt to the jungle . . . makes too clear a target for the blowguns."

"Uh-huh," Quilla said, helping Beatrice to her feet. "But I got your back, Steve. If I see a little pygmy, I'll whop 'im with a stick."

"Oh dear . . . pygmies," Beatrice said, blinking rapidly at the thought. "I saw one last week at the florist. He was hiding in the bamboo."

Beatrice then pulled two letters from her purse and tried to get the bag-check man to mail them. Alexis, who had volunteered to watch out for Beatrice, gently took her by the arm. Together they walked off to find a drop box.

With lots of time left before boarding the commuter to Atlanta, the others also began to wander. Asbury and Maurice strolled into a bookstore. Quilla went out to the observation deck to watch the incoming flights. Steve headed to the men's room with a faded green softball jersey in hand, intent on changing into something that would blend with a rainforest.

Left to sit in the lobby together were myself and the unusually quiet Darcy. Coupled with her olive T-shirt, her tied-back blonde hair made her look like she was about to model outdoor clothing. Adding to the runway look was her detached expression.

"Okay, friend," I said, sprawling to her right in a lobby chair, "you're the only one who isn't smiling."

"Oh . . . it's nothing."

I was about to leave her alone when the urge to leap right in took over. "You and Steve?"

"We're fine."

"Bugs in the jungle?"

"I brought spray." She crossed her left leg over her right and bounced it up and down like she was nervous. Then she sighed and stared at the floor. "It's my father, Neil. He thinks you, me, Steve, and everybody else on this team are insane to give up vacation time to go help out Jay and Allie. My dad thinks the gospel is just propaganda from an ancient textbook. He yelled at me and said he forbid me to go."

It was an odd moment, waiting on a flight as the leader of missionary wannabes and listening to one of the team members spilling her beans about the atheistic family from which she'd sprouted. I was trying to be the leader, trying to be serious, but I kept thinking of Darcy's beans as lime green. I gathered my thoughts and tried to reason with her. "But you live on your own, Darce. He can't forbid you to do anything."

Now she was kicking her leg even faster, staring out the lobby glass at a refueling truck with such concentration that I thought she might ignite not only the truck but the entire airport. "He has lots of power, Neil. My father loves his power."

"This isn't about money, is it?"

"I'm fine. Don't you need to go round up the rest of the team?"

I glanced down the long expanse of the lobby. The team was nowhere in sight. "Yeah. But is there something I can do here, right now, to help you deal with this? I mean, we all want the fun-loving Darcy who races down mountains."

She tried to smile, but the weight of the issue pulled her smile into a frown. "Last night when I stopped by my parents' house to get a camera for the trip, my father told me that if I went, he might not give me the . . . I'm being bribed, Neil."

Parental bribes? I was not qualified to discuss this stuff. "Not that it matters much, but what kind of money are we talking about here?"

She spoke to the blue carpet, and she spoke very slowly. "Twenty thousand dollars if I want to start my own business, plus six months of living expenses."

I had no clue what to say, having never been in such a position. "An entrepreneur . . . I thought you liked your career in the ad world."

Darcy paused before explaining her reasoning. "I'll work the ad world by day, manage the Cellar on weekends. That coffeehouse sits right in the heart of downtown and could be such an outreach to the community." She took a breath and continued. "Someone needs to take charge of that place and renovate it, and I'm thinking that person is me."

I'd never seen this side of her. "Just what has gotten into you? Did signing up for a mission trip invigorate you?"

She stared out at the tarmac. "It's my nature. I press the limits of my car, my relationships, even my time." Darcy cocked her head to the side as if a new thought had rushed in. "Ya know, I really think I could do it—hop between ads and the coffeehouse like Alexis hops between Baptist and Presbyterian."

I rocked back in my chair and laughed. "Okay, so your parents are manipulative and don't want you serving God, but you want their money so you can serve better mochas."

"Correct. I just need their money." She glanced meekly at me. "You see, Neil, I'm not a saver, so I have little money of my own."

The first boarding call echoed through the terminal. Way down the corridor Maurice and Asbury had gathered everyone and were walking them toward us, Alexis in front, Beatrice in tow. Darcy was looking at me without expression, so I tried to give her a vote of confidence. "Somehow I think you'll have what it takes to handle two jobs."

She crossed her legs the other way as the boarding call repeated. "God gave me a functioning brain, so I intend to use it." She glanced over my shoulder at our approaching friends. "And one more thing—I'll renovate the Cellar with or without my father's money."

Darcy rose from her seat and walked like a detached, jungle-clad model onto flight 227, bound for Atlanta.

Steve was bound for Darcy. From behind me he rushed past, hustled down into the tunnel, and brought her back out into the lobby. Preacher Smoak had volunteered to ask a prayer of protection for us, so the Looney Tunes gathered into a circle and did their best to show reverence. I removed my Ecuador cap and pointed at Steve, who removed his Cubs cap and pointed at Maurice, who removed his captain's hat and pointed at Beatrice, who pressed her straw hat firmly into place. "I have bad hair today, dear."

Alexis held my left hand; Asbury had my right. He used Psalm 91 for his reference and prayed the kind of prayer that scares you because it reminds you of how vulnerable you are. He mentioned every risk taker he could think of, including Dr. Martin Luther King, Jim Elliot, and Jesus himself. I thought Asbury was about to say amen when he squeezed my fingers hard and asked God to also protect his boat, seeing as how hurricane season was at hand.

An hour later our team walked single file into Atlanta International, Quilla out front and swinging her left arm like she was clearing a path. The changeover was uneventful except for Alexis and Maurice walking up the down-escalators for fifteen minutes—they claimed it was good exercise for trekking in a jungle.

Before we boarded the 757 for Ecuador, I had a few minutes with Alexis, who was breathing hard after her workout. We sat against the lobby glass, shoulder to shoulder, watching hordes of harried travelers get rustled like cattle through the inspection line. I asked her what she thought of the team's unity.

"Everyone likes everyone else," she said in a rare moment of calm, "but I think Darcy is a basket case."

I clutched her hand. "And I always thought you were the basket case."

The slap across my wrist came quick and girlish. "Stop it, Neil. I'm being serious. Darcy didn't think her dad would carry through with his threats, so now she's dancing with reality." She looked across the lobby at her friend. "Steve is probably the best thing going for her now. Did you know that this week he bought two original hubcaps for her Cadillac? I mean, look at them over there, he's even carrying her bags for her. You didn't carry my bags."

"I've got Beatrice's bags. Gimme a break."

She winked at me, then stood and said, "Lead the way, O Great Team Leader."

For sheer efficiency I'd retained all the boarding passes. Together the two of us tried to come up with a plan for seating arrangements for the long flight to South America. We'd been given three seats each in rows eighteen and twenty, two seats in row nineteen. Our goal was to equally divide four men, four women, and an incalculable amount of personality into those three rows.

Much debate preceded the decision. But Alexis figured it out, explaining in a tidal wave of oration that Steve and Darcy should surely be seated with Asbury in row twenty, if for no other reason than wise counsel, and that she, Quilla, and Beatrice were an inseparable threesome for row eighteen. This would leave Maurice and me to plop down in row nineteen.

At takeoff, the three with window seats—Beatrice, Maurice, and Asbury—all gazed out at a shrinking Atlanta. I wondered how many of my teammates realized that our ascent from concrete would be so radically offset by a descent into twisty green acreage, a jungle that, according to Jay, couldn't care less if you hailed from the land of prosperity. I wondered who would adapt and who would cower in their hut. I wondered about my own sense of comfort, if I'd miss hot showers. We were above the clouds, somewhere over the Florida panhandle, when I let it all go and decided to simply trust God with the details.

When the FASTEN SEAT BELT sign reversed its opinion, everyone loosened up except for Maurice, who was already snoozing, his head against the window. My nudge roused him.

"Huh?" he said, stirring in his seat. "I'll have me a Diet Pepsi and some pretzels."

I told him they weren't serving drinks yet. He shut his eyes and told me to wake him when they were.

In the forward row, Quilla, Alexis, and Beatrice were discussing, well, pretty much everything.

The sheer volume of their chatter reawakened Maurice, and in a burst of curiosity he tapped Alexis on the head and asked her if he'd heard right—that she had ordered a trampoline. She spoke over her shoulder. "When we get back, you can jump with us."

"I'm gonna jump," Quilla said. "I love to jump. Uh-huh."

Maurice reached up and gripped Quilla's headrest. "But what if you get maimed by pygmies?"

Beatrice interrupted. "Did you say the pilot's name was Rigby, dear?"

"No, Beatrice. Pygmy."

"The pilot is a pygmy? Oh my . . . how does he see over the steering wheel?"

By this time Maurice was so tickled he couldn't talk. Then, somehow—maybe it was because of the altitude—the women got on the subject of art. When Alexis mentioned a painting that she had hanging on her bedroom wall, Maurice and I leaned forward to listen to the responses.

"I do graphic art on my home computer. Uh-huh. Yep, shaw do."

"Dear, my favorite is Van Gogh."

"He's great, Beatrice," Lex said. "But have you ever seen the Sistine Chapel?"

"The sisters have chapel? Oh my, I didn't know sisters were allowed to preach."

"Uh-huh. Sisters preach in my church all the time. I've affirmed plenty of sisters in my red robe."

Beatrice peered out the window. "I don't see any red road, dear. It all looks like ocean to me."

All the way across the Gulf, for five more hours, we were engaged in such discussions. The topics included jungle food, Southern food, soul food, country music, rap music, and gospel music, plus Quilla's monologue on the deforming nature of face-lifts. The talk only stopped when the pilot announced that we were approaching the colonial city of Quito. Conversations faded. Heads turned toward windows. Then, deep into our descent, I saw familiar mountains, looked down on familiar rooftops. Furlough had come full circle. A wobbly circle, sure, but still a complete revolution.

Inside Quito's Mariscal International Airport at 5:15 in the afternoon, our luggage was piled in the middle of the terminal, a mound of suitcases and duffels heaped like garbage.

I found a young employee and convinced him with Spanish words and American dollars that we still had another flight left. After a dash down the main corridor, he returned with a clunky-wheeled cart, loaded the luggage, and followed our team through the terminal. Steve even dropped back and helped push.

Our circus had made it three-fourths of the way. Just one more carnival ride, a last flight on a puddle-jumper from Quito that would take us above the Andes, over the outskirts of the rainforest, and down into the jungle town of Coca.

At the far end of the airport sat a twin-prop, red-and-orange airplane. Vintage, possibly World War II. I suspected that the paint job had been slathered on just to comfort the tourists.

It did not comfort Darcy. Both she and Asbury had reservations about boarding. Steve, however—the man with the gift of logic—took Darcy by the hand, spoke softly to her, and led her up the skinny stairs and into a seat.

Maurice did not take Asbury by the hand, nor did he speak softly. He slapped the preacher on the rump and told him to think of this next ride as just another day on rough seas. Asbury said nothing. While the wind whipped what little hair he had left, he walked to the back of the plane and looked up at the tail. As if the aircraft had failed inspection, he shook his head and boarded hesitantly, muttering another string of *Oh, Lordy*'s as he climbed the stairs.

Quilla and Maurice helped Beatrice up the steps. Alone on the tarmac, I looked up and saw the wrinkled eyes of my gardening friend peering out an oval window. Beatrice had the glint in her eye that I'd seen on the lawn of North Hills Prez. She stared across the runway at rich farmland as if she couldn't wait to subdue it with her trowel. I shifted my glances to the other windows and realized that we were one short.

The team had lost a member; I had lost my new girlfriend.

Propellers sputtered then spun into warm-up mode as I waved with both hands and caught Steve's attention in his window. *Where is Lex?* I mouthed.

Steve shrugged, squinted, shook his head. Then I saw the pilot waving at me from the pilot's perch. He pointed to his right, and across him I saw her hand waving—Alexis had talked her way into riding shotgun. Tinkerbell as copilot. Perfect.

At takeoff we climbed at such a steep angle that carry-on bags slid down the aisle. The plane had seating for twelve, legroom for five, and all the turbulence of Darcy's family life.

Within five dubious minutes we had passed over a range of snow-covered peaks, and the engine noise was so severe we had to yell to communicate. We then dropped altitude and headed for the wilds of the Amazon Basin. I knew my fellow travelers were grasping reality when we'd been in the air for half an hour and neither Maurice nor Quilla nor Beatrice had said a word.

Everyone stared out from their oval windows, astonished at the serpentine flow of rivers carved into the earth. Each tributary appeared smothered by a jungle canopy that extended into the far reaches of South America. An out-of-comfort-zone experience is what Maurice had predicted. Comfort zones were nowhere to be found, having parachuted out somewhere between Atlanta and the Gulf of Mexico.

Then, with no warning at all, the plane dipped, rolled sideways, dipped again. Seven gasps combined to suck the air from the fuselage.

"What was that?" Steve asked, wedged into the rear of the plane with Darcy.

"This isn't Delta Airlines, son," Asbury said, looking anything but calm himself.

From behind me came the expected affirmation. "Uh-huh. Shaw ain't."

We tilted right, wobbled, tilted again. Lower now, we were at least leveled off.

Out my window the sky was an unblemished blue, and below the wing the greenery appeared as a blank Ecuadorian canvas on which our team would leave its mark. I tried to picture an end result of coordinated artistry, but what I really pictured was a smudged finger painting drawn by eight hyperactive kids.

Deep into its descent our plane began vibrating. The runway crimped and the jungle shook. One hundred feet above ground, then fifty, then ten, and none of us could draw a breath. My anxiety was buffered by a single thought: Allie Kyle was expecting professional carpenters, and at best I'd brought Daffy, Tweety, and Pepé Le Pew.

The equatorial sun showed no mercy, even at 6:15 p.m. A sweaty Alexis departed the copilot's seat with two whoops and a fist pump. She pulled her black cap low on her head and grinned when I helped her down off the wing. Then she bounced on her toes and held me at arm's length. "I learned how to read the instrument panel, and the pilot even let me take the controls for three seconds. Didn't you feel that little dip and swerve? Well, guess what . . . that was me!"

I bounced on my own toes. "Oh yes, Lex. We felt it. Darcy and Quilla got dizzy, and Asbury nearly barfed up his beef jerky."

Coca's runway was surrounded by lush rainforest spilling across the perimeter fences. Above the jungle swooped incoming planes, all of them in bright, buglike colors, looking like giant mutations of Amazon flies.

Our team watched two landings before helping the pilot haul luggage off the plane and onto the tarmac. We roasted out there for fifteen minutes—Beatrice taking cover under a flowery umbrella—until a burgundy van pulled around the side of the terminal. The driver rolled her window down and honked the horn.

I had only seen Allie's picture once, when Jay showed it to me in language school, but there was no mistaking her. She looked lithe, tan, and glad to see us. Her brown hair flowed back beyond her shoulders, and she was dressed in classic jungle attire: thick beige shirt, full of pockets. She honked again, pushed open the van door, and smiled sheepishly. I'd never been great at reading expressions, but hers seemed to say "Thanks for coming to rebuild the huts that I burnt down while trying to cook spaghetti for orphans."

She jumped from the van and hugged Darcy first. Then she hugged every one of us, even Quilla and me, whom she'd never met. "Welcome to Ecuador, folks. Now who remembered to bring my dark chocolates?"

Quilla dug some from her backpack. "These are for eatin', not throwin'," she said. "Maurice told me all about you and food."

Steve and I tied the luggage to the roof of the van, then looked down to see Allie handing the van keys to Darcy. Steve winced. Allie took Darcy by the hands and said, "Well, friend, you've always said you wanted to drive through the jungle."

Despite the fearful thought of Darcy driving in this terrain, I was determined to work hard for seven days, restore the village, and get everyone safely back to South Carolina.

That was the plan, anyway.

# 29

Instead of seeing an Ecuadorian sunset, we saw trees and vines and plant life so thick that the rays had no access. Allie was navigating from the front passenger seat as Darcy drove unusually slow, steering us around potholes and washouts in the dirt road. Several times she either drove the van around them or crept through, one tire at a time.

"You have no idea how much I appreciate you two organizing this team," Allie said to me and Alexis. "Now, which ones are the carpenters?"

I glanced nervously at Alexis. "Um, Maurice can swing a hammer, and Steve can read a blueprint, and Quilla can ward off looters with her bat, and Asbury says really good prayers." My conscience scolded me as Darcy steered us through a curve of bad road. "Okay, we assembled a ragtag team after Alexis volunteered me at North Hills Prez."

After a moment of bumpy deliberation, Allie nodded her head as if she understood. "You do know that Jay wasn't qualified to be serving as a missionary. He was just . . . willing."

Alexis reached up and squeezed Allie on the arm. "That's all we brought, Allie. No carpenters, just wills. A broad assortment of wills."

Allie smiled at Lex, surveyed the team, and said, "They'll do just fine."

Deep into the journey Allie rolled down her window, and the incoming scents nearly knocked Beatrice from her seat. Filling the van was not the balmy tonic of the Carolina coast nor the ecosystem passing gas. This was something far more potent.

"Oh my," she said, sniffing the air from the third row. "Those aren't gardenias."

"Ain't no ocean either, Bea," said Quilla, who had decided some miles previous that Beatrice needed a nickname.

Darcy lowered her own window. The entrance to the jungle reeked from the moist dirt of a thousand regenerations. The smell was of growth overtaking decay, moss piggybacking tree trunks, and an ever-evolving zoo thriving without borders. Shadowy birds were its noisy gatekeepers, and surely a fugitive life-form could hide here and never be discovered.

We were still a long way from the village when Alexis leaned forward and whispered for Darcy to speed up. Maybe we could see the monkeys before dark.

It was the hour to debate headlights, and Darcy switched them on and off several times before leaving them on bright. Surrounded by foliage—the trees and plant life brushed the van on both sides—we tried to guess what Jay Jarvis would be doing when we arrived.

"He'll be asleep," Asbury said.

"He'll be making a carpentry schedule for all of us professionals," Darcy said.

Steve disagreed. "He'll be cleaning fish he caught in some river."

Quilla, who had never met Jay, offered a fourth opinion. "He'll be hiding all the matches from his girlfriend, uh-huh."

Allie smiled and shook her head. She knew Jay best, and she told us what he'd be doing—slicing bananas and mango and making us a salad.

Whatever he was doing, Jarvis was not waiting to greet us. We drove into a dark village, where a lone bamboo torch lit the five huts to our left, which someone had numbered 1 through 5. Down the right side were the remnants of disaster, a sprawling heap of black boards bulldozed into a pile. Stilts from three of the eight burned huts had survived, and new stilts protruded from the ground on the remaining plots, evidence that

282

someone, probably Jay, had been hard at work. Beyond the heap were stacks of new plywood and two-by-eights awaiting installation.

Darcy parked the van in the middle of the dirt road and left the lights shining. But there was no one milling about. Our arrival was suspended in a surreal moment—headlights beaming through the village and into banana trees, a black heap illumined to our right, the five remaining huts standing like privileged survivors to our left. "He's got to be around here somewhere," Allie said, peering through the windshield. "Honk for him, Darcy."

Darcy tooted the horn twice.

From behind the blackened heap came Jay, wearing jeans, sneakers, and a University of Texas T-shirt. He held a scorched oval of plywood and a hammer, which he waved at us. I would always believe that wave signaled more than just hello, perhaps his way of preparing us for what lay ahead.

Jay went over to one of the new stilts and nailed that plywood oval to the top. Though charred from the bottom up, some of the writing on it remained. Only the first of three stanzas was still legible:

> Sand dunes blown with heavenly breath
> Make for fleeting, aloof congregations.
> The hot winds are vocal, the sermon is swift
> And the grains do not wait for amen.

The rest was black crust.

Allie opened her door, looked back at us, and said, "I just hate it when I compose my own irony."

Jay turned around and waved us all out of the van. Hugs, handshakes, and an outdoor dinner followed. Beatrice even hugged Jay twice, like a long-lost grandchild. True to Allie's prediction, Jay had a salad waiting, and even some bread and cheese donated from the emergency shelter in Coca. Without unpacking, the team gathered around the one picnic table that had survived the blaze. We spent an hour eating by torchlight, drinking strange juices and getting reacquainted with old friends. The scent around us was no longer of rainforest, however—more like ashes and smoldering wood.

Allie and Darcy, at one end of the table, quickly moved on to old-friend topics. They were talking of the need for extended vacations and a trip they'd talked of but never taken. Allie said she craved a break, and Darcy dittoed her craving, saying surely a torching was reason enough to someday visit Australia. Opposite Allie, Jay was being swarmed by Asbury and Maurice, who asked him, with no restraint whatsoever, about jungle life, jungle food, and jungle romance. But all chitchat ceased when Allie pounded on the table and said we needed to introduce ourselves, just in case somebody didn't know somebody else. She motioned for Steve to start.

Steve cleared his throat. "My name is Steve Cole, I'm an engineer, and I'm Presbyterian."

In copycat fashion, the intros came quickly: "My name is Darcy Yeager, I work at an ad firm, would like to renovate a volunteer coffeehouse, and I'm usually Presbyterian."

"My name is Quilla Jones, I work in juvenile corrections, and I sing and play church softball for Pentecostal Holiness."

Alexis, who'd been unusually quiet for several minutes, seemed to wake up as her turn arrived. She blew her hair out of her eyes and stuck her chin in the air. "My name is Alexis Demoss, I sell real estate, serve in that coffeehouse with Darcy, and am undecided as to denomination."

I shouldered up to her and said, "My name is Neil Rucker, I teach Spanish in a language school for missionaries, have endured the wackiest furlough in the history of missions, and in Quito I belong to a nonde-nominational Bible church."

Beatrice adjusted her straw hat. "My name is Beatrice Dean, and . . . oh dear, I used to attend First Baptist. But then I did the scope and got fired by Presbyterians, so now I'm a gardener who needs a new project."

"My name is Asbury Smoak, I preach at Pawleys Island Baptist, and by the grace of God I co-captain an offshore fishing boat in Georgetown, South Carolina."

"My name is Maurice Evans, I'm an ex-janitor, a deacon in Smoak's church, and by the grace of God I'm co-captain of his boat." Maurice pointed a thumb at Asbury. "And I know more fishing spots than he does."

Asbury coughed loudly.

"My name is Allie Kyle, and I became a sinner, a Southerner, a Christian, and a missionary, in that order."

Jay put his arm around Allie and winked. "My name is Jay Jarvis, and I became a sinner, a Southerner, a stockbroker, a churchgoing girl-scoper, a Christian, and a missionary, in that order."

For a moment everyone looked approvingly at each other, nods dominoing around the picnic table. Then something furry bolted beneath hut No. 5.

Quilla jumped to her feet and pulled a flashlight from her purse. "I saw 'im, uh-huh. Who else saw that little varmint?"

I raised my hand. "I saw it, Quilla."

"Me too," Jay said.

"I'm glad I didn't see it," Darcy said, clutching her arms.

"I didn't see no varmint, Quilla," Maurice said.

Beatrice turned from her salad and pushed up the brim of her straw hat. "What color was the garment, dear? Was it a blouse?"

Alexis and Quilla, in their best snoop posture, tiptoed over to hut No. 5. Quilla shone her light back and forth over the steps. Lex stooped down to look under the hut. "Could have been a baby coyote," Alexis said.

"I see tracks," Quilla replied, shoulder to shoulder between the huts with my equally curious girlfriend. "Yep, little bitty varmint tracks. Looks like he was eatin' on that bad banana Asbury tossed out."

The Looneys had arrived in Ecuador. Quilla and Alexis searched for ten more minutes before showing signs of fatigue. Lex returned to the bench, snuggled up against me, and began speculating with the older women on the colors they'd see the next morning. Quilla expected surroundings like she'd seen in a Tarzan movie. Alexis just wanted to see the monkeys. Beatrice was the only one with classic taste. Candlelit, she swallowed a bite of salad and dabbed at her mouth. "I'm telling you young folks, it'll be like Van Gogh's greenhouse."

Tarzan or no, the reality of where we were had struck Steve the hardest.

He hadn't spoken since we departed the van, save for the introductions. He had been born and bred in Carolina and had never ventured outside the South. Wide-eyed, he kept looking around, silent, like he just could not get comfortable with where we were. I couldn't blame him. With the lack of amenities in this village, I wasn't at ease myself.

Near midnight the girls rose from the table, carrying their conversations toward the left side of the village, into huts No. 1 and No. 2. Allie, Darcy, and Alexis settled in No.1, Quilla and Beatrice in No. 2. The third hut, which had sea-green walls, offered only two single beds and a grass rug. Maurice and Asbury hauled their gear inside.

Since No. 5 was filled with tools and supplies, Jay, Steve, and I were left with hut No. 4, which, to my surprise, contained not beds but three hammocks, hung across the room and spanning wall to wall. I got the second one, with Jay to the back wall and Steve to the fore.

The moon rose to where a faint light shown through our lone screened window. Too pumped up to sleep just yet, we swayed in the hammocks and listened to the bugs conduct their high-pitched auditions. The volume was outrageous and, like everything else here, of Amazonian proportion.

Finally Steve cleared his throat and brought up "The Topic." "Okay, Jay, what's the status of things between you and Allie?"

Jay's hammock creaked in hesitation. "I'm not going first. You gotta tell me about you and Darcy. I mean, what a shocker to see you two holding hands when you climbed out of the van. I almost fell back in the rubble heap."

Steve wouldn't give in. "If you think Darcy and I are a shocker, wait till you hear what your former language teacher has been up to in Greenville . . . Go ahead, Neil. Tell 'im."

"I'm not tellin' anything."

"C'mon, Neil," Jay begged. "We won't go to sleep until everybody knows everybody else's business. You know the girls are already on chapter 19 of everybody's business."

"More like chapter 44," Steve said.

Just to get it over with, I blurted it all out. "Okay, the very one you warned me about, Alexis—we're a, um, a thing. She's the one who turned out to be the most spontaneous, who feeds milkshakes to the homeless and makes a mean she-crab soup. I knew I wanted someone who was compassionate; all the other stuff was the big surprise."

Jay let the news sink in for a moment. "Neil, Neil, Neil."

"What? You don't approve?"

"Miss Hopscotch herself?"

"Maybe she's repented."

Jay was struggling to accept that I would go for the very one he'd warned about. "When you stepped off the van, Neil, I thought you two were just friends. So it's you and . . . you and Alexis?"

"They kissed on the beach," Steve said.

Another pause. "Neil, Neil, Neil."

"We were having fun. Plus the waves were lapping against the pier and there were eighties lyrics carved in wet sand. It was . . . romantic."

"You kissed her on the shore? Don't tell me it happened on your first North Hills beach trip."

"Worse than that," Steve said. "It was on their first night."

"Goodness, Neil, that must've really been some great soup."

"Awe inspiring. Now, what about you and Allie?"

"Yeah," Steve said. "What about you and Allie?"

"We hold hands."

"Aw, here we go. Vague Jay."

"Okay, the first time I kissed her was way up in a bird tower. But only about once a week, when we hike out there and the sun is going down and she gets the . . . the feeling."

"The feeling," Steve said slowly, trying the phrase out for size. "I wish Darcy would get the feeling more often."

"She used to keep her feelings and romance invisible," Jay said. "No crow's nest rendezvous this year, I suppose."

"All that must have changed after Darcy broke up with him," I said, "because we all know that dating Steve is like water-skiing behind a canoe."

Steve's pillow jarred the side of my head. "It just took awhile for me to realize that Darcy and I have true feelings."

The moon had risen farther, and now its light cast ropey shadows across the wood flooring. I gripped both sides of my hammock and centered myself in its womb. "You been practicing the Spanish, Jay?"

"*Sí,*" he said. "You been talking to God on any rooftops lately, Neil?"

"Of course. Was on Steve's just last night."

"You were on my roof?" Steve asked. "How'd you even get up there?"

"Wasn't easy. And I didn't stay long. Lots of bird poop on your roof."

"Okay, guys," Jay said. "What's everybody been talking to God about?"

His question rang of a growing maturity, and it caused us all to sway quietly in our hammocks before offering any answers.

Steve spoke first. "Mostly Darcy, struggles with my thought life, and if I want to be an engineer for thirty more years."

"Mostly Alexis, and if I'm qualified to be leading this mission trip."

Jay swayed awhile longer. "Mostly Allie, adopting an orphan, and if I'll spend the rest of my adulthood in Ecuador."

We chewed on each other's responses for several minutes as the bugs continued their one-note serenade. Swaying inside hut No. 4 in a remote, Ecuadorian village, we were just three guys with three different futures and three very different girlfriends. Despite the variables, my guess was that we all had the same basic fears and the same basic hopes. We wanted the companionship and the intimacy and the soul mate—and we were scared of messing it all up. The bachelors were silently calculating the future, lost in the algebra of relationship. Perhaps a week in the jungle would bring clarity . . . if the jungle didn't eat us, that is.

I considered my surroundings—huts without showers, a road without pavement, and a rainforest without a zookeeper—and wondered if all these city people could complete this project. Out of sheer overconfidence I'd promised Elder Kyle that we would get the work done, although I could not remember the last time I'd used a power tool.

It was nearly 1:00 a.m. when Steve stirred in his hammock. "Jay?"

"Huh?"

"Neil's girlfriend is reading Song of Solomon. I heard her talking about it in church."

Jay's hammock creaked its disappointment. "Neil, Neil, Neil."

# 30

The pounding of a hammer woke me. I rolled over in my hammock and reached into my pants pocket for my watch. Then I peered through the screen of my hut and saw that Maurice was on the job at 6:50 a.m., already nailing joists between the stilts. Beside him, in a camouflage shirt, Asbury picked through drill bits to find the proper size. I was embarrassed that the old guys had beaten us to the site, and I scrambled out of the hammock to wake my roommates. Jay was already gone, so I thumped Steve on the foot and opened the door to a green and humid Amazon morning.

Jay and Allie were preparing breakfast together at the picnic table, he slicing bread and bananas, she pouring a red juice into plastic cups. Alexis wandered out from her hut, yawning as she admired the surroundings. I walked past the smoldering bamboo torch as she bent down to tie her shoes. "Late night?" I asked.

"Four hours of sleep," she said. "Allie kept us up till 3:00 a.m., talking and throwing marshmallows. And you guys talked about us girls, right?"

I pulled her to her feet, and we turned toward the food. "Oh, we'd never do that."

Breakfast was hurried but filling. We drank the red juice and made faces at its tartness. Then Alexis left to brush her teeth in Allie's bathroom among the trees, the designated jungle spot for females, as our hosts referred to it.

It was only 7:30, but Jay had beach music playing on an old boom-box, and the village was awash in production. Both Steve and Asbury had brought drills and cordless screwdrivers, and in the whir of their efficiency the first boards were affixed to stilts and screwed into place. Inept at handling power tools, Quilla and I were demoted to the role of helpers—carrying boards to the whirring affixers.

Quilla was a strong woman, and despite her flamboyance she was determined to make a contribution. "Hurry up, Fish Stick," she said, toting another board toward Asbury. "At your pace we'll only get one hut built this entire week."

Someone had to be designated as foreman, so after Jay called a brief halt to the work, we took a vote. The unanimous choice was Maurice, who was inside the frame of No. 7, pounding nails into plywood at a machine-gun pace.

The village looked like a rural version of the haves and have-nots—the prospering left side boasting huts 1 through 5 and ending at a thick stand of banana trees, the disastrous right side longer and tightly spaced, eight clusters of stilts looking hatless and incomplete. Maurice and crew had begun near the village entrance, at huts Nos. 6 and 7, and I envisioned lots of sweat and blackened thumbnails before we reached No. 13.

Alexis returned with sparkling teeth, and after helping Quilla and me for a while, she walked back across the village and began knocking on the door to Darcy's hut. Shortly before 9:00 a.m., both Darcy and Beatrice managed to make their appearance from the Hotel Ecuador—but not to do construction. The two of them spent twenty minutes wandering the perimeter of the village. Hands on hips, straw hat on head, Beatrice stared in awe at the size and scope of the surrounding flora, cocking her head to the side as if stunned by the abundance. Darcy followed her like a tall apprentice, saying she'd never seen anything like this on the cover of *Southern Living*. She waited for Steve to stop drilling and yelled across the dirt road. "Don't you think this yellow-and-red plant would look good in my apartment?"

Steve paused from the construction. "I think it would eat your apartment."

Darcy smiled at him, then recoiled at a voice shouting from the trees. Alexis and her adrenaline had discovered a patch of wild plants out beyond the designated spot for females. Beatrice immediately summoned Darcy to begin the landscaping phase of village renovation.

Darcy took her by the arm. "It might be the mother lode, Mrs. Dean."

"Call me Beatrice," she said, shuffling along. "And if there's even a hint of brown on the petals, we must reject it. Did you hear me, dear? Not even a hint of brown."

The duo marched off together behind hut No. 2, trowels in hand, intent on digging up and transferring the most exotic plants Ecuador had to offer.

Allie proved to be a gracious and appreciative hostess. She brought us drinks at regular intervals but mostly remained at the picnic table, planning lessons for the orphans and trying to remember her burnt poetry. At her request Asbury had used Jay's saw to cut eight small squares of plywood, on which she wrote with a red marker. She was adamant about getting the village back the way it was, down to the poems and verses she had crafted for each hut. What surprised me about Allie was that she—the cause of the blaze—seemed to have recovered so quickly from her guilt.

While lifting another sheet of plywood with Jay, I shared my observation about his girlfriend. We had the sheet overhead, walking in its shadow, when he said, "Neil, that girl surprises me every day."

Our team had divided the duties among itself well: The preacher, Maurice, Jay, Quilla, Steve, Alexis, and I were rebuilding the huts; Darcy and Beatrice were landscaping; and Allie remained in charge of hospitality, medical attention, and recollecting burnt poetry. No one was complaining, so I lifted another two-by-eight and deemed us all to be in harmony.

Harmony lasted about another ten minutes.

A scream curled the leaves of the banana trees. It wasn't a Spanish scream, nor was it native. This was definitely a Southern-girl scream. Jay and I dropped a sheet of plywood beside hut No. 6 and hustled across the village and into the undergrowth. We found Darcy scared pale, shaking in the shade of the jungle, afraid to move backward or forward. She pointed beyond a moss-covered log. "I came back here to get another one of those wild plants like Beatrice told me and, and . . . it slithered across my sneaker." She pointed again, her hand trembling.

I picked up a stick and poked behind the log. Nothing moved.

Jay kicked the log and got a similar result. "It was just passing through," he said.

Lex and Beatrice closed in behind us, peeking through low-hanging limbs.

"But it . . . it slithered across my sneaker!" Darcy repeated. She glared at the log as if no snake had the right to slither without at least a week's notice.

Jay patted her on the back. "Lots of critters pass through the village, Darcy. Very few have a taste for blondes."

Still annoyed by the snake, Darcy stepped gingerly through the foliage as we escorted her back to Landscape Central. "It was big, Neil," she said, spreading her hands wide.

"I'm sure it was."

"I mean it was really, really big."

"Of course."

Calmer now, Darcy grabbed a hammer and spent an hour nailing plywood with Alexis, the two of them talking about how it was good practice for renovating the coffeehouse.

Beatrice, lost again in her floral world, just kept planting colorful stalks of wildness around the circumference of the village. On her knees one minute, she'd step back the next to get the grand view. "Neil," she shouted, using her trowel to swat a fly. "God has given me a second chance at Tribes of Many Nations, and I'm not going to let him down."

Lex saw me toting another two-by-eight to Asbury, and I could sense what was coming. She wiped the sweat from her brow and narrowed her eyes at me. "Neily, all I've seen you do is tote boards. Why won't the men let you use the power tools?"

"Just hammer your nails, Lex," I replied, pointing at the wall she and Darcy were erecting.

"But O Great Team Leader is such a handsome board-toter."

I knew she was kidding. But I also knew that even on the first morning of this mission, God was beginning to reveal a truth about my abilities. I could take an English phrase and make it Spanish, and I could take a Spanish phrase and make it English, but I could not seem to take a power tool and drill four evenly spaced holes. Now that construction had commenced, I didn't feel much like a team leader. But I didn't really care—it was enough just to be a part of this clan, never mind the titles.

At noon Jay called another halt to the work, explaining that our seven-day schedule would proceed according to a plan he called Five-Four-Three. We were to work the five hours until noon, take four off to eat and nap and roam the jungle, then work three more in the cooler hours of late afternoon. No one objected, especially Maurice and Asbury, who had discovered a pair of old fishing rods in the supply hut. Jay knew a shortcut to the Rio Napo, and before I knew it the three of them had walked off without inviting anyone else. Behind the stilts of hut No. 12 I saw Jay pull back a limb and point Maurice down a path. The preacher followed, both rods bouncing on his shoulder as he whistled a tune.

*Discovery*, it seemed, had become the operative word for our first day—as the fishermen left, Beatrice and Quilla discovered that Allie knew of an observation tower out in the jungle, built by bird-watchers. They insisted on seeing that tower. So at 12:30 the three of them strolled out of the village and down the dirt road and disappeared into the rainforest.

Not to be outdone, Alexis shared her own discovery—during a morning trek to uproot outrageous flora, she'd found a path behind the banana trees. Gathered around the picnic table, she, Darcy, Steve, and I drank from a water cooler while Lex explained. "Y'all, on this path there's a little wooden sign about knee-high that says PERU: 61 MILES."

"And . . . ?" I asked, knowing she likely had another wild idea brewing.

"And I say we walk it for a couple hours and look for Inca ruins."

"But sixty-one miles would take us four days," Steve said, ever the calculating engineer.

Darcy held up both hands like a cop. "Hold it, gang. The only way I'll go hiking a jungle is if I get to walk in the middle. I'm not going first, and I'm definitely not gonna be the caboose."

"Choo choo," Alexis said, motioning for Darcy to follow her. "Now let's get changed into hiking clothes."

They ran to their hut as Steve and I looked at each other in confusion. "Hiking clothes?" he asked, pouring water on his head, "Why can't they just wear what they have on?"

"Beats me."

Within minutes Darcy and Alexis returned in jeans—jeans were a command from our hosts, given the potency of the insects—and T-shirts. Darcy wore a lime-green "I Love Litchfield Beach" tee, and Alexis donned her pink Bahamas tee, declaring that the color and the adventure would make this a double date to remember.

I grabbed Alexis by the hand, and we led Steve and Darcy through the banana trees and onto the path. Sparkling domes of greenery shaded the forest floor, and birds we could neither see nor name cackled from above. The smell was of rainwater and fresh vegetation, of wild mangos so plentiful that a sneeze would fill your basket. I had double-dated in movie theaters, restaurants, and even once at the Virginia State Fair, but I'd never double-dated in a rainforest.

Shortly we came upon the sign, which was weathered and crudely made. Upon second glance Steve pointed out that it read PERU: 61 KILO-METERS, not miles.

Miles to kilometers . . . there was a percentage to apply here, although that too was not taught in language school.

The jungle tried its best to give warning. For the fifth time in a minute I pulled a stubborn vine out of the way and handed it back.

"Neil?" Alexis asked, tugging me along.

"Yeah?"

"Somehow I don't think we're going to find any eighties lyrics scrawled out here."

The path narrowed to where we had to walk single file. Alexis insisted on going first, so I followed behind, Darcy third, Steve the caboose. We stumbled on roots and jerked our ankles through ground cover. Blue-winged flies teased our faces. Soon the path curved left around a rotting stump, where Alexis stopped, gasped, held a hand to her mouth. At shoulder height between two limbs, an orange-and-white spider with an extra hump on its body lay suspended in its web. In the filtered light of the jungle, the spider nearly glowed.

"Is it pregnant?" Steve asked.

"I think it has a tumor," Lex said, leaning closer.

Darcy made the icky face and called it the humpback-camel spider.

I declared it female and speculated she'd just eaten the male, thus the hump. Mired in disagreement, we moved on, tromping along in silence until Steve announced that the rainforest was just one humongous salad.

From rooftops I'd seen many profiles in cloud cover, but a jungle presented a whole new assortment of mind tricks. I saw warriors, green Martians, even pygmies. Steve knew what I was thinking. "There are faces in these trees," he muttered.

Darcy stopped and peered above. "Please tell me they're nice faces." For extra precaution, she began stepping in my footprints.

"We're getting closer," Alexis said, lifting her nose to the sky. "I can smell the Inca ruins." But she was the only one talking. Along with the mile-to-kilometer computation, fear had entered the equation. Without a guide to lead us, what had begun as a normal single-file hike had become a squished-together, hand-on-back, single-file hike. We might as well have been exploring a haunted house.

In contrast, I imagined Maurice and Asbury being instructed by Jay to "step here, don't step there," as he led them to the Rio Napo. I imagined Allie expertly leading Quilla and Beatrice down the dirt road, into the jungle, and safely up to the bird tower. But we, the footloose foursome, had unwittingly begun playing Road Trip again, only this time without letters. Instead of lazy Earl, there were oblong spiders. Instead of red tomato juice in brown paper bags, there was brown goo on red porous mushrooms. And instead of detouring into the sleepy town of Pomaria, we were hiking unescorted toward the wilds of Peru. I trudged on and hoped the others weren't thinking as I was—that if we turned around we'd discover that our path had vanished, dreamlike.

Alexis urged us to continue our hot and shaded hiking, and we did—until we came upon a second weathered sign: PERU: 57 KILOMETERS.

"Anyone bring a compass?" I asked, my hand on Alexis's back.

"I brought a whistle," Darcy said, still gripping my shirt.

"I brought a pack of Asbury's beef jerky," Steve added.

I had my harmonica, but I wasn't about to play—might provoke the faces in the trees.

Alexis stopped, turned in the path, and licked her left index finger. She held the moistened digit in the air. "East," she said, resuming our trek. "We're definitely heading east."

How Alexis talked Darcy into walking up front with her was, like all things concerning Alexis, just a blur. But hand-on-back and urging each other along, Pink and Lime led Logic and Spanish along an ever-narrowing path.

Steve and I decided to lag behind the girls and speculate on how the fishermen were doing. "No telling what swims in that river," Steve said.

I kicked the head off a red mushroom. "Asbury might have a pot of crocodile gumbo stewing when we get back."

Steve spotted a second shroom and booted it soccer-style. "Or Jay and Maurice are making catfish perlot."

That sounded interesting. "What all goes into catfish—"

The shrill of Darcy's whistle startled even the birds.

She and Lex quickly backpedaled toward Steve and me, stopping right on top of our feet.

Shaking, Darcy pulled Alexis to her side and pointed. "Y'all, it's . . . enormous." In a marvelous display of voice inflection, Darcy had managed to accentuate all three syllables.

I rushed around them to see the culprit. Steve was right behind me. Ten feet ahead of us a slick, green-and-gray body slithered across the path, its skin stretching and recoiling like a train of never-ending boxcars. We stared open-mouthed as lengths of sleek belly glided over loose dirt, the front and rear hidden within a leafy undergrowth.

Darcy burst into full retreat. She ran toward the village and blew her whistle, yelling "Allie, help!" between blasts. Her long legs produced quite a stride, and we struggled to keep up. Back past the sign that read PERU: 57

KILOMETERS, Steve caught Darcy by the shoulders and told her that jungle snakes never eat people over five feet tall.

"He's right, Darce," Alexis said, hands on hips and breathing hard. "I read that in *National Geographic*."

We settled into a brisk walk, and though I didn't tell anyone for fear of creating panic, I knew a boa constrictor when I saw one.

When we arrived back in the village, a lone figure was fitting a piece of plywood onto hut No. 8. The upturned mustache, the cowboy shirt, and the trademark pointy-toed boots were all there. He had not changed in the two and a half years since we'd worked together in the soup kitchen in Mexico City. José Cepeda, my mentor since I'd been on the mission field, had shown up after all. Beside him on the ground lay a suitcase and a sack of fruit.

I nearly tripped as I ran across the dirt road to greet him. "Two and a half years," I said, bear-hugging him first then shaking his hand. "And new boots too."

He released my hand and pointed at the others, who were walking over to meet this stranger. "Ah, young Neil. Look at you, working hard in the jungle for your God. You have made many friends in Carolina, yes?"

I waved the others over. "More than you know. Most of 'em are still out wandering the jungle."

After introductions and cold drinks, we spotted Allie and Quilla and Beatrice strolling up the dirt road, which led to more introductions. Then everyone commenced to hammering and sawing and replanting. Even Allie grabbed a hammer. I imagined that most jungle missionaries, by necessity, were jacks-of-all-trades.

A while later she and Alexis dragged the water cooler over near hut No. 9, where they were attempting a girls-only framing with Darcy. "I forgot to warn y'all about something," said Allie, filling her cup. "There's a path out beyond those banana trees, and on it are signs that reference Peru. Now don't go down that path, 'cause it's full of snakes and the reason I know this is because Jay and I put the signs out as a joke and we've marked it all the way to 44 kilometers but have no idea where the path leads." She

297

washed down her warning with a gulp of water and set her cup on the ground. "So, what was that whistle I heard earlier?"

"It was me," Darcy said, without looking up from her hammering, "greeting another critter passing through suburbia."

Jay and the co-captains did not walk but positively sauntered back into the village. A sweaty Maurice held up a stringer of fish, Asbury and Jay grinned, and applause broke from the work site.

Asbury let Jay and Maurice tend to fish cleaning and assisted me in lifting a pair of two-by-eights. We attached the boards across the stilts in an X, and Steve proved efficient with his power drill.

Progress was slow, however, and even after Jay and Maurice had cleaned the fish and I had made a third round of introductions to José, I could tell we would be hard-pressed to finish our project in one week. This was in contrast to Beatrice, who had already bordered three of the surviving huts with the rainforest's tallest and most exuberant flowers.

Our most efficient worker might have been José, who teamed with Steve and me in building the steps. We had one side of a board notched when he paused and flicked sawdust from his mustache. "Young Neil, perhaps your team would consider a work week in Mexico City. We have many needs."

*The Looney Tunes in Mexico City?* I nodded hesitantly, wondering if he was serious.

We were finishing a second set of steps when he paused again and tapped my foot with his hammer. "Before the week ends, Neil and José will have a talk, no?"

It had been this way ever since I'd known him; no visit was complete without some offering of wisdom. "Yeah, sure José. And this talk will involve me and a girl, right?"

José smiled and went back to work.

Near quitting time a red macaw appeared atop hut No. 3. It watched us work across the dirt road and looked surprised by all the commotion. Jay hoisted another board over his shoulder and told us he'd given the bird a name. He called it "Officer." A drenched and grimy Steve paused from his hammering and asked Jay why anyone would name a macaw Officer.

"He rules this dirt road," Jay said. "His full name is Officer Theologian, named after a South Carolina patrolman who knew what kind of car Jesus would drive."

I dropped a board at my feet and looked at Jay in disbelief. "You have got to be kidding me."

Jay pointed at the macaw. "Me'n Allie trained the bird. Throw him a berry, and he'll say, 'Lincoln, Lincoln.'"

Steve laughed so hard he missed the nail on his next three attempts.

Ecuador's setting sun not only bathed the village in soft orange light, it caressed the leaves, massaged the bananas, and deposited to all a promise—that whoever survived until tomorrow would get to do it all over again. For José, this promise included a well-deserved nap. For Steve and myself, this promise included another cold shower in the wooden structure behind hut No. 5, the designated jungle bath for males. Hot water remained very much like Peru—known to exist but not within walking distance. I was addicted to hot showers, and their absence quelled my desire for long-term jungle missions.

"This soap Jay gave us feels like compressed whale blubber," said Steve, who had beaten me to the shower.

I leaned against the outer wall, a towel draping on my shoulder. "Then please save Uncle Neil some blubber."

Before the team gathered for dinner, I walked cleaner and fresher to the site of the former kitchen and joined Preacher Smoak in grilling the fish. Jay had built the grill out of river stones. The stones were stacked hip-high in a crude circle, a caveman grill fashioned of necessity after Allie had torched the kitchen while trying to cook spaghetti for orphans.

Asbury set another filet above the flames. "Don't even ask what they are, Neil. We're just assuming they're edible."

I borrowed his spatula and poked at the filets. "Didn't Jay tell you which fish were okay to eat?"

"Jay approved the brown ones. The ones with the gold scales he wasn't sure about. But I sampled a piece 'fore you got here, and I haven't felt any pain yet."

I almost asked him to shape my filet like a flounder, but I didn't want to be accused of harassing the clergy.

Dusk seeped into the village and across the picnic table, and after everyone was seated, Quilla asked the blessing. It was a powerful blessing, one in which her substance, her volume, and her parallel construction lifted everyone into the light of grace, the scent of grace, and the presence of grace. When I opened my eyes I noticed the blisters on my hands. My skin was telling me, with no grace whatsoever, that it preferred me in language school.

After the last piece of fish was consumed, Allie stood and announced that we needed a few minutes of story time. Silhouetted by torchlight, she banged her spoon on the table. "Truth matters not out here in our village, and facts are relative. Now, who has a story?"

Everyone looked at everyone else. Then José rubbed his chin, as if he did not know quite what to think of all this.

"The fishermen have a story," Maurice said. Jay and Asbury nodded, as if they knew what was coming.

Maurice took a last sip of red juice then looked at each person to make sure he had total attention. "Okay, all right. After we'd caught enough fish to feed y'all dinner, Asbury cast one bait way out into the Rio Napo. How far, you ask? Waaay far. Logs were floatin' in the river, and when Asbury saw an odd ripple beyond a log, he tugged his bait to lure the fish. The fish bit hard, so hard that not only did the fish pull the cork under, but it swam under one of the floating logs then jumped back over the log twice, so the line would loop around and get tangled."

Quilla waved her hands to interrupt. "And I bet the fish swam to the east, didn't it, Maurice?"

"It did," Maurice said. "Now tell the team why it swam east."

Quilla turned to her audience. "Because only the great white shark goes to the west. It's a quirk of nature, uh-huh."

"That's right," Maurice said. "The fish went east, up the river and against the current, towin' both the log and the line off the preacher's reel. Asbury handed the rod to Jay, who gritted his teeth and sunk ankle-deep in black mud. Then Asbury went running up the bank of the river to get ahead of the fish that was swimmin' upstream and towin' the log. The preacher climbed out on the limb of a tree, and when the fish swam by with the log in tow, he—"

"Wait a minute," Allie said. "What were you doing during all of this, Maurice?"

"Recording details for the story. Now listen up. The fish was towin' the log, and Jay was now knee-deep in the river, tugging on the rod as hard as he could. Ten feet above the river, Asbury shimmied out on the limb, where poisonous lizards with purple eyes were sneaking up toward his leg. The fish came swimmin' upstream, and just before the lizards got to Asbury he jumped from the limb with perfect timing. He cleared the log, splashed down, and grabbed the fish around the neck. The preacher had that fish in a calf-ropin' hold, and the tail was whoppin' him in the back like wet leather. Then with his other arm Asbury grabbed the log and told Jay to crank on the reel. The fish pulled Asbury underwater three times, but each time he surfaced he'd catch a breath and grab the log. Jay used all his muscle to pull the fish, the log, and Asbury to the muddy bank. The fish then tried to bite Asbury, but Asbury subdued it with both hands. It was a one-hundred-forty-pound Venezuelan carp. Jay said a Venezuelan carp tastes like grilled licorice, so for your benefit we let the fish go. But not before it clamped down on Asbury's hand. The preacher even has the swollen thumb to prove it."

Asbury held his right thumb up near the torchlight, and everyone leaned in to look, led by Quilla. "Uh-huh, that's a carp bite."

"Oh dear," Beatrice said. "Remind me not to wash my bloomers in that river."

"That's not from a fish," Alexis said. "That's where you hit your thumb with the hammer."

The preacher winked at Allie. "Facts are relative."

Maurice folded his arms in satisfaction. "Next story," he said, pointing at Darcy.

Darcy shook her head and pointed at Steve, who shook his head and pointed at Jay, who said he could never keep up with Maurice in anything involving words.

Finally José raised his hand. "José has no story, but in Mexico the carp is said to taste like grilled whitewall tire. We feed it to cats."

In this jovial moment, among the camaraderie and the remote setting, I saw not just teammates but perhaps the makings of family, a clan with whom I could envision spending future furloughs. I even considered the possibility of not returning to language school but looking for a job teaching Spanish in South Carolina. But laughter shook me from reflection, and I looked around and smiled at everyone like I was totally in the moment . . . just like Alexis, who really *was* in the moment, high-fiving José and giggling at the moon.

Soon levity had faded into the night air, and Beatrice yawned and tipped up the brim of her straw hat. "Now, I don't dispute the Venezuelan harp, but it's time for ol' Beatrice to go to bed. I just want y'all to know that today Allie and Quilla and I almost bungee-jumped off the observation tower. But the views were grand so we wrote ourselves a poem instead."

"Uh-huh," Quilla said. "Guess y'all have to hike out there by your own selves and climb up and see what we wrote. Ain't that right, A.K.?"

"Indeed," Allie said. "And Quilla named the poem herself. Tell them the name, Quilla."

Quilla sat up straight and spoke to the heavens. "Diverse Women 237 Steps above a Rainforest."

Beatrice said, "That's a lovely name, Q. It would make a grand name for a flower."

"Shaw 'nuff."

Allie smiled. "Uh-huh."

# 31

On the fourth day of rebuilding, the team switched scenery during jungle exploration hour. The tug of leisure was strong, and as Jay had told me at breakfast, out here time came with hand brakes, and urgencies arrived with rubber bumpers . . . except, of course, for fires.

Darcy, Steve, José, Alexis, and I went to the river but caught not a single fish. Quilla and Allie took Beatrice to get pictures taken in front of the sign that read PERU: 61 KILOMETERS. And Asbury, Jay, and Maurice hiked out to the bird tower before returning to confirm that something impressive awaited all visitors.

While opening a new box of nails I wondered how ol' Stanley would have behaved on this trip. Maybe he'd have set a ten-minute limit on hikes and fishing trips. Who knew, but such limits might have been a good idea—the week was moving quickly and we had only three of the eight huts walled and floored.

By now everyone was dealing with small cuts, banged thumbs, splinters, and the equatorial heat that seemed to melt the accent from your voice. Beatrice and Quilla soon complained of bad backs and agreed that a nap would be nice. The two of them ambled into hut No. 4 to doze in the hammocks.

In a gray T-shirt, shorts, and black shades, Alexis returned from the designated outdoor bath for females, making a hammering motion as she saw me measuring boards. Together we managed to climb up and nail one sheet of plywood to an A-frame roof, even though the walls were still just two-by-fours. Completing a hut, however, was not our main goal. Man and woman had made shade.

Beside partially roofed hut No. 8, we played cards in the cool of angled shadows before tiring of our game and deciding to draw a map of South America in brown dirt. She etched the shapes of Brazil and Peru; I added Chile and Argentina. While etching, I thought back to the rooftop in Quito, when I'd reminded God that he'd said it was not good for man to be alone. I had forgotten to say thanks.

I was admiring our earthen map when I remembered that we'd left off Uruguay. Alexis cared nothing for learning the whereabouts of Uruguay; she was already tamping dirt clods with a hammer. She scooped a handful of grains and sprinkled them on my foot. "Neil, just for the memory, can we please kiss just once while we're in Ecuador? It's almost like we've adopted a no-kissing rule."

I reached for her hand and rubbed her fingers. "Smooching on a Presbyterian mission trip . . . yeah, this'll be one for the memory bank."

She scooted closer. "But why the worried look?"

"I was just wondering how many countries you've kissed a man in."

"Only the U.S. and—" She leaned forward and pecked me right on the lips. "And here."

"I'm very flattered."

"You should be," she said, pulling away to lean back against a stilt. "But then, I should admit that I've kissed boys in North Carolina, Georgia, and, oh lemme see . . . New York."

"New York too?"

"It was a drama team field trip in junior high."

"Oh. So you kissed Peter Pan?"

"It was the week before I tripped him. That pretty much ended things."

These were our first moments alone since we'd arrived, and we held each other's gaze for longer than we had at the beach. Behind her I heard Jay and Allie giggling over something he'd written. Jay was lending his expertise to Allie's recollection of burnt poetry, and at the picnic table they were half-working, half-snuggling.

Then, in matching olive tees, Steve and Darcy went walking off hand in hand, down the dirt road and past the banana trees. They were strolling in the middle of the road, however, avoiding the lush edges as they would an electric fence.

And I thought we were only here to build huts.

The next morning Allie hopped in the van, drove herself solo to Coca, and returned at noon with Isabel, the village's recovering fire victim. They stepped from the van, and I saw a thick bandage covering the little girl's left forearm.

Tentatively Allie walked her past the picnic table and into the middle of the village. Darcy and Alexis had just returned with a handful of exotic plants, and they dropped them on the ground and rushed over to greet Isabel. At first the little girl turned her head from strangers. Then she refused to look at the rubble heap. In the middle of the dirt road she hugged Allie's leg and said, "No."

After a quick tour of the landscaping, Allie pointed Isabel to Maurice and Steve hammering away. They looked up and waved, but again the little girl turned and said, "No."

This happened five more times—Isabel could not look at her former place of residence. The accident was too recent, too visceral. After holding her for a long while, Allie tried to get her to walk over to greet Jay and me, who were working on hut No. 9 with Asbury. "Isabel needs to be reacquainted with the site of the disaster," Allie said, rubbing the child's back. "She needs to witness the rebuilding, see new boards replacing old. But mostly she needs to experience the sight of helpers sent by God."

Again Allie pointed the girl to our work site. Again Isabel turned away.

"I have an idea," Jay said. He handed his drill to Asbury and went over and took Isabel by the hand. He walked her away from the construction and over to the front of hut No. 3, to where her back was turned to the disaster. He pointed to the roof. The red macaw peered down at them.

With her good arm, Isabel waved at the bird. Jay led her around the hut, and they returned to the front with a wild berry. Jay tossed it underhanded, and Officer snatched it in its beak.

"Lincoln, Lincoln," it squawked.

Isabel was bouncing in her sneakers, like she wanted to jump.

"I shoulda thought of that strategy," Allie said, smiling her approval at Jay.

The three of them strolled quietly around the village, Allie pointing at familiar objects and doing her best to reacquaint the girl, and Jay stroking Isabel's hair and reciting bad Spanish platitudes. After a while they all three went walking out of the village, hand in hand, Allie giving the child a run-on narration of how all the strangers came down from South Carolina. Down the dirt road they walked, out toward the general direction of the bird tower.

For a moment I stood on the remaining stack of plywood and watched the three of them growing smaller with each step. In a kind of Ecuadorian mirage I didn't see Jay with Allie and Isabel, but me with Alexis and a little girl with lighter skin, darker hair, and lots of energy. It could have been the heat, but the mirage soon faded into still another couple, this one Steve and Darcy; their child was tall, blonde, and very independent, even for a six-year-old.

That's when Quilla hit me in the butt with a rock. "Stop your daydreamin', Fish Stick. We ain't even halfway done."

I had no idea where my thoughts had originated. In fact, such blissful ponderings scared me so bad that I went into overdrive and started working harder than I had all week. José and Asbury even shooed me away from hut No. 10, saying that I'd brought more sheets of plywood than they could handle.

In all of our busyness—between the child's emotions, the construction, and my domesticated thoughts of someday—only Darcy noticed that Landscape Central was missing a member. She rose from a row of yellow flora and called Beatrice by name.

The first echo was barely noticed, and everyone continued working.

Darcy called out again, and again the jungle echoed.

With my head between the frame of hut No. 9, I yelled across the road to Alexis, who was on her knees and packing dirt around a sidewalk of river rocks. "Lex, where did she wander off to?"

Alexis stood with hands on hips and looked around. Loudly, she called Beatrice's name four times. Darcy hurried behind the supply hut, where they'd been digging just minutes earlier. She came around the other side, arms in the air, the give-up signal.

Then Alexis ran into hut No. 2 but came out shaking her head at me. "I thought she might be taking a nap," she said, worry creeping into her face.

I fought pessimism by picturing Beatrice wandering off to pluck some rare species from its habitat, intent on dragging it back for everyone to see and simply losing her way.

Everything was oddly quiet. Steve's drill whirred to a stop. Quilla dropped a board. Asbury and José tossed their hammers aside. It seemed all creatures had scurried to their safest habitat, and even the birds had stopped cackling.

In that instant, that breathless, where-is-Beatrice instant, the air felt both hot and cold, electric and tingly. My arm hairs stood up. "Nobody panic," I said, as much for myself as the others. "Let's cover the perimeter of the village and keep calling her name."

All eight of us fanned out around the village, checking behind the huts, under the huts, inside the huts. After ten minutes of searching, no one had found Beatrice.

Faces turned pale. No one would look anyone else in the eye.

I hopped up on the picnic table and shouted Beatrice's name. The jungle echoed, but it was only an echo. One by one, the others gathered around, speculating. I fought the impulse to blame Alexis for not watching Beatrice more closely.

I yelled again, and this time the echo came back trembling. Around me Alexis, Darcy, and Steve exchanged nervous glances. Clockwise I turned, silently praying that God would let Beatrice walk out of the jungle and back into the village. Then, from behind the new huts came Asbury and Quilla and José, palms up and shaking their heads.

I stepped down and met my girlfriend's gaze. Pure fear stared back. I took her by the hand. "It'll be all right, Lex. We'll find her."

"But what if . . . what if . . ."

My legs went wobbly as I turned toward a crashing noise through the banana trees. Maurice was pushing through the greenery, carrying Beatrice in his arms. Her legs dangled limply over his right forearm, and her head bobbed only to his footsteps.

Alexis grabbed me about the waist. "Neil, please tell me that she's . . ." Her voice faded into a bog of unspoken possibilities. She grew uncommonly still.

Maurice continued toward us, but Darcy couldn't look. She hid behind Steve, who, like the rest of us, could only stare in disbelief. I glanced once at Asbury and Quilla and José, who all stood zombielike in the dirt.

Quilla began mumbling a prayer. "Sweet Jesus, if there be any way . . ." But her voice trailed off as I pried loose from Alexis and took a step toward Maurice. Then I froze, unable to go any farther. I was afraid to face the truth. We all were—Lex in her stillness, Darcy in her slide for cover, Steve unable to summon logic into the unfolding reality.

Maurice had his head down as he brought Beatrice closer. Though his hat shielded his face, his body language spoke of fear.

I hurried to the shaded picnic table with José, and we swept it clean of cups and paper plates. I motioned for Maurice to set Beatrice down. But he held her there and shook back his hat. His raised eyebrows and sweat-drenched face contained any number of possible interpretations.

"Too close," he said slowly. "Way too close."

Lex buried her face in my sleeve, and Darcy tried peeking between the shoulders of Steve and José.

I had never given much appreciation or thought to the tiny muscles that open and close the human eye. So when Beatrice opened her wrinkled, jittery left eye, I praised God for the finesse of his creation.

Alexis pinched my arm and grinned. "She's breathing, Neily."

"Oh, Bea, you still with us," Quilla shouted, shaking her hands toward blue skies. She broke into some sort of charismatic dance, and in the process reached over and tried to get Asbury to join her. He nearly fell down at his first step and quickly retreated to being a Baptist.

Maurice stepped forward and set Beatrice on the bench. Her right eye jittered and opened, and she squinted around at all the faces leaning over the table. Her gaze swept past Darcy and tried to land on Quilla's bouncing hair beads. "Oh my, I thought the pygmies had got me, but Maurice tells me it was only the heat." She turned her head to glance at her gardening project. "Now, which one of you dears will get an old lady some water? I have work to do."

There was no more construction on our fifth day. No more landscaping either, just lots of whispers and time alone in hammocks. The young girl had humbled us, and the elderly woman had scared us into reflection. Asbury and the women tended to Beatrice, who lay in her bed in hut No. 2, fanning herself with a paper plate and sipping red juice. I was in the doorway when she asked for a chunk of Asbury's beef jerky, but he told her to wait a day and to settle for Psalm 91, which he read to her while seated beside her bed. I went in a bit later and played her a tune on my harmonica, and by the third chorus she had fallen asleep.

When Jay, Allie, and Isabel returned to the village, they were not only concerned but downright scared over what had happened in their absence. The host missionaries and I held a private, impromptu meeting atop the plywood stack.

Allie spoke first. "We can't risk her health, guys."

Jay wiped sweat from his brow and nodded his agreement.

I brushed sawdust off the stack and pondered our options. "It's in moments like this when I have a hard time being the so-called team leader."

Allie reached over and squeezed my shoulder. Jay thumped me on the knee and told me what I already knew—someone was going to have to leave and escort Beatrice back home to South Carolina.

# 32

I didn't expect to lose over half the team. Over a torchlit dinner of Allie's jungle soup, bread, and cheese, we sat around the outdoor table on the evening of our fifth day and discussed what should be done with Beatrice.

"Do we all go back?" Darcy asked between nibbles.

"We're committed to finishing what we started," Steve said. "But some-one has to go."

Maurice cleared his throat. "Our first priority is—"

"The health of Bea," Quilla interrupted. "If no one wanna go back with her, then I'll go."

"Or I'll go," Maurice said.

José shrugged and tried to join in. "To this Carolina and back to my Mexico City is a long ways, no?"

Asbury assured José that he was exempt from consideration. Then the preacher pointed at his co-captain. "We need you to be the foreman, Maurice."

"Uh-huh," Quilla said, "and we need you, Smoak, to keep Neil away from the power tools."

Alexis and Darcy tossed "I go/no, you go" glances back and forth. Then Alexis waved her spoon in the air. "Okay, everybody," she said, tapping the table to command attention. "I invited Beatrice to come, so I'm responsible to get her back. I hate to leave you guys, but I'm the one who should escort her home."

Darcy put an arm around Alexis. "I'm going back too. I'm the least qualified to build huts." She winced, looked around the table. "And to be honest, I've now seen four snakes and five of those double-humped, orange-and-white spiders. No offense, but this place is starting to scare me pretty bad." Darcy looked at Allie. "I love travel, girlfriend, but maybe the jungle just isn't for me."

I took Alexis by the hand, and together we went and sat on the dwindling stack of plywood. It was dark there, and across the village our teammates' shadows flickered beyond the torch. "Lex, that's big of you to sacrifice your trip to help Beatrice. I can't wait to get back to Greenville after this is over . . . Maybe we'll get to the beach again?"

Her eyes searched mine for sincerity. "Are you sure you're coming back?" she asked. "I mean, you're already near your own stomping grounds."

"But I still have four more weeks of furlough. After these huts are built I'll be on the next plane to—why are you crying?"

She sobbed on my shoulder, and sobbed between her words. "I just . . . wish . . . we could have spent . . . more . . . time together here."

I ran my hand through her hair and kissed her forehead. "I'll just be a few days."

Another sniffle. "Promise?"

"Promise."

At lunch hour of the sixth day, and in the partial shade of hut No. 9, Steve looked glum over the news of Darcy's leaving. Jay's countenance had changed too, given that Allie needed to get Isabel back into Coca for treatments for her burn. Allie told us they wouldn't return to the village for at least a week.

An artist painting this scene would have brushed onto his canvas three downcast bachelors standing in a dirt road, mourning the imminent departure of their women. No one else but José would have been in the painting, for Team Looney Tune was unraveling—quickly, and one by one.

Quilla had succumbed to back spasms. She returned from the designated outhouse complaining of pain, walking all crooked and bent to the side. Rather than complete the last two days she, too, decided to leave. "I gave it my best shot, Fish Stick, uh-huh. We'll see you back at the marina." Her voice hadn't changed, but her smile was gone.

Maurice then came out of his hut with his duffel bag over his shoulder, a frown on his face. He tossed the duffel in the back of the van before turning to speak to me. "Neil, if my wife finds out that I let Quilla travel back from Ecuador with a bad back and didn't escort her home, I'll get whopped on the head with a skillet every morning for the next ten years. Roberta made me promise to watch out for Quilla every minute. I'm really sorry 'bout this."

I almost frowned, but I shook his hand and said I understood. "We got four and a half huts built, Maurice. I figure the team we have left can finish the job."

Behind me, Asbury coughed loudly.

I turned and saw that he, too, had his bags packed. "Neil, I've been over at hut No. 10 trying to grip my tools. I can't do it, son. Look at this thumb, not to mention my index finger." He held up both digits, purple clouds of bruise expanding under swollen skin.

"Painful?" I asked, trying not to show my disappointment. We needed the manpower, and losing Asbury's skill would slow our progress like his boat losing an engine.

Asbury put his left hand on my shoulder. "Son, I hate to do this to ya. But besides the hand, I keep getting sick from eating all this jungle fruit. By Monday I have to be healthy. I got clients from the governor's office signed up to go out on my boat. Can you forgive a preacher for checking out two days early?"

I glanced at barren stilts. I glanced at José over at the water cooler. I glanced at Steve and Jay, who were huddled with their girlfriends on the steps of hut No. 1. I called out to the guys. "Can the four of us build the last three and a half huts on our own, including the long one where most of the orphans will live?"

Steve flexed his arm muscles. "Absolutely."

José gulped his water and shrugged. "Sí. Then Neil and José will have a talk, no?"

But Jay ran a hand through his blonde hair and looked off into the jungle, doing math in his head. "I don't know, guys . . . maybe, but I dunno. We can try."

"I've got another week of vacation I can take," Steve said. "I'll stick around until we're done. What about you, Neil?"

I thought of Deacon Stanley and his desire for all projects to go just right. "I'm accountable to Presbyterians, man. I'm staying as long as necessary."

Soon our entire team, plus Jay, Allie, and Isabel, had gathered in a circle in the shade of the banana trees. Hand in hand we prayed, one and then another, thankful for what was done and hopeful for what was yet to be completed.

After the prayer Preacher Smoak gave Isabel a tiny whale that he'd carved from a block of wood. She hugged his leg and said, "*Gracias,* Señor Asbury."

The preacher grew teary-eyed over this, so he took a masculine reprieve and asked Maurice and me to help him load the remaining luggage into the van.

It was all so mushy after that. Mushy good-byes, mushy hugs, mushy memories. I led Beatrice into the van, where she promptly handed me an orange flower and kissed me on the cheek.

"Neil, I may have messed up by coming here," she said, patting my hand. "There are limitations to being eighty-one, and it took this journey for me to find that out."

I patted back. "We're all learning things this week. Maybe back in Greenville you can offer Stanley some more help."

"Dear, when I get back to Greenville I'm gonna get my gardening club to roll Stanley's yard."

I shut the door smiling, unable to tell whether or not she was kidding.

Steve walked Darcy to the front passenger seat and kissed her good-bye. Jay walked Allie around to the driver's side and out of sight. At the rear of the van, Alexis hugged me long, then kissed me five times in three seconds.

I took hold of her hands. "You've been incredible this week."

"You've worked too hard."

"Just know that my favorite memory is you leading us toward imaginary Peru. That's one for the scrapbook."

She hugged me again. "You're an adventure, Neil Rucker."

"You're an epic journey on rollerblades, Alexis Demoss." And I kissed her one last time.

All the women, the two co-captains, and little Isabel were now piled into that burgundy van. Jay, Steve, José, and I stood in the dirt road and waved through the dust as the van pulled away into an Amazon afternoon. Allie honked once, and in the distance someone's hand waved from a window.

After they were out of sight and the dust had settled back on the road, only José felt like working. The rest of us didn't even feel social. Without comment we wandered into separate huts.

Discouraged and lonely, I loped into hut No. 3, where the sea-green walls did little to cheer me. Nor did a plywood sign that said GOD SPENDS AN INCREDIBLY BRIEF AMOUNT OF TIME BLOWING OUR THESIS TO BITS. I wondered if Jay had written that.

Before trying to take a nap I scanned this humble *casa*, unable to imagine how Jay lived here year round, given the sparse amenities. An hour later I was still missing Alexis, and in the next hut Steve's hammock was creaking in its sway.

# 33

The following Tuesday a mail truck passed through the village. The driver set a few letters on the picnic table, honked his horn, and kept going. Nearly a week had passed since the other team members had left, and our daily dose of cuts, bruises, and sunburns had us welcoming any sort of communication.

But we were in the middle of framing the twelfth hut, so we kept working. While we hammered plywood to the south wall, Steve and Jay and I took turns telling José our stories of finding romance in Greenville. He listened intently as we worked, smiling at the way Jay described leaving the brokerage world for Allie and the rainforest; grinning as Steve recounted his and Darcy's breakup and getting back together; and giving me two thumbs up as I told him about crabbing on the dock with Alexis at Pawleys Island.

We were now just one and a half huts away from completion, from shaking hands and heading home.

Soon Jay scrambled out of the construction site to inspect the parcels. I had slim hopes that there was anything for me. Mostly I was craving a rotisserie chicken.

Jay opened one letter and then another. Finally he held up a light blue envelope and waved it in the air. "Do we all miss our girlfriends, or are we just sick of construction?"

"I'm sick of missing my girlfriend," Steve said, covered in sawdust and wiping his eyes.

Jay opened the envelope and drew out two sheets of paper. "Looks like your girlfriend sent you an email, Neil. Allie printed it out and mailed it."

Hearing this, José stopped hammering. "Ah, young Neil, receiving romance from the *correspondencia electronica*?"

I hurried past him. "It's quicker to just say email, José."

"*Sí*. But José survives without this bother of email."

Excited over getting mail, I accepted the papers from Jay, propped one foot on the picnic bench, and read my first message.

Neily, I'm forwarding this to the village's email address that Allie gave me. I hope someone will get it to you soon. Just know that everyone who left early wants you to lead the next trip. Miss you! Lex.

Ladies of the Quest,

It's funny what a mission trip will do for a girl's outlook.

After two years as your secretary, I decided to study our spreadsheets and total my personal results. Over these past two years I heard 27 Baptist sermons and had two Baptist dates that went nowhere. I heard 16 Pentecostal sermons, got some good exercise, and had 3 Pentecostal dates that went nowhere. I heard 7 Methodist sermons, got asked out by the choir director, but he was a grandfather and so I said no. I heard 6 Episcopalian sermons but never quite caught on to all the ceremony, so all 6 times I scarfed their free donuts and left. Largely due to my friend Darcy, I also heard 31 Presbyterian sermons, had several Presbyterian dates, got invited on two infamous beach trips, and read one and a half pages of Tolstoy.

So there you have it—87 sermons in 2 years, but no husband or boyfriend came from my astonishing game of hopscotch. I have a new method to recommend. It involves faith, coffeehouses, Pawleys Island, chicken necks dipped in fish blood, Sinatra, and foreign missions. All other details I leave to your imagination.

Good riddance to your quest, ladies. I've retired at the ripe old age of

25 and have signed up to serve on the missions committee of North Hills Presbyterian.

Alexis Demoss, former secretary, Ladies of the Quest

P.S. Has anyone seen our little redheaded friend Lydia? Last I heard she had sailed off with a Pentecostal at Litchfield Beach. If you're out there, Lydia, you need to check in with the Ladies. You're obligated to give an update.

During her time in the jungle, Alexis had not seen the monkeys, but perhaps she had seen the light. Reading the note made me want to see her that much more, so I refolded the first message and unfolded the second.

But the second page wasn't addressed to me. The second message was an email from Darcy. I summoned Steve from his power drill. He brushed himself off and came over to read his note. When I handed it to him he turned slowly sideways, trying to keep me from peeking. "Did you read my message, Neil?" he asked, not looking up from the wording.

"I did not. But we're all hoping that you'll read it to us."

"We'd really like to hear what Darcy said this time," Jay chided. "No secrets."

José dropped his hammer and came over to join us. He leaned in close to Steve. "This Darcy, she is your woman of interest, yes?"

Steve nodded and kept reading, taking slow steps away from us, concentrating on the words and walking without a destination. Then he folded the paper in half and went and sat on the other picnic bench. He had his elbows resting on his knees, his head in his hands—the posture of contemplation.

The rest of us hurried near. "C'mon, Steve," I said, taking a seat beside him. "What's the matter, Darcy break up with you again?"

"Hardly. I can't believe what she did."

Jay thumped him on the back. "Well, are ya gonna keep us guessing or are ya gonna confess?"

"I just can't believe she did this."

José stood over Steve, curious as ever. "Baffled by the printed words? But truly we will not pressure Señor Steve." José walked back over to the construction site and picked up his hammer, but he kept glancing over to check on us.

Jay and I were not leaving Steve until he told us what the note said.

After staring blankly into the jungle for a moment, Steve unfolded his message and began to read to us:

Hey handsome. I'm sure by now you guys could use a home-cooked meal. Just so you know, we got Beatrice home, and she's resting at her house and taking fluids. Says she'll try Alaska next. By the way, thanks again for the hubcaps. I put them to good use. Just read on.

Sunday at North Hills Prez, Wade spoke to the singles class about doing what's required, even when it hurts. He used Abraham's sacrifice of Isaac for an example. Well, Steve, let me first say that sometimes God will let you slay your beloved. Which brings me to my plans for renovating the coffeehouse—I think it's going to happen.

You see, while I was in Ecuador I saw how Jay and Allie had sacrificed to provide for those orphans, and also how Neil had sacrificed his furlough to organize the team. By the second day I realized that I, Darcy Yeager, had never sacrificed for anything. You know that I have little savings. And of course my father did as expected. He's not returning my phone calls, and mom is just his pawn. Which is why I did what I did.

Yesterday evening Alexis and I went to the Monday night classic car show on Laurens Road. There were hundreds of people in attendance, and one by one, folks would drive their classic to the front so everyone could have a good look. I took note of how Old Mustangs and Camaros were bringing big dollars, so I left Lex for a moment and went over and sat in my Caddy and prayed to God about what I was thinking. I was thinking wild thoughts. Really wild. I kept watching the crowd lust after those shiny paint jobs and big engines. Then I thought about how the Cellar might go under if someone didn't do something to afford repairs. Then I said no, someone else will make that happen. But who?

Last night I cranked Sherbet's engine for the last time. I turned up the radio loud. I propped plastic Elvis on the dash. I even stuck my hands in the air like Allie always did. Then I drove slowly in front of those hundreds of strangers and honked the horn. The auctioneer came over and asked me what my minimum bid was. I had no idea what to tell him, so I just added up a few thousand for repairs and a few thousand for decor, $3,000 to buy myself something driveable, a little extra for a trip I want to take, plus a hundred bucks to buy you some nicer shirts. So I told him my minimum bid was $10,000. The first bid was $11,200, and the bidding went up from there, $50 per bid, until a stocky man with a crew cut stopped all the bidding by saying he'd pay $13,000 for my Caddy. The auctioneer took 5 percent, and so I netted $12,350. Steve, you'll never guess who bought my car. That cop. The one who gave me the ticket last year and the same one who was in Pomaria when my hubcaps got stolen.

Yes, I cried. Alexis hugged me, consoled me, then told me no way was she selling her 280z. Together we watched the officer drive off with my car. He was waving over his head as he left, hollering something about V-8 power meeting heavenly glory. So Lime Sherbet rumbled off into the sunset . . . and I let her go, my metallic Isaac.

Steve didn't read anymore. He just folded the paper again, stuffed it in his pocket, and went and stood under the banana trees. Jay and I figured he just needed to be alone.

Wearied by the jungle, we retired to our hammocks at nightfall and lost ourselves in the welcoming weaves. After a long hush—just the sound of Steve snoring—Jay spoke in a near whisper. "Neil, we're short on money."

I turned toward him. "The rebuilding money?"

He lay on his back, his hands under his head. "The long-term money. Giving is down, and now we've had these extra expenses. Plus medical for Isabel. I might have to spend a month raising support back in the States. And then, of course, I'll probably take the second semester of language school."

"But who would pick up the slack down here?"

"Hopefully the natives. Allie's overworked for sure. But we know the kids need us, so we're sticking with this mission." Jay just swayed for a moment. "I bet you language teachers never have these kinds of worries."

It was getting late, and I almost didn't bring up the next topic. "Do you ever miss Wall Street? The life you could have had?"

"Sometimes I think about it. But I'd have turned out shallow. I would have never pursued Allie and never been the kind of guy who talked to God from rooftops." After he said that he rolled over and faced the wall. Nearly a minute passed before he spoke again. "Sometimes I think it's guys like you, Neil, guys who prepare so many people to go serve, who turn the wheels of foreign missions."

I could not think of what to say. It had been a long time since I'd felt like part of the ever-flowing whole. Me . . . a ripple.

Sometime around midnight, I left my sleeping roommates and walked out into the middle of the village. Into the stillness of night I walked, focused mainly on the height and breadth of hut No. 6. Sitting vacant and complete across the dirt road, it looked easy enough to scale. Tonight I had things to say.

With the help of four bricks and a two-by-eight, I climbed to the roof, sat straddled on its center, and turned my back to the village. Beneath moon and stars I pondered creation, and soon the bugs' monotonous drone had faded to background music. I looked skyward and began speaking. "Here I am, back in Ecuador, and once again, you've sent me down roads unrecorded by Rand McNally. I was all set to work in Georgetown on a charter boat; you sent me to a rainforest to build huts. I thought Alexis and I would be strolling a sandy shore; you sent us hiking toward Peru. I don't know what has been more exhausting—building huts, keeping up with Lex, or trying to decipher your plans. So I think I'm going to stop trying to decipher your plans. It stresses me, don't ya think?"

I searched the sky for any sign that I'd been heard. I knew I'd been heard—I was always heard—it was just that tonight I was hoping for something more from the galaxy than random twinkles.

To the north, in the general vicinity of Colombia, I admired a dense group of stars whose sheer brilliance turned my thoughts appreciative. "I forgot to thank you for providing these new friends from Carolina. And I forgot to thank you for answering my request about meeting an interesting woman. She is most interesting." I rewound to the crabbing dock, kissing her bottom lip, our zany conversations, and how Lex was constantly pushing me into new experiences. "But one more question—how do you, as an all-knowing but very busy God, keep up with Alexis? Do you have extra seraphim assigned to her?"

I stared into the night sky and listened for any hint of a voice.

And I heard him.

This night I really did hear a voice—and it spoke Spanish. Only it wasn't God speaking; it was José. I looked to my left and saw him atop the roof of hut No. 8, his pointy-toed boots straddling the center. In the moonlight I could tell that he'd been watching me.

"Young Neil remembers José's lesson, yes? Five years of roof-talk is a good thing. A very good thing."

That was all he said before turning his attention back to the heavens.

I squirmed to get comfortable. "Ever since I saw you climb on the roof of your soup kitchen in Mexico City, José, I've been emulating you."

His attention was elsewhere, his voice low. "You, Neil . . . always the observant one."

For the next few minutes two voices addressed their creator in two languages. José sounded like he was offering more praise than questions, so I made a mental note of this and began to think of more things for which to be thankful.

Finally José stopped talking to the heavens and turned his attention back to me. "You, Neil, growing up without parents; me and my lovely Maria childless. Truly you and I are a matching from God, yes?"

I thought back to the first day that I'd wandered into his soup kitchen, how he'd tossed me an apron and put me to work. "Yes . . . yes we are."

Nothing else needed to be said. Like the galaxy above us, the relationship between José and me seemed fixed, a thing established long ago, back before I was parentless and before he knew he'd be childless.

But José being José, he just couldn't let the moment stay quiet. "Young Neil, there is more."

"What's that?"

He breathed deep from the night air and shifted on the rooftop. "This God we share, he sends many mentors in a lifetime."

"Yes, he does."

"You must pay attention for them. This Asbury with the bad thumb, he too is to be listened for. But this Maurice and his poisonous lizards, well, José is not so sure about him."

"He might make a decent fishing mentor."

We sat quietly for a while, then I began to speak to the almighty about Alexis, my future, furlough's remaining weeks, and what to do about it all. In mid-sentence I was startled by a scraping noise from farther down the row. A stocky silhouette had climbed onto hut No. 10.

José turned to his left and waved. "Welcome, Señor Steve."

Steve sat in silence and pondered his new altitude. Then I looked behind me to the ground and saw Jay walking slowly to the end of the village, moonlight like a nimbus on his blonde head. He climbed atop hut No. 12 and said, "I've been living here for nine months and never thought to do this."

José waved again.

On every other rooftop—Nos. 6, 8, 10, and 12—was a man sharing concerns with his maker, a staggered form of reverence that required frequent repositioning of our derrieres. All I heard were hushed tones, punctuated by frequent pauses, José in the middle using breakneck Spanish. After ten or fifteen minutes, I wasn't listening anymore. I was talking too. Then listening again.

José was the first to break the silence. He looked to his right, at me, then to his left, at Steve and Jay. "There is sadness in the Ecuadorian air. Tonight José senses heavy thoughts. Young men on rooftops, pondering young women . . . is this true? Of course it is true. When your women were present, they were accepted for granted, no? Now the women depart, and there is sadness."

Balanced on the rooftops, no one else said a word. So José, as was his habit, picked up his own conversation. He spoke toward the jungle. "Many young men do not gather counsel for their concerns. But you, Señor Jay, and you, Señor Neil, and you, Señor Steve . . . you are wise. You exit from your sleep and climb up and address your God. Then you hope for wisdom from José. Perhaps each of you teeters on the same confusion. You think, 'Ah, is the greenest grass before me now, or do I leave this grass and possibly rust in loneliness like an old lawn mower?'"

Again, not one us could think how to respond to José. He was a man of odd wisdom and convoluted English. He spoke our language, and yet . . . he didn't. He looked to his right, at me, then slowly turned and looked at Steve and Jay. "Truly this grassy issue is stronger than the tongue. I now expose the root, but I must dig with the pointed question: Señor Jay, could you see yourself together on a rooftop with your Allie, twenty years from now, talking to God?"

From all the way down at hut No. 12 came Jay's voice. "I could, José. But she'd be reciting poetry."

José nodded his approval. "Señor Steve, could you see yourself together on a rooftop with your Darcy, twenty years from now, talking to God?"

A bit louder, from hut No. 10, came, "I could, José. But she'd prefer a nicer roof."

Again José nodded. He turned his gaze on me, but I just stared up at the moon. "Señor Neil," he said, a hint of persuasion in his voice, "could you see yourself together on a rooftop with your Alexis, twenty years from now, talking to God?"

*Hmmm. Well, I'd rather not rust in loneliness like an old lawn mower.* "Hold it, José. I've only known her for three weeks, so gimme a break. But if Alexis does end up on a roof with me twenty years from now, she'll be humming Sinatra and hopping on one leg."

Moonlit, José smiled with pleasure, as if the interview phase of the Mexican Dating Game had concluded to his satisfaction. He then rose to his feet and began climbing down from the new construction of hut No. 8. He dropped the final two feet to the ground, looked up, and scanned the rooflines. One last nod at the three of us. Then he ran the point of his boot through the dirt and refocused on me. "Rich wisdom is better even than rich soil, young Neil. José sees now that you grow in wisdom like a weed in manure."

And José strode across the dirt road to hut No. 3 and went to bed.

My mentor. My friend.

# 34

At midmorning on the fourteenth day of construction, Steve and I finished framing and plywooding hut No. 13, even adding a "welcome back" sign to the inner wall. José fashioned the steps to the front, and Jay paused between hammering to calculate how many shingles he'd need to complete the project.

A plan had come together, so we broke for an early lunch of peanut butter and jelly sandwiches, cold showers in the designated spot for males, and naps through the broil of midday.

Soon José was knocking on our hut. He entered without waiting for a response. Today he wore new blue jeans and a plaid cowboy shirt with a thin leather lanyard around the collar. He looked at us swaying in our hammocks and asked if there was a place in the jungle where a man could see the horizon.

Steve told him he thought we'd seen plenty of horizon the previous night.

Jay rolled over in his hammock. "Yeah, José. A short ways down the dirt road there's this path that leads into the rainforest and to the base of an observation tower. It's for bird-watchers, but we use it all the time. It's a good place to confess sins. Feel free."

José shook his head. "You misread. This horizon is not for José or sins." He pointed at me and clapped his hands. "Now, young Neil, out of your hammock and into your shoes!"

Embarrassing, being called out like this in front of roommates. But I put on my hiking boots and went along.

I imagined how the red macaw, perched on new digs atop hut No. 9, might have viewed our trek: Two blue-jeaned men walking a dirt road into the jungle. Laborers on break? Amigos walking for their health? On that sunlit afternoon, however, I had no clue what was on the mind of my pointy-booted friend from Mexico City.

The two of us walked on, side by side, like gunslingers without guns. Skies were blue and equatorial. Footprints came and went. Some of the prints looked female, some male, and one set appeared to be those of a young girl.

"This way," I said, pointing to José's left. We stepped off the dirt road and unto an unmarked path grown over with vines, elephant ears, and stringy weeds pretzeling into impossible shapes.

In a small clearing ahead I saw the base of the observation tower. The steps were numbered, just as Jay had told us, and mold was multiplying on the stair rails. Shadowed and sweaty, José pointed up into the canopy and began his climb. I followed closely, at a loss as to why we were going to see the horizon.

We climbed past step one hundred, up into the middle of the trees. Then José paused and turned to face me. He looked worried. "Truly no bungee cord hangs up here?"

"Who knows, José. Just keep climbing." I kept trying to guess what he was up to, but aching thigh muscles blurred my deliberation.

He stopped again. "Young Neil, do Señor Jay and Señor Steve have mentors?"

"I doubt it. Just keep climbing."

He said "Hmmm" and strode higher. Then he paused a third time. "Perhaps I can offer wisdom to your friends as well."

Through the tree limbs and into warm air, I saw above us the floor of the tower—sturdy, wooden, and not particularly large, but big enough to hold the two of us comfortably. Open-air with a tiny roof over its center, the tower boasted chest-high railings and stomach-tingling height. We breathed hard and glanced beneath us at treetops. The views were otherworldly: snowcapped peaks in one direction, endless jungle in two others, and the Rio Napo twisting to the east. Here the air felt stripped of its fat. For a while we just gazed out at the peaks, then watched a hawk soar on the currents. Soon José turned south and said, "Ah, someone has been here."

I spun around and saw for the first time six lines of poetry in red magic marker, scrawled on a piece of plywood.

José put his hands on his hips and read the poem. After he was done he looked confused. "You will explain this verse?"

I backed up against the railing. "Well," I said, reading the words, "I suspect that Señorita Allie wrote it, but I think it's not only about her but also Señora Quilla and Señora Beatrice."

José read the poem again. "Few words, but deep of meaning, no? I can tell that the words are of women. This is clear."

I could picture Jay coming up here, touching the first line, and saying, "That's my girl."

In her lofty chair
Next to dark, flamboyant hair
She's admiring a Van Gogh.

Today she feels forgiven
Today she feels flamboyant
Today she feels very ... Van Goghy.

A.K., B.D., Q.J. 7/17/03

José pointed to the last line. "This Van Goohee, he hammered with your mission team, yes?"

"Not this year."

"No matter," José said, turning his back to the verse. "We gather for a purpose of seriousness."

Sunlit and confident, José asked me to stand against the railing, my back to the Rio Napo and the mountains of Peru. The tower creaked. The sun felt warm on my neck. Then José raised his index finger but did not speak, as if he were searching for the right word. "Young Neil will listen closely?"

"I'll do my best."

"Last night on the rooftop was a special time for José. Yes, a very special time. Never before have I the feeling of a son—a son of whom I am proud. So strong was my feeling that I retired to my hut with emotion, thinking of your future. But one question haunted me through the night, and even today, on this tower for birds, the question still pursues. Can you guess the question?"

I wiped my brow and pushed away the matted hair on my forehead. "No, José, I cannot."

José scruffed a pointy-toed boot on the wood flooring of the tower. His mustache frowned at the middle but stayed happy at the tips. Then he stared out across the Amazon Basin before focusing back on me. "When it is time to commit to a woman, will you be a man and do the right thing?"

I nodded my agreement.

"And when this time comes, you will decide with an act of confidence?"

"I hope so."

José reached into his pants pocket and brought out a tangelo. Under my nose he held it in his palm, allowing the sun's rays to highlight the orange skin.

I stared at the fruit like it might explode. "José, please don't ask me to do the pitching motion again. Besides, Alexis is back in South Carolina and she's already agreed to date me."

José jiggled his hand. The tangelo wobbled. "When a man becomes sure of the right woman, Neil, thoughts of frightening may clog his head. Then he must decide to throw away his independence that he has stored for years, no? And he must do this with an act of confidence, so the fruit is sym . . . eh, sympto . . . José forgets the word."

"Symbolic?" I asked, trying to help.

He smiled. "*Sí.* Sym-bo-lic."

I turned and glanced at the jungle floor. "So the tangelo is hurled to symbolize the throwing off of a man's independence?"

José smiled again. "*Sí.* But which fruit is used plays no matter, though the tangelo fits well in the hand. So, young Neil, when the time of commitment comes, you should take a fruit and picture this fruit containing all of your selfishness and independence, then throw it with all your might. You may throw it against a tree, a building, or just watch it soar from a bridge. When I got engaged to my lovely Maria, my own father gave me a lemon. But now in my fifties I have no taste for lemons."

I gripped the railing on both sides and tried to make sense of this, his oddest wisdom yet. "José, are you saying that symbolic fruit-tossing has been passed down through the men in your family for generations?"

This time he grinned. "Since before the Alamo."

Maybe this wasn't numbskull advice. Maybe one day I too would be in a position to counsel a single man. Maybe he'd be a little guy and require a grape, or a huge guy and require a melon, or be named Johnny and ask for an apple. All I knew was that ever since I'd tried to find belonging by going into mission work, this amigo from Mexico City had done his best to help make sure I was ready to meet life and, more importantly, to stay in frequent contact with the Lord.

José took two steps back, looked behind him, and stepped down onto the stairs. "Young Neil, when it is the right time for you, I want you to act with confidence and let your *sí* be *sí*. Wherever you are, I want you to rear back and throw, a true signal to your bride and to your God that you are ready for the journey where two walk as one."

"I'll heave it high, José."

"Only you will know the time." And he tossed me the tangelo.

By the time I had caught the fruit and held it up to the sunlight, José was tromping down the stairs. He had left me to my thoughts, and I listened to his footsteps as he descended through the treetops.

Alone on that creaky tower, I thought of Alexis. I rubbed the fruit in both hands. Then I looked out across the far reaches of the jungle, where birds looked paired off and clouds looked paired off and where even the body language of the trees made them seem to be flirting with each other.

I gripped the tangelo like a major leaguer.

I thought of Alexis again.

I even began a pitching windup.

Then I did what I'd wanted to do ever since José had pulled that tangelo from his pocket.

I ate it.

Up there in that bird tower, I peeled and ate the tangelo and thanked God for his provision, for providing new family after he'd taken my first, for providing someone to date after he'd kept me quite lonely, and for helping me realize that while rooftops are okay for questions, many of the answers are found in relationship with people on the ground, in simply taking my eyes off of Neil and making myself available.

My plan was to return to South Carolina, not knowing if I would stay or go back to language school. Jay had left the South for Ecuador; perhaps I would leave Ecuador for the South. Summer still had another month to go, but already I could claim a surrogate family, a nutty and loyal bunch I'd nicknamed the Looney Tunes. And one of them I missed terribly.

Before descending the stairs I glanced again to the east, at the broad headwaters of the river. In its many ripples bobbed a snippet of summer's lesson—that Looneys of every nation are invited into the ever-flowing whole, a community where submerged things can be exposed regardless of previous tides and rusty, life-choking anchors; and that none of us, whether we be engineers, language teachers, jungle missionaries, soup-kitchen owners, coffeehouse renovators, preachers, gardeners, boat captains, or real estate agents, is ever really on furlough.

That afternoon I was atop hut No. 13, installing a flagpole, when I glanced down into the middle of the village and saw Jay and Steve, both in jeans and T-shirts, walking down the dirt road with José. The three of them had been sitting around the picnic table, talking for hours. Steve, unshaven as usual, looked up and told me they were heading out for the bird tower, though he knew not the reason. José strode in the middle of the two bachelors, urging them along, and in his hands he carried a pair of tangelos.

I stood tall on the roof, where across the banana trees and a hundred yards of jungle I could see the top of the tower. Minutes passed, and soon in the distance three heads appeared above the railing.

I reached down for my hammer and tried to imagine the conversation taking place on high. I imagined the convoluted English. There was no time to imagine anything else—when I looked up again, someone had heaved the fruit.

Against a blue sky the tangelo rose swiftly, first opposing gravity, then submitting, caught up in the velocity like a ripe comet streaking toward the bonds of matrimony. In its arc flew the virtues of commitment and loyalty and passion, followed by the afterburners of summer—amorous and ablaze. Faster the tangelo descended, an orange blur, poetic, expensive, at once brunette and blonde, rotating so fast that its skin appeared tan, then pale, then something luminous, the color of love.

I wondered how any of us would explain such ceremony to the girls. But perhaps the throw was a male-only event, to be spoken of only in the company of men. Regardless, I could not help but speculate on what the girls were doing at that moment—Allie with the orphans, Lex selling real estate, Darcy perhaps painting the walls of the coffeehouse, and all of them thinking we were just building on the last hut.

I followed the fruit's descent into treetops, green leaves fluttering down in a prologue to rice. I could stand it no longer. Across the banana trees I yelled, "Who threw it?"

But no one answered; Steve and Jay and José had leaned over the railing, watching as the tangelo landed, *thud*, on the jungle floor.

What struck me was the sound of that reentry, how the fruit landed with such finality, as if it had been shot out as a last blast from the furnace of singleness—and the door to that furnace had slammed shut.

I was still inside the furnace, but so were lots of people. The God of all rooftops would not let me be hasty and miss the way. Indeed, it was only within the way—this delirious furlough and its many tangents—that I'd discovered that what I was looking for was more than simply a mate. I wanted to belong, to feel a part of that ever-flowing whole. The ultimate key of G, the key of *grace*, had proven all-sufficient, music to live by.

As for Jay and Steve, I was excited for whichever of them had thrown off his independence. But again, today was just a male-only event. There was still the matter of getting the girl to say yes.

One more height to scale for a Bachelor of the Quest.

# Acknowledgments

Many thanks to the readers who have emailed their encouragement, urging me to continue writing after the release of *Flabbergasted*. Your support means so much, and it energized me to complete this second book of a loosely connected trilogy.

"Surf's up" greetings to the island gang of '03. Mike and Colleen, Aimee A., Mike and Amy, Scott, Annalee, my parents, Charles and Phoebe, Dana and the 3 J's (who are a Team Looney Tune unto themselves), and to the Midnight Shark Fishermen: Tony L., Matt K., Sandy C., Mike H.

"The SoulFixers" were a Friday night street band in Greenville during the summer of '02. Its members included Martin on guitar and vocals; Gretchen on vocals and tambourine; and Holly on harmonica.

Jeanette and Kristin at Baker Book House once again steered me down wise paths. Jodi Brinks lent her Ecuador experience to my research. Jennifer Chappell read and critiqued the manuscript with insight, encouragement, and the keen eye of someone who knows all things "coastal." Also in the role of distinguished test-reader: Aimee Aird, Whitney Brown, Holly Grant, Ken Harris, and my mom, Phoebe, who taught Beatrice everything she knows about gardening. Dad, the writing table held up through another book—*gracias*! Brandy in Dallas sells my books with great enthusiasm. Ditto for Monica in Calgary. Amy of Taylors First Baptist came up with the Act 1 "misfit" epigraph.

Hi to Ed and all the mountaintop gang in Tennessee.

Roger married Amy at sunrise . . . beside a lake. Wow!

Wes, you're supposed to step *over* the stingrays.

Somewhere there is a preacher who thinks no book should sell for more than five bucks. *Ahem*.

Allie's "Van Gogh" poem was partially inspired by "apricots" by Carolina's Lee McAden, 1971.

Special thanks to the Open Book in Greenville, S.C., for hosting my first book signing. Also to Rick Hoganson of Hoganson Media for his promotional efforts. Kudos to singer/songwriter Andrew Peterson for reading the audio version of *Flabbergasted*. Prayer support led by John and Shari Horner, Brian and Debi Ponder, Bradley and Kathy Wright.

She-crab soup (in its many variations) courtesy of Phoebe's Diner, Haubert's House of Flying Shell Fragments, and Lands End Restaurant, Georgetown, S.C.

The Carpenter's Cellar coffeehouse recently reopened after extensive renovations. A diversity of up-and-coming musicians entertain us on weekend nights. A few even play the harmonica.

Music credits: "Hey Baby" by Maurice and the Zodiacs; "Rio" by Duran Duran; "Come on Eileen" by Dexy's Midnight Runners; "Tainted Love" by Soft Cell; "Me and Bobby McGee" by Janis Joplin; "My Way" by Frank Sinatra; "Carolina Girls" by Chairmen of the Board, Surfside Records, Charlotte, N.C.

Ransom buys his surfboards from Surf the Earth, Pawleys Island. Darcy buys her whistles at Wilson's Five 'n Dime. Steve donates his beige, logoed shirts to Goodwill. Jay orders his beach music from Horizon Records. Allie sells her jungle beads online at www.ddpdesigns.com. Neil buys his harmonicas at Pecknel Music. And Alexis, well, she buys her chicken necks at Piggly Wiggly.

And to all who have inquired—Asbury and Maurice's charter boat is booked solid for this year.

**Ray Blackston** lives and writes in Greenville, South Carolina. His grandfather, the late Reverend A. F. Smoak, served as pastor of Pawleys Island Baptist Church. Ray invites you to read more of the background for his two intertwining novels, *Flabbergasted* and *A Delirious Summer*, at his website, www.rayblackston.com.

"Thank you, reader, for turning the pages of Ray's second novel. Rumor has it there's a third one on the way."

**My name is Quilla, and I made my man throw a pumpkin.**

**Uh-huh.**

**meet Jay—**
new in town, successful,
and not afraid to plop
down in a pew to scope
out the females. But
the unusual assortment
of friends he finds
launch events that
leave him thoroughly
flabbergasted.

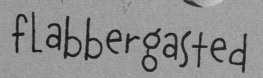

A NOVEL

flabbergasted

RAY BLACKSTON